Terror Unleashed

by **Roger Marshall**

with Cathy Newman

iUniverse, Inc.
Bloomington

Terror Unleashed

iUniverse books may be ordered through booksellers or by contacting:

iUniverse
1663 Liberty Drive
Bloomington, IN 47403
www.iuniverse.com
1-800-Authors (1-800-288-4677)

ISBN: 978-1-4502-9473-7 (pbk)
ISBN: 978-1-4502-9475-1 (cloth)
ISBN: 978-1-4502-9474-4 (ebk)

Printed in the United States of America

iUniverse rev. date: 2/8/11

DEDICATION

This book is dedicated to my parents, my children, and my best friends.

My Dad, Wayne Marshall, is no longer walking on this planet. He died between the publishing of book one, Terror Within, and this book, Terror Unleashed. Although Parkinson's won the physical battle, his spirit will live on forever.

My Mom, Janet Marshall, has been an unending source of support and inspiration. What else can I say?

My two daughters, Alison and Veronica, keep me young by always challenging me.

With regard to this book 3 women greatly helped me through this effort. I thank them deeply. Kathryn Davis played a big role in helping me through book one and book two. Without her I would not be here. She literally saved my life. Ko Barrett also was an unending source of inspiration always telling me to push on and demonstrating that drive in her own life. And last but far from least, Debra Cooper. Debbie has been a dear friend for over 15 years. Debbie was an unending source of support and encouragement through book one and through book two.

Thank you all.

Roger

Terror Unleashed

by **Roger Marshall**

with Cathy Newman

Contents

Contents

CHAPTER ONE

Arrested

"Stop him! Stop that — that . . . mutant!!!"

The Military Police gave chase, but Harland had a good head start. He weaved through the pedestrian traffic in the basement labyrinth of the Pentagon, banging into some, though avoiding most. Soon he slammed into a three-star general that turned, gaping in affront, to find out what peon had the gall to assault him. Harland's survival instincts were at full throttle with the fight-or-flight control fixed firmly on flight. With avian reasoning instincts, he knew the way to freedom was up, so he headed for the nearest stairs. Edging by the general, respectfully, the MPs broke into a sprint trying desperately to capture Harland.

"Subject is heading for the stairs to the first floor and will most likely try to make a break for the nearest door. . . . Cover all exits," the lead MP said into his microphone without breaking stride. "Subject is a mutant bird man wearing a major's uniform. He is considered highly dangerous and wanted for murdering a nurse. Approach with weapons drawn, using all caution."

Klaxons blared overhead warning all personnel to evacuate the hallways and close themselves into locked offices. Following Pentagon protocol, people began in orderly fashion to proceed to designated emergency areas, clearing the way for the military police to enter. With their weapons drawn, they entered and moved quickly

1

through the halls. After 9/11, the military brass realized that the Pentagon was vulnerable, so they instituted emergency procedures to deal with every contingency they could imagine.

Harland's devolution allowed him to almost fly up the stairs. With his mind focused on going up, he headed towards the roof of the inner ring of the Pentagon instead of towards the exits at ground level. There he hid in a restroom as MPs pounded past on their way to covering all the exits. The Pentagon is a huge place where even someone who has worked there for many years can get lost if he or she wanders out of his or her routine path. Harland, however, had spent many long, lonely years in the basement working at a dead end job, and had taken to exploring the different levels and rings during his breaks to add some interest to his days. Although there were many areas his clearance would not allow him to enter, he had managed to find many nooks and crannies, not to mention places that were continuously under construction where a quiet man could hide, unnoticed. He made use of the information he had gathered to dart from one hiding place to another as he slowly made his way towards his goal.

It was true that Harland now had many features of a hawk from taking enhancement pills to correct his vision. Most of the feathers that now covered his body were covered by his uniform. There were many majors in the building. He was not the only person in the building who had taken the pills and who had experienced the devolution track of taking on the characteristics of birds. In the confusion, many clueless people were stopped and held at gun point until it was ascertained that they were not Major Harland Parker.

A tedious office by office, ring by ring, level by level search was begun by the MPs with the investigated areas sealed off so Harland could not slip behind them to escape. All the exits were blocked by fully armed MPs. Slowly; the noose was drawing tighter, leaving Harland fewer choices of places to hide and the MPs fewer places left to search.

Harland decided that it was time to make a break for it and head for the final set of stairs that would take him to the roof. He cautiously opened the door and peeked around it. About 30 yards down the hall, a squad of MPs headed away from him. Harland decided to give them a few more seconds to get around the bend in the corridor. However, as he tried to quietly ease the door shut again, his talons were not able to maintain a firm grip on the smooth doorknob, like a human's hand can easily do. The doorknob slipped from his grasp and clicked loudly. Harland held his breath, not daring to move, hoping the MPs were too far away to hear the noise, and listened for the sound of their boots moving away.

Harland's luck had just run out. One of the MPs had turned around — about to say something — and he not only heard the sound of the door, but also saw a slight movement out of the corner of his eye. He signaled for the other MPs, making them freeze in their tracks. Putting a finger to his lips, the alert MP motioned down the hallway to the closed supply room door. Checking their drawn weapons, they began a swift turn, nearly in unison, but they were too late.

Harland, with the extraordinary hearing and response time of a startled bird, had heard the footsteps stop and nearly flew out of the trap of the supply closet and was halfway up the stairs across from it before the MPs could complete their turn. Though their orders were to capture Harland and bring him in, one of the MPs thought the flash of Harland's extra long talons was the barrel of a gun, and began firing. Trusting the lead of the first shooter all the MPs brought their weapons to bear and opened fire.

Harland was part way up the stairs when the barrage of fire started. With the maneuverability of a bird he dodged back and forth as he leapt up the remaining steps and was out of sight of the MPs as he headed for the roof. Because he had moved to the inner rings to escape capture early, he was far from the perimeter of the building as he exited onto the roof. He started across what looked like the length of a few football fields to get to the edge, each step taking him closer to freedom.

The MPs pounded up the steps after him, stopping at the top to regroup. Their assumption was that Harland would aim towards another downward stairwell, following on the idea they had that he would eventually dash for an exit door on the first floor. With all the heating and air conditioning units, communication equipment, and security apparatus on the roof, it was hard to tell which direction Harland had gone. Not only was their vision blocked, but it was noisy on the roof and they could not hear Harland's light footsteps.

Running flat out with large leaps between steps, Harland felt encumbered and he shed his jacket and tied his shirt around his waist. He kicked off the shoes he had bought in increasingly larger sizes as his foot talons grew. Regardless of the bigger size, they now felt too inhibiting. If he had the time to stop, he would have gotten rid of his pants, too, but he knew there was no time to waste. He had heard the MPs reach the roof, and though puzzled at why they weren't following him, he was glad for the lead this afforded him.

Reaching the edge of the building, Harland found a high ledge and climbed out onto it. As he scrambled up, discovering that climbing was not an easy skill for him, one of the MPs spotted his movement.

"He's over there!" the MP shouted, abandoning any pretense of stealth. "He's on the ledge and it looks like he plans to jump."

"No one could jump from that height and live," scoffed another MP as they all hustled in and out between the obstructions on the roof.

"Halt! Stay where you are or we'll shoot!" shouted the MPs closest to Harland.

Harland shot a quick glance back and stood upright.

"We promise you won't get hurt if you come down now," reasoned the MP, now about 50 meters away and slowly closing in.

Harland ignored him, along with the others. Centering himself and calling up all his avian instincts, he raised his arms.

"He's going to jump. . ."

Bending his legs, Harland leapt into the air, causing the MPs to immediately fire. If Harland had actually gone airborne, maybe a shot would have connected. Though Harland had internalized his bird persona, his body had not lost its humanoid form. While his chest muscles had deepened and feathers had grown, his wings were still not developed. He had arms and flapped them as much as he could, but still he plummeted towards the ground.

The MPs rushed to the ledge and climbed gingerly up it with all their weighty gear on. Shooting down at Harland was an exercise in futility and most watched in gaping horror, knowingly shaking their heads wisely, anticipating Harland's tragic and gruesome death.

Harland hit the ground, but there was no loud splat, no guts bursting out in all directions. Harland's bones had hollowed like a bird's and he was extremely light in the air currents of the downward trajectory. And, though he didn't have full wings yet, he did have his feathers free to provide some drag, slowing his descent as he fell, thanks to his foresight in removing some of his clothes. Stunned for a second, Harland lay motionless, while the MPs above nodded to each other at the proof of their certainty that no one could sustain that fall. Then, Harland got up, gave himself a little shake and ran off, putting his shirt back on as he went, leaving a host of surprised faces in his wake.

*   *   *

"I've got him on picture phone," Erin Blaine called out, wearily, brushing her straggly hair out of her eyes. Brad Cho, another analyst in Homeland Security, and Jamie Whiteman, the Deputy Director of HSA, abandoned their own tasks to gather around her as she spoke to Zack McHenry — thousands of miles away in Argentina — where he was monitoring the start-up attempt by Rita Perez to genetically reverse the course of devolution.

Homeland Security had quickly claimed jurisdiction in the hunt for Harland Parker after he successfully eluded the Pentagon security the day before. With egg on their faces, the Pentagon personnel gladly washed their hands of the whole mess and tried to fade into the background out of public scrutiny. The more covert their operations, the more effective they would be in the long run to round up dissident mutants and put them in containment centers.

"Hola, buenos dias," Zack said brightly, munching on a fat strip of bacon, "Que pasa?" The food at the huge spread owned by Rita's parents, Ronaldo and Eva Perez, was as outstanding as the wine their vineyards produced. Normally quite taciturn, Zack couldn't help being a bit mellowed on his current assignment.

"There's no time to waste, Zack, so get serious!" Jamie barked, impatiently sweeping empty coffee cups out of her way. It had been a long night of expanding the search for Harland. First checking the usual places — like his home and friends — the search quickly encompassed all of Washington, D.C. and Annapolis, soon spreading out to cover the whole Eastern Seaboard. All transportation on airplanes, trains, buses, and boats was being monitored, but so far all the leads that had come in turned out to be false.

"Harland Parker, one of the original band of terrorists, has turned savage and violently attacked and killed a nurse at the Pentagon," Jamie told him, tersely. "We have been considering the possibility that he might try to join his fellow conspirators at the Patagonia Estates where you are in Argentina. Have you had any sightings of him?"

Snapping to attention, Zack was all business as he answered, "No. There are no sightings down here."

Needing to put in his two cents, Brad piped up. "Has anyone been acting strange? Maybe he has been in contact with Rita, Sandra, or Nate and you don't know it."

Affronted, Zack put on his most forbidding face. "I think I know what is going on in my own backyard. Rita is focused on getting the new complex set up so she can really get going with her research. When he is not watching the stock market, Nate has only eyes for Sandra and visa-versa. They are so lovey-dovey it makes me want to puke." He looked scornful, while purposely suppressing all thoughts of how luscious Rita looked and how he could barely keep his own eyes off of her.

"Well, okay," Jamie said, giving Brad an annoyed look as she resumed control. "Be on the lookout for any contact from him. Brief the security detail you brought with you, and monitor all the ways he could use to enter the country."

"Yes, Ma'am, I'll get right on it," Zack replied, and the transmission ended.

"At least that base is covered," Erin announced as she looked at the empty coffee cups scattered across the floor. Deciding it was not her job to pick them up; she headed for the coffee machine, only to discover that it would be her job to fill it again for the hundredth time since the siege began.

"I've got to get to a meeting," Jamie declared, straightening up her navy designer suit that had begun to hang loosely. There was nothing like coffee and a non-stop crisis to work off those extra pounds. How was Erin always able to look so polished and so crisp, like she had just walked out of a spa, while she felt like she had just driven 48 hours without a break? "Keep up the search and let me know the second you hear anything." She headed out the door without a backwards glance.

* * *

Trying to appear like anyone else out for a stroll in Theodore Roosevelt Island Park on the Potomac River, Harland proceeded cautiously to the rendezvous he had arranged with his 10-year-old son, Sterling. Fortunately for Harland, Sterling had been staying with a friend and was not home when the HSA forces raided it. Uncannily, since Sterling had also been taking the enhancement pills along with his father and had been mutating along the same path, few actual words were required for communication between them. Harland was able to give Sterling instructions on how and where to meet him without actually saying much.

It was impossible for Harland not to notice the many mutants on the island. Though he had been taking the pills longer than anyone else, it was evident that other people were also transforming quickly, following the course of various animals. Like he had done at the Pentagon, many were gradually shedding their clothes — some out of comfort — but many because traditional human clothing no longer fit their changing shapes.

The volume of mutants seemed disproportionate to the percentage in the general public, but then maybe he had a heightened awareness because of his own status. How he blended in was crucial to his continued freedom. Then again, maybe the mutants were gathering together purposely on the island. It was reassuring to him to see how well he fit in with the others. Whatever the reason for the amount of mutants on the island, Harland did not have the time or inclination to pursue the matter further. By nature, he enjoyed solitude, so as he developed more hawk-like characteristics it felt even more natural to play a lone hand, except for when his son was concerned. He had a fierce instinct to protect his only child.

"Dad, over here," Sterling hissed. Enjoying the thrill of evading capture, Sterling had hidden himself in a section of dense bushes. Forgetting the game, he launched himself at Harland.

"Son, I am so glad you made it here," Harland said, briefly hugging him. "We have to look like everybody else, though, and not draw attention to ourselves, so no more hiding, okay?"

Giving a sharp, birdlike nod of his feathered head, Sterling acknowledged what Harland had said. Then they began to casually stroll along, quietly discussing their plans. The immediate plan was to walk the island paths, acting like the other tourists. When the park closed at dusk, they made their way towards the footbridge to the west side of the Potomac where Harland had parked the car he had boosted, a skill he had managed to acquire during his youth in the auto shop class in high school. However, it became increasingly apparent that Roosevelt Island had not been overlooked in the search plans for Harland.

"Dad, look," Sterling said, excitedly, pointing to a couple of armed men who were approaching everyone on the island with a concentration on people with avian characteristics. Without wasting time on words, Harland grabbed Sterling, ducking into nearby brush. Deciding there was no time to lose, Harland headed through the woods to the footbridge.

Fortunately, not enough men had been assigned to the island since it was deemed a low priority destination for Harland, and the footbridge was not guarded. Just as they were about to step onto the bridge, a helicopter could be heard coming up the river. They quickly hid as the helicopter slowly passed overhead and continued down the river. Harland and Sterling abandoned all pretenses and ran flat out to the other side of the bridge, Harland's shoeless talons clacking noisily. Once in the parking lot they wasted no time jumping into the car. Having to change his plans on the fly, Harland figured that they needed to hide out until nighttime, so they could travel by night. He found a multi-level parking garage in Arlington and parked the car in a spot furthest from the elevator and hunched down to keep a low-profile until dark. As he waited, in clipped tones, Harland outlined for Sterling why they were on the run and what he planned to do, picking through Sterling's feathers as any concerned parent would do.

As the streetlights came on, Harland decided they were reasonably safe now, figuring those running the search would think they were long gone from the local area. After going through a fast food drive-through and ordering a dozen burgers (all rare), half a dozen fish patties, and extra cups of water, because both of them were extremely ravenous and thirsty, they pointed the car west. The goal was a remote cabin in the Appalachians that Harland had inherited from his great-uncle and had never discussed with anyone at the Pentagon. The cabin was so far off the beaten path that the dirt track that led to it was not shown on any maps. Travelling quickly on Route 66, they were just another dark car in a stream of dark cars pouring out of D.C. to suburban homes during rush hour. As the traffic thinned, they abandoned the major roads and sought the narrow, winding roads through the farmlands and foothills leading to the mountains.

"We're here, son," Harland announced as he shook his son awake. He was tired as he pulled up to the cabin after a long, safe trip.

"Are we there yet, Dad?" Sterling mumbled as he rubbed his eyes awake. "I'm starved again. When do we eat?"

Harland was also hungry again. As they had gotten out into the country where less people had been exposed to the enhancements, he had been afraid they might be spotted by law enforcement if they tried to stop and shop for food. Even if the word of his escape hadn't made it into the back woods areas, he would have been memorable walking barefoot with his long talons through the store. Getting gas had been risky enough. Thank the greedy gas station owners for following the trend of self-pay pumps to keep a bit more money in their pockets rather than paying a person to pump gas. Harland ironically thought about how gas prices had not dropped when the pumps changed to self-serve. Take away another local job and up the profits.

Food, however, was not going to be a problem. Though the cabin lacked plumbing and electricity, these amenities were becoming increasingly irrelevant to Harland and Sterling.

"See that river, Sterling. Let's go catch some fish and drink some of that cool and refreshing water. It's funny how much I love sushi now! And, there are plenty of small rodents in the woods. It'll be fun to figure out ways to catch them together," Harland said, stretching his lean dark frame to get the kinks out. The shirt felt so restrained after the long trip that he shed it, shaking his beautiful silver feathers free in the air. Without a second thought, he stripped out of his pants too, for the first time feeling completely unencumbered. Quizzically, Sterling gazed at him and then quickly followed suit, prancing around as free as a bird.

"In fact, a bug flew into my mouth the other day, and it was actually tasty," Harland added thoughtfully. For a moment Harland became aware of how much he had changed from his previous human likes and dislikes, but then he shrugged it off. Deep insight and introspection were alien to him now.

"Race you to the river," Sterling yelled to his father, leaping off as fast as he could before the words were out of his mouth. Harland took off after him.

* * *

The dolphin broke the water as it paced the 45 foot homemade wooden sailboat off the coast of Brazil.

"Gabe, come here and look at these dolphins," Marti urged as she leaned over the edge watching as the dolphin easily sped up to join its compatriots zigging and zagging under the bow of the boat.

Gabe gave her a small wave to acknowledge he had heard her but didn't move another muscle. He and Marti had partied hard at their stopover in Rio as they headed up the East Coast of South America after leisurely cruising from the Patagonia Estates where they had left their friends behind. During the days in Rio, they had played the tourists, seeing all the sights and the glorious beaches, even tramping up to see the famous statue of Christ. What was that called anyhow? It bothered him briefly that the sharp journalist mind he had when he worked for the Annapolis Triangle was not holding onto details the way it had in the past. He put it down to the Jim Beam and Coca-Cola he had been steadily sipping as they lazed about on the deck of the boat. He didn't put any effort into coming up with the name of that statue. Marti would know and he could ask her later.

They must have spied out every little corner bar in Rio in the evenings, Gabe mused. Though they had shut down most of the hot spots they tried, he couldn't help but feel none of them measured up to the bar in the Marina Hotel where he had anchored down his own stool for over 30 years, and where he had met Marti. He gazed at her fondly, even now not able to keep from admiring the way her curly auburn hair glinted in the sunlight, and the way she filled out those scraps of green fabric she called a bathing suit. On the other hand, today Gabe was feeling every one of his 65 years, and just didn't seem to be able to move. Maybe, he surmised, he was just tired from all the traipsing and nightlife.

Marti was having none of it. "Get up, you lazy old codger," Marti said fondly as she firmly removed the drink from Gabe's hand and began tugging on his arm to get him up. "You have got to see these dolphins," she insisted.

"I've seen dolphins before," Gabe protested as he obediently got himself up. "It's not like this is the first time I've been sailing in my life."

"Well, I haven't, Mister Gabriel Channing," Marti retorted, playfully sweeping his still lush blond and gray hair out of his eyes. "I say we stop this old tub and go for a swim with the dolphins."

"Well, Miss Marti Svonski, I don't feel up to paddling around in this big pond with a bunch of fish, even if it is as calm as a lake,"

Gabe responded, knowing he had lost the battle the second he gazed into her deep amber eyes.

"You know darn well that they aren't fish," she answered heatedly, falling neatly into the trap he had set. "They are mammals, and exceptionally intelligent ones at that, probably smarter than you even!"

"Today I wouldn't doubt it," Gabe said, not being able to hide a bit of a twinkle in his eye from being able to bait Marti so easily. Normally he wasn't able to put anything over on her, since they had known each other too long. Now that he thought of it, it amazed him how long it had taken for them to get together.

The water was as calm as the proverbial lake. They had not even been able to raise the sail, but had been motoring along for the better part of the day. Moving slowly, Gabe went and turned off the engine, hoping that without a bow wave to ride, the dolphins would take off for other dolphin pursuits and spare him from having to go in the water. However, the dolphins seemed to have no inclination to leave and Marti was already putting on her snorkel gear. Sighing, Gabe joined her and gave a hearty spit into his mask.

Marti rolled her eyes. "You could use the spray," she said in exasperation.

"Nothing works better than a good spit," Gabe declared, situating his mask on his head and reaching for his fins. "I've been doing it that way —"

"Yeah, yeah, I know! Since the dinosaur age or before," Marti teased, and without waiting for his answer, she jumped into the water. Shuffling over to the side, Gabe reluctantly followed her in.

At first the dolphins kept their distance as Marti and Gabe paddled. As they got used to the presence of these strange creatures with their long tube-like noses coming out of the top of their heads and their long ungainly side flippers and split tails, their natural curiosity and friendliness brought them closer to explore. Before long, a whole pod of dolphins was cavorting around Marti and Gabe, leaping into the air and diving down, swimming underneath them and coming up alongside with a little kick zooming on past.

The most enchanting moment for Marti was when a mother dolphin escorted her baby over for a closer view. Though she had the mouthpiece of her snorkel inhibiting her, Marti cooed away at the baby, for all she was worth. The baby came straight at her and butted her mask with its nostrum. Marti, who had never experienced the joy of motherhood, was transported with the sheer bliss of that moment.

Gabe, meanwhile, was eye to eye with the male leader of the group. This large dolphin would whack the water with his tail every once in awhile, and give a mighty snort from his blowhole. He stayed right next to Gabe, matching speed with him. Tentatively, Gabe reached out a hand. The dolphin eyed it carefully, but didn't move away, and for one magical second Gabe touched the softest skin he had ever felt — including Marti's — before the dolphin powered away.

Gabe and Marti would've probably stayed forever with the dolphins, but the dolphins must have echolocated on a distance group of fish and were gone in the blink of an eye, leaving empty water, but strong feelings of exhilaration and peace in Marti and Gabe. Just as suddenly as the dolphins had disappeared, Marti and Gabe suddenly realized they were famished. They had been in the water with the dolphins for hours. Feeling comfortably drained, they stroked over to the boat.

Marti started up the ladder first, but playfully decided she would pretend she couldn't make it up. "Oh, Gabe, I am so exhausted, I don't think I can climb another step," Marti said as she leaned back into him. Gabe gave her a half-hearted shove on her bottom, and disappointedly, Marti trounced the rest of the way onto the deck.

"Marti, I, I don't think I can make it into the boat," Gabe panted, resting his head against a rung.

Impatiently tossing her curls, Marti said, "Oh, you wouldn't play that game with me, but now you expect me to play it with you."

"No, Marti, please, I'm serious," Gabe pleaded, faintly, not even raising his head.

Beginning to be alarmed but still not putting it past Gabe to be trying to put one over on her, Marti reached out a hand to Gabe. He reached out to take it, but his grasp was weak so she grabbed him under his arms. Marti had all she could do to manhandle him onto the boat. He collapsed like a beached whale, breathing heavily and holding his fist to his chest.

"Oh no, Gabe! Are you having a heart attack?" Marti asked, now in a panic. Dropping rapidly to his side and uselessly fluttering her hands, she tried to decide what she should do first.

Gabe dropped his hand from his chest, but didn't answer immediately. Marti started to get up to head for the ship-to-shore radio, when Gabe reached out and restrained her. "I'm all right Marti," he said feebly. Then he bellowed to her, using a stronger voice. "Seriously, Marti, I'm fine now."

"Oh Gabe, you are so scaring me. I think we need to call for help," Marti replied, fearfully.

Struggling into a sitting position, Gabe pulled Marti into a rough hug. Gabe said, "See, I'm fine now. I think it was just the combination of too much sun, too long without food, all that exertion with the dolphins, and too many Jim Beams."

Wanting to believe him, Marti rested in his embrace, gradually letting go of her fear.

After eating some filling sandwiches, they motored into a bay and dropped anchor close to land. Resting on the deck in each other's arms, they watched the lavender and orange sunset over the coast of Brazil.

"Marti, I've been thinking about those free pills we were given," Gabe brought up, casually, winding a strand of Marti's hair around the fingers of his hand. "Maybe we should try taking them."

"Why would we want to do that?" Marti queried lazily, her mind more on the brilliant streams shooting up from the dying sun than on their conversation.

The episode that occurred when they had gotten out of the boat had bothered Gabe much more deeply than he had let on to Marti. Gabe knew he wasn't getting any younger, so the thought of a heart attack like the one that had taken his father loomed large in his mind as he remembered that sharp pain he had felt in his chest.

"Well, it might be nice to be able to swim with less effort with all those dolphins," Gabe said, trying for nonchalant. What he really was thinking is that there were pills that slowed aging, claiming to strengthen and improve blood flow to the heart.

"Yes, it would be nice to be able to swim faster and longer without tiring," Marti agreed. "Speaking of the pills, it's been a long time since we made contact with Rita, Nate, and Sandra. I think we should give them a call."

That wasn't where Gabe had intended to go with the conversation since he had more romantic plans in mind. He was quick to agree with her, realizing they had all the time in the world now to do whatever they wanted to do for the rest of their lives, including conversations about pills and romance. The million dollars he had pocketed from his portion of the sale of the technology for the enhancement pills Rita had developed, coupled with the money he made from his story in *Playboy*, would keep them afloat forever. Then there was the money Marti had made from selling the bar. Being an old chauvinist, Gabe didn't count that as living expense money. With Nate handling the investments for them, he felt certain they were secure for life.

"Okay, Marti, let's give them a holler." He jumped up and headed in to the radio.

After a long gabfest, with the women doing most of the gabbing, and Nate filling them in on their current portfolio status, Gabe asked if anyone had heard from Harland.

Sandra, who had met with Harland and his son for lunch before heading for Argentina, filled Gabe and Marti in on that get-together. "You wouldn't believe what has happened to Harland and his son," she said. "They have feathers all over their bodies from taking the hybrid pills. Holly and her daughters joined us and they have started to grow feathers too, but they aren't as far along as Harland and his son. What freaked me out even more was that Harland, whom you remember was quite a drinker, only wanted water!"

"Well, maybe he was just practicing moderation in front of his son," Gabe suggested.

"No, I don't think so," Sandra disagreed. "He hadn't even noticed the change in his drinking habits until I mentioned it. Sterling only drank water too, and what kid do you know that doesn't want a Coke?"

"Maybe it was just an unusual side effect that a few people had," Marti hypothesized.

"That's not it at all," Sandra stated, emphatically. "This is a world-wide phenomenon. Boy, you two lovebirds have really been out of touch. Didn't you see the news of the demonstration that occurred around the world?"

"We've been avoiding the news," Gabe, the old newshound admitted, a bit shamefacedly. "What was that all about?'

"People gathered in front of major monuments in every country of the world, and all of them had mutated to different animal characteristics," Sandra informed them.

"What do mean "different animal characteristics"?" Marti asked.

"Well, like Harland, some people have become birdlike, while others have taken on aquatic features, like gills. Others have developed long necks and legs. Oh, there are too many changes to enumerate them all. Believe me, if you can think it, it has already happened," Sandra said.

Thinking of his fears of aging and serious medical conditions, and his discussion with Marti on the possibility of taking the pills, Gabe did not want to readily let go of that option. "I'm sure the manufacturers of the pills are responding to the outrage about that, and are trying to quickly create cures for the conditions. They're definitely reworking the supplements so that won't happen anymore," Gabe sounded off.

"Gills sound sort of cool," Marti piped in, thinking of how much easier it would be to swim with the dolphins if they could get rid of that mask and snorkel and be able to breathe underwater without having to worry about it.

"That's just it," Sandra explained, impatiently. "The people who have mutated are not complaining at all."

"Then why were they protesting?" Gabe asked. His journalist instincts aroused.

"They weren't protesting at all. They just sat or perched there," Sandra said in frustration. In fact, the quote that all the papers picked up was, "that they did it just because they could."

"That doesn't have much of a ring to it," Gabe said, critically. "I could —"

"Never mind that," Sandra interrupted. "I got out of there as fast as I could. I think these mutants are going to take over the world. I wanted to get as far away from civilization as I could."

"Oh, like seeing Nate again wasn't a factor in your decision," Marti said, coyly. "I don't see what the big deal is. As you said, these mutants, as you call them, were peaceful and seemed content with who they are. As Gabe said, I'm sure the manufacturers will have to do something to change the pills for people who want the enhancements without developing animal characteristics. It'll all work itself out, just as things usually do."

After a few more general comments, the call ended. Marti, not particularly worried about what was going on in the rest of the world, and happy with Gabe in their own little boat world, looked forward to their next planned stop in Barbados. Gabe had many nagging reservations, and more personal interest, not only as a former journalist who couldn't shake the habit of wanting to know all the news, but also on a personal level due to his private health and aging concerns. As Marti threw her arms around his neck and gave him a long meaningful kiss, Gabe's mind turned to more immediate matters.

* * *

Holly settled down wearily on a stool in the bar she had bought from Marti in the Marina Hotel, which she had gotten with some of her million dollar take. Was it her imagination or was Jasmine (the piano player) having difficulty with her playing, since she had started to develop webbing between her fingers?

17

Running a bar was a more work than she had ever imagined when she was a limousine driver for the hotel, enviously dreaming about owning a business herself one day. Going into partnership with Carley, a former waitress in the bar, had been the next best decision after buying the bar, Holly thought. Carley had the hands-on experience of the everyday routine in the bar and an intimate knowledge of the regulars and their drinks of choice. As Holly gazed around the bar with satisfaction, her eyes lit on Gabe's old bar stool. She chuckled as she remembered Gabe actually buying and installing his own stool in the bar, complete with a brass name tag. Regardless, it still startled her to see total strangers sitting on that stool. She idly wondered how Gabe and Marti were doing on their lazy cruise to wherever their fancy took them.

Picking up a newspaper a customer had left lying on the gleaming mahogany bar, Holly was going to throw it away when a headline caught her attention: "Mutant Birdman Evades Capture After Brutally Murdering A Nurse". Self-consciously, Holly smoothed the feathers on the back of her neck which blended attractively into her short brown hair. Reading further, she gasped out loud when she came to Harland's name, remembering their time together on Gabe's sailboat when the six relative strangers bonded together to evade capture by Homeland Security.

Despite the obvious tension and uncertainty of the situation, Holly couldn't help but find herself attracted to Harland, darkly handsome in his major's uniform. They had casually flirted together, even discovering that both of them had children. They had gotten back in touch after Harland returned to the States. Holly started taking the enhancement supplements after she heard Harland rave about how the pills had eliminated his need for glasses, how his son was excelling in school, and how they both were invigorated with health.

She couldn't believe that Harland had done what they were accusing him of, though she had to admit she had noticed changes in his behavior the last time she, her daughters, and Carley had met Harland and his son (plus Sandra) for lunch. She glanced uneasily down at the tiny brown feathers on the backs of her hands. She felt like she was still the same person and hadn't changed whatsoever. She wondered if anyone else thought she had changed, and decided to ask Carley as she reached for her glass of water. It was peculiar how much she liked water now. She never realized what she had been missing. And, of course, water was so healthy for anyone.

I wonder if Sandra, Nate and Rita have heard about Harland, Holly thought to herself. With sudden decision, she hopped off the stool and headed to the office where she clipped out the article, scanning it and emailing it off to her friends in Argentina, hoping they would have some insight into what was going on.

* * *

"Hey Zack," Rita called out as she entered Zack's office in the administrative building. It was in a complex that was being built to research a cure for the devolution process that was affecting millions of people around the globe.

"Oh, hi Rita," Zack said, stretching his arms in a fake yawn as he casually tried to hide his delight in seeing her. He saw her many times a day, but the attraction, at least on his part, was increasing exponentially, with every moment away from her more and more hard to bear. As he looked in the deeply mysterious hazel pools of her eyes, wanting to fall into them and float there forever, he failed to see anything approaching a reciprocal affection for him. Sighing, he brusquely asked, "What can I do for you, I'm pretty busy here?"

Ignoring what Rita perceived as just part of Zack's usual abrasive personality, she responded. "I wanted to show you this article about Harland that Holly just emailed to us, to see what you think of it."

"I already know about it," Zack answered, unthinkingly, as he noticed the way her khaki shorts and shirt emphasized her shapely assets. Other guys might drool over nubile young women in their 20s, but Zack preferred a woman like Rita any day!

"What do you mean you know about it? This hasn't made the local news that I know about," Rita said, suspiciously narrowing her beautiful eyes.

Uh-oh, Zack thought, I'm busted. "I was informed of Harland's actions yesterday morning by Homeland Security, and was asked to be on the lookout for him in case he tried to come here. You haven't heard from him have you?" Zack asked, going on the aggressive to avoid being put on the defensive.

Going for the jugular, Rita ignored his tactic. "I thought we were supposed to be a team down here. How could you hide this from me?" she demanded, waving the article under his nose.

"You know I have to keep secrets from you," Zack said in exasperation, running his hand back and forth over his military-cut hair. "I'm with HSA, not some Hollywood gossip website. Sure, we are collaborating on your work, but that doesn't mean I share every part of my job with you that doesn't impact what you are doing."

"Well, I would say this news exactly impacts my work," Rita declared. "Up until now devolution has seemed to be a peaceful process. While it is insidiously bringing physical changes to the people who take the pills, there have not been any violent personality changes to the subjects that would pose a direct threat to others around them. This changes everything. It makes my work more crucial and the need for a solution more pressing!"

Wow, what a woman, Zack, thought. I love it when she gets fiery. Pulling his thoughts back to the matter at hand, Zack decided that he needed to lay all the cards on the table for Rita to really know what they were up against, so she would know what was at stake and what she needed to do about it.

"Have a seat, Rita. This is going to take a while. It's time I explain everything to you. You are aware of the nuclear testing that the United States conducted in the Marshall Islands, sixty-six tests in all from 1946 to1958. The nuclear fallout created changes in the people who lived on the islands," Zack began in laborious detail.

"Yeah, yeah, I know all that," Rita said impatiently with a wave of her hand. "Gabe covered all of that in his article for *Playboy*. He also exposed how the US herded all those people to an undisclosed spot and used them for experiments to create the perfect warrior. That's why we sold the technology to the United Nations, so that the whole world would have it and the U.S. would not have a secret, unfair advantage over everyone else."

"Ah, but that's where you are all wrong," Zack said, sadly shaking his head. "We had already found out that when the DNA changed in the islands' natives causing them to devolve, it also caused all the characteristics of civilization, peaceful coexistence, brotherly love, building a new and better tomorrow, whatever terms you want to apply, to be wiped out too. Eventually, even perpetuation of the species fell, since everyone devolved in a different, unique manner, there was no personal identification to anyone else, except barely their own offspring, and then even that disappeared. They were all turning on each other until we had to restrain them to keep them from tearing each other apart."

Misinterpreting Zack's sadness for supercilious superiority, Rita interrupted hotly with righteous indignation. She said, "Then someone got the brilliant idea that with a little more genetic manipulation from innocent scientists, like me, being kept in the dark and used as patsies, you could revolutionize the parts of the code you needed to make your mutants more manageable, creating the perfect killing machines. Well, we put a monkey wrench in your precious little plans."

"You still don't get it. We weren't interested in developing walking weapons. We were looking for a way to reverse the devolution process. What you were working on in your GenXY lab was a way to turn DNA that had previously been 100% human and had devolved into something much less than human, back to *being* human," Zack said quietly, his dark brown eyes registering sympathy for Rita as it hit her.

Slumping back in her chair, Rita whispered, "Oh, no, what have we done? Instead of stopping the US from being able to wage war on other nations with an unfair advantage, we have provided every other country in the world with the ability to create hybrid monsters."

"And even worse," Zack sad ramming the point home, "innocent civilians are being genetically devolved into vicious mutants under the benevolent guise of enhancement supplements."

"Do you think that is all a plot by a foreign government?" Rita asked naively.

"No, Rita, everything is not a conspiracy. All of this is just a huge, horrible mistake. This is what happens when governments and corporations rush in to take advantage of new technology without finding out in advance what the consequences might be," Zack answered, looking sorrowful and stern at the same time.

"Just like we rushed in," Rita admitted, avoiding Zack's gaze. "However, you are not without blame here either Mr. Zack McHenry. The government should not have kept all of this a big secret, and trusted the scientists working on the project."

"And then what?" Zack demanded, getting up and walking agitatedly around the office. "Surely word would leak out and there would be a panic."

"At least we would've known not to sell the technology to other countries," Rita retorted, jumping to her feet and getting in his face.

"Don't kid yourself, sweetheart," Zack sneered, for the moment not even registering how close Rita was to him. "The more people who were in the loop, the greater chance of a leak, and then other countries would secretly have controlled the genetic formulas and would be doing their own experiments that we wouldn't even know about, or have a way to protect against. At least now we know that everybody has it and we know what we have to prepare for."

Looking down at the article that had started this whole conversation, with tears in her eyes, Rita mumbled as if to herself, "and what exactly are we up against? How can we ever begin to measure the damage that has already been done?"

Looking up at Zack she said, "Promise me that there will be no more secrets!" Having said that, and without waiting for a reply, she turned and fled out the door. She knew that she, more than anyone else — with her work ethic and training — was responsible for the unleashing of DNA mutating pills on the unsuspecting inhabitants of this planet.

Giving a desk leg a swift kick, Zack thought, way to go McHenry. That sure went well. You could have been a bit more sensitive about how you broke it to her knowing ruefully that he had the sensitivity of that proverbial bull in the china shop. His wiry, muscular frame nearly hummed with the desire to run after Rita, but he plopped down in his desk chair instead, rubbing his hands on the black jeans he had put on this morning. After being at the ranch for a couple of weeks, he had allowed his uptight D.C. style of dress to relax with the climate, but he still wasn't used to it, or quite sure what exactly fit in with the local culture but still looked like he was working.

Give her some time to cool down, he instructed himself, turning back to his computers. Dames, can't live with them, but sometimes it seemed like it would be better to live without them. Besides, with all this acreage who knows where she is by now. Determinedly he put her out of his mind and concentrated on the work before him.

Rita had instinctively headed for the high estate vineyards on horseback where the grapes were still sparkling from the sprinklers' watering. Wandering aimlessly down the shady rows, drinking in the sharp, sweet, plumy smell of the thin-skinned grapes grown as bush vines, Rita felt herself centering, as she had for all the years growing up when she used this as her sanctuary in times of distress. She had used the genetic manipulation program that was now threatening the world to genetically enhance the organically grown grapes in her father's vineyards years ago, giving them an increasing reputation as the best of the Argentinean Malbecs. How benign that all seemed now.

The shock and horror of the enormity of what she and the others had done was beginning to sink in and Rita realized it would take her a long time to come to terms with it, if she ever could. Throwing herself into her work and trying to reverse the de-evolution process they had unleashed onto the world would be a start in the right direction. She knew she couldn't do it just by herself. Instead, she would have to enlist the aid of her brother, Pedro, a mechanical engineer, who had written the initial program to streamline change-orders in mechanical designs, not DNA, by reducing a blueprint to its basic parts and then reconfiguring it to any combination that was desired. With some adjustments Rita had been able to reform the application to analyze and manipulate the DNA sequencing. I'm not waiting for the lab construction to be done, she decided, burying her face in a cluster of purple orbs. There's plenty I can get started on immediately, she thought, as she hopped back onto the horse and trotted off to find Pedro.

* * *

"Can I open my eyes yet, Nate?"

Nate had wanted to keep the new ranch he had bought, in the foothills near the waterfall where he and Sandra had first kissed, a secret to surprise her. But when it came to secrets, the large estates shrunk to the size of a small village where everyone was related. The next best thing he could do was to not allow her to see his plans for it, let alone visit it before everything was done. Sandra had begged and pleaded and batted her long eyelashes at him. She tried to sneak peeks over his shoulder when he was working on the blueprints. She had even tried his door when he was up working at the site, only to find it was locked. She knew he had bought a place by the waterfall, but for all her machinations, she had not been able to come up with a single other detail. Nate had held firm.

But, finally the day had come when he was ready to show it to her. They had mounted horses at daybreak, a time of day Sandra was not fond of, though she was gradually adjusting to getting up at that time. Rather than taking her directly to the waterfall, Nate turned off on a dirt drive that looked like it had been recently graded. Before they reached a bend, they dismounted and tied the horses up to a tree. Under protest Sandra had agreed to keep her eyes closed and let him lead her from there on foot, adamantly refusing to be blindfolded. As they walked, it seemed that they were actually getting closer to the waterfall, at least by the sounds of it.

"Wait one more second," Nate pleaded, as he swiveled her around, pointing her back towards the thundering waterfall. "Amazing how much louder it sounds when you can't see it," she thought absently, pushing her Alice-in-Wonderland blond hair out of her face.

"Okay, you can look now," Nate announced somewhat anxiously, his golden retriever brown eyes searching her deep ocean blue ones, which widened appreciatively at what she saw before her.

Tucked into the hillside in front of her was a Spanish-style adobe ranch of peach clay. Twirling around, Sandra could see there was a clear view to the top of the waterfall, but thankfully not to the pond below, where she and Nate had gone skinny-dipping after their first kiss. As if he could read her mind, Nate blushed on cue. Giving him an amused smile, Sandra threw her arms around him and exclaimed, "This looks like a favorite dream of mine. Pinch me so I know I'm awake."

Nate obliged with a soft pinch on her rear, earning himself a playful slap.

"Show me everything, right now," Sandra commanded, grabbing him by the hand and leading him up the embedded marble chip walkway.

"Hey, who's leading whom?" Nate yelped, surging into the lead. Though short, Nate was full of kinetic energy, and was a great sprinter. He'd built up some strong leg muscles from all his winter ski trips to Aspen, but so had Sandra, allowing her to keep pace with him.

"This doesn't look like a new house, "Sandra said, stopping in front of the ranch.

"It isn't. It has been on the market for a long time, and I was lucky enough to buy it," Nate responded.

"Then what have you been doing up here all this time that was so mysterious?" Sandra asked.

"For a start, I installed those," Nate said proudly, pointing to the solar panels on the roof. "I took a page from Rita's father and made this whole place environmentally friendly and self-reliant. Let me show you."

Taking her hand a bit self-consciously, he led her around his new estate showing her the wind turbines, and fuel cell generators that provided power to the house. He even showed her the beginnings of an organically grown vegetable garden. There was a stable that was still in the process of being refurbished. The setting for all this was breath-taking, with glimpses of distant mountains; the ranch had its own stream that wrapped partially around the estate after passing over the waterfall. There was a separate spring-fed pond that had icy, delicious water, providing all the water needs for the ranch. There were meadows and forests, with much of the land still virgin. Sandra oooed and aaahed at everything she saw, clapping her hands in wonder like a child in a magical land. Nate was more than rewarded for his efforts by her evident delight. They picnicked by the pond with the food they had packed in with them.

"I can't believe all you have accomplished in such a short time," Sandra said, twining flowers into a wreath and placing it on her head.

"And that's just the outside," Nate said proudly. "Wait until you see what I have done inside." He jumped up and pulled her to her feet, and they wound their way back to the house.

Inside, Nate eagerly showed her that he had outfitted the house with all the latest and best in electronics and communication equipment. Sandra dutifully showed her interest, but her eye was more on the spaciousness of the rooms done in earthy, masculine style. "It's obvious this place could do with a feminine touch," she thought.

As if reading her mind, Nate said, "This ranch belonged to an old bachelor. I haven't touched anything yet as far as decorating goes. I haven't a clue what to do with it. I thought maybe you would be willing to help me out with that?" He suddenly felt shy and lacking in self-confidence. "Suppose I am moving too fast," he worried.

"Oh, I'd love to decorate this place. I've never had a place where I had total freedom to go wild with my ideas," Sandra enthused. Then realizing she was being a bit presumptuous, she backpedaled. "This is your house, so I would need to know what you would like."

"Hey, be my guest. Go wild and tack a whack at it! I'm serious about not having the first idea of where to start or what would look good. These are my babies," Nate said, patting his equipment fondly. "But now, how about we go for a swim?"

Sandra fell silent, remembering their last swim. Misinterpreting her silence for reluctance to repeat the skinny dipping experience he said stammered quickly, "I stocked the guest room with an assortment of bathing suits. I'm pretty sure you could find one to suit you."

"If you want me to wear a bathing suit I will," Sandra teased with a devilish sparkle in her eyes, "but that seems like a step backwards to me. I'd rather pick up right where we left off."

And leaving no doubt in his mind to her intentions, she started shedding clothes as she ran down towards the pool they had had their first swim in. Nate lost no time in following suit. They spent a beautiful afternoon paddling around, standing under the waterfall, splashing and dunking each other, and just floating quietly, absorbing the trills of birds and the distant sounds of animals going about their business. The sun was pulling away from the land, as they pulled themselves away from the water and returned to the house.

"I should probably be heading back to the Perez place," Sandra said, obviously not meaning it.

"Wait," Nate urged wheedling, brushing his damp, sandy, blond hair out of his face. "I've prepared dinner for you."

"How could you do that?" Sandra scoffed, collapsing in a comfortable arm chair. "You've been with me all day. There was no time."

Going to the freezer, Nate triumphantly pulled out a large casserole pan, and popped it into the oven. "I made it yesterday. All it needs is to heat up. We can have a glass of Ronaldo's excellent wine while we wait." Suiting actions to words, he pulled out a couple of bottles he had stocked for the occasion.

"Um, Nate. You do remember that I am a vegetarian don't do?" Sandra said quietly, not wanting to break the mood, but refusing to back down on her principles.

"How could I forget? You've been reminding everyone at every meal for months now," he laughed. "I have prepared a vegetarian recipe that I remembered my mother making. It's a spinach casserole. My satellite phone came in quite handy for getting her timely help yesterday."

"Well, in that case, bring on the wine," Sandra said in relief.

They dined on the covered porch overlooking the waterfall with the sun setting behind it. The spinach casserole was delicious, filled with hard-boiled eggs, cheddar cheese, onions, and a Portobello mushroom puree. After the long eventful day, Sandra's appetite matched Nate's. Nate had provided a platter of local fruits that were in season, as well as Eva's homemade bread to go with it. They dawdled over the food and wine, both reluctant to break the mood.

"Not too bad for a steak eater, especially with a wine that is so steak-friendly," Nate trumpeted his own horn.

"No, it was absolutely perfect," Sandra assured him, with a contented sigh. "I really pigged out. I didn't know you had it in you to concoct such a terrific vegetarian meal. Too bad you don't cook this way all the time."

"Whoa there! I may have cooked this meal, but it was a real stretch for me. I did it just to please you. Normally I'm just your regular meat-and-potatoes type of guy, though I admit a vegetarian meal now and then makes a nice change," Nate protested. "How did you become such an avid vegetarian anyhow? Were you raised that way?"

"No, I was raised in the normal American way of eating heavy amounts of meat," Sandra answered. "From the time I was little it always bothered me that I was eating an animal that had been killed. By the time I was a teen, I could not look at meat anymore without seeing the pleading eyes of the animal every time I took a bite. I knew that if I had to look at a beautiful calf and kill it myself, I'd never be able to do it. It seemed just as morally wrong to let someone else do it for me. It was only after I had become a vegetarian myself that I learned about the horrendous practices that are used to store and raise, and then kill the animals. That only served to harden me in my beliefs." Sandra gave a shiver, thinking of how calves were kept in tight boxes so they couldn't move any muscles that would toughen the meat, and then hit on the head when they were deemed right for butchering.

Misinterpreting her shiver, Nate said, "You're getting cold, let's go inside." And he pushed his chair back, effectively ending the discussion.

"Nate, I really need to be going," Sandra said half-heartedly, knowing there was no way she could follow those trails after dark all alone.

"I was kind of hoping you would spend the night here," Nate said, and then with an embarrassed confusion added, "I mean, I have so many guest rooms, that there is plenty of room for you. I could ride back down with you in the morning."

"That sounds great," Sandra responded in relief as they made their way in the cavernous living room towards a fireplace made of river stone that was already laid for the match. "You think of everything," she added, eyeing the fire Nate was starting. Eschewing a chair, she fell gracefully into a lotus position in front of the hearth.

Not quite gracefully, Nate plopped down next to her, wine in hand for a refill once he had a nice blaze going. Suddenly a bit tongue-tied at the intimacy of the moment, he searched for a neutral topic to talk about.

"So what do you think about that new email that came in today on Harland's attack on that nurse?" he started.

"It's horrifying. At least now I'm sure I made the right move in leaving the States to live down here," Sandra replied. "When I had lunch with Harland and his son I could see that he was losing his human nature and becoming more like an animal. I couldn't help but assume that the internal changes were keeping pace with the physical ones. If Harland had been the only one, I could have looked at it as an aberration, but from the demonstrations around the world, it appears to be the norm rather than the exception. I had no real clue that people who mutated would turn violent, but I felt that at some point there would be a confrontation between them and us, and with the sheer numbers of people popping the pills I wasn't confident about the outcome. I decided the farther away I could get in a rural area, the better the chances of surviving the inevitable. My first thoughts were to come here. You haven't taken any of the enhancement supplements have you?"

"No, I haven't thought about taking them much. I'm pretty content with who I am," Nate answered with the vanity of a 25-year-old in excellent shape. "I've been viewing them more in terms of an investment, and I have to tell you that my stock portfolio has gone through the roof since I put most of my pennies in that hat. I don't see the market bottoming out in the foreseeable future, either. More and more people are going to want the benefits of improving aspects of themselves they are not too happy about, or just taking on new abilities for the fun of it with the ease of just taking some pills."

Shaking her head, Sandra disagreed vehemently. "It may look like that to you down here in the cozy safety of the foothills of Argentina, but in the real world things are changing fast. Normal, regular humans, and by that I mean people who have not taken the pills, are being turned off quickly by the changes they see in those who have taken them. No one wants to give up their human form and turn into animals, no matter what the benefits. I think you need to sell off your stock as fast as you can. I don't see more people taking the pills at all. In fact, I expect there to be a backlash to the pills soon."

A bit miffed at being advised about what to do in the arena where he was an expert and had made millions while most people were still getting their feet wet, Nate declared, "I guess time will tell."

"Don't you feel guilty that we are the ones who started all of this? If we hadn't blithely sold Rita's technology to the United Nations none of this would be happening."

Sandra continued. "I know sometimes I feel weighed down by my part in what has happened especially since I have spent my whole life fighting for the environment, and trying to encourage mankind to live in harmony with nature and each other. Now I have set loose a means of tearing apart the normal course of evolution, wreaking havoc on the natural course of things and pitting man against mutant. I have betrayed myself and all of humanity," Sandra said, overwrought with emotion, her tears began falling from her lovely eyes.

Nate put his arms around her. "It's not your fault, Sandra. It's not any of our faults. We didn't know what we were doing. We thought we were doing the right thing and making a buck at the same time. I was all in favor of the making a buck part," he said facetiously, trying to lighten the mood. He liked having his arms around Sandra, but hated to see her in such distress.

"That's the whole problem," Sandra said, rebuffing his comfort. "We didn't know what we were doing. We just rushed in, where angels fear to tread. We are no better than the companies who pushed plastic baby bottles on the world and caused a whole generation of ADHD children. New technology needs to be scrutinized for a long time to see what the long range repercussions might be."

"If every new technology had to go through years and years of government mandated testing nothing would ever change, there would be no leaps forward. If we were afraid of every new development that was made, mankind would never have survived as a species," Nate protested, his own conscience beginning to twinge. "Throughout most of history the technology to test new things properly hadn't even been invented or thought of yet. We wouldn't get anywhere as a civilization, we'd be stagnant if we didn't boldly push forward. What was that line? To boldly go where…."

"It's easy to generalize like that," Sandra said, standing up and then pacing in agitation. "What about Harland and his son? Do you think they really would have chosen this for themselves if they knew what would happen to them beforehand? This is a friend of ours and a little boy. Now they are on the run, hunted like animals, all because of changes in their bodies they had no control over."

"He had the same choice to not take the pills as the rest of us did," Nate asserted.

Their conversation continued back and forth into the deep hours of the night, all thoughts of romance brushed aside in the weighty discussion of the pros and cons of introducing new technologies into the world, and more specifically, the ramification of what they had done by introducing the mutating technology on the world. At least on Sandra's part, the romance was forgotten. Nate, however, being a normal guy, seldom had it far from his mind and in a small corner of his brain he mourned the evening's loss of romance.

*   *   *

Harland munched contentedly on a rat. It had been a great couple of weeks hanging out at the cabin. Since it was winter, they had huddled together in the cabin at night for warmth, though Harland was noticing more and more that he didn't like to be confined in enclosed spaces. He liked the wide open sky above him, and to be able to see for miles in all directions. The higher he was, the better he felt. He often found himself climbing to the top of the tallest tree and sitting there gazing in the distance for hours. It was also the best vantage point from which to spot prey. Speaking of trees, he hadn't seen Sterling for a while and that was probably where his son had also traveled, up into a tree. Sterling's devolution was not as advanced as Harland's, so he needed lots of practice to sink his talons into the tree trunks and climb. If only they could fly! He was thinking vaguely that he should go check out what his son was doing when he heard a scream.

Dropping the rest of his meal, he made his way up the rise to check out the commotion. As he got closer to the Appalachian Trail, he slowed and approached cautiously. He had told Sterling at least a hundred times to stay away from the trail. Hopefully, the screaming had nothing to do with Sterling.

Unfortunately for Harland, it did have to do with Sterling. Against his father's orders, Sterling had chased a plump, juicy hare down the trail just as a couple of hikers had come along. On seeing a naked bird creature running full tilt towards them, they started hollering and brandishing their hiking sticks at him trying to ward him off. Sterling had stopped in confusion, not knowing what the fuss was all about. Harland, whose parental instincts were strong, jumped out from the underbrush in front of Sterling, squawking menacingly at the hikers. The hikers took one look at the fully grown naked bird-man and took off back the way they had come as fast as their sturdy legs would carry them. Harland turned to see if Sterling, who was now quite shamefaced, was okay. Then he proceeded to lecture him, hoping that the hikers would just shrug it off as they got further down the trail. Regardless, the damage was probably done.

Grabbing Sterling, he hustled him back to the cabin, trying hard to think what they should do now.

The hikers did not just forget about their harrowing experience, one they would probably dine out on for many moons to come. Just that morning they had seen a wanted poster at the Rangers' station a quarter mile up the trail, warning hikers to be on the lookout for two mutants with bird features. There was a picture of Harland the way he used to look when he was human and a photo of how he looked on the day he fled the Pentagon. Though he had changed significantly, he still bore a resemblance to the picture. Soon, the hikers burst into the Rangers' station to report the sighting.

The three rangers at the counter set down the inventory sheets they had been working on with gratitude at having an excuse for abandoning, even temporarily, such a boring task, and gave the hikers their undivided attention. With lots of gesturing and exclamations, the two hikers drew a portrait of a vicious attack by the mutants that they had barely escaped from with their lives. Quite a bit of heroics on their part fitted into their story.

Checking the bulletin, the rangers saw they were supposed to contact HSA immediately, monitor the mutants from afar, but under no conditions were they to approach them because they were considered to be highly dangerous. The bulletin also stated that HSA would come and take the lead in their capture. Upon calling HSA, they were reminded in no uncertain terms to keep their distance. HSA wanted these mutants captured alive and they insisted that only they had the experience to get the job done. Hanging up the phone, the rangers looked at each other.

The hikers continued to be hysterical, insisting that the mutants were a threat to anyone on the trail. In fact, in their fantasies they had them already advancing onto the ranger station. Despite their experience with wild hiker tales, the rangers knew there could be danger to innocent hikers on the trail, and that at least some action was required from them. They also didn't like the insinuation on the part of Homeland Security that they wouldn't be able to handle a couple of mutants. After all, they had handled bears and mountain lions in the past. What challenge would a couple of bird-men be to them, especially since one was just a little kid?

The lead ranger, Bob, jumped up and went to the weapons locker, extracting an assortment of specialized equipment. "Molly, you stay here and watch the station."

"You're making me miss all the action because I'm a woman," Molly challenged.

"Don't pull that feminist crap on me now," he answered with disgust. "I need you to guard these hikers and the station, maintain communication between us and HSA, and warn off any other hikers coming along the trail."

With that, the two men were out on the trail and before long they came to the spot the hikers had described. It was easy to see there had been a disturbance in the undergrowth to one side of the trail, and with prudence they stepped into the forest to follow the path of broken twigs and crushed leaves. There was also some snow on the ground, making it easier to follow their human-sized footprints with long talons.

With ingenuity and luck they rapidly found the cabin but it was plain to see the footprints leading away from the cabin overlapped those leading in. Harland's superior auditory ability had heard the men approaching, and he knew the cabin would be a trap. He decided they would be better out in the forest where they could run and have options, so he hustled Sterling out just before the rangers arrived.

Walking was no longer a natural way for Harland and his son to move. So, they merely hopped along the ground though they did not have the necessary speed to keep ahead of the determined park rangers. With his head darting back and forth, Harland thought they should climb up into the trees. With barely a chirp to Sterling, he signaled his intent and climbed up the next tree, hiding in the dense evergreens. Sterling picked his own tree and leapt into it, fluttering his arms as if he had wings, something both of them had been doing with increasing frequency. However, his claws had not developed to the extent of his father's, so he slid down the tree, his talons screeching as he tried to dig in. He landed with a soft thump and jumped up to try again, when the rangers burst onto the scene.

Bob, the tall and solid lead ranger, without stopping to think, threw a net over Sterling that he had thought to bring from the weapons locker. Sterling hissed, and squawked piteously, pecking at the net with his teeth and trying to rip the net apart with his fledgling claws. Harland, in full raptor attack mode, all his thoughts on protecting his young, dropped from his tree and slashed at the ranger holding the net, as he shrieked at him at the top of his voice. Harland lashed out with his right hand talons and cut the arm of the ranger, causing him to drop his hold on the net. Harland's weight, light though it had become, carried the ranger down underneath him. The second ranger, a sturdy Iowa farm boy named Tom, jumped on Harland's back, trying to pull him off Bob. With lightening speed, Harland pivoted and bit him in the shoulder. Bringing his right foot up, he raked his foot talons down the guy's leg. Screaming in pain, Tom, grabbing his leg, backed away from Harland, who was advancing to attack, and fell to the ground. The distraction was enough to allow the Bob to get back up and draw his tranquilizer weapon. Without hesitation, he shot Harland in the back. Then turning, he shot Sterling, who was still fighting his way out of the net. Both father and son hit the ground, tranquilizer darts, sticking from their backs.

"Well, that's one way to subdue these mutants without hurting them, we'll just show those snooty Homeland Security guys we know a few tricks of our own in the park service," Bob remarked boastfully as he bent over to check out his partner. "You doing okay, Tom?" Together the rangers examined their wounds. While deep and nasty, none of the slashes or the bites had hit any major arteries or veins. They'd need a few stitches, but they could hold out until help arrived. They called in to the station with their GPS coordinates, tied up Harland and Sterling, and shook their heads at what the world had come to. Then they sat back and patiently waiting for the HSA cavalry to arrive.

CHAPTER TWO

The Breakdown Begins

The cell doors clanged shut on Harland and Sterling as they were shoved into adjoining cells in a small jail close to where they had been apprehended. The effects of the tranquilizer darts had worn off of them while in transit. While Sterling worriedly curled into a ball, his father kept stewing. Harland kept hurling himself against the divider between the front and back seats in the police car, unwilling, or possibly unable, to understand that escape was no longer an option. They had been placed in shackles and cuffs before they woke up, but Harland continued to try to bite through the barrier. Because the cops doing the transport had never experienced such voracity from a restrained prisoner, they experienced a new fear as they drove the mutants to the jail.

They radioed ahead to voice concern that it might not be possible to peacefully transfer the prisoners from the car to the cells without risk of injury. Muzzles were discussed, but no one could be confident they could get one on Harland before being bitten. The thought of rabies, though unspoken, was on everybody's minds. With Harland and Sterling devolving to animals, could they now have animal-transmitted diseases too?

Finally, there seemed to be no alternative but to tranquilize Harland again, and slip a muzzle onto Sterling. Fortunately, the fight instinct did not seem to have been triggered in Sterling yet.

He was still in the highly dependent stage of a fledgling bird. This plan had gone off without incident, and now they were safely in small holding cells.

Higher level government officials had greater concerns. Consistent with the usual government policy of keeping everything close to the chest and away from the public, first and foremost on the minds of those in charge at HSA had been the desire to keep the location of where Harland and Sterling were being kept a secret. They wanted to prevent a storm of media from descending on the jail. They also wanted to buy time to decide how to handle the legal ramifications of mutants as killers. Their official position was that secrecy was needed to prevent the public from panicking. But, as was usually true, the real reasons had to do with jockeying for power and control, and covering their collective posteriors.

Another question being kicked about at a more local level, but with the oversight of Homeland Security, was whether Harland and Sterling should be jailed as humans with other humans, or if they had devolved so far that they were merely animals and should be put under animal control. Homeland Security had many practical concerns, like how could mutants interact with other prisoners and staff. What they would eat? Certainly raw rodents were not on the prison nutrition plan. How would they even use a toilet? Could they even still recognize a porcelain throne or would they just let loose in whatever direction they were pointed when the urge hit? How could they safely exercise? Could they actually fly with those feathers they were growing? Were their talons capable of helping them climb out of the exercise yard? It was quickly decided that no one had enough authority yet to take away the rights they had been born with as human beings and citizens of the United States. Until a court ruled on their status, the mutant prisoners would be treated like all the others, though everyone knew that was going to be difficult. There would be all kinds of specialized care that would be needed, providing them another reason for holding them in a small facility where more personal attention would be given. Big on everyone's minds was the necessity of doing this right, so that no one could accuse them of violating the prisoners' rights so they could be released back into society on a technicality. At the highest levels, they knew that precedents were being set that would be used to guide future cases with only the naïve doubting there would be future cases.

Soon, a carefully worded statement was issued to the press, downplaying any differences between this case and those of other murderers. Obviously, the media wasn't fooled even for one instant. Before long, *The Washington Post*, the *New York Times*, and every other major newspaper had picked up the story. Then, the *Associated Press* brought the news to the TV newscasters, and major newsmongers like CNN used it within a continuous rotation of stories. Later, the story grew internationally, led by the BBC.

As a story with great potential to increase ratings and subscriptions, the media jumped on the theme of debating about the rights of arrested mutants. Experts in the field, a misnomer because the field was too new to have any yet, were called in to espouse opposing views to keep the dialog raging. In Harland's case the debate centered on whether Harland was still a human or not. If he was no longer a human, then did he have the rights to be tried as a human?

A few caring people queried, with great concern, that if under all those feathers and behind that squawking beak Harland was still actually a human. Were his thought processes human? Was his emotional make-up human? What about his socialization needs, including his personal dreams and plans? No one saw a way to find out these things, since Harland was barely able to communicate even his most basic needs, and these protests died out from lack of a means to validate them.

Some argued that Harland was still human, but that he should be treated as if he was living with diminished capacities. The bleeding heart liberals cried out that he needed a guardian appointed the way children, the mentally challenged, and the elderly who had various forms of dementia do. A sub-argument of this was whether it should be a legally appointed guardian of the court, or a relative of Harland's, or both.

The churches, spying a way to sermonize, weighed in on the issue of the soul. Ponderously, they declared that the soul was the part of humankind that was spiritually formed in the image of God. Though there was a side debate among them about whether the soul was present at birth or at conception, they banded together in insisting that a person could not ever lose his soul. Therefore, Harland remained human because he had a permanent soul. A few individuals, especially teary-eyed little girls, cried out that animals had souls, too. (Thus, to them, Fluffy and Rover were indeed in Heaven!) The idea that animals might have souls, too, muddied the waters too much. Church leaders never put that topic in the spotlight, especially since it would beg the question about whether the Easter Bunny actually had a soul and whether or not it would then be ethical to kill and eat an animal with a god-given soul.

If Harland was a non-human, should he be treated as an animal, or some new form of species? If he was an animal, he surely had some limited rights, depending on how he was classified, to protection from abuse the same as house pets have. Drag a dog behind your car and a jail sentence was pretty much a given. However, if that same dog has perfume sprayed into his eyes in a laboratory it is not considered to be abuse. Until recently, animals on endangered species lists, like the Bald Eagle, could not be hurt in any way, but must be allowed to live in their natural environment, free and wild. Some argued that Harland seemed to be on the track towards becoming a bald eagle, and maybe he had some protection therein as our national symbol.

The vegetarians saw their opportunity to grab the limelight and talked loudly about the rights of animals used for food. Where were the laws to protect animals from abuse when it came to force-feeding geese to produce foie gras? What about the practice of cutting off the beaks of egg-laying hens so they couldn't peck, then keeping them stuffed together in overcrowded cages where many starved to death or dehydrated when food and water were only steps away because they could not move within the crowded space? What about the way veal calves were treated? On and on went the list of atrocities they could cite. They had no real agenda where Harland was concerned because no one proposed he was edible, but they saw an opportunity nonetheless to get their platform out there. Fortunately, at least they added to the whole discussion regarding rights for living beings in general, no matter what form they took.

Many prominent scientists were enamored and vocal with the idea that Harland might be a new species and as such needed to be preserved and studied in controlled conditions. It was vital to civilization to see how this new species would affect the fragile ecosystems, whether they could be replicated, either through natural reproduction, or through cloning. Plus, how would they even come up with a mate? The ethics of Harland being treated like a lab rat were happily bandied about by this group.

Far to the right were the ones who believed that Harland was none of the above and had no rights under any status. After all, fetuses before they are viable do not have any rights. This stand confused the poor Pro-Lifers because, at the same time, they wanted zygotes to have rights. They loudly argued that while he was a human at one point, he no longer was now, and that his rights as a human had devolved along with his physical and mental devolution.

As a prisoner, Harland had lost many rights, to heck with the presumption of innocence until proven guilty. He was incarcerated and every moment of his day was monitored and controlled. Americans would shudder to think that they would permit an innocent man to be held in sensory deprivation. Sitting in a solitary cell, Harland was deprived of almost any stimulation other than what his bird brain was able to concoct.

Recognizing that there was no way, except for a secret military tribunal, to keep the details of this case out of the eye of the public, and it was a little too late to put that cat back in the bag, Homeland Security took the case away from the military and assigned it into the hands of the U.S. Attorney's office. Richard T. Chambers, the brightest star of the prosecuting attorneys was chosen to try the case. Dick, as he was fondly, and unfondly, known, was an arrogant man, centered only on how this case would build his career. He realized that he would be making history and setting the precedent for how all mutants would be tried in the future. Unconcerned about

Harland's mental capacity, he wanted to ensure that mutants would be punished to the full extent of the law.

Prosecutor Chambers proclaimed on every news show that would interview him, "Mutants should be treated no differently than the law treats people who commit crimes when 'under the influence.' In fact, those particular crimes are frequently judged more harshly. Major Harland Parker voluntarily took the supplements not knowing or caring how they might impair his judgment and actions, and he is responsible for his actions before the law. There will be no plea bargaining in this case. It has to go to trial, so mutants will know that they are going to be held responsible for their actions."

Meanwhile, Sterling was also sitting in a jail cell, creating an even bigger problem. Initially, Sterling had been placed in a separate, though adjourning cell to his father. He continuously cried, and refused to eat. No one could bear to look into his mournful, big chocolate eyes. Then, they felt forced to move him into the same cell as Harland. That had improved matters immediately, not only with Sterling, but with Harland, too, who had been throwing himself against the bars separating him from his son. Huddled together, Harland groomed Sterling reassuringly.

Had Sterling even committed any crime? Sure, he aided and abetted his father when there was a warrant out for his arrest. But, did Sterling know that his father was wanted before meeting with him? After all, he did hide with his father, but did he have any understanding of what he was doing, even if he was thinking as a normal ten-year-old boy, let alone if his mental capacity had devolved beyond his ability to reason? He also had resisted capture, or at least had tried to climb the tree. He had never willfully struck out at an officer. If there was no warrant out for him, how could he even be captured let alone incarcerated?

Many had questions about what to do with Sterling. Gleefully, the media hyped the plight of this young man, and the public gladly took up his cause. Normally, a minor would have been released to the custody of his nearest relative. In Sterling's case, though, no one could be found that was willing to accept his special needs. All the same questions about rights that were raised about Harland were rehashed, though this time with greater sympathy. Should he also be treated as if he had human rights?

The authorities scratched their heads as they tried to find a foster home, a group home, or a detention center for his care. Privately, some even considered zoos or wildlife sanctuaries. The idea of a juvenile detention center, when discovered by the ecstatic press and righteous public, led to speeches and marches in town squares to free the boy, especially since many people believed he had done nothing wrong. Regardless, either a guardian or care-giver needed to eventually care for him. Could he even live in a house anymore? Would he devolve further and require some kind of pen that would prevent him from flying away? Should he just be allowed free, his age no longer judged by the standards of a human child? As he had shown when they captured him, he still seemed to be dependent on his father.

Ending the debate, the news reported that a wealthy business mogul, Robin Birdswell, who had such a fascination for avian wildlife that she had created an aviary on her estate, stepped forward. She agreed to hire experienced human and avian care-givers to live with Sterling in a converted cottage on her sprawling farm in Virginian horse country and care for him until the authorities could make up their minds about him. If he devolved further and developed wings, the aviary would give him room to exercise them safely while he learned to use them.

To the cameras, she solemnly vowed, "I will continuously adapt his living conditions to his evolving needs. I am immediately hiring a team of renowned attorneys to sue the government for his confinement and to plea for his rights to freedom once he is able to care for himself."

"Daddy!" Sterling squealed heartbreakingly as officers gently tried to pull him away from Harland's grasp. Harland screeched as four strong, male officers restrained him. There was nothing he could do to prevent them from taking his son away. He knew he needed to fight and to protect his son, but he dimly realized he could do nothing as the little boy was dragged away, weeping uncontrollably. Frantically remembering his long unused practice of human communication with words, he squawked out a rusty, "Please — my son!"

* * *

"Oh no, what can I do? Oh, poor man! Poor boy!" Holly moaned softly, wringing her hands as she paced back and forth in the bar.

Holly had gone to the local law enforcement agency to see if she would be allowed to visit Harland and Sterling, and then be able to post bond for them. She had difficulty communicating to the desk officer who, glancing at the feathers in her hair had been brusque with her when he informed her that Major Parker was being held in an undisclosed location without bail. She had returned to the bar disconsolate and was now pacing agitatedly.

Trying to be discreet because the last few stragglers from the lunch hour were still there and she did not want them disturbed, Carley strolled casually over to Holly and put her arm around her, steering her towards the kitchen. The partnership in the bar had come as quite a surprise to Carley and she was determined to make a success of it. That was becoming increasingly difficult as customers noticed the devolutionary changes in the appearances of Holly and Jasmine and tended to shy away from them, some because they were disgusted by the changes in their appearance and behavior, others because they were afraid that they might be contagious. Still, others knew they had taken the supplements themselves and dreaded the reminder that they themselves were also changing. Whatever the reason, patronage of the bar was decreasing, as it was for the hotel too, and Carley did not want any further disturbance to the business.

"What's wrong, Sweetie?" Carley asked, stroking Holley's head of soft dark curls and tiny feathers with one hand and giving her a glass of water with the other.

"It's Harland," Holly blubbered. She tried to collect her thoughts to explain to Carley what was on her mind, but nothing would come out. Holly had been cautious about taking the pills when they initially came onto the market, but Harland had boasted so much about them when he got back from Argentina. He bragged about how well he and Sterling were doing on them, especially with his improved eyesight. Truth be told, that man sure looked fine, with the ruddy glow he had acquired in South America. He boasted about his increased strength, and with a sly wink hinted at his increased prowess in all areas. Holly had blushed at the implications of that last thought, her mocha latte complexion gaining a touch of strawberry.

He earnestly told her of how much better Sterling was doing in school, and how healthy he had become. Holly was enamored. When Harland offered her the pills that he was taking, she took them with no hesitation and also gave them to her 6-year-old twin daughters, Reva and Vera. All that happened before the devolutionary traits of the pills were known. At that time, there were no physical changes apparent to anyone. Since Harland had been the first person to take pills, and he was in such great shape, obviously there was no one to reveal the danger the pills actually posed.

Holly had been carefully following the news coverage of Harland and Sterling's predicament. She had been about to step forward and offer to take Sterling herself, when that bird lady whisked him to an undisclosed location. Bird lady, she thought, what does she know about birds, where are her feathers? Since her daughters were also taking the same pills, she felt sure she knew how to handle Sterling much better.

At first, she had not believed everything the media had said about what Harland had done or the extent of his devolution. She felt sure that they were sensationalizing the story just to keep the public's attention. Part of her did not want it to be true. She had started to fall for Harland in a big way and did not want to think he was capable of such an atrocity. She was also concerned about her own devolution path and that of her daughters. While she thought her sprinkle of feathers was kind of chic, she had not imagined simultaneous changes to herself internally. She didn't want to think that she or her daughters could become like Harland. Secretly, she knew she was starting to fantasize about the taste of small mammals eaten raw, which made her feel uneasy. She resolved to stop taking the pills at once and not to give them to her daughters. Maybe the process would reverse itself, or at least arrest when she ceased taking them. She could live with the feathers, but she didn't want to change any further. She would call Rita and ask about that, but now when she needed to confess her fears and worries about Harland to Carley the words would not emerge. Were other changes occurring inside of her that she was not aware of?

At least Carley was able to understand her predicament, without putting it into words, having been a barmaid for a decade, and learning to read between the lines when her customers confided in her. Though tiny of stature, Carley had a huge heart and was more than willing to share it with this business partner of hers who had given her such an amazing gift and was now in such great distress.

Carley had never taken the pills. At thirty-one, she had learned enough about life not to try something new, especially in pill form, until time proved whether it was safe, or whether there were unexpected side effects. That started after she'd tried St. John's Wort back when that was a fad, only to find out that the companies out to make a buck were making the pills from parts of the plants that didn't even help depression. Then, studies came out that showed St. John's Wort could even deepen depression and contribute to suicidal tendencies. She had learned that the field of health supplements was unregulated and there was no guarantee of what you were getting when you took them, which was a shame, because it would be nice to use natural substances instead of prescription medications created in a laboratory. It was nice to learn that the pharmaceutical companies were looking more to Mother Nature for answers. Their pills had to go through rigorous testing and approval by the FDA. Even then, look at how medications like Vioxx slipped through the net. Was it better in the long run for time and lawsuits to be the final test of a product's viability?

Carley was in excellent shape and had no medical problems she felt compelled to fix. Carley sat back, waiting and watching, and when Holly and Jasmine began undergoing physical changes, she congratulated herself on her restraint. She was justifiably quite vain about her porcelain skin and her shimmery brunette hair that she wore in a short tousled look, her jade eyes, and her tight birdlike figure, but without the feathers, thank you very much. She sighed with relief that she had practiced wisdom in waiting, something she had not done in many areas of her personal life, though her heart went out to her friends who had fallen for the lure.

"You can't help but care about what is happening to Harland, can you?" she sympathized.

"Lawyer. Harland needs lawyer," Holly sobbed.

Carley grabbed a newspaper. "It says here that one has been appointed for him."

"Good lawyer," Holly managed to get out.

"Oh, I see what you mean," Carley said, now reading the article. "I see. They are giving him a public defender, but you think he needs a better lawyer than that."

Holly nodded her head gratefully.

"Let me just think for a minute," Carley said, scratching her head as she attempted to reach a solution. Neither of them could afford an expensive defense attorney for Harland, even if they put the bar up as insurance. Carley didn't know about the $900,000 that Holly had stashed in Swiss banks from her part in the sale of the original technology for the genetic manipulation, and it was likely that Holly had forgotten about it herself by now from the mutation process. And, it was evident that no one new Harland also had a cool million stashed away from that same sale. Harland was certainly in no position to communicate his wishes regarding his money, a defense attorney, or anything else at this point. Even if they could afford an attorney for Harland she had no idea how to go about finding one who could knowledgeably handle the issue of a mutant committing a crime. For that matter, who knew anything about mutants? This was definitely ground-breaking law. "I've got it! Let's call those friends of ours in Argentina, since they know more about these pills than anyone else. Maybe one of them has some ideas on how to hire a good lawyer for Harland, especially Sandra with her do-gooder connections. Say, come to think of it, isn't Sandra a lawyer herself?"

Holly agreed vigorously and gave Carley a big hug, then pulled out her cell phone and handed it to Carley with a pleading look. "Can you call for me?"

Carley took the phone and wasted no time dialing Sandra's number. "Hello, Sandra? This is Carley. Holley and I are calling about Harland."

"Oh hi, Carley. We have been hearing all about Harland's problems down here, too. Nate is right here with me, and we were just talking about it, trying to think if there was something we could do to help him. Let me put you on speaker phone," Sandra replied.

"In fact, that is just why we called," Carley responded, briskly. "We were wondering if you know a good defense lawyer for Harland? All they've given him is a public defender. Not to disparage public defenders, but you know how many cases they get. They never have the time or resources necessary to do a thorough job for their clients. From the ones I've met, they seem like they're all underpaid and overworked. Harland's defense requires someone who has plenty of time and knowledge to put to good use. It seems like a tricky case, at least from my perspective. We were also trying to remember about you, aren't you a lawyer yourself?" Carley pressed the speaker button on her cell so Holly could hear.

"Yes, I am a lawyer, but not a defense lawyer. I just do litigation work, suing Corporate America for abusing the environment," Sandra explained, shaking her head. "Harland is going to need a great criminal lawyer."

"I hadn't thought of that," Carley acknowledged. "What criminal lawyer is going to know anything about mutants or the genetic changes that are occurring in their bodies? We figured you at least have a better working knowledge of all that than anyone else."

"Wel-l-l, I don't know much about it myself either since it's an unknown field. Actually, the person with the most understanding of that field is Rita. Maybe she would be willing to be a consultant for me and I could tag team with a top criminal lawyer. At least I have a track record of defending the underdog," Sandra said, thoughtfully. "Let me make some calls and see what else I can come up with. I have a few chips out there I can call in."

"That's great, Sandra! We'll be waiting to hear from you," Carley said in relief.

Holly chimed in with a garbled, "Thank you!"

Carley hit the end button on the phone. Then she and Holly did a high five, Holly's emerging talons clacking against Carley's salon-styled nails.

* * *

Nate, who usually had a fast opinion about everything, was uncharacteristically silent during the phone call. Sandra looked at him quizzically, with her eyebrows raised. "I can't believe I'm already heading back to Virginia. Lucky I didn't sell my condo when I left so precipitously!"

Nate spoke angrily, "Are you sure you are doing the right thing? You left because you were sure that things were going to turn ugly up there. You were afraid for your life."

"But, this is Harland's life we are talking about. I can't turn my back on him. Think of the opportunity to fight for all mutants who had their lives changed without knowing it was going to happen. Plus, I'll be helping to develop new case law. I'm just worried whether I know enough to be of real help," Sandra finished, biting on her left pinkie nail as she sank into a comfortable armchair at Nate's ranch.

Twirling on a high bar stool by the counter to the kitchen, Nate reassured her, though he continued to look troubled. "As you said yourself, no one knows anything more about mutants than you do in the legal profession. Rita, who is not a lawyer, is your friend, making her far more likely to consult easily and better with you. I have no doubt that you are the perfect choice for this job. I just wish you weren't," he said in frustration. "I don't like the idea of you going back up there, though I know it's none of my business."

"That was such a sweet thing to say," Sandra exclaimed, jumping up and planting a kiss on Nate's cheek. He responded by kissing her back, naturally. Kissing had now become a common practice between them. In fact, there were not many nights that Sandra made it back down to the Perez' estates after having spent a day at the ranch.

"I'm going with you!" Nate declared, holding her tight. "I'm not letting you go up there and face, who knows what, all by yourself."

"I'm a big girl," Sandra said, dryly, "I've stood in front of bulldozers that were going to plow down ancient redwoods. Believe me. I'm used to taking care of myself. However," she added hastily as his brow darkened, "I would love the company, and it might be a good idea for you to see for yourself what's happening up there."

"Have laptop, will travel," Nate sang out, hugging her tighter as he chuckled.

"Meanwhile, big boy, " Sandra said, batting her long lashes at him vampishly, "I need to get started on some phone calls and see if I can rustle up a strong criminal lawyer to have at the table with me. Then I need to get busy on some of the arguments we can use for Harland's defense. I'm thinking 'diminished capacity' at the least, but I would really like to get to 'temporary insanity.'" Walking absently away, she pulled her phone out and started calling in her favors.

*   *   *

Hopping into a taxi, Marti and Gabe directed the driver to the Queen Elizabeth Hospital. They had arrived in Bridgetown's Deep Water Harbor on the southwest end of Barbados the night before and spent a pleasant evening exploring the Careenage, a trendy area of converted waterfront warehouses that had been turned into boutiques, restaurants, and lively nightspots. They had tried to have a great time, but in the back of their minds, keeping them from totally relaxing and enjoying the ambiance, was this planned trip to the hospital the next day.

After Gabe's chest pain incident, even though he seemed fine afterwards, Marti had prevailed on Gabe to get a checkup next time they were in port. Gabe had contacted his doctor back home, who barely remembered him, since Gabe hadn't been to a doctor in many years, and that had only been for a tetanus shot after he stepped on a roofing nail. His doctor had done some research and referred him to a Dr. Gupta, a cardiologist on the island of Barbados, their next planned port of call.

Having been a former British colony and still a member of the Commonwealth, Barbados, the easternmost island of the archipelago spanning from Florida to Venezuela, had a literacy rate of 99%. The 600+ bed hospital at Queen Elizabeth Hospital had a cardiac surgery unit that was highly recommended, not that Gabe had any plans for surgery. He was only getting this checkup to stop Marti from pestering him about it, so they could continue their trip without her continuing to nag him. He appreciated that Marti cared about him, but after so many years of being a self-reliant bachelor, he was having trouble getting used to the cloying and clinging aspect of a relationship. He just wanted to go back to the carefree spirit they had felt when they had sailed off from Argentina.

As they rode through the town, they noticed a few traffic lights weren't working, cars that hadn't been moved out of the way were stopped in the middle of various roads, and most of the shops were closed. Brimming trash cans were still out on the curb and gave the appearance of not having been emptied for days, causing garbage to litter the sidewalks and gutters. As they passed through residential areas, they noticed that in some places lawns were nicely mowed, while in others it looked as if nothing had been done to the yard for awhile. At one house the lawn mower sat in the middle of the lawn, apparently abandoned during a mowing. Mail had piled up in front of some houses, strewn carelessly about. In some places people stood around blankly looking off into the distance, as if they had no idea what to do with themselves.

"I thought this place was supposed to be immaculate with everything shipshape and oh so British," Marti observed.

"We must have just hit on a bad day, or are going through a section of town that isn't as well maintained," Gabe responded absently, his mind on the tests he'd be undergoing, not on the signs of disorder along the way.

"Tch-tch, I will report these problems immediately to the government," chimed in the taxi driver in proper British English, worried that these Americans might affect the lucrative tourist trade enjoyed by Barbados if they went back home and told everybody about the slovenly appearance of the island. "Do not worry. It will be taken care of right away. We Bajans are proud of our home."

At the hospital, Marti and Gabe hurried over to the information desk only to find that it was not manned. Fortunately, the signs were all in English, so they managed to find their way to Dr. Gupta's office by following the arrows and studying the floor plan layouts. When they finally found the cardiology suite it gave every appearance of a busy, thriving practice and Gabe and Marti were reassured. After the usual intolerable wait that many doctors' offices around the world subjected patients to, Gabe was led away to begin his testing, while Marti was left to leaf through year-old magazines. She lucked upon one that heralded the attractions of Barbados, the "Little England" of the Atlantic Ocean, but her mind was too full of worry for Gabe to settle down and plan out a fun-filled exploration of the island.

Without first seeing the doctor, Gabe was led around from one testing room to another by polite and friendly technicians. After running some blood tests, he had an EKG, then, they put him through a stress test. Gabe had heard about having to run on one of these tricky treadmill machines, while being hooked up with leads, but he had never been on one before. Being a bit nervous and quite a bit out-of-shape he tried to bluff his way through with humor, but the locals didn't seem to get his jokes, even though they smiled and nodded all the time. There did seem to be a bit of scurrying about, and if he knew the culture better, he might've thought they were undermanned and hassled. Once during the test, the power went out, and they had to start the test all over again, but Gabe was too focused on what the machines were showing and whether he was okay to devote any time to questioning what else was going on in the hospital. Honestly, he was a teensy bit worried since he had a history of heart disease on his father's side of the family. After a final echocardiogram, Gabe returned to the waiting room to sit and wait with Marti for the results.

Three hours later, a nurse ushered them into Dr. Gupta's office. Gabe had insisted that Marti come along so that she could hear right from the doctor herself that he was okay.

"Thank you for seeing us on such short notice, doc," Gabe started. "If you'll just tell my lady here that my ticker works just fine, we'll be on our way and not waste any more of your time." That earned him a stab in the ribs from Marti's elbow.

"Please have a seat Mr. and Mrs. Channing," the doctor said suavely. Gabe and Marti did not find it necessary to correct the error of Marti's status, though Marti sent Gabe an amused eyebrow. "I'm afraid it is not as simple as that. Your tests show that some time recently your heart sustained a small myocardial infarction. It has lost about 5% of its function, but as we are now learning, it might repair itself. Your major arteries appear to be about 70% clogged with plague. A heart catheterization would be recommended for that. My best guess is that what you experienced on the boat was a clot that got momentarily stuck in one of the arteries and caused a temporary blockage of the blood supply, causing your heart to seize."

"Are you saying I had a heart attack?" Gabe demanded, unbelievingly.

"Yes sir, in layman's terms that is what I am saying," Dr. Gupta confirmed. "What I would recommend is that you have stents put in."

"It can be scheduled for like three to six months from now, right?" Gabe asked.

"Yes, you can wait, but there are risks in waiting. Meanwhile, I will give you a prescription to start lowering your cholesterol so that the plague build up will slow down. I also want you to take two low dose aspirins to thin your blood and help prevent further clots from forming."

Gabe sat with his mouth hanging open, not believing what he was hearing, so Marti jumped in with questions. "Are you saying we need to go back to the States right away? Is Gabe in danger of another heart attack now?"

Dr. Gupta was cautiously reassuring. "There is no way we can tell if Mr. Channing will ever have a heart attack again. He could have one tomorrow, as could anyone, or he might never have another one. These medications are to help minimize those chances for him, but he needs to be monitored by a competent cardiologist and will require yearly blood work and other tests as your doctor deems necessary. If you don't have your heart monitored and take the medication prescribed, chances are that your arteries will get further clogged with plaque and then you will be at risk for a serious heart attack, maybe even a life-threatening one."

"Say, listen here, doc. Marti and I are on a long vacation by sea. We have no plans to return to the States any time soon. I don't mind taking those pills, but you'll have to give me a good supply," Gabe blustered, trying to take control of the situation and his life again.

"I am not comfortable with giving you more than a three month's supply, but I will contact the doctor who referred you and see if he will authorize more, if you will check back tomorrow," Dr. Gupta suggested. As Gabe started to rise, thinking the consultation was over, the doctor said, "Please sit down another minute, Mr. Channing. There's another matter I want to discuss with you. The best way to take control of your heart's health is by adjusting your diet, eating less red meat, avoiding fatty foods, and eating more vegetables. You also need to start an exercise program. If you smoke, you need to stop. If you drink, you need to limit it to two drinks a day. That small amount of liquor is good for the heart, but more is not. This is important if you want to live a long, happy life." He glanced meaningfully at the small overflow above Gabe's belt. "My nurse will be in to provide you with handouts giving the guidelines for how to do this. It was my pleasure to be of assistance to you." Then, he shook Gabe's hand and was out the door before either Gabe or Marti could get in another word.

It was a dejected pair that headed out of the hospital after the nurse had cheerfully given them the handouts. They were quite subdued and hardly spoke a word as they took a cab back to their boat, not even noticing the many visual signs that all was not right on the island.

Back on the boat, they sat on the deck and examined the handouts.

"This says you a need a good regular exercise program, walking at least 30 minutes for 4-5 days a week," Marti read.

"Yeah, like that's going to happen on a boat," Gabe responded, truculently, since he was in a surly mood after the bad morning news. His life, which had seemed to stretch gloriously in front of him, with adventure-filled days of sailing the seas and exploring new places with Marti, suddenly seemed threatened. He faced the idea of mortality, and he did not like it at all. He was only 65 years-old; he shouldn't have to think about dying for at least another 25-30 years by his estimate. Now, this foreign doctor had thrust death right in his face. He resented the way the doctor had looked at his mid-section, too. He knew he didn't have a six-pack stomach, but compared to the average American he was in moderate shape. He didn't smoke but had been known to enjoy an occasional cigar. He had no intention of giving up his Jim Beam and cokes, either. "And I am not going to become a vegetarian like that Sandra. Not a chance."

"Come on Gabe, you've got to try to work this out. I want you around for a long time," Marti wheedled, giving him a pat on the cheek, her eyes brimming with tears.

"Hey, don't cry, Babe," Gabe said, while momentarily forgetting about his own problems. He gathered her in his arms and patted her back.

Sniffing, Marti calmed down and just enjoyed the cuddle for a moment. Then she pulled back a little and said, "How about we figure this out together? Instead of walking, we can swim. It's a great form of exercise, too. You don't have to become a vegetarian, either; you just have to eat less red meat. You can still eat pork, chicken, and fish. With all the sea travel and islands we'll be visiting, there will be plenty of tasty seafood dishes to try."

Wanting to placate her, Gabe agreed, albeit a bit grudgingly. "That sounds doable, but I don't want to go back to the States just to get more pills. In no time at all I'd become tied to having to see a doctor all the time, just to get my prescription renewed."

Marti paused before she spoke. "Well, what about the supplements we were sent? If I'm not mistaken, one those bottles says that it will improve your heart's health. If you take those specific pills you don't have to be monitored by any doctor ever again. Besides, we are entitled to a free lifetime's supply of them."

Gabe had been thinking the very thing after his incident on the boat, his heart attack. He needed to face up to that's what it was – a heart attack. Now he had second thoughts, "Remember all the side effects that Sandra was telling us about on the phone, how people were taking on animal characteristics? Remember how she said Harland had changed? Sure, I'd like to get my heart strengthened and keep from aging, not that I'm old yet," he said, sucking in his gut, "but I don't want to develop a giraffe's neck and a duck's webbed feet."

"You are right. We can't take the first batch of pills, but I'm sure Rita and scientists like her have already corrected all those side effects, making them safe to take," Marti replied. "Let's give them another call and see how things are going with improving the supplements." She picked up the satellite phone to do just that.

After greetings and a bit of hemming and hawing, Gabe got to the point of his call. "Hey there Sandra, we were wondering if there have been any new pills developed that do not have the same side effects the earlier versions had. You know that little incident I had off the coast of Brazil? It turns out it was a mild heart attack. I was thinking maybe if I took the pills I could get my heart back into shape without having to mess with doctors and prescription medications all the time. What do you think?"

"Oh, Gabe, I'm so sorry to hear about the heart attack. Gosh, don't you guys ever pick up a newspaper? I wish I had good news for you, but it is not simple side effects that people are having from the pills. They are devolving, and at alarming rates, too. There is no way you want to start taking those supplements. Instead, throw them overboard as fast as you can, and forget you ever thought about using them. Do you remember how I told you Harland had changed? Well, he attacked a nurse, trying to eat her. He is under arrest now, and I am flying up with Nate to lead his defense. That is the first sign of violence, but social order and every form of civilization is starting to break down," Sandra explained to them in great detail, Marti gasped in horror the more she heard. Gabe's lips tightened and he kept shaking his head. This was not what he wanted to hear.

"Now that you mention it, things have appeared a little off here in Barbados, too," Marti said thoughtfully, vaguely remembering the signs of disorder and neglect along the way to and from the hospital in the taxi, and the subtler signs that things were not up to par in the hospital.

"I'm sure it is taking more time to hit the islands," Sandra said, "but the technology we gave the UN was distributed world-wide, and there are few corners of the globe where the pills haven't been marketed. Barbados, being so cosmopolitan probably got them soon after we did."

"But, Sandra, where do we go from here, where will it be safe?" Marti cried out.

"I wish I had a good answer to that question, Marti," Sandra said in near despair. "All I can tell you is that Rita and other scientists are working day and night to try to find a cure for this, and that people are being warned not to take the pills and to stop taking them if they already started, not that we know if that will do any good. Stay out on the boat and keep safe until all of this is over. That's all I can recommend at this point."

On that mournful note, they said their good-byes. As Marti looked at Gabe, she said, "That's all well and good for Sandra to tell us to stay at sea, but we obviously have to come into port for supplies and fuel." She purposely did not mention Gabe's need for prescription refills, but it was on both of their minds.

"We'll just have to do the best we can. We'll lay in as many supplies as we can possibly store and carry extra fuel. We'll try to stop in only out-of-the-way places and make sure my gun stays loaded," Gabe said, stoutly, squaring his shoulders and recognizing that he still had an important job to do in keeping Marti and himself safe and alive.

"Things aren't that bad here in Barbados," Marti said, resolutely. "Let's try to have a little fun here before we start laying in all those stores you are talking about. We might as well start on your healthy diet by trying the national dish of couscous, flying fish, and okra."

Marti had remembered something from that long wait for Gabe in the hospital.

"Do I have to catch it first?" Gabe joked.

"Only if you can fly at 30 miles an hour," Marti joked back, gamely. Linking arms, they set off to explore the coral and white, sandy beaches, and to dine to the sound of calypso watching the sunset, trying for carefree fun while they still had time.

* * *

Nate, Sandra, Rita, and Zack were relaxing on the front porch at Nate's ranch after eating a scrumptious dinner of eggplant parmesan and fresh baked bread served with extra virgin olive oil, fresh ground pepper and freshly grated cheese, a salad with Italian dressing prepared by Sandra with a full-bodied Chianti to go with it, Nate having exhausted his meatless recipes in the one meal he had made for Sandra.

Rita and Zack were seeing the ranch for the first time. After Rita began working such long hours trying to reverse the mutations from the supplements she had not been able to take the time off for the trip up there. Once Rita hit a waiting point in the experiments, Sandra and Nate had persuaded her to take a break and visit them. Rita had praised Nate for all the improvements he had made to the ranch and for picking such a fantastic setting. Zack was impressed with the array of electronics that Nate had installed, thinking that the private sector could afford more than the government provided for him. They were effusive in their thanks for the meal, though Zack wished he could've sunk his teeth into a nice Argentinean steak instead of eating so much rabbit food.

"We got a call from Marti and Gabe today and they mentioned that they could see signs of disorder in Barbados when they toured the island," Sandra informed them. "They had kept themselves away from any newspapers. Isn't that hard to believe of an old newspaper man? They didn't have any idea of the mess Harland has gotten himself into or the chaos that is starting to occur back in the States and other civilized countries. I'm going back to the States to defend Harland, and Nate is coming with me."

"I want to see for myself what is going on," Nate scoffed, his arm casually around Sandra's shoulder, her waist-long golden hair covering it like a blanket. "I don't believe things are nearly as bad as the media is saying. I'm sure they are just sensationalizing everything to pump up their sales on slow news days."

"From the reports we've been getting, the underlying infrastructure of civilization is falling apart," Rita said dramatically, agreeing with Sandra. "Mutants just walk off their jobs, forget how to do their jobs, or just simply don't show up for work. Take one small example — air flights. Pilots don't show up to fly the planes, or their computer systems are all screwed up because the mutants inputting data have forgotten how to do it, causing baggage to be put on the wrong planes or just left in the terminals. Flight controllers are not showing up for work either, or are making beginner mistakes when they do show up. The public is in an uproar and the industry is effectively paralyzed. That is just a small example of one industry. Multiply that across every business and aspect of life and you will begin to get an idea of how bad everything is."

Still not convinced, Nate shook his head but made a mental note to charter a private flight to and from Virginia. All he could see were the numbers in his investments getting higher and higher day by day. He had not taken Sandra's advice to bail on them, but was still secretly riding the wave, sure he would know the right time to sell — but it wasn't time yet.

"Things are not only bad already, but they are going to get much worse," Zack said authoritatively, wishing wistfully that he could put his arm around Rita as easily as Nate had put his around Sandra. He felt pretty certain he'd get his arm cut off if he tried. "The HSA hired consultants to formulate predictions on where this technology would go once every country in the world that wanted it got it hands on it. While we were never developing hybrid soldiers, there was a high probability that other countries would rush to do so. Even as we speak here, I am positive that hidden armies of superior warriors are being bred in countries that are hostile to the US. While countries like China continue to espouse friendship, we know their track record on human rights. They are probably conscripting people as fast as they can to build up a force of hybrid troops."

They went on to predict that the development of various sub-human races through tinkering with DNA with the limited knowledge currently available would lead to creating at least one race, and probably many, that would be stronger and more cunning than humans and would prey on humans, causing worldwide destabilization. They further predicted, that even when a cure was found, it would take decades to undo the damage that had been caused.

Rita burst out into tears, and Sandra leapt up and went to put her arms around her, giving Zack a dirty look. Nate gave him a dirty look too, though he was doing it because Sandra was no longer cuddling with him.

"Now, see what you've done," Sandra said, venomously.

"He's just telling it the way it is," Rita sobbed. "I can't get over what I've done and I've no idea whether I can reverse it. It seemed as simple as flipping a switch when I was playing with it at GenXY. But, I am finding it is much more complicated than that to restore DNA to the way it was."

"You mean what we've done," Sandra said, quietly, rocking Rita and patting her back. "Remember, turning your data over to the UN was my idea. We are going to do everything we can to turn it around. You are working day and night to reverse the devolution. I am heading north to help defend the poor people who have been unwittingly sucked into this genetic nightmare. At least we aren't profiting financially from it anymore." She threw a significant look at Nate.

Nate was immediately interested in a squirrel running across the lawn. He pretended to not be aware of the turn in the conversation. Inside, he was feeling a twinge of guilt, and decided that he would at least respect Sandra's wishes about her own investments, and since she had entrusted their management to him, he would sell off everything in the biogenetic fields for her tomorrow, but he would be darned if he was selling off his own investments until he was good and ready. In some ways, he was beginning to realize that Sandra could be a little zealous and pushy about her convictions.

"I was just calling a spade a spade," Zack said, defensively, realizing he hadn't improved things with Rita and that he would probably be in trouble with his bosses if they knew he had been so open with his friends tonight. Being open with the public was not a comfortable government policy. However, he was pretty sick of the whole bureaucracy. If it wasn't for the opportunity to help find a solution to the genetic pandemonium he was working on with Rita, he most likely would've told them to kiss off long ago. He did have some personal motives for staying down here in Argentina with Rita, too. He wondered if he would still be welcome on the Perez estates if he no longer worked for the government.

"Hey, everybody, how about some more wine?" Nate asked, not waiting for an answer to start the refills. They all complied with the distraction and turned their talk to lighter matters of interest.

* * *

Carley slammed the phone down with a sigh, her mop of hair in more disarray than usual. "I can't get a hold of any of the waitresses or bartenders on the phone. If I'm lucky, I get their voicemail, but most of the time I get a 'no signal' message, or just empty air." She turned to Holly in exasperation, her dark eyes flashing. "Holly, are you listening to me?"

Holly, who had been standing still, appeared to be gazing out the window, looking at people. Thinking about how the people who were walking by were transforming into non-people, she gave a start, and turned towards Carley. "There are no napkins," she said.

"Holly did you hear what I said? We have no one to work the bar this evening. Last night we only had one person come in, and tonight looks dead. What do you mean we have no napkins? Is that something else that wasn't delivered, along with most of the beer, liquor, and pretzels?" Carley ranted.

"I am afraid," Holly whispered, not meeting Carley's eyes.

Intent on her thoughts, Carley replied, "I'm afraid too. It looks like we don't have enough supplies or employees to run the bar. How are we going to open for business tonight? Sure, with the one or two customers we have showing up most nights now, you and I could probably handle things for a couple nights, but we can't do without supplies. I guess, then, I'll have to try to get some emergency stuff in. Maybe the hotel restaurant can float us some of their liquor until I can get a delivery in here." She turned back to the phone, trying to reach the restaurant next door. "Now all I'm getting is a ringing signal. I'm going to run over to the restaurant next door and talk to them in person."

Without waiting for a reply from Holly, Carley ran out of the bar and went to the hotel's restaurant. On the door was a sign, reading, "Temporarily Closed for Business." She peered through the stained glass inserts in the doors, but it was apparent that all the lights were out and there was no activity inside. Gloomily, she went back to the bar. Holly was still standing in the same position, but Jasmine, who had now come in, was opening up the piano. She gave Carley a small wave and began to play "Wild Honey" by U2.

"They're closed for business Holly. What do you think of that? I hate to say this, but I think we are going to have to close down until we can think of a way to get more supplies," Carley announced in great frustration. It was not in her nature to quit, and she had been so excited about being a part-owner of the bar. She hated to go down without a fight.

"I'm afraid," Holly whispered again.

"It doesn't help matters that you keep saying that," Carley said, losing her patience.

With great effort, Holly responded, "I am afraid that I am becoming like Harland. I think I am like Harland." Great tears began to flow down her face.

"Oh, is that what you are talking about?" Carley said, immediately turning her attention and sympathy on Holly. "What do you mean you are like Harland? I don't think you're anything like him. You don't have a mean bone in your body, unlike Harland, who was a trained killer. In fact, his Dad was a trained killer, too. You're as different from him as a morning dove is from an eagle."

Mutely, Holly raised her hands, and Carley could see right away that the nails were looking more like talons. Carley saw Holly every day, so the changes had snuck up gradually without her really noticing them. Now, looking closely at her friend, she could see that she was losing weight. In addition, the weight she had was redistributing differently, forming a heavier rib cage. Her cute little feathers had now grown out into long feathers on as much of her body as Holly let be seen.

"I thought you had stopped taking those pills," Carley said, in irritation. She felt quite perturbed that Holly would be so irresponsible after what had happened to Harland, especially with the business of the bar depending on them both. Carley felt a bit put upon.

"I did stop," Holly managed to get out, each word an effort. "The changes did not stop. My daughters are fighting. The school is closed."

"Oh, Holly, do you mean you are still mutating even though you stopped taking the pills?" Carley cried. "Oh, honey, we need to do something to help you and your girls. I think we need to call Rita and see if she has any answers."

Jasmine had been trying her hardest to eavesdrop on the conversation. She, too, had stopped taking her supplements, though to no avail. The webbing between her toes had widened her feet so that she was no longer able to wear shoes. Because of that, she had been coming into work with wide sandals on and fortunately was able to hide her feet nicely under the piano. She couldn't hide the webbing between her fingers, though, so she pretended to play the piano, while surreptitiously with Carley and Holly's approval she played a CD of piano pieces, not that anyone cared. The only customers for the last few weeks were a couple of diehard drinkers who never put anything into their bodies unless it had some potent alcohol. In time, she casually worked her way closer to where her bosses were talking.

Picking up the phone again Carley made the call, which luckily went through this time.

"Hello, this is Rita Perez."

"Hello, Rita. This is Carley and Holly. Holly is in bad shape. She stopped taking the supplements a couple of weeks ago, yet she has continued to mutate. We were wondering if there is anything you can suggest. She is really worried that she will become like Harland, since she was taking the same pills he took," Carley poured out the moment Rita came on the line.

"I'm so sorry to hear about Holly," Rita began. "Unfortunately, it fits in with what my research is showing. For some reason, stopping the pills has no affect on the devolution. Think of it like flipping a switch to turn on a light. Once the switch has been turned on, the electricity just keeps flowing. You don't even have to keep turning it on for the light to show. What we need as a society right now is a way to flip the switch to off, and so far I haven't been able to discover how to do that. It isn't just reversing devolution that we're dealing with. Instead, the devolution is actually a new evolutionary path, but I don't think you're interested in the science behind it all. The bottom line for Holly is that whether someone takes more pills or stops taking them, the mutation will continue indefinitely."

Just then, the window shattered and shards of glass flew everywhere, a brick landing on the carpet. Still holding the phone, Carley dove behind the bar. Holly continued to stand where she was and began to pick small pieces of glass out of her feathers as Jasmine darted back towards the piano.

"Holly, get down here," Carley screamed. Without waiting for action on Holly's part, she grabbed her and pulled her to cover just as more bricks came flying through the window.

"Carley, Carley, what's happening? Are you all right?" Rita yelled through the phone.

"We are under attack," Carley gasped into the mouthpiece. "Somebody is throwing bricks through the windows. We are all out of supplies, and none of our employees except Jasmine has showed up for work in days. We can't reach anybody on the phone either. I don't know what to do!" Carley had been trying for weeks to hold everything together, but she was finally realizing that sheer willpower was not going to do the trick.

"Come down here," Rita invited her, with sudden inspiration. "Maybe if Holly was here and willing to try different things I come up with, then I could find a way to help her. You will all be safe here."

The barrage of bricks stopped as suddenly as it had begun. Peaking out the window, Carley saw a gang of mutants heading down the street, focusing on their next target. She turned to Holly and repeated Rita's offer. "Rita has offered for us to go down to Argentina because she says it will be safe there. She is even willing to work with you on trying to stop your mutation, if you are willing to let her experiment with you, as a guinea pig."

"My girls!" Holly croaked.

"Of course, she means your daughters, too," Carley said, impatiently.

"I want to come, too," Jasmine said, timidly. She had worked her way back to where they were without them noticing her, holding out her hand in the process. "I stopped taking the pills, too, and look at what is happening to me. Please ask Rita if she has room for one more guest."

Carley reached out and patted her arm, looking at Holly who emphatically nodded her head. "Rita, we would love to accept your invitation for Holly, her twins, and me to come down to Argentina. I hate to impose on your hospitality, but do you have room for our piano player, Jasmine to come with us? Jasmine has been taking pills, too, though she didn't start as early as Holly did. . She took a different kind and she has been developing aquatic characteristics – webbed hands and feet, and just now she showed us gills in her sides."

"Yes, yes, we would be glad to have her. We have plenty of room. If she will let me work with her, that will increase the sample for my trials," Rita responded briskly, both gracious hostess and keen scientist at the same time.

"I think we have one other problem," Carley admitted, feeling that she was imposing, but not seeing any way around it. If it was only for herself, she probably wouldn't be so bold, but she thought of Holly's young girls, and pushed on. "I don't think we can get a flight out of here anymore. From the little news that is getting through, it sounds as if most flights have been grounded because personnel are not showing up to work. Even if we can get a flight, I'm not sure it would be safe, since there have been many crashes lately."

"Funny you should mention that," Rita said. "I was just using the chaos of the airplane industry as an example of the problems that are occurring in every area of life these days. It surprises me that you have hung on as long as you have with everything falling apart in the States. However, don't worry about any plane trip. My father has his own private jet, and we have been meticulous in not allowing any of our employees to take any of the supplements. We will just send it to a private airfield near you right away. Just gather up whatever you need to bring and meet the plane there. We will be anticipating your arrival."

"Oh, Rita, I don't have the words to thank you," Carley said, tears streaming down her face in relief and gratitude. Holly and Jasmine were holding onto each other sobbing, too. "We'll gather up the girls and be there as soon as we can."

Not bothering to close up the bar, knowing that a lock would do no good now that the windows had been breached, the three women walked out.

CHAPTER THREE

London Bridge is Falling Down

"Ahoy, is anyone there?" Gabe shouted. "Permission to come aboard?"

Having just emerged from the water, Gabe was admiring Marti's dripping-wet figure in its red and orange swirled bathing suit, when in the distance, Gabe spied a cabin cruiser lying idle.

Gabe and Marti had slowly been sailing from Barbados towards the Panama Canal. They had established a daily routine of anchoring to the leeward side of small islands in calm bays to swim and snorkel with many exotic species of fish, as well as more encounters with friendly dolphins. Everything was fun for them, but it also was an important part of Gabe's cardio exercise. They had learned through the handouts that they were given at the doctor's office that aerobic exercise was important to help oxygen flow to all parts of the body, which includes getting to the heart. They also realized that many women died from heart attacks because they never recognized that they like men also have unique symptoms frequently different from men, and many of the same risk factors. So, Marti agreed to follow the cardio routine alongside Gabe. Besides, a buddy system made the exercising more fun and more consistent, with less likelihood that it would be skipped.

Like a deflated balloon, Gabe had given up the bluster after hearing the news that he had suffered a minor heart attack and had plaque in his arteries from Dr. Gupta in Barbados. He had acquiesced to everything Marti and he could think of to improve his heart health. Exercise was a key component of the regimen, along with a heart-smart diet. They tried to make that fun too, by searching out new recipes online and trying them one by one. At times, they had to get creative to put together ingredients from the supplies they had brought aboard, but that was all part of the fun. Marti was determined to make an adventure of it all and Gabe played along with her, grateful to just have a companion that cared about his health and was willing to go to such lengths to help him. Marti had an ulterior motive for keeping everything carefree. She knew that reducing stress was just as important as all the other components of healthy living. Thus, for Gabe, she was intent on keeping the worry and work of trying to live healthy as stress-free as possible. She wanted this guy in her life for as long as possible.

For the third time in their leisurely trip, they had come upon a boat drifting aimlessly. By now, it was becoming a familiar routine. Each time they had called out, and after determining that no one was on board, they had shrugged, called it in to local authorities, then headed on their way. At first, they hadn't given the drifting boats much thought, so intent were they on their own problems. Their assumption was that the boats had gotten loose from their moorings and the owners hadn't found out yet. This time, though, Gabe was beginning to get suspicious of the circumstances, so he decided to investigate, his rusty journalistic nose beginning to sniff out more to the story.

"Is anybody aboard?" Gabe hollered, throwing out his fenders and then tying up to the cabin cruiser. "I'm going aboard to see what's going on, Marti. You stay here."

"I don't think it is a good idea for you to go there alone," Marti argued.

"If anything were to happen, it would be best if you could get on the satellite phone and dial for some help," Gabe answered her, climbing onto the other boat without waiting for any argument from Marti.

Marti was not waiting for more argument, either. She scooped up the sat phone and followed him. Sometimes Gabe's male chauvinism, or gallantry as he preferred to call it, was a pain in the neck. She could always use the phone to brain anyone with wild ideas.

After examining the boat from top to bottom, they found maps set out and marked as if the boat was on a cruise. In the cabins, they saw signs of clothing strewn on the floors as if people had strangely stepped out of their clothes and walked away from them.

"That's just typical male housekeeping," Marti scoffed. "Guys just drop their clothes wherever they land and leave them right there. My guess is it was probably an all-male fishing trip."

"If that was the case, there would be more than just one set of clothing on the floor," Gabe answered, seriously. He moved into the galley. "Aha — look at this!" On the counter was a plate of molding sandwiches, some with a couple of bites taken out of them.

"To me, it looks like someone was in the middle of eating when he just disappeared," Marti surmised, seeing more signs of haste in leaving the kitchen nook. "What do you think happened to all these people, Gabe? There aren't any signs of a struggle whatsoever."

"I'd say that they left suddenly and peacefully," Gabe guessed. "Maybe the engine died, and they accepted an invitation of another boat to take them in to port."

Gabe hurried up top to check out the ignition. As he had begun to suspect, the key was still in the ignition. Why? With only a brief hesitation, he gave it a turn, and the engine caught right away. "Obviously there was no mechanical reason for them to leave the boat," he told Marti as she joined him topside. "I'm wondering if this has anything to do with mutants."

"What do you mean?" Marti asked, quizzically.

"I'm trying to remember the things we've heard from Sandra, and read online about the mutants. Maybe they mutated to the place where they just abandoned the boat," said Gabe.

"Oh, I've got some ideas of my own," Marti piped up. "Remember how I was thinking how nice it would be to develop gills so I could swim with dolphins? I bet they did just that . . . and swam away forever." She nodded, pleased with herself.

It was then that Gabe noticed there was also a ship's log on a table nearby. In it, recorded each day, was the boat's journey, including a description of weather conditions and major details of the trip. For some reason, everything abruptly ended just two days ago. Not disagreeing with her, Gabe suggested, "Why don't we take that log and read it, seeing if it gives any facts to support your theory. Besides, it doesn't look like anyone is going to be missing this any time soon."

"Gabe, don't we need to report this to the authorities, like we did before?" Marti said, uneasily, as Gabe grabbed the log.

"I don't think it will matter if we take a couple of minutes to read this first," he asserted, climbing back to their boat, with Marti following him.

Within minutes, they sat together on the deck, perusing the journal together, arm in arm. While most of the journal was dry facts of latitude, longitude, distance travelled, sea conditions, and weather conditions, there were signs that the writers' handwriting was deteriorating, the letters larger and wavering with each entry. Gradually, the captain began using fewer words making it more difficult for others to understand. When they turned back to the beginning of the journey, they found something that gave support to Marti's theory.

It read: "We have all taken the supplements that will improve our ability to stay under water longer and longer each day. We have increased our endurance and strength in the water. We love water!" It was dated before Harland had been arrested, before the devolutionary aspects of the supplements were widely known.

"Looks like you were right, Marti. Those poor people turned into fish and swam away, not knowing any better," Gabe declared, shaking his head.

"Or, maybe they turned into dolphins," Marti suggested. "That might not be a bad life at all."

"If it would clear my arteries and give me a strong heart and I didn't have to treat lettuce as a food group, it might not be all that bad," Gabe agreed, jokingly. He closed the journal with a slam, and got up and took it back to the other boat. Marti lifted the sat phone and began a report on the abandoned boat. That accomplished, they went to their galley to fix some of that lettuce Gabe had complained about into a new and tempting salad of the day.

They continued on their way until they reached the city of Colon, in Panama, where they had a reservation at the Yacht Club. Inside the club they met with the handling agent who had taken care of all the registrations necessary to transverse the Panama Canal. They paid the exorbitant transit fees and all the other miscellaneous fees, still secure in their financial independence and trusting Nate to keep growing their money.

The agent had arranged for the four line handlers who were required, plus the advisor they had to take onboard with them for the trip through the canal. They were able to get volunteer line handlers who could make the trip back and forth on the canal for the ride including the free meals and all the beer they could drink when they were in port. Since Marti had the foresight to research all of this online and book an agent in advance, they only had to wait one day in port before starting their 51 mile journey through the canal.

Using that day to take on more fuel, because it was required that sailboats motor through the canal, they also stopped at the post office to pick up mail that was being held there.

Picking out a large manila envelope, Marti waved it teasingly in Gabe's face. "This is just what I've been waiting for, big boy."

"What's that?" Gabe played along, grabbing for it. Marti danced away before he could get it.

"Never you mind, I will show you once you are back on the boat," Marti responded, continuing to keep it out of Gabe's reach on the walk back to the dock.

Marti led Gabe into the cabin where the DVD player was located. He then opened the mysterious package as she popped a DVD into it, announcing majestically, "This is going to transform your life."

"Oh no, you don't," Gabe protested, getting a swift look at the screen. "I'm not doing yoga."

"This isn't yoga," Marti sniffed." It's Qi Gong. I contacted Sandra, since she is into all that healthy living stuff and asked her if she had any ideas for exercise that we could do on a boat that would be good for your heart, besides the swimming, of course. Qi Gong is the foundation for Tai Chi, you know?"

"Oh, come on, Marti, you know I don't want to do that stuff. All I need to do is some swimming from time to time," Gabe protested, refusing to look at the screen.

"You know that there are plenty of days that we can't swim, Gabe," Marti calmly answered. "Even though the weather in the Caribbean has been glorious, we do run into the occasional rough water when we can't swim. Besides, this is a whole body workout that opens the flows in the body of blood and oxygen to every part of the body, signaling the body that it is alive and healthy. It is considered a meditation with movement, which is more beneficial than weight training and aerobics."

"Sounds like you got yourself brainwashed pretty quickly," Gabe sneered.

"I am excited about it, not only for you, but for myself, too. It will build my abs and flatten my belly with the diaphragmatic breathing that it has you do. It will increase tendon strength, and super oxygenate my brain, so I can be as smart as you are. It also relaxes you into a deep state of rest, which will remove the stress you have been feeling since you got your diagnosis from the doctor. We can do it together," Marti wheedled, twining around Gabe and giving him a full body squeeze.

"Your abs and tummy are just fine the way they are," Gabe said, giving her a once over while sucking in his gut. "I guess I can give it a try for awhile and see how it goes." Marti's powerful physical presence did much more than her words could in breaking Gabe down. "There's nothing much wrong with your brain, either. You can twist me around your finger anytime. I just don't want to get so relaxed that we spend all our time sleeping." Gabe gave her a meaningful leer, followed by a deep, long kiss that effectively ended any further discussion.

That evening, they were rafted together with three other boats and taken through the first three Gatun locks to spend the night nested with the other boats in Lake Gatun. There was supposed to be a fourth boat, but it mysteriously never arrived, never even called to cancel. Gabe's reporter instincts were aroused, making him wonder if devolution had anything to do with it. He was so caught up in the excitement of transiting the Panama Canal, which he considered to be "The Eighth Wonder of the World", that he wasn't interested in thinking about much else. The other boaters were party people, and all of them had a lively time before settling down for the night. When they were partying, it was evident to Gabe and Marti that there were changes occurring in some of the other boaters, like how much some of them liked to swim and how deep they could dive into the water.

Early in the morning, the new advisor came on board for a little while and they began their journey up the canal, which was normally a nine-hour trip. Since they had already done the first set of locks, which raised them 85 feet above sea level, the second part of the trip would take less time. With rainforests were on both sides of the canal, Marti kept binoculars handy in case she would see monkeys in the trees. Although Gabe kept teasing her about it, she wasn't dissuaded from her pursuit. After all their time alone at sea, it was strange, though also comforting, to have other people on board, so they spent a lot of time talking to them, and wining and dining with them. Fortunately, the handling agent had brought a prepared picnic lunch from a local restaurant so that Marti and Gabe did not have to waste time slaving in the galley cooking, allowing them to enjoy their trip.

All too soon they stepped down through the Pedro Miguel Lock and the Miraflores Locks that brought them back down to sea level and ultimately into the Pacific Ocean. Gabe was fascinated with the mechanism of how the locks worked, but after sitting in one lock for two hours watching water rise, or lower as the case might be, Marti quickly grew bored and was glad to have her binoculars with her, though she never did see a single monkey. She did spot ape-like mutants and wondered if the normal animals were being killed by the mutants.

They docked briefly in Panama City and enjoyed the exciting nightlife, sampling Pan-American cuisine at one of the many excellent restaurants, making the whole event a folkloric show. They couldn't help but notice that there were problems similar to those they had encountered in Barbados, though at a heightened scale. They now realized mutants were affecting the culture of lovely, exotic Panama, too. They set sail again, stopping briefly for the renowned snorkeling off Cobia Island and the Pearl Islands, before heading on to the Galapagos Islands.

* * *

"Hi, Rita, are you busy? There's something I need to run by you," Sandra announced as she entered Rita's lab. She perched on a stool at the counter where Rita was working, pulling her golden hair back into a haphazard ponytail. "Whew, it is warm in here."

"That's because they are still working on installing the AC," Rita said, fanning herself with her hand. "They'd better hurry up because all this electronic equipment doesn't do well in heat. So, what do you have on your mind? Is Nate with you?"

"Now why would you assume Nate was with me?" Sandra said, her delft blue eyes merrily twinkling.

"Because he follows you around like a puppy dog," Rita retorted, putting a white mouse into a cage.

"Yeah well, if Nate is my puppy, Zack sure looks like yours. Why do you think he volunteered to work in Patagonia? Anyway, Nate mentioned something about going down to the stables while I talk with you," Sandra replied, uneasily eyeing the caged mice. "Say, would you mind talking in your office? I can't bear to be around these captive animals."

Good-humoredly, Rita led the way into her office. "Would you rather I experiment on humans to try to reverse the DNA devolution?"

"No-o-o, but I can't bear to see innocent animals hurt in any way. I guess there is no easy solution to this madness," Sandra responded, following her.

"If what I'm doing works, there is no harm to any of the animals. It isn't my intent to hurt any of the mice either, you know," Rita gently explained, perching on a corner of her desk.

"From the start, you had to make them mutants. . . . Oh, never mind, that isn't what I came to talk to you about," Sandra said, waving her hand as if to wave away the previous discussion as she plopped down in the nearest chair. "What I wanted to talk to you about, though, is Harland. I've been asked to take over his defense, and I need you with me to do it, since you are the only one who truly understands the process of the devolution from A to Z."

"I wish I understood it that much, myself," Rita said, ruefully, looking down dejectedly at her jean shorts and sleeveless blue blouse. "If I did, I'd be able to reverse the process, or at least stop its progression. How can I help you? Don't you need to go up to Virginia? I have to stay here where my laboratory is."

"We'll bring your lab with you so you can run it from a remote location. You only need to testify on one day," said Sandra, airily, waving her hand again, this time to encompass everything around them. "Through some friends of mine, I've located a big empty ranch in Virginia horse country that we can use for the duration of the trial. There's a separate building there that you can set up as your lab. Nate will come with me to see firsthand how out of control everything has gotten in the States. He's not the type of person who believes things unless he sees them for himself. I guess that comes from being a hard-headed financial sort." She shook her head fondly as if perplexed by it.

"I just got off the phone with Carley and Holly, giving them permission to come down here. Holly and her daughters are in a bad way; they are following the same devolutionary path that Harland went down since they have been taking the same pills that he and Sterling took. They also want to bring their piano player, Jasmine, who took different supplements that brought on sea life characteristics. I've agreed to do whatever I can to try and help them. The fact that Holly's daughters are identical twins sets up an interesting study for me," Rita's changeable eyes glowed green at the thought. "I'm sending my father's plane up to get them, since the airports are in upheaval and are unreliable."

Thinking fast, Sandra said, "Wait. I've got a better idea. Why not just have them come to the Virginia ranch and we can take the plane up there to meet them?"

Rita, who was used to methodical, scientific approaches to major decisions, was taken aback by the suddenness of Sandra's solution. "What about Zack?" she spluttered. "He is responsible for overseeing my research and providing security for it."

"Bring him too," Sandra declared recklessly. "How big is your father's plane?"

"It's big enough. That's not the problem," Rita answered slowly, trying to think what was the problem, besides leaving her family and home after just having gotten settled in and comfortable here again.

"Well, then, what is the problem?" Sandra asked, trying to be patient, a trait that did not come easy for her.

Defeated, Rita shook her head. "Okay, I can see why you need me to help Harland's defense, especially since I'm responsible for this whole mess. I need to do whatever it takes to help out the first victim from it." Refusing to cry about it anymore, she purposely squared her shoulders and looked a bit fierce.

"Let's not keep rehashing that," Sandra said, trying not to look guilty. "Since there is enough blame to go around, sitting and pounding our chests about it is not going help anything."

"I'll get back on the phone to Carley, and let her know of the change in plans. What is the status of Harland's defense right now?" Rita responded, picking up a pen to take notes.

Sandra gathered her thoughts. "I just got off the phone with the public defender who was appointed by the court for Harland. He walked Harland through the arraignment and pled not guilty. With no protest from either side, and pressure from the government to get this over with quickly, the judge set an early trial date. I may have to try to get a continuance though, since I am coming in at this late date as lead counsel, but that may be an unwinnable battle. The public defender recommended a number of well-known criminal defensive attorneys and I intend to meet with a couple of them as soon as we get to the States. I haven't done much on the criminal side of the law in the past, so I need someone to prop me up in that department. Surprisingly, money is not an issue in this case. To get the publicity from such a high-profile case, many lawyers are now clamoring to be a part of his defense team. In addition, animal and human rights organizations have banded together to handle his costs."

"Have you decided what your defense is going to be?" Rita asked, curiously.

"Well, coming this late into the game, some things have been decided already. Obviously, they have decided that Harland is going to be given human rights and not merely treated like an animal; otherwise there would not be a trial. That's a good thing since animals that attack people get put down. I was thinking along the lines of diminished capacity or temporary insanity?" Sandra's voice rose in a question to Rita with her last remark.

"Well, I'm not sure of your legal definitions for either of those defenses," Rita answered, slowly, tapping her pen on the desk. "Obviously, Harland no longer thinks like a human. Is that 'diminished' capacity or just an 'other' capacity? As for being insane — what he did was most likely a natural and logical action for a predatory bird who felt threatened. We can only hope at this point that the change in Harland is "temporary," though I have no clue yet as to how to reverse the whole process."

"Rita, you are knocking down every argument before we get started, which is not helpful," Sandra admonished, playfully shaking a finger at her. She jumped up and began pacing around the small, sparsely furnished office.

Rita spread her hands with a shrug. "Hey, someone has to play devil's advocate and help you think of what the prosecutor is going to throw at you."

"That's what I'll have my defense team for," Sandra retorted. "What I need you for is to help explain the science in layman's terms for the jury and judge, and to help me come up with a defense that has a shot at persuading the jury."

"Well, just like you, I won't know more until we get up to Virginia and I personally have the chance to evaluate Harland and his unique situation. Comparing his condition to Holly and her girls' will be a help, too. I'd better go talk to Zack and my parents about this. My folks aren't going to be too happy to see me leave again, especially not to go back to the States where it's so dangerous. Besides, I have to call Carley back," Rita enumerated, unhappily. She was committed to going, but emotionally she wasn't fully on board yet.

"I'll go see where Nate has gotten himself to, and then get packed. The sooner we can leave, the sooner we can get started on this long process," Sandra declared, hurrying out the door. Privately, Rita thought she could keep working in her lab until she needed to take the stand.

Nate was down by the corral, ostensibly watching the horses get trained. In spite of his interest, he was continuously busy on his Blackberry, selling off all his shares in biotech companies and reinvesting them into time-tested commodity-type stocks, like oil, gold, and food. He had obediently sold Sandra's stocks when she had told him to, but he was stubborn about his own stocks. From what he was hearing on the news and the information on the stock markets, it wouldn't be too long before people would stop buying the supplements, making it likely that the bottom would soon fall out of that market. He wasn't even too sure about the stability of the world market, in general, especially with the upheavals he was hearing about. While selling off his holdings in biotech firms, he also transferred all of Marti and Gabe's stocks. He had just finished placing all his orders when he saw Sandra heading his way, causing him to quickly slide his Blackberry into his pocket.

"Hey Nate, Rita has agreed to go with us. We will all fly up to Virginia in her father's private jet. Do you need to get back to your ranch for anything?" Sandra said, a bit breathless from jogging all the way to the stables. Her white cotton tank top and short khaki shorts molded nicely to her fantastic figure, causing Nate to be bemused enough to not pay much attention to her words.

"Yeah, I packed a bag based on what you had said before I came down. Have Blackberry, will travel," he answered a bit facetiously as he patted his pocket.

In less time than anyone had thought possible, they were all on the plane ready for take-off. There was an emotional good-bye between Rita and her family, but eventually they were off for the long flight to the States.

Everybody, even Zack, was uncharacteristically quiet for much of the trip. Zack was busy trying to figure out what he thought and felt about this sudden change in plans. He had been enjoying his laid-back assignment in Argentina, once he got used to the slower pace of doing things there. He had tried to hide his growing disillusionment with Homeland Security, as he wrestled internally with his continued employment with them. On the one hand, his conscience bothered him about the way HSA manipulated people and the truth for their own ends. On the other hand, he wanted to be involved in helping to handle the disaster brought on globally by the DNA changes to people from the supplements.If he wasn't working for the agency, how would he be able to remain informed and be able to personally work on the threat to mankind? He firmly believed that they were involved in a horrendous war that threatened the existence and future of mankind, and so he needed to be on the frontline. Then there was Rita. He was confused about his feelings for her, but he knew he wanted to be near her, and the only way he could continue to do that was if he continued to work for HSA to protect her work. Of course, he wasn't only there to provide security, he was also there to watch her, which made him feel duplicitous and like a cad. Now that he was going back to the States, he would be back under the close scrutiny of his bosses and be subjected to their every whim. All in all, Zack was not a happy camper as he tried to muddle through the maze he found himself in.

"Look everybody," Sandra called, pointing out the window as Rita and Nate hurried over to her. Zack shook himself and went over too, craning his neck with the rest of them. Far below them on the sea was a mammoth cruise ship travelling in tight circles with helicopters buzzing around it. Some of the helicopters were news choppers with their call stations in big letters on the sides. Other choppers were military choppers and seemed to be trying to put forces down on the liner. The railings of the passenger liner were jammed packed with passengers in life jackets. They could see that some figures were trying to lower life boats over the sides for some reason. Before they could see more, the jet had flown past the commotion, heading to another site.

"See if you can get anything on the news," Rita said, calling out a station name she had seen on one of the news helicopters. Zack fiddled with the plasma screen remote while Nate checked his Blackberry and Sandra booted up her laptop. Before long they had the story. Many of the crew on the ship had turned into mutants and were now sabotaging the ship. Some had just forgotten their jobs and had done things wrong accidentally, but some were gleefully playing with controls. Others were running rampant among the passengers, many of whom were themselves in various stages of mutation. It seemed like the military was involved in trying to seize control of the ship while simultaneously staging rescues of as many passengers as they could. However, they were seriously undermanned and it was not known how many servicemen were affected by the supplements and whether the choppers themselves were safe. One station went off the air as they were watching it, and a few seconds later, it was reported on another channel that the helicopter from that station had crashed from mutants disrupting the station's signal.

As they passed over the area they saw more and more boats that were aimlessly drifting. When the plane came back over land, they saw massive fires burning out of control. Not only were there forest fires, but there were fires at airports too, where crashed planes were burning. There were also fires in cities where whole blocks were in flames. In some places, it appeared that no one was even fighting the fires. The major highways were jammed packed with motionless cars. Along the way were burning cars, others with all their doors open, as if suddenly abandoned. Trains were stopped on the tracks and in some places were overturned. In one place, a train hung off a bridge, dangling into a river. Everywhere they could see, people were running in all directions, seeming to have no purpose or plan to where they were going.

On the jet, they wandered wide-eyed from window to window as the news coverage played on a television in the background. With each new newscast, they kept looking at each other in wide-eyed horror. Were they really heading right into the center of all this chaos?

* * *

As Zack turned on the BBC channel . . .

FRENCH NUCLEAR PLANT EXPLODES
- BBC

Reports are coming in of a massive explosion at a nuclear power plant in France that has released radiation into the atmosphere. This meltdown is being attributed to mutants, though it is not clear whether it was negligence or sabotage that caused it. Expected fail-safe measures did not operate as planned.

Due to the current wind patterns, the radiation is expected to spread in a southwesterly direction over southern Europe. The Prime Minister of England is assuring the public that his country will not be exposed and that no one should panic. However, radiation shelters are being prepared in case the wind changes direction and the radiation is greater than estimates have declared.

It is reported that airports, highways, and trains across mainland Europe are jammed as people try to flee in advance of the radiation cloud. There are projections that hundreds of thousands of people will stream into England and Ireland to flee from the targeted area. The Prime Minister has called an emergency session of Parliament to decide how to handle this influx of fleeing people and to predict the long-term effects from the explosion. In addition, the military is on high alert, in case the situation grows worse.

Switching to CNN Zack caught . . .

This is Rake Yardley breaking in with a live report from China. Just in — an oil tanker has gone aground near Shanghai, China and is spilling hundreds of thousands of gallons of oil into the sea. According to experts, the ocean currents are bringing the oil directly towards mainland China. The Chinese government is vowing to contain the oil spill before too much environmental damage has been done.

Wait, I've just been handed another report. It seems that another oil tanker is on fire in the middle of New York Harbor, blocking all marine traffic to that area. The oil spilling out of this tanker is on fire, preventing special spill containment vessels from getting close enough to work on stopping the leak. There have been eyewitness reports of men on fire jumping from the tanker. Unlike China, in New York Harbor, every direction the current flows will take the spill towards land, making it imperative to extinguish the fire before it reaches land. Mayor Lionel Rosencrantz of New York City is asking all citizens to stay off the waterways and roads leading to the harbor. Traffic is blocking the efforts of firefighters and rescue teams to get through. All hospitals are on standby to receive the injured from the tanker.

This accident will cripple the New York shipping industry for some time to come. All ships coming into the harbor are being diverted to ports southward, creating backlogs in those ports, too.

Both of these accidents, the one in China and the one in New York, appear to be from actions of mutants. It is still not known if they were intentional or not.

Environmentalists report that there will be untold damage to sea life and the environment from both spills. Environmental experts in this field are on their way to both sites to help up with the cleanup efforts. The President of the United States has pledged federal dollars, declaring an emergency, to help with cleanup efforts. He has also offered to collaborate with the Chinese government in how to best go about minimizing the damages.

Meanwhile, a search is underway to apprehend the mutants responsible for these accidents. Anyone with information is asked to contact their local law enforcement agency which will forward the information to the lead investigators at Homeland Security.

Continuing his scan of TV stations . . .

Reporting live from the scene of the levee breaks in New Orleans, this is Kimberley Kando of MSNBC. We are flying over one of the breaks in our news helicopter so that you can see from our live cameras the news as it occurs. Millions of tons of water are pouring into the low lying areas that were rebuilt after Hurricane Katrina flooded New Orleans in 2005.

The new levees were guaranteed by the Army Corp of Engineers to withstand Category 4 hurricanes, but due to global warming the water level has been rising and putting increased pressure on the levee system, creating tiny cracks that are barely visible to the naked eye. From the break you can see the water level rising inside the levee with your own eyes.

There are people on their roofs waving to us. On one of the roofs you can see a sign that says, "PLEASE SAVE US". As we zoom down for a closer look we can see people in boats. On the right side of your screen you can see a mob of men trying to get in a boat that is already filled to capacity with people. Oh, no, the boat is tipping over and everybody is falling out. You are seeing it here first and live at MSNBC.

There are people swimming in the water, some are sitting on top of stranded cars with the water lapping up at their feet. Dogs and cats are paddling desperately alongside the people, with no place to go. We don't see any signs of help, though we have received a report that a state of emergency has been declared by the Governor of Louisiana and that the National Guard has been called out. There is some question whether there will be many guardsmen available since most of the National Guard have been deployed to the ongoing war in the Middle East.

Look, in the upper center of the screen. Is that a body floating in the water? Yes, that does appear to be a body. You may be seeing the first casualty of the catastrophe live here on MSNBC.

Word just in of a rumor that these breaks in the levees have been caused by mutants, but it is too early to tell. There seems to be a trend towards blaming every major disaster in the world on mutants, so we have to caution that at this point it is just a rumor.

Live now is a close-up of another break in the levee. It does seem highly unusual that so many sections of the levee would break through at the same time without a carefully timed plan.

And now you can see the traffic jam of cars stalled and overheated on the major highways flowing out of New Orleans. Cars are trying to head outbound on the incoming lanes, preventing help from being able to enter by land, slowing down the response time and limiting aid to helicopters flying in.

There are widespread reports of power outages and riots. Many of the hospitals are isolated and surrounded by water themselves. We are flying over St. Agnes Hospital right now and you can see that they have patients in wheelchairs and on stretchers hooked up to IVs and other equipment on the roof. They are waving at us to help them, but of course, there is nothing we can do to help them, except get the news of their plight out to the millions of

```
people who are glued to their TV screens watching
this story. We will now go to a short break from
our sponsors. This is Kimberley Kando reporting.
Stay tuned for more news of the levee breaks in New
Orleans as it happens.
```

* * *

Some news reports were still getting out, but as media systems broke down, affected as much as other industries by the actions of mutants, less and less information was getting through to the public. Reporters might still be on the job broadcasting, but local affiliates were off the air. Opportunists were taking advantage of the chaos and lack of communication between law enforcement to stage riots and break-ins of homes and businesses for personal gain. Some justified their actions as necessary for survival as they raided supplies to hunker down for the long haul. In every civilized country and city across the globe people were panicking because they had no way of knowing if danger was right around the corner. Some barricaded themselves in their homes, weapons ready, while others fled their homes, not sure where it was safe to travel, though many instinctively headed to rural areas, believing those areas were safer.

* * *

Slapping down the folder she had been reading, Jamie Whitehead looked grimly at Brad Cho and Erin Blaine. Brad crunched his long lithe frame over the folder in front of him and pretended to be absorbed in what he was reading. Erin, however, jumped a mile and gave her startled eyes to Jamie, who immediately zeroed in on her. "Erin, would you care to summarize this latest report on national defense?"

Trying to look alert, Erin shoved her stringy dark hair out of her face and adjusted her glasses on her thin nose. It felt like she hadn't had a shower in months, let alone any sleep. Her stomach growled, and she added food to the list. It didn't seem fair that Zack was relaxing in sun-drenched Argentina while all the pressure was on those stationed Stateside. "This report states that our National Defense is severely compromised by mutants in the ranks. It is estimated that approximately 25% of all branches of military and agency personnel are infected. This figure has been extrapolated to the general population. The mission of defending the country is compromised by personnel going AWOL. Mutants who do arrive for duty either forget how to perform their duties, or are causing accidents, or are purposely sabotage their areas of responsibility, though it is difficult to define which incidents are accidental or purposeful."

"That is beside the point," Jamie interrupted. "It doesn't matter what the motivation is behind the actions, all that matters is that they are occurring."

Erin, prided herself on her intuitive ability, and had been hired to do profiling, so she was miffed by Jamie's rebuff though she tried not to show it.

Clearing his throat for attention, Brad said helpfully, "We need some way to be able to distinguish who is and who isn't infected."

Smiling at him as if he was the teacher's pet, Jamie responded. "How right you are! How do you think we should go about doing that? Have everyone stand in line and be strip searched for physical signs of devolution?"

"That wouldn't work," Erin rushed in. "If personnel had just started taking the supplements there wouldn't be any physical signs for a while." Noticing Jamie's smirk, she blushed, "Oh, I get it. That was a joke. I think I need another cup of coffee." She jumped up in a flurry and rushed over to the coffee pot. It was becoming increasingly evident that Ms. Whitehead was baiting her and that Brad was her golden boy who could do no wrong. Erin didn't know what to do about it, and felt trapped having to work in this environment. Regardless, the issues at hand were vital to the security of the country and she was determined to stick it out by doing her part.

"Of course, personnel have been told not to take the pills," Jamie steamrolled on, "but we can't just take people at their word about whether they have taken the pills or not. I suppose we can administer polygraphs, though that would be time consuming and some people can fool them on rare occasions. Who knows, maybe mutants wouldn't show reliable test results anyhow." She looked at Brad, expectantly.

Combing his hands through his glossy, black, straight hair, Brad was aware of the dynamics at play. He didn't like them either, but he couldn't figure out what he could do to change them, and he valued his career as much as Erin. "How about a test — I don't know — like a blood test, that shows whether someone is mutating or not?"

"That's a great idea," Jamie fawned, wondering if Brad minded the 20-year age difference between them and if he liked older, mature women, with more life experiences. "This sounds like something we should get Rita Perez working on. Right now, it is more important to know who is infected and who is not. We need to be able to separate out people who are mutating. That is much more important than finding a cure for this; we'll put that on the back burner for now. Take care of that, Erin, get in touch with Zack and bring him up to speed."

Feeling reduced to a mere messenger, Erin gave a barely perceptible nod.

Rolling right along, Jamie said, "The next question is what to do with the mutants once we have identified them? As you can see from the consultants' report, they agree that we must concentrate the mutants into central locations, where they can be monitored, for our safety and for theirs. Where are we on the construction of the containment centers?"

Tapping away at his keyboard, Brad answered, "We have a dozen completed, with a capacity for 2,000 detainees each. Another dozen are 50% complete, with plans for 100 centers to be completed by the end of the year."

"That is unacceptable," Jamie declared. "We need to put a rush on getting the ones under construction completed ASAP. Divert whatever resources are necessary to accomplish that pronto, Brad! The future ones that are still on the drawing boards need to be expanded to hold larger numbers." She ran numbers in her head. "One hundred times 2,000 equals 200,000. We need facilities to house 75 million mutants."

Erin was afraid to speak up, but couldn't contain herself any longer, "Can I ask what the criteria will be for being incarcerated in these detention camps? Surely, we aren't going to put all 75 million mutants in them, especially since many mutants are harmless."

"Nonsense," Jamie asserted. "There is no such thing as a harmless mutant. You can see by the report that even if some of the mutants are not intentionally destroying systems they still do so accidentally by forgetting proper procedures and tasks they are supposed to use. Either way, systems are failing everywhere, not just in the military. Mail is not getting delivered, water sources have failed, power grids are down, and fuel is not getting through for transportation needs. That's just a few examples in the private sector, alone. We don't have fuel for our military aircraft, ships, transports, and that is certainly more crucial than the private sector. We can't tell if the pilot getting into the cockpit is going to crash a billion dollar fighter jet. Heck, no one can even tell if the next person who walks in the door is going to try to take a chunk out of his or her neck. We must start rounding up all the military that have been infected and get reliable and uncontaminated humans, into all the vital positions. Then we will progress to the civilian critical positions. Until further notice, everybody infected will go into the containment centers."

"What about government officials who have been infected?" Brad asked, brightly.

Jamie looked momentarily uneasy. "We'll have to sell them on the idea that it is patriotic to get tested and that they need to set an example for the public. We need to convince the public that they want to know if their leaders are subhuman or not. If we can maneuver voters to insist on testing their leaders, then people will not question the intentions of the HSA. Our first job is to get a cohesive military, since it looks like we might have to impose martial law on the country in short order," she finished, grimly.

Both Brad and Erin gasped, exchanging shocked glances.

"Brad, you get the procedures in place to round up the known mutants and get them into the completed camps. Erin, you will be responsible for getting in touch with Zack and giving him the marching orders for Rita to come up with a test to distinguish who is infected and who isn't." She marched out of the office to report to Eric Collier, Chairman of Homeland Security, on the actions she had taken.

Now avoiding each other's eyes, Brad and Erin turned to their assigned tasks.

"How is it going in sunny Argentina?" Erin joked as she got Zack on the video phone.

"Oh, haven't you heard? You must be out of the loop," Zack teased. Erin gritted her teeth, knowing that it wasn't a mere oversight that she wasn't aware of Zack's status. "Even as we speak, I am over Georgia, heading to Virginia, with Rita, Sandra and Nate."

"What about Rita's research?" Erin exclaimed, hating that she looked stupid but she needed to quickly get up to speed.

"Sandra has found a spread out in horse country where we will be staying. She is going to defend Harland Parker, and she needs Rita as an expert witness. There is a guest cottage that Rita will be using for a temporary lab. Plus, she figures she will have more humans willing to volunteer for trials here in the States, where the pills were more popular so there is a larger representative sample population. Let me assure you that her absolute goal is to reverse the genetic devolution," Zack explained, good-naturedly. He'd seen firsthand how Jamie used Erin as her whipping girl, so he had a suspicion that was still going on.

"That's all changed now," Erin explained. "It is imperative that Rita's research go in a different direction for now. She needs to develop some kind of test, maybe a blood test, that can be administered to find out if a person is infected or not. It needs to be something that can be mass-produced immediately, too, because we are going to test all military personnel to secure our armed forces. Then it will be given to civilians in key positions, and eventually administered to the general public."

"I don't think Rita is going to like this change in plans at all," Zack said, shaking his tousled hair. Before Erin could respond, he called out, "Hey, Rita, Erin Blaine from HSA has something she needs to discuss with you. I'll put her on speaker phone."

As Rita came into view on the video feed, Erin gave her formal instructions. "Deputy Director Whitehead has ordered that you begin working on a way to test people for whether they have taken the pills or not. This needs to be done ASAP, and in a way that is easily mass produced so that we can administer it to the military, and on from there. This is of the highest priority and takes precedence to whatever else you are doing."

Rita shook her head, her golden eyes glinting, "I definitely am committed to reversing the mutation. First I have to help these poor people. Can't you just ask people if they have taken supplements? Besides, what is going to happen to the people who are identified as mutants?"

Erin secretly agreed with Rita. Erin said, "It is believed at the highest levels that mutants are not to be trusted to be honest about their involvement with supplements. Our first priority is that it is necessary to solidify the military as quickly as possible. It is not your concern what the plans are for the mutants once they are identified. Let me repeat my order. You must stop any current research and concentrate exclusively on developing this identifier test. These are your new orders and Zack is responsible for seeing they are enforced! Zack, you will be reporting on the status of the test to me."

Rita looked at Zack, incredulously. She knew she was under contract to HSA, but she hadn't realized until now that they could order her around or that they would even consider changing the focus of her research. Zack was miserable. He could feel himself being sucked back into the whirlpool of Homeland Security red tape. He knew about the containment centers from past planning sessions at the agency, but, at this point, he also knew he had no other option than to follow orders, even if Rita would hate him for it. "Yes ma'am, Erin. I will ensure that Ms. Perez gets right on developing a testing procedure once we get settled in Virginia." He broke the signal before anyone could say anything else. Then, he turned to Rita to try to reason with her, but Rita turned in a huff and walked to the other end of the plane.

Zack might have agreed to what she was expected to do, Rita thought to herself bitterly, but she hadn't. There was no way she was going to abandon Holly and her daughters, and millions of other trapped people like them. Somehow, she would figure out a way to work on both initiatives at the same time, even if she had to hide her work from Zack.

*   *   *

"Look Mom, look at all those people down there," Reva exclaimed as leaned across her identical twin Vera and pointed at a group of people gathered near the river's edge. At least Carley was pretty sure it was Reva, since she had memorized which of the identical twins sat where in the back seat of her car. Holly could tell them apart, but Carley had not been able to see any differences yet. They even seemed to be mutating identically. She imagined that as she got to know them better she would be able to identify them as quickly as Holly could. Carley, from her position as driver, craned her neck to try to see what the girls were pointing at from the right side of the car. Holly, who was in the passenger seat, barely glanced out the window.

"Those people look like they are becoming fish, like you Jasmine" Vera announced, frankly comparing the changes to Jasmine, sitting with them, to the people by the river. "They look even fishier than you do."

"Vera, where are your manners?" Holly stirred, looking severely over the seat at the girls.

"Sorry, Ms. Jasmine," Vera mumbled, looking up under her long, dark eyelashes.

"That's okay, honey," Jasmine said. "You didn't hurt my feelings. You only spoke the truth. I'm not as far along as most of those people are, but looking at them gives me a good idea of where I'm heading if Ms. Perez can't help me." Jasmine reached across Reva to pat Vera, trying hard to keep her spirits up and not show her revulsion to the aquatic mutants they were passing. Some of the mutants had jumped into the water and were cavorting in it as if it was their natural home, diving deep and not surfacing for many minutes. A group of teenagers were holding races, while smaller children were darting after minnows and swallowing them whole when they caught them.

"Eeuuw! Did you see that?" Reva said. "That boy just swallowed a fish live!" She shuddered and turned away.

Holly had held off from taking supplements for weeks after she had heard about how great they were from Harland. Then, once she tried them, she waited another couple of weeks before taking a second dose to make sure she didn't have a bad reaction before starting her daughters on them. Unfortunately, during the time she waited no physical mutation effects had occurred. She felt brimming with new life and energy and wanted all the benefits for her daughters that Harland had proclaimed were happening to Sterling, so she began giving the pills to her girls. They were just at the stage now where they were showing a small amount of downy feathers, like baby birds, on their arms, legs, and necks. Holly had stopped the pills for both herself and the twins the minute she started noticing physical changes in herself, before anything had changed for the girls. It was evident that the genetic process was continuing regardless of the fact that they had stopped taking the supplements.

"Mom, tell Reva to stop leaning over me," Vera whined, pushing Reva.

"I'm not hurting you," Vera responded, giving her a push back. "I can't see out the window from where I'm sitting if I don't lean across you."

"Girls, stop fighting," Holly screeched at them, startling everyone in the car with her ferociousness. The girls looked at her wide-eyed, forgetting their arguments in their concern about their mothers hollering at them. Holly was normally a soft-spoken person who believed in calmly reasoning with her girls when they acted up in the rambunctious way of typical seven year-olds.

Carley looked over at Holly warily, wondering if her assessment was accurate that Holly would not turn violent. "Hey, Holly, it's okay; they are just being typical kids. This is a long ride they have to put up with, going out to Virginia to meet with Rita and the group." She reached over and patted Holly's arm.

Holly looked at Carley, beseechingly, "They are fighting, Carley. I am afraid they are becoming violent like Harland." She hung her head in despair.

Holly got protests from all sides.

"We're not fighting, Mom," the twins piped up in synch, throwing their arms around each other to articulate the point.

"They are just acting like normal kids," Carley insisted. "A little squabbling does not mean anyone is going to get violent from those pills. You have to stop worrying about that, Holly."

"How about you and I change seats?" Jasmine suggested to Reva. "I can sit in the middle, and then you will have your own window to look out of. There is a different group of mutants on this side. In fact, they seem to be ape-like."

"Okay, Ms. Jasmine," Reva said eagerly, almost jumping over Jasmine so she could see the ape people. Vera was a bit jealous now because she couldn't see them from her window. "Oh-h-h-h look, there are ape men up in the trees."

No sooner had she said that when an ape-like mutant jumped out of a tree in front of the car, landing agilely on his feet and pounding his fists on his chest in a threatening manner. Carley swerved the car to the right just in time to miss hitting him, but not far enough to prevent the guy from giving the car a hard whack as it passed by him. Everybody was shaken to the core, speechlessly looking back-and-forth at each other and watching the trees fearfully ahead. The fact hit home that this was not a sightseeing lark they were on. Carley gripped the wheel hard and kept her eyes focused tightly on the road, trying to spot further problems before they got too close.

It was fortunate that she was so vigilant because most of the traffic lights were out and most of the other vehicles were plowing through the intersections without watching for crossing traffic. They came upon abandoned cars stopped in the middle of the road, some of which were vandalized, with graffiti on them and stripped of resalable parts. Driving was like traversing an obstacle course. Carley tried switching to lesser travelled side roads, avoiding major highways, but no matter where they drove, they encountered more problems.

Many gas stations and businesses were closed, making Carley eye the fuel gauge more often than normal, not knowing if they had enough gas to make it to where they were going. Buildings were on fire everywhere. People in all stages of mutation were wandering, singly or in groups, all to be feared because their intents were unknown — alien to the human way of thinking. Carley instinctively checked the locks on her car doors, whenever she spotted trouble.

"I think it would be a good idea if you girls crunched down below the level of the windows," Carley suggested in a tone that was immediately convincing. The girls complied, but normal curiosity had them bobbing their heads up for little peeks every few minutes.

"I see a bird girl on that bridge, just like us," Vera informed everyone, forgetting she wasn't supposed to be looking. "She's standing up on the railing." Everybody in the car looked out to see. As they were watching, the mutant started flapping her arms and leaped into the air, trying to fly like Harland, who was the most advanced mutant. Since she didn't have developed wings yet, she landed with a huge splash in the water, aquatic mutants quickly swimming over to her. She partially climbed onto the back of one of them and was pulled to shore, as many people cheered.

"See, Holly," Carley was quick to point out, "not all mutants are bad. That fish person just saved that bird girl's life. Even animals have different personalities."

Wounded, Holly looked at her.

"Not that I'm saying you are an animal, because the truth is nothing of the sort," Carley said hurriedly, giving Holly a guilty look. "I just meant that you and the twins and Jasmine all have your own personalities, and that will probably not change."

Jasmine nodded her head in agreement, though Holly still looked skeptical.

"It was silly of that girl to think she could fly without wings," Vera scoffed.

"Do you think we are going to grow wings, Mom?" Reva asked, half fearfully and half entranced by the idea. She lifted her arms and looked them over carefully.

"Aaargh!" Holly cried.

Carley hastily replied. "That's why we are going to see Ms. Rita, so she can change you back to the way you were. Don't you want that?"

A bit regretfully, Reva grudgingly agreed as she inspected her arms.

Spotting the turnoff to the ranch just ahead on the left, Carley gratefully pulled in, relieved that her responsibility to drive everyone there had ended, wondering what the future had in store for all of them.

* * *

Robin Birdswell led a group of people to the door of a large aviary and opened it for them to enter. "This is the aviary where Sterling can practice flying safely if and when he feels so inclined. We let him spend some time in here every day so he can watch other avian creatures and learn from them."

It had been an emotional meeting when Holly, Carley and Jasmine met up with Rita, Sandra, Nate and Zack at the Virginia house in horse country. It had been difficult for the Argentinean contingent to hide their shock at the transformations in Holly and her daughters. They'd heard talk of the changes in people, even seen pictures on TV screens of them , but this was the first time for all of them to see a mutating person up close and personal, let alone people they all cared for.

For Nate especially, the whole trip to this point had been one eye-opener after another. He realized now that Sandra had not been exaggerating the upheaval occurring in society and in law and order. He had now seen it with his own eyes, so he was thanking his lucky stars that he had sold his biotech stocks near the top before the bottom fell out. He did have a thought to invest immediately in the cure, if and when one was found. He was hoping Rita would be on the cutting edge of that discovery, so that he could get in on the ground floor. Then, looking at Reva and Vera dancing around with their fledgling feathers, he at once felt guilty for thinking greedily of his investments at a time like this when so many people were personally affected.

After just a couple of days, before they could all settle into a routine, Holly had started agitating about Sterling. She insisted that they needed to see him, to make sure he was alright. She worried that no one would be able to understand his needs. She talked about poor Harland being alone in jail and worrying about how his son was, and what was being done with him. She cried and cried as if her heart would break. Soft-hearted Sandra decided to find out where Sterling was being kept. As Harland's lawyer, she had standing to find out. They had heard about Robin Birdswell in the headlines when she had taken Sterling, but they didn't realize that she was only a few miles from where they were now. After Sandra called her and explained the situation she had graciously invited them to her spread. It was quite a crew that rode over to visit.

Walking into the spacious aviary, it was hard to spot Sterling right away because it was so large. There were plants and birdhouses and perches everywhere, as brightly colored birds of every size and shape flew or perched in every direction they looked.

Holly's sharp bird eyes were the first to spot him. "There he is," Holly exclaimed, pointing with her right index talon to the far corner where a figure was huddled, too large a figure for a bird, but small by human standards for a 10-year-old boy. The rest held back, not wanting to overwhelm or scare him, as Holly approached.

"Hi Sterling, I'm Holly. Do you remember meeting me with your father?" she said gently, reaching out a clawed hand to him.

Sterling, who had been squawking with his head down, raised his head slowly to look at her. There was a gasp from most of the group that they could not hold back when they saw him. His teeth had begun to fuse together and jut forward, while his lips were retracting, forming the beginnings of a beak. His eyes, small and beady, were mostly hidden amongst the gray feathers on his face. His nose had also retracted. His legs were short and spindly; his arms were flat and covered with luxurious feathers. It was still possible to see fingers, though they had shortened and were more talon-like than flesh-like. His chest had rounded and enlarged, too. Invisible to them were the internal changes. Sterling was probably the second person to take the pills after his father Harland. Thus, his advancement along the track of devolution was the most progressed any of them had seen. Nate turned away, unable to look anymore. Rita, warring between her human shock and her scientist's eye, forced herself to study him, as dispassionately as she could manage. Sandra was outraged at what had been done to this poor child. Day by day, she was more resolved with her view that mutants needed rights. Zack's position was more in terms of defense. He didn't see the boy as much of a threat, but he realized how powerful a beak on a fully-grown man could be, especially if flying was added to the equation. Not to mention three-inch-long talons. Shocked, Carley and Jasmine looked at each other, thinking about how Holly and the girls were going to change like this in the near future.

Holly and the girls, however, experienced no revulsion at seeing Sterling. They flocked around him, the girls chattering to him like magpies.

"Hey, Sterling, remember us?" Vera said.

"Wow, you have longer feathers than we do," Reva jumped in, holding her own arm up to Sterling's to compare. She was always a bit more forward than Vera.

Sterling squawked and hid his head under his arm as Holly pulled her hand back.

"Girls, give him some room to breathe," Holly ordered, pulling the twins back a bit. "Give him some time to see who we are. Just feel comfortable with us!" Turning to Sterling, she murmured, soothingly, "There, there, we aren't here to hurt you. We care about you and want to help you. You can trust us." She approached him slowly, watching to see if he was okay with her doing it.

Sterling peeked one eye out from under his arm, fearfully eyeing everyone, and then settling on Holly. He nodded slowly, as if he was dimly remembering her, and picked his head up all the way.

Holly held out her hand again and Sterling cautiously reached out and took it. Slowly and carefully, Holly put her arms around him and began to rock him, crooning to him softly.

"I can't figure out why he just stays in the corner like that," Robin Birdswell spoke up. She was a tall, solid woman, with a mane of heavy brown hair that hung wildly down her back. She still favored the hippie age with her high-waisted gauzy blouse over jeans and her granny glasses. She honestly thought she was helping Sterling. She had devoted her life to studying birds and caring for them, so she felt like it was an honor to be the first one to actively help a mutant acclimate to an obviously new yet natural environment.

"Can't you tell he's afraid?" Sandra said, outraged and ready to begin fighting.

"Oh, no, that's not it at all," Robin asserted. "He's just overwhelmed by all you folks. It is pretty overpowering to have so many of you just come in like this and surprise him."

"Why are you keeping him caged up?" Carley asked, her tender heart thinking of the child being treated as an animal.

"That's not the case at all," Robin Birdswell heartily replied, her good-will undiminished. "He has a house that he stays in, all his own, with people to take care of him. Here, come with me and I'll show you."

Most of the group turned to follow her, but Holly stayed protectively holding onto Sterling.

"What about Sterling? Can he come, too?" Rita asked.

"Of course he can!" Robin said, cheerfully. "Come on, Sterling. Come show everyone where you live."

Sterling glanced up at her, and then sidled across in front of everybody, taking her hand and leading the way to his house, an oversized four-bedroom guest house on the property. Three caregivers lived there full-time with Sterling in a house with furnishings that were constantly being modified to fit his needs. The girls pranced around, exploring the house and pulling Sterling along to show them everything. After a hesitant look back, he went with them, for the moment being a child with other children.

"This looks nice," Sandra said, mollified as she brazenly looked around, peering into cupboards and looking behind closed doors.

"Are you keeping any records of the changes you noticed in him?" Rita couldn't help but ask the question.

"Oh, yes, we are being quite scientific about all of this," Robin answered, nodding her head. "I have studied birds for years, and I've always kept careful notes of their habits and behaviors."

"Would you mind if I have a look at your records?" Rita asked. "And I'd like to have access to spending time with him. I'm working on a way to reverse the process and Sterling is the most advanced mutant not in captivity. I'd love to work with him."

"Well, I certainly don't mind letting you see my notes, or having you visit him," Robin responded, affably. "I'm of a mind to let nature take its course. What will be, will be. If Sterling is going to turn into a bird, then that is perfectly fine with me, and we should accept him for what he is."

"You are treating him like a lab rat," Jasmine blurted out, thinking fearfully that her turn was coming when she would be treated that way.

"He's just a little boy who needs love," Carley added, putting her arm around Jasmine. "We all need love!"

"He gets plenty of attention around here, as much as he wants, in fact," Robin insisted. "We all love birds and are dedicated to giving him a fully enjoyable life."

"You had him in a cage," Holly spit out, aggressively.

"NO, no, you misunderstand me! The aviary is just for his safety. If he starts flying, he might blunder into things and hurt himself out in the open. The aviary is meant to be a safe environment for him to learn in. He can observe the other birds, too, and see how they fly, helping him to learn how to do it," Robin protested, throwing her mass of hair around. "He doesn't have to be in the aviary, since he can leave whenever he wants to. You see the lovely house I have provided for him."

"I suppose the other birds in your aviary are free to go whenever they want to," Sandra asked, thinking about the rights of all birds to fly free without cages.

"Well, no," Robin acknowledged, uncomfortably. "Most of the birds we get have been injured or abandoned as babies and couldn't survive in the wild. I provide companionship, food, and plenty of space for them to fly. I have all the comforts they need with none of the dangers involved. Remember, being in the wild, is certainly not a picnic. They are constantly in danger from predators out there."

Before Sandra could engage in battle, Zack broke in, "What about security? How are you keeping reporters from finding Sterling and what will keep him from running away?"

"We have tried to keep this location hidden from the press, but I doubt that will last long," Robin answered. "At least I have the whole estate surrounded with electric fencing and motion sensors. I have a private security force that I don't think even a determined reporter can get through. As for Sterling, we keep a pretty close eye on him."

"He's a prisoner," Holly said triumphant at proving her point.

"No, he's not a prisoner. He's a minor child that I am obligated by the court to care for, just like any other child who is a ward of the state," Robin asserted, her good will beginning to be taxed under the attack from all sides. "Maybe you would like to bring your girls over to play in the aviary with him."

"Because we are all birds, you want to put us in a cage, too," Holly said, incensed.

"Not at all," Robin said, regally. "I just thought he might like to play with other children, especially children who are experiencing the same things he is."

Before Holly could launch herself at Robin, Carley put a restraining arm around her friend. Rita spoke up. "Hopefully, we will be able to change all of that soon."

Nate had kept quiet through most of the visit, feeling out of his element, though he was glad he had the opportunity to see just how advanced the devolution was. He could not even begin to imagine how Harland looked now. Speaking up, he said, "We all thank you for letting us come visit Sterling. If you don't mind, we will continue to visit him, though we promise to come in smaller groups from now on. It is obvious to me that you are doing your best in a difficult situation."

Mollified, Robin showed them all out after Holly gathered up her children and gave Sterling a fierce hug. As they left, looking back they saw Robin with her arm around Sterling as they waved good-bye.

After discussing Sterling's situation animatedly on the way home, each of the friends went their separate ways. Rita and Zack went to the lab. Sandra headed to work on Harland's defense with Nate going along to keep her company while he watched the markets. Jasmine, pleading a headache that was really an anxiety attack, went to lie down.

At the pleadings of the twins, Holly and Carley took them out to a pool, where the girls jumped in joyfully, splashing around to their hearts' content. Not wanting to go in themselves, Carley and Holly retreated to a table with an umbrella, carrying tall drinks of water to keep them cool. The girls tried to splash them occasionally, shrieking with laughter every time they got one of the adults wet.

"We need to get Sterling out of there," Holly said, without preamble.

"I can see how upset you were about Sterling's situation," Carley said, soothingly. "It really got to me, too."

"She treats him like an animal," Holly hissed. "She keeps him in a cage."

"It must be hard for her to know exactly how to take care of him," Carley temporized, a bit uncomfortably.

"He needs to be with people like himself. Harland would want him to be with me," Holly insisted, talking slowly. It was an effort for her to speak a lot and to put all her thoughts into words.

"I know you understand what he is going through better than anyone else does," Carley said, supportively, as she played with a bead of water on her glass.

"I do. My girls do. Sterling would be happy with us. Rita could help him, too," Holly continued, struggling carefully to get sentences out. "You must help me rescue him. I must do this for Harland."

"I'm not sure the others would go along with that," Carley said, uneasily, feeling caught between wanting to help her friend and that poor, scared child and not knowing what was right legally.

"We can't tell them," Holly replied with a little squawk, running her talons along the table.

"Sandra would be put in a horrible position as an officer of the court and Nate would not want to hide anything from her. Zack, as part of Homeland Security, would immediately notify his superiors," Carley reasoned. "We might be able to trust Rita to keep it quiet, since she would want to help reverse his mutation. Jasmine would probably help us and keep it quiet, too."

"Don't tell Rita until afterwards when we have Sterling," Holly said. "Jasmine can watch the girls for me."

"Okay, I'm in, but where do we hide him since this would be the first place they would look," Carley responded, inwardly wondering what she was getting herself into, but knowing she had to stand by her friend.

They sat there, scheming by the pool, puzzling out how they could work out their planned rescue without anyone being the wiser.

* * *

Looking in the mirror in their cabin, Marti admired her tan and how fit she had become from swimming every day and doing Qi Gong when she noticed a few white hairs among the golden red. She frowned, pulling them out, as she discovered more and realized she wasn't going to be able to pull them all out. Of course, Gabe had plenty of silver among the gold, since he was a good 17 years older than she was. But, his silver blended in so beautifully, and these white hairs of hers stood out in stark contrast to the fiery red of her natural color. Would Gabe mind, or would he think she was starting to look old? Surely a few white hairs wouldn't matter to him. In fact, maybe she needed to get some hair dye, though she didn't want to spoil her natural color either. She then bent her head down, trying to see how many hairs showed from the top, holding a hand mirror up for a better look at it. Speaking of Gabe, what was taking him so long in the bathroom, anyways? The shower had stopped quite awhile ago and she was waiting to get in there to rinse herself off.

"Gabe? You about done in there, honey?" she called out.

"I'll be out in a moment," was his muffled reply.

Shrugging, Marti decided to run into the galley for a drink while she waited.

His hands pressed to his chest, Gabe sat on the closed toilet wondering what to do. He had been having chest pains off and on since they went through the canal, but attributed them to angina. He had surreptitiously popped a nitro pill each time, though, not letting Marti ever know what he was really doing since he didn't want to worry her. He was well aware of how much older than Marti he was, and didn't want her to think he was an old man with nothing but medical problems. Worse yet, he didn't want to disrupt their vacation and go get an endless barrage of tests, especially since they were having such a good time. The doctor had said he might get angina pains, and that's all this was.

This pain though, this pain, was hurting a bit more, and he could feel it down his left arm. He had even broken out in a sweat after having a nice cool shower, which made no sense to him. His nitro pills were in the cabin, and he didn't want to go get them while Marti was right there to see. . He didn't know what to do. Oh, good, he thought, she was leaving the cabin and heading to the galley. Quietly, he staggered out of the bathroom and got to his dresser, fumbling to open the nitroglycerine tablets' tiny bottle. Sitting on the bed he put a nitro pill under his tongue, hoping Marti would stay gone until it dissolved and took effect.

CHAPTER FOUR

What Makes a Human?

"Good thing we got here early," Nate whispered to Rita, twisting on the bench seat behind the defense table to look at the full courtroom. "If we'd been any later we wouldn't have gotten seats."

Rita nodded, quietly glancing at the crowd, though her mind was more on the testimony she had to give than on who was attending the trial. Her eyes quickly turned forward, unseeing. Zack, sitting next to Rita, looked straight ahead, uninterested in the people around him and completely focused on the trial.

Nate observed the scene as if it was a circus put on for his entertainment. At the back of the courtroom were four rows reserved exclusively for media outlets, though the judge refused to allow cameras in the courtroom. Therefore, there were half a dozen sketch artists seated in various strategic areas in the courtroom, allowing them maximum visual capability. Soon they were busy drawing sketches of anything they thought might be of interest in the room.

The court crowd was divided down the middle. All the seats on the left side behind the defense table were filled with mutants supporting Harland, while the rows on the right behind the prosecution table were filled with normal humans who showed no signs of mutation. Harland spotted Holly, Jasmine, and Carley sitting in the back of the room on the defense side. Carley was stoutly there to support

Harland, but it was apparent that she was uncomfortable as one of the only non-mutants sitting among the mutants. Nate caught her eye and gave her nod as if to say, see I'm on this side too. Carley gratefully nodded back.

People had come out for a variety of reasons. Many non-mutants had arrived, wanting to see that justice was given to the mutant who had killed a beautiful human nurse. Others were there just for the show, to see up close the now-famous creature that had devolved into a birdman, the most mutated person on earth. It was their opportunity to drink in the drama and get high from the excitement. Some had even brought their children, taking them out of school for the day, thinking this historic trial would be an educational experience for them. The mutants were there to see that Harland was treated the same as any other human would be, with the full rights afforded to any human. They were divided on whether he should be found guilty because he had the same responsibility as any other human being, or whether as a human he was suffering from a condition that prevented him from being in full possession of his faculties and as such should not be found guilty.

Because everybody was buzzing with anticipation and opinions, it wasn't too long before the two sides started exchanging words back and forth.

Normal people would jeer. ""What are you crazy mutants doing in this courtroom? This is a place for human justice. You aren't humans, but mutants . . . animals, even! None of you belong here, but should be put in cages!"

The mutants would yell back. "We are humans, too, just higher evolved than you are. All of us were born human, so we have the same rights that you do. We want to be sure Major Parker is given his equal rights."

It quickly became a madhouse with people/mutants jumping up on each side, getting into each other's faces, and beginning to get physical with those they were arguing with, shoving and pushing. It caused parents to rethink their decision to bring their kids to court, with some even heading for the exits when the bailiff and court officers came in and demanded order in the court. Everybody settled down, especially when the officers threatened to start throwing people out. No one wanted to miss out, though Nate was disappointed because he had been enjoying the show.

Just then, the doors at the back of the courtroom opened and Sandra and her team entered, walking down the long center aisle to the defense table. Nate did a double take at Sandra. He had gotten used to seeing her in casual shorts and tank tops, her hair blowing free as she rode on horses and swam in streams and pools. By contrast, he had never experienced the professional Sandra. That morning, she was awake and out of the house before he had even rolled out of bed. Her long, honey hair was fastened to the back of her head in something Nate vaguely remembered hearing called a French twist. She had on a conservative dove gray linen suit, with a white silk blouse. Nate was used to seeing her long legs exposed in shorts, but somehow, with hose and high black heels, they seemed to go on forever, and Nate couldn't stop looking at them. He felt a nudge in his ribs from Rita, and switched from staring at Sandra's legs to looking at her face and trying to figure out what was different there. Sure, she wore a touch of make-up, which she normally spurned in everyday, casual persona, because her features were so finely chiseled, fresh, and dramatic. At that moment, the make-up enhanced her beauty, but there was something more that increased his attraction to her. He just couldn't put his finger on it, though. With the expression on her face showing determination and experience, it was an entirely different side of Sandra that he had never seen before. Should he treat her differently in the future because of it? After all, he now realized she was a woman he didn't fully know or understand. Just then, Sandra turned around, her eyes scanning the crowd as if looking for someone. Then she spotted him! Her intense gaze immediately melted into her soft and familiar face, causing her to smile in delight. Nate smiled back and gave her a slight wave. She was still his Sandra underneath that professional exterior. He hadn't lost her. He was just seeing more aspects of who she was.

There was a big stir from the audience and Nate, along with everyone else, craned to see over or around the people who were half standing to see what was happening. Down the aisle came

Richard T. Chambers and his team, strutting as he looked from side to side as if acknowledging accolades being thrown at him. Although not a tall man, he seemed to fill the room to the point where no one noticed the team that followed him in. He had a bulldog face, complete with jowls, and sharp brown eyes that pierced right through you from behind his tortoise shell glasses. Though on a public salary, he still managed to own a high price hand tailored suit, complete with navy tie and a light blue shirt that also was tailored carefully to fit his solid build. The press had made much of the fact that the lead prosecutor himself would be trying this case. It was obvious as Chambers scanned the media that he bemoaned the lack of cameras in the room. With great fanfare, he proceeded regally to the prosecution table.

The crowd was ready to settle down again when there was a loud whisper. "Look, it's the Navy nurse." Everyone's head went on the swivel to view the new diversion. With her head held high, Joann walked down towards the front of the courtroom and then stopped, not knowing where to go. Chambers hurried to her and grandly helped her to a seat in the row behind the prosecution table, where the other prosecution witnesses were sitting. She wore her dress blue Navy nurse's uniform and looked highly competent, a formidable witness. There would be no question that Harland had actually performed the deed with her testimony to corroborate it. She sat stiffly, her face forward, aware that every eye in the court was on her.

Soon a new distraction caught everybody's attention. From a side door near the front of the courtroom, Harland entered the court in shackles. Nate knew that Sandra had tried to get Harland to wear normal clothes, which would have added comedy to the circus. There was no normal men's clothing, or any kind of clothing that fit him anymore. It was immaterial since Harland had refused any of the clothes she had brought for him, preferring to be in the baggy prison clothes, which gave him room for his un-human shape. The crowd gasped as Harland shuffled to the defense table in his orange jumpsuit, his bare-footed talons clicking on the wooden floor as he walked. His face had an almost perfectly formed beak, the tissue still slightly puffy where it hadn't yet hardened. His ears had receded to mere openings among the feathers; whereas short white feathers covered his head. His forehead protruded and his eyes drifted somewhat to the sides, increasing his peripheral vision. There was no longer any white or iris in his eyes, either, since they were now pure black. From his sleeves long brown feathers surrounded a minimal arm, and there were mere vestiges of fingers left.

"Momma, he looks like a bald eagle," piped up one youngster in the audience who was quickly shushed by his mother even as many in the courtroom nodded in agreement.

The officers brought Harland to the defense table and there was a flurry of discussion between them and Sandra. Nate could hear Sandra insisting that Harland's handcuffs and shackles be removed. The officers refused, citing Harland's tendency towards violence. "It's for your own protection, ma'am," one was heard saying. Realizing they were at a stalemate until the judge came in, Sandra tried to get Harland to sit down. The backseat area of his jumpsuit puffed outward, and it became evident that Harland could no longer sit the way humans do, so he had to remain standing. Nate suspected that the "puff" was actually scrunched tail feathers. He had seen many things since coming back to the States, but Harland's condition rammed home to him how physically different mutants were from humans. The jury had quietly filed in while everybody's eyes were fixated on Harland. All were startled as the bailiff called the court to order.

"Hear ye, hear ye. All stand for the Honorable Judge Terrence Blackburn."

After the spectacle of Harland, and the swaggering entrance of Richard T. Chambers, the judge was a major disappointment for the crowd. Judge Blackburn was a small elderly man with a white fringe of hair around his bald head. He seemed consumed by the black robe, as he made his way to the bench. He peered through his bifocals as he timidly pounded his gavel, telling everyone in a meek voice that they should be seated. Nate gave Rita an incredulous look, and she shrugged, thinking that you shouldn't judge a book by its cover.

In a low voice that the audience had to strain to hear, Judge Blackburn dispensed with the pretrial motions. He ruled that Major Harland Parker was a human being and as such entitled to a fair trial under the current laws of the United States.

People in the audience were angry, yelling out random comments. The shouts came from both sides, as well as the gallery that had filled to standing room only.

"He's a freaking mutant!"

"He's not one of us!"

"He should be put down like an animal!"

"He's not just a human anymore, he's more evolved!"

The judge pounded his gavel, and in a loud stern voice that surprised everyone he barked, "Order, order, the next person who makes a sound will be ejected from this courtroom." He glared, sternly, at the ringleaders who sat down in stunned silence.

Sandra took the opportunity to plea to the judge. "I request that Major Parker's handcuffs and shackles be taken off, and that it be put in the record that I object to the prison uniform as it biases the jury to perceive him as a prisoner, instead of as a Navy officer."

Without getting up, the prosecutor responded. "We have a record from the prison that Major Parker is taken with sudden fits of violence, such as throwing himself against cell doors and fighting the guards who escort him. It is for the safety of those here in the court that we request his restraints be kept on. As for his clothes, we have received a report that Major Parker no longer fits into his military uniform and that it is his own desire for comfort to remain in his jumpsuit. Just look at him. Does it look like he could wear regular human clothes?"

There was a buzz from the crowd that was quelled by a glance from the judge. "I order that Major Parker remain in restraints and prison garb. The jury is reminded that they should not be swayed by this in their decision. Ms. O'Callahan, you may proceed with your opening statement."

Smoothing her skirt as she stood, Sandra approached the jury — and meeting each person's eyes in turn, she began. "Your Honor, and members of the jury, today we intend to prove that Major

Harland Parker is not responsible for his actions. The fault lies with the United States government. [There was a gasp from the audience.] The fault also lies with the United Nations and the big pharmaceutical companies. Let's view these one at a time. The United States government knew that human DNA had been genetically modified by their nuclear testing in the Marshall Islands. Rather than being open about it, they tried to keep the information secret and attempted to develop technology to repair the damage they had caused. When the United Nations found out the United States had this advanced technology available and were not sharing it with the rest of the world, they disseminated it equally to everyone. This led to abuse of the technology by the big pharmaceutical companies. In their eagerness to get their products to market before their competition did they took shortcuts and didn't fully test the products to ensure their safety. Then they began marketing personal enhancements proclaiming that they were safe. Major Harland believed their advertising and took those supplements, trustingly, thinking they were harmless and beneficial. He had no previous knowledge that the supplements would cause irreversible changes to his DNA that would cause him to permanently evolve. Look at him." Sandra dramatically threw her arm out and pointed at Harland, who was ignoring her and everything that was occurring in the court. The jury obediently shifted their gaze to Harland, some of them nodding along with Sandra.

"It is evident what the supplements physically did to him. Do you think a certain Navy major would purposely choose this look for himself and his only child?" Many in the jury shook their heads in agreement with Sandra while others tried to look enigmatic and impartial. "However, the changes are not only external, they are also internal. Major Parker not only looks like a bird, he has the behaviors, thoughts, desires, and needs of a bird. He had no free will regarding his behavior on that day. Instead, he was programmed by the mutated DNA to act the way he did, like a bird recognizing food and unthinkingly eating it. Since he was not in his human mind at the time, we will show that by the legal definition of sanity, Major Parker was definitely insane, and, thus, not responsible for his actions regarding the tragic death of the Navy nurse. Ultimately, we are all responsible for our eagerness to exploit this new mutation technology without worrying ourselves about the consequences." After another deep look at each of the jurors, Sandra resumed her seat. Many of the jury seemed as if they had already made up their minds.

"Mr. Chambers, we are ready for your opening remarks," the judge whispered.

Mr. Chambers sat for a few seconds until the courtroom was silent. Then he stood next to the prosecution table, turning to point at Harland. "He killed a nurse. When a person kills another person with a gun, we don't say it was the gun's fault and let the individual go on his merry way. This was a vicious and unprovoked crime, with the victim being an innocent, caring nurse who was trying to help him at the time of her death. Major Parker killed that nurse, and not the supplements nor the companies that sold the supplements — and certainly not the United Nations or the United States. How desperate is the defense to try to claim conspiracies by our government?" He pointed again at Harland. "He chose to take supplements, just like the person who chooses to drink and then drives and kills someone. Not knowing what effect the pills would have on him is no excuse for any irresponsible behavior on his part. In this country, each individual is held responsible for his or her actions." Nodding pontifically, he approached the jury, sweeping his hands out to include them all. "I will prove to you that Major Harland willfully committed this heinous crime. Your job as a jury is to send a message to all the mutants that they don't have the right to run around killing ordinary folk without consequences. You need to let them know in no uncertain terms that if a mutant kills a human he or she will be held to the same standards as any other person. If the evidence bears it out, you must insist on the death penalty when human life is extinguished so wantonly and brutally." Again, many heads on the jury nodded in agreement, some of the same ones that had nodded in support of Sandra.

Mr. Chambers gave the jury one more challenging look, and then swept to the prosecution table. The crowd was in an uproar. Forgotten by now were the commands of the judge. The humans were chanting that Harland should be put to death as the mutants yelled that he should be freed. The judge pounded his gavel, hollering for order in his court. The court officers hustled to the rabble-rousers and began ousting them from the courtroom. Through it all, Harland stared off into space, unaware or uninvolved in what was happening around him.

* * *

This is Rake Yardley reporting live from an undisclosed location near the Alaska pipeline, raking up all the news of the day for CNN news. "We have been bussed to a location close to the break in the pipeline. I can't say exactly where we are because officials want to keep the exact location secret. You can see oil gushing out of the pipeline just behind me. It is unknown at this point whether the break occurred naturally from mechanical failure, stressed parts that should have been replaced through scheduled maintenance that has not been performed, or from sabotage. Fingers are pointing at mutants as possible saboteurs, or at the mutant workers who failed to do their jobs to maintain the integrity of the pipeline. Isn't that the case everywhere in the world now? It has become almost a given that when anything breaks down mutants will be suspected.

At this point experts cannot get close enough to the break to inspect it for the cause. Meanwhile, millions of gallons of oil have already poured out, creating a river of oil flooding the Alaskan Wildlife Sanctuary. Environmentalists are up in arms, claiming they have been predicting this type of disaster for decades. This will have devastating effects on wildlife and the fragile ecosystem of the area. The bald eagle will be flying around looking for food and the caribou will be looking for food. . .

"Hold on a moment, I am being informed right now that there is not just this one break in the line, but that there are three other breaks, hundreds of miles apart from each other. This would seem to argue for a planned attack being conducted simultaneously along the line. Surely, sections of the pipeline so far apart can't coincidentally break down at the same time! We have had no word from any group as yet claiming responsibility, but the pattern has been that mutant caused destruction goes untrumpeted by the perpetrators. They seem to have no interest in publicity, and no agenda to espouse. It would appear obvious that there is organization involved for these breaks to have occurred at the same time. What the purpose for this is, we are left to speculate. Are mutants activist environmentalists? Are they intent on undermining the infrastructure of the country? Do they want to take over the country? We now turn to our CNN expert on mutants. This is Rake Yardley, raking in the news live as it happens on CNN."

Back at the studio, the broadcasters talked amongst themselves, in consternation. "No way would an environmentalist purposely destroy the environment. I don't know what Rake is thinking? It could be mutants, could be something else."
"Like what?"

"Shifting terrain. . . . According to satellite imagery, it appears that the melting permafrost may be causing some shifting of surfaces that have been held in place by its once-permanently-frozen state."

* * *

Kimberley Kandu reporting for MSNBC from high over the San Andreas Fault, giving you a live view of the traffic along the major highways in California. As you can see, the highways heading east are more like parking lots than channels of escape. Since increased seismic activity was reported this morning, with the prediction of the long dreaded "big one", Californians have sought to escape the area before it hits. Airports are clogged with all flights full. Passengers are rioting in the terminals, demanding more planes and fighting over seats. The train stations and bus depots report the same chaos. All transportation is stymied by mutants who have sabotaged equipment or have not reported to work. Few planes, trains and buses are operating, forcing people to their cars. As you can see as our helicopter drops lower, no one is able to get anywhere by car, either. It would seem impossible to blame a pending earthquake on the mutants; however, the abandoned vehicles blocking almost every road are certainly the work of mutants. The increasing chaos to the whole transportation system can certainly be blamed on them. Who knows how many lives will be lost because people can't get away from the epicenter due to mutant sabotage or abandonment — purposeful or not.

We have gotten reports that seismic activity is increasing. We need to head back to base to refuel and determine if it will be safe to fly over the danger zone any longer in the buffeting air currents. Please be assured that MSNBC will bring you the fastest and most complete coverage on this breaking story. Why is the helicopter bucking? Kimberley Kandu out for now.

DIKES BREAK IN HOLLAND
-BBC

Where is the little boy to put his finger in the dike? The problem is there are not enough boys and these are not little holes in dikes, either. The dikes and seawalls comprising the canal structure in the Netherlands have breached spontaneously, in hundreds of places. The pressure from one break has created a domino-effect on the rest of the system. The water is not trickling into the lowlands, but is pouring into them, flooding much of the countryside. Water levels have risen to above the first floor level of homes, with many homes and businesses being swept from their foundations. The death toll from drowning is rising, too. Suddenly, cars were unexpectedly flooded while people were driving them along the seawalls. Bridges have been washed away, too. In all, it is estimated that the death toll could reach into the thousands.

There has been talk by the environmentalists for years that the rising sea levels from global warming were putting too much pressure on the infrastructure which once protected this low-lying nation, but the government was slow to act, which has led us to the situation in which we are today.

It is highly unlikely from the extreme extent of the damage that sabotage could be behind it since it would take days for even a small group of people to break through some of these seawalls. No matter how much officials would like to blame this on mutants, it is too incredulous to be true. This had been an insidious problem that has been undermining the canal structure for years.

However, mutants are taking advantage of the flooding to swim anywhere they please. Regardless, this is hampering the escape routes of people trying to flee by boat. There is total chaos as the ocean continues to flow into the country and a mentality of everyone for himself exists. Government and law enforcement officials cannot be reached. Thus, it is surmised that they are busy saving themselves, considering the reality of the situation.

Many of the displaced people are headed to England, which is already strained to the seams from the displaced people of the nuclear disaster in France. Belgium would normally be expected to take up part of the load, but they were also inundated with displaced people from France.

People have found every kind of boat they can commandeer and are trying to cross the English Channel, in some cases with no more than a rowboat. Boats are capsizing and the Royal Navy is overwhelmed in their attempts to rescue people. Helicopters from all neighboring countries have been put to work to try and save as many stranded people as possible. It is estimated that millions will have lost their homes before this crisis stabilizes, and these people must have refuge elsewhere.

* * *

"I demand the floor!" shouted the ambassador of Switzerland.

"The chair recognizes the Ambassador from Switzerland."

The words of the president of the general assembly of the United Nations were drowned out in an uproar as representatives of the 192 member countries of the U.N. vied for attention. Forgotten were the rules of order, ignored the need to wait for translations, everybody was now talking at once.

The agenda called for discussion and open debate on how to deal with two important issues affecting the globe: global warming and mutants. Global warming was an old topic that had been rehashed repeatedly and was now at an emergency level due to the changes in, climate, proliferating diseases, and elevated pollution levels. The second issue was the proliferation of mutants and mutant technology. Most countries did not want the issue of the technology looked into too closely, since every nation had access to it and was busy devising their own secret projects that they didn't want to have come under close scrutiny. However, the actions of people infected with RHV (Regressive Human Variance), in diplomatic circles the term "devolution" was considered improper and insulting, was of major concern to highly developed nations where the distribution of the supplements had been widely spread. The meeting had begun sedately with a discussion about global warming, which neatly settling into previous well-worn arguments, though admittedly heated beneath the surface. Thinking that topic was sufficiently exhausted, President Hassera Arwadi had called for tabling the matter and proceeded to the topic of genetic engineering.

The Secretary General, Duncan Faust, had read a prepared a brief opening statement into the record. "We did nothing wrong by releasing the DNA technology to the whole world, giving everybody an equal opportunity to benefit from studying it." Eyebrows were raised by technologically advanced nations. They knew there was no equality among the nations. True, the information was out there for everyone, but it took big bucks to experiment and study the material. The world giants had the money for that, which would keep them ahead of all the third world nations. They kept quiet because they didn't want this inequality to come to light, which it might with open discussion. The poorer nations of the world did not want what they were tinkering with to be exposed to public view, or to do anything to jeopardize their meager piece of the pie, so they kept quiet and the discussion was tabled.

What created the uproar was the question of how to deal with RHVs, as they politely called the mutants. Many of the diplomats at the UN were among the first people to have the opportunity to take the pills marketed by the big pharmaceuticals. In a huge publicity ploy, the big pharmaceuticals had sent free samples to all the delegates. Greedy to have an evolutionary edge over their brethren and ensure their higher positions, a majority of the diplomats had taken supplements and were starting to show signs of RHV themselves. There was a lot of sleeve tugging as those infected with avian changes sought to hide their feathers. A lot of hats were suddenly in fashion, as were turtlenecks. People remained sitting so their footwear was not visible and hands were often tucked into pockets. No one seemed eager to shake hands. So this topic, brought up by the Ambassador from the United States, where the most people were infected, was loudly shouted down by all the delegates who were infected.

"Move all the mutants to Australia," was heard above the roar, coming from a European diplomat who wanted the whole problem to go as far away as possible.

The Australian ambassador became incensed at this and forgoing any diplomatic procedures went head to head with the Italian contingent who had made the suggestion.

The previously level-headed Swiss ambassador, who had tried to follow protocol, hollered, "Every country must deal with their own RHVs in their own way." His country had been cautious in trying something untested and there were few mutants there. Besides, Switzerland was brokering deals left and right with all the money being made from the sales of the supplements and the technology; they wanted to keep the river of money flowing towards them.

With the total confusion going on, many countries lost the thread of what the topic was. Jacob Btok, Ambassador from the Solomon Islands, who wanted the topic to return to global warming because the islands were being flooded over, shouted out, "Our homes our being wiped away. All this chaos from the mutants, I mean RHV's, is increasing the rate of global warming exponentially."

Ambassador Jonathan Summers of the Marshall Islands, who was sitting near Btok and was able to hear him, nodded gravely. After all, the nuclear tests that started the mutations had occurred on his islands and it was evident the rise in sea levels had increased faster than any scientist had predicted. His islands were flooded, too, so it made sense that there must be a connection.

Others in the vicinity shook their heads at this circular thinking, since they were too intensely involved in the melee to pick up on this side circus. The Chinese delegate, showing clear signs of aquatic adaptation, pointed out that the Ambassadors from the Marshall Islands and the Solomon Islands introduced the bio-technology of RHV to the United Nations.

Even with much gavel hammering, the Secretary General could not restore order to the session. Secretary General Duncan Faust and the Assistant Secretary General, Ingrid Johansson, slipped out a side door. The President recommended the agenda items to the Security Council and formally announced the close of the meeting to the individual taking minutes. She called security and slipped herself out, as the guards began to break up the rest of the diplomats and send them on their way. The mutant diplomats silently congratulated themselves for avoiding any official sanctions and actions against them.

In an emergency session, the Security Council met to discuss the agenda items that had been before the General Assembly. Each of the five permanent members of the Council had coastline that was affected by rising sea levels from global warming, so this was an important topic for them. It was still old news and they could think of nothing new to do than what they were doing already. They issued a proclamation that all nations should step up their schedules for reducing pollutants and dependence on fossil fuels. They were careful not to point fingers at the greatest offenders.

On the subject of genetic engineering, as in the General Assembly, no one wanted their hands exposed to the table. They agreed to make a general statement suggesting that genetic engineering should be monitored and tested extensively by anyone working on it. It was nebulous enough, with plenty of wiggle room to make everybody happy.

However, when it came to the mayhem that was occurring from the RHVs, they all agreed that something needed to be done. They decided to authorize a study into how this could best be accomplished. After much debate over whom and how such a study would be conducted, it was agreed that they should put the project out for bid so that there would be no appearance of favoritism in the selection of the consultants. Pleased with what they had accomplished for the day, they disbanded.

* * *

"Yoo-hoo, Rita, are you here?" Zack called out as he entered the lab. Yoo-hoo, he thought, jeez, she's got me in such a tizzy that I can't even talk or think straight around her. Self-consciously, he looked down at his clothes, khaki slacks with a green dress shirt, with sleeves casually rolled up to the elbows. It was hard enough getting used to the climate and horses of Argentina. Now he was in old money Virginia horse country, but had to be available to his bosses at HSA on a moment's notice. He'd never worried about what he wore before. He surmised this was Rita's fault, too.

"I'm right here, Zack," Rita answered without looking away from the large computer screen on the wall. "I'm in the middle of something right now. Can it wait?"

As if I'm invisible, Zack thought sourly. His tone was more aggressive than he had intended to be. "I'm sorry to interrupt, but this is important. Deputy Director Whiteman is on my back for a report on your progress in isolating the mutated genes in RHVs?"

Turning to look at him, Rita gestured grandly towards the screen. "Look for yourself."

Zack looked uncertainly at the wall. To his woeful lack of science training, it looked like gibberish. "Uh, I think you'd better walk me through it," he said.

"Let me recap a bit first," Rita said, sighing at having to suspend her work and risk losing her train of thought. "As you know, all military and government personnel have to register their DNA upon enlistment or being hired, so Homeland Security was able to provide me with a sample of Harland's DNA prior to the RHV developing. They also provided me with a sample of his DNA after he became infected, though I don't like that choice of words, it isn't a flu bug he caught. In addition, I have a sample of Sterling's DNA after he was caught with his father. If you look at the left side of the screen, you can see the results from the pre-test of Harland and on the right side the post-test. You can see that they are obviously different." She looked at Zack for confirmation.

Shaking his head in bewilderment, he said, "I'll take your word for it."

"Well, you would think we could just derive a test based on the difference observed in the data, wouldn't you?" Rita continued more to herself than to Zack. "Let me show you what happens when I put Sterling's mutated DNA up on the screen next to Harland's. They are different. So a test used to detect mutation that works for Harland would not show the mutation in Sterling." She looked at Zack expectantly, as if it were clear as crystal.

Thinking it was as clear as mud, Zack asked, "Um, why is that the case?"

"How do you think? We all are different from each other in so many ways they can't even be enumerated. Well, everybody's junk DNA is unique, so the bottom line is, if someone's DNA is mutating, I would require before and after samples of that individual's DNA to be able to state that person has used the supplements and has DNA that is devolving. Each person's DNA would have to be submitted separately. There does not appear to be any standardized way to separate out RHVs based just on a current sample of DNA from using Harland's pre and post as a model."

Zack was still lost and trying to figure his way through what she was saying. More importantly, how was he going to say it to his boss? "You said there doesn't appear to be a test you can devise at this point. Does that mean you might be able to in the future?"

"I used an open-ended statement because as a scientist I can't say definitely what new sciences of the future will be able to do what can't be done today. As for what I can accomplish with today's science, it is impossible to create a test that will tell if any individual is devolved. Each person would have to be tested singly with a comparison pre-test on that person."

"This is not good news," Zack said, shaking his head at Rita.

"I know," Rita admitted, helplessly. Then with firmness, she said, "This is why it is more important that I find a cure, a way to reverse the process or at least arrest the regression. My energy is better spent on that than on mindlessly testing thousands upon thousands of individuals."

Putting his hands up as if to stop an attack, Zack responded, "Hey, I'm just the messenger. I'll be sure to pass your educated opinion on to the deputy director. In fact, I'm off to do that right now." He took in Rita's neat form, shapely even in a lab coat, but frowning; she had already turned back to her computer, trying to recapture her place in her work when he had come in.

Trudging glumly back to his office, Zack's own thoughts warred between realizing he was getting nowhere fast with Rita and wondering what he could do about it, and trying to figure out how to rephrase Rita's dire results to Jamie Whiteman so that he didn't lose his own head in the process. Choosing not to delay the inevitable, he called her up on his media screen.

"I hope you have good news for me, McHenry," Jamie said, greeting him.

Opting for formality, since he knew his words would be recorded, Zack answered her. "Deputy Director, I am reporting to you that Dr. Rita Perez has discovered that each person's devolution is as unique to the individual as that person's DNA is unique from all others. Given current capabilities in science, she reports that there is no way to devise a test that tells definitely that someone's RHV is devolving. This can only be determined on a case-by-case basis, when there is a comparison DNA taken prior to infection."

"Let me get this straight," Jamie said, sitting straighter in the chair. "We can't just take a sample of someone's DNA and know if the RHV is occurring?"

"That's correct," Zack agreed, warily. Deciding to take the plunge and get it on the record, he continued. "Dr. Perez feels that her time would be better utilized if she concentrated on finding a way to reverse or at least halt the devolution process."

"Esoterically, in the perfect world of the laboratory, that makes sense," Jamie said, sardonically. "However, we have live people in sensitive positions, and I need to know if they are suddenly going to go whacky on me; pardon the French. I am ordering that everyone in the government who has a DNA sample on record should be tested for comparison immediately. All personnel who don't have a DNA profile on record must submit one for a baseline test at once, to be followed with weekly samples for comparison." Turning her head and speaking over her shoulder, she called out, "Erin, I want you to head this up, and arrange for all the testing." Turning back to Zack, she continued, "And you will follow up with the samples as they come in to Dr. Perez for testing. Report to me ASAP on anyone with known DNA changes. Oh, and Erin, we might as well get complete physicals and blood work on everybody at the same. Yes, I know this will be time consuming and costly, but this is a matter of national security. Do you want a mutant's finger near a missile trigger?" And swiveling back to Zack, " I want earlier warning signs if I can't get DNA. Tell Rita to work on isolating cells at their earliest stages of change once the physical changes become apparent, like the start of gills, webbing, and feather developing. The RHV process happens so quickly that maybe it occurs simultaneously with cell changes. Keep me informed. Out."

Zack slumped in his chair. That woman was the most exhausting whirlwind he'd even encountered. At least he'd been able to get Rita's protest on record. Now he had to go break the news to her that she was going to be doing what amounted to highly skilled technician work, rather than being able to focus on a solution. He groaned as he thought of her fiery Latin temper. Regardless, he looked on the bright side because now at least he had a legitimate excuse for seeing her again, maybe even for lunch.

*　*　*

121

Joann calmly and professionally related the events leading up to the nurse's death. The jury and audience sat spellbound. This was so much better than watching it on TV. "Major Parker had indicated he was hungry, and had saliva dripping from his mouth. I poured a glass of water from the faucet and handed it to Clare. Clare held out the glass of water to Major Parker and asked him if he wanted a drink. Then he reached out and grabbed Clare's neck, breaking it. At that point, I ran from the room, screaming for the MPs."

"I know this is hard for you, even though as a medical professional you are used to seeing trauma cases. Can you describe what Major Harland did to Clare?" Prosecutor Chambers asked, solicitously.

"Objection, Your Honor," Sandra said, bouncing up from her seat. "The defense stipulates to the fact that Major Parker caused the death of Lt. Flicker. There is no need to subject the court to the details."

"On the contrary, Your Honor," Chambers smoothly responded. "It is important that the court recognized how heinous and brutal this attack was."

"I'll allow it," the judge mumbled. "Proceed."

"He grabbed Clare with those long nails he has and kept squeezing harder and harder as she fought him and begged him to stop. She began bleeding profusely, but nothing stopped him. He kept squeezing until her neck snapped from the force," Joann said, her breath coming fast as she strove to control her emotions.

"The prosecution has no further questions for this witness," Richard T. Chambers stated somberly, as if he was weighted down with grief over the untimely death of this young vibrant nurse.

Sandra got up sedately and approached the witness with a sympathetic manner. "That must have been quite traumatic for you. I noticed you called Lt. Flicker, Clare, through your whole testimony, Capt. Waters. Were the two of you close?"

"We had worked together for eighteen months before she was murdered," Joann answered, succinctly.

"Move to strike the word, murdered, as prejudicial," Sandra said quickly.

"Motion granted. Jury will disregard the word, murdered," the judge whispered.

Nate grimaced to himself. He knew Sandra had to protest the term 'murder' as a judgment call on the part of the witness that was reserved for jury deliberations. But, by calling attention to it, she had only succeeded in having the word repeated two more times, planting it more firmly in the heads of the jurors.

Sandra continued, "Weren't you two friends on a social level as well?"

"We occasionally went out together," Joann responded suspiciously, not sure where this line of questioning was going. The prosecutor looked equally baffled.

"Isn't it true then, that you have a personal stake in seeing Major Parker convicted?" Sandra asked, giving the jury a knowing look.

"How dare you impugn my professional judgment," Joann said, loudly, losing her professional cool just as she was defending it. Unfortunately, she realized too late that she had fallen into Sandra's little trap. She quickly made her back ramrod straight and composed her face into practiced experience.

Hiding a smirk, Sandra switched gears, "Could you describe for the court Major Parker's physical condition before he reached for Lt. Flicker's neck?"

"Major Parker had feathers on his head, arms, and chest. Those were the only areas we could see. His fingernails had grown long and curved inwardly, growing thick like talons. He had lost half his body weight based on our records from just two years ago. As I stated before, he was salivating constantly, repeating over and over again that he was hungry, regardless of any questions we asked him," Joann reported.

"Regardless of the questions you asked him, he kept repeating he was hungry over and over again," Sandra emphasized. "In your professional opinion, would you say he was non-responsive to you and Lt. Flicker?"

Reluctantly, Joann admitted, "I would have to say he was marginally responsive."

"Can you describe for the court the behavior of Major Parker just prior to the incident in question?" Sandra prompted.

"He began twitching with his neck jerking from side-to-side. Then he sat straight, looking at Clare, I mean, Lt. Flicker, and noticeably swallowed his saliva," Joann answered, her eyes forward, as if looking into the past.

Sandra zoomed in for the kill. "In your professional opinion, does this sound like someone in control of his behavior?"

Struggling to remain objective, Joann tonelessly said, "No, it did not appear that Major Parker was fully in control of his bodily responses at that time."

Wow, Nate thought, Sandra is really defusing the prime witness' testimony. 'Diminished capacity' sounds like a shoe-in judgment. He tried to catch Sandra's eye, but she was fully into the tempo of her cross-examination.

"Can you tell us what Lt. Flicker said to you during the examination of Major Parker, prior to the incident?" Sandra asked, looking expectantly at the witness.

Jumping to his feet, Prosecutor Chambers roared, "Objection. . . . Hearsay."

"Your Honor," Sandra said, primly, respectfully turning to the judge. "This can be admitted under the dying declaration rule."

"I'll allow it for now and see where it goes," the judge said, quietly. The audience strained to hear.

"Clare, Lt. Flicker, asked him if he was hungry, and if he would like some water,' Joann answered, snapping her mouth shut.

"Permission to treat this witness as hostile, based on her personal relationship," Sandra petitioned the judge.

"Granted."

Oh, so that's why Sandra wanted to establish a personal relationship, Nate said to himself. He wanted to exchange glances with Rita or somebody, but Rita, or rather, Zack, had decided her time was better spent in the laboratory until it was time for her expert testimony.

"Didn't Lt. Flicker say that Major Parker acted like he wasn't human. In fact, didn't she actually call him sub-human in front of him?" Sandra attacked, reading from the deposition in her hand.

"Well, yes, she did, but it wasn't like he could understand what she was saying. He didn't seem to understand much of anything," Joann said, defensively.

"Wouldn't you say that was extremely unprofessional for Lt. Flicker to be saying derogatory remarks about a patient in front of the patient? Wouldn't you say these kinds of inflammatory remarks could have exacerbated Major Parker's already fragile state?" Sandra pressed in.

Chambers was on his feet, talking over her. "Is counsel testifying herself?"

"I'll withdraw my last comments," Sandra said, smugly, knowing they had already sunk into the jury's minds. Turning away from Joann, she announced, "I have just one more question for this witness. Captain Waters, you are a trained military officer. You are combat trained. You are a martial arts expert, a black belt, I believe."

"Yes," answered Captain Waters.

"So, my question is: did you try to stop Major Harland? Did you try to save, Clare, your friend, or did you run?"

"Objection! Objection!"

"Withdrawn. No further questions." Sandra moved regally to sit at her defense table. Dropping her pencil, she gave Nate a slow wink, as she turned to pick it up.

"All of us have inactive DNA in us from birth. Indeed, we go through the stages of evolution during gestation, and all of this junk DNA remains in the body. What has happened from the supplements is this DNA has been turned back on, signaling the body to regress to previous evolutionary stages, dependent on the particular manipulation used by the drug companies and each person's DNA blueprint." Rita droned on and on, explaining the science behind the mutation in laymen terms so the jury and judge could understand, while at the same time, sounding like the expert she was, not an easy juggle.

After a lunch break, the prosecution had called Rita to the stand. As the person who had achieved the original successful manipulation of the genetic material, she was a key witness to both sides. Aware of her relationship with the defense, Mr. Chambers handled her carefully.

"According to the law, a drunk driver is held responsible for his or her actions, even though the body chemistry has changed significantly to the point where that individual has no control over his or her actions. Wouldn't you say the change that Major Parker experienced is similar to that of a drunk driver?" Chambers asked respectfully, knowing that Rita's expert opinion on this would carry great weight.

"It is true that in both the cases of the drunk driver and Major Parker, their bodies underwent changes that affected their judgment and ability to control their actions," Rita nodded. "However, in the case of the drunk driver, the effects of alcohol on driving ability are well documented; the person drinking has foreknowledge of the possible consequences of driving after drinking. In Major Parker's case, he had no way to know in advance the harmful effects of the supplements he was taking. He took—"

Hastily, the prosecutor interrupted Rita. "Move to strike the last part of that testimony as unresponsive."

"Your Honor, Mr. Chambers opened the door himself. He can't close it just because he doesn't like what comes through it," Sandra was on her feet with a quick protest.

"Sustained. You will have your turn to exam this witness, Ms. O'Callahan," the judge ruled, mildly.

"No further questions for this witness," Chambers said, trying not to show that this testimony hurt his case and would continue to do so under cross examination. He took his seat grandly as if he won an important point. The jury looked at him in puzzlement, but quickly switched their gaze back to Sandra, admittedly a prettier view, as she got up to question Rita.

"Dr. Perez, would you please continue the statement you were making, as to how Major Harland's condition is different from that of a person who chooses to abuse alcohol," Sandra said, eyeing the jury meaningfully, so they would know this part of the testimony was of paramount importance.

As if she had never been interrupted, Rita continued. "Major Parker took the supplements based on the advertisements of the big pharmaceutical companies that claimed the supplements would only enhance desirable traits. No mention was made in any of the literature of any undesirable side effects from the supplements."

"Would you say then, that Major Parker was in fact attempting to increase the skill level of the judgments he made?" Sandra asked.

"Definitely," Rita agreed, nodding her head strongly. "It says right in the literature that the supplements will increase mental acuity."

"Would you also say that the blame for Major Parker's alleged behavior lies squarely on the pharmaceutical companies that marketed the product?" Sandra asked, trying to focus the jury on the culpability of the drug companies.

"It is evident that big pharmaceutical companies rushed these products to the market without the proper testing and the government let them get away with calling them health supplements instead of controlled substances that require FDA rigorous oversight and detailed long-term studies of long-range effects of the drugs. Everyone was so eager for the supposed benefits of these enhancements, and greedy for the money and power they generated, that they ignored the need for controlled testing. Genetic engineering is a new field, still in its infancy. That alone should have been a warning to go slowly." As Chambers got to his feet to protest the lengthy answer, Rita circled back to Harland, saying, "Major Parker had no way to know the effects these supplements were going to have on him. To the best of his knowledge he was doing something that would improve his life and his responsible interaction in society."

"Some people would argue that Major Parker should have discontinued the supplements the second he noticed negative changes occurring," Sandra suggested.

"I am the leading authority on Regressive Human Variance, or RHV since I am the one who programmed the manipulation that started the process. I have worked non-stop to reverse the process, or at least halt it, ever since I found out about the devolution. Similar to a missile button being pushed, there is no way to stop the regression once it has started. You can't un-launch it. Even if Major Parker had stopped taking the supplements after the first day, he still would have devolved. There was nothing he could do about it," Rita insisted, emphatically, holding her head up high while trying not to give in to the weight of her shame.

"Surely he should have sought help for his condition once he noticed it," Sandra asked, innocently, her eyes large and wide.

"It is important to remember that internal changes are taking place at the same pace as external ones. In Major Parker's case, he externally took on the aspects of the avian species. That means that mentally he was thinking and processing information as a wild bird. A bird does not think that anything is wrong with its appearance or behavior. It just is what it is. It all feels natural to the bird. This is how it all seemed to Major Parker. All his actions seemed normal to him," Rita declared, triumphantly.

"I have no more questions for this witness," Sandra announced to the court, trying not to appear gleeful as she returned to her table. Mr. Chambers doodled busily on his pad.

"Call your next witness, Mr. Chambers."

"The prosecution rests, Your Honor."

"In that case, we will resume tomorrow with the defense's first witness." Judge Blackburn said, smacking his gavel lightly on the podium and shuffling quickly out of the room before anyone knew he was gone.

"Dinner tonight?" Nate called out to Sandra.

Turning to Nate after watching Harland being dragged off in chains, Sandra said distractedly, "I'm sorry Nate. I have to prepare Harland for his testimony tomorrow morning. Maybe I'll see you back at the house later." Gathering her papers into her briefcase, she followed after Harland without looking back.

"I'm sorry, too," Nate muttered, mournfully, as he turned to join the rest of their group who were busy congratulating Rita on her testimony.

*   *   *

"The defense calls Major Harland Parker to the stand," Sandra announced, dramatically.

Harland continued to stand at the defense table, oblivious to what was going on around him. The guards finally took it upon themselves to move him along to the witness box. A huge gasp went up from the spectators and jury alike as they got their first good look at him out from the cover of the defense table. They could see his feathers sprouted out in all directions. They could see the wingtips with residual finger stumps coming out of his coverall sleeves. They could discern the redistribution of weight to the chest, with what were probably tail feathers straining at the back seat area of his jumpsuit. The legs of the overall had to be cuffed because his legs had shortened and appeared spindly and hairless. The feet were what got their attention, first. Unable to wear any kind of shoes, Harland was barefoot. Everybody, except those in the last rows, could see that one of his toes was pointing straight backwards, and that all four of his toes now formed a claw. Yes, that is right — four of them. One of his toes had somehow disappeared. As he turned to stand in the witness box, Harland was unable to sit like a human. Another gasp went out. Harland's face, which they had only previously seen in profile view, was now fully visible — beak and all. The judge reached for his gavel, but everybody settled down at once, since no one wanted to miss any of this by being thrown out of the court.

A major problem arose when the clerk tried to swear in Harland, who was totally unresponsive to the clerk. Harland ignored the Bible placed in front of him. In fact, the clerk was worried because Harland looked at her like prey. In panic, she abandoned the attempt as swiftly as she could. Sandra quickly requested a side bar. After a muted discussion with the judge and prosecutor, that everybody strained to hear but could not, it was decided that they would forego the swearing in for the time being. Inwardly, Sandra was ecstatic. Harland had already done half the work for her before they even got started.

.

"Major Parker," Sandra began, trying to establish eye contact with Harland. "Can you tell the court why you are here?"

Harland's head bobbed back and forth from side to side, ever watchful but unengaged with Sandra.

Sandra tried again, needing it to be on the record that she had done her utmost to elicit a response from her client. "Harland, I'm Sandra. Can you answer me?"

For a fraction of a second, Harland's eyes touched hers. Sandra thought she saw a glimmer of recognition, but then it was gone. Harland continued his vigilant scanning of the room. He made sounds, and some thought he was trying to answer, but most thought it was sheer gibberish. It was on par with the sounds any raptor would make, all totally unintelligible to the human ear.

After utterly failing to make any meaningful contact with Harland, Sandra turned to the prosecutor and said, smugly, "Your witness, Counselor."

Chambers, who thought it was all an act agreed on in advance by the defense and the client, went right away on the attack. "Major Parker, tell the court why you took the supplements?"

Harland was unresponsive.

"Major Parker, did you kill Lt. Flicker on purpose?"

Harland looked to the galley and squawked loudly.

"Your Honor, please direct the witness to answer the questions," Chambers demanded.

"The witness is directed to answer the question," the judge said, with a sly grin.

Harland never glanced at the judge but seemed intent on the upper galley. Agitated, he squawked again. Rita, who understood the internal changes better than anyone, wondered if his avian mind was worried about others being at a higher level than he was. He felt surrounded and thus needed to get to high ground. As if he read her thoughts, Harland began beating his arms (or wings) as best as he could within the restrictions of the restraints. All the while, he kept squawking loudly.

"Let him go!" came shouts from the galley. The cry was promptly followed up by an outcry from many mutants. "Set him free!"

An immediate contrary response came from the human side of the aisle. "Execute him! He's a danger to society. Fry him!"

The judge came to life, pounding his gavel and sounding almost like he was squawking in tune with Harland. The court guards raced up the aisle and started grabbing the loudest offenders. Again, the courtroom erupted into brawls. The prison guards hustled Harland out of the courtroom, and court was suspended until after lunch, though it somehow was doubtful anyone heard the judge's announcement.

*   *   *

Richard T. Chambers posed in front of the jury as he began his closing argument. "There is no question that Major Harland Parker brutally murdered this young nurse in the prime of her life." He pointed dramatically to a large picture of Clare Flicker, prominently on display. "We have the eyewitness testimony of her superior officer, Captain Joann Waters, who was present in the room throughout the whole incident. The defense has stipulated the fact that Major Parker did kill in fact Lt. Flicker. There is no question whatsoever that Major Parker is guilty of murdering Clare Flicker, who was just trying her best to care for him. That only leaves you the decision of what we are going to do about it.

"This is a landmark case, the first trial of a mutant, a hybrid through RHV, being charged with a crime. As you know, we don't allow excuses for murder. Defense lawyers have tried to blame alcohol, drugs, childhood abuse, and society in general for people committing crimes. The American people have refused to accept these defenses and ruled to hold defendants responsible for their actions. This case is no different. Major Parker chose to take a substance that facilitated vicious behavior on his part, and he should be held accountable for it.

"The eyes of the world are on you, thus you will set a precedent for other cases where mutants cruelly attack normal citizens going about their everyday business. It is your responsibility to send a clear message that we are not going to tolerate any horrific crime. I'm asking you to find that Major Parker is responsible for his actions and judge him guilty of murder," he concluded pontifically, before taking his seat.

In a friendly manner, Sandra approached the jury for her closing argument, though no less professionally. "I'm sure that each of you knows someone who has taken these supplements." She paused as nods came from the jurors. "Think about these friends, relatives, and acquaintances of yours. Did they know ahead of time the consequences of taking these supplements that were highly touted so highly in commercials, on billboards, and in magazines? Indeed, everywhere you looked, there were messages that enhancements would improve their lives. Certainly the pharmaceutical companies and the government allowed these supplements to be hurried onto the market, as our expert witness, Dr. Perez, has told us. In fact, the United Nations, itself, was quick to hand out this technology to benefit the world, as was publicly proclaimed. Major Parker, as the first person to take the supplements, was the least likely of anyone to know or suspect that they would have a negative effect on him. This is not like alcohol and drugs, where the effects are widely known by the users. Certainly no one in the whole wide world knew what would happen from those supplements."

"You have heard expert testimony that there is currently no cure for this process; no stopping RHV. No way could Major Parker have prevented the regression once he started the pills. Our expert, correction, their expert stated that the changes were internal, as well as external, giving Major Parker no control over his behavior. The eye witness, who was a personal friend of the deceased, as well as an experienced medical professional, admitted that Major Parker was obviously not in control of his body, and was only marginally responsive, if that."

"We do not dispute that Major Parker unwittingly killed Lt. Flicker. What we do dispute is that he was aware of his actions, as Major Parker's own behavior on the stand has made perfectly clear. Major Parker is to be pitied for what has happened to him, through no fault of his own. He needs to be cared for, until such time as science is able to reverse the terrible effects these supplements have brought on him, and millions of other innocent people in similar situations. I am asking you to find Major Parker 'not guilty' by reason of insanity." Sandra took a deep look at each juror and returned quietly to her seat, the sound of her high heels the only noise in the courtroom.

* * *

The group of friends was finishing lunch in a nearby diner when word came in that the jury had returned. Nate gave Sandra's hand a squeeze as they hurried back to the courthouse. Normally Sandra would've waited out the verdict with her client, but Harland gave no indication of recognizing her or deriving any consolation from her presence. So, to Nate's pleasure, she joined her friends for the wait. Even though she was understandably distracted, it was nice to be able to spend some time with her.

The judge abandoned his meek pose and sternly warned the spectators that there were to be no outbursts when the verdict was read. Since most of the hecklers had already been thrown out, he had hopes for a civilized ending to the trial. Looking over the crowd, Nate was not so sure. The courtroom was still packed, as many new people were now able to get in, and some of them looked ready for a fight.

The foreperson of the jury handed the verdict over, and the judge read it silently, as the courtroom held its breath. Even the children seemed to know something important was about to happen. Then the judge asked the foreperson, a chunky grandmotherly person, to read it out loud for the record.

"We the jury, find the defendant, on the charge of murder, not guilty. On the charge of involuntary manslaughter, we find the defendant guilty. Further, we find the defendant to be criminally insane."

As Nate expected, the crowd erupted. The mutants were incensed, yelling, "We are not insane!" The unaffected humans hollered back, "He's a criminal. He needs to be punished for his crime. He should be in prison, not some cushy hospital." Each group moved towards the other, ready to go head-to-head.

With chaos everywhere, the judge pounded his gavel. No one heard him repeat that Harland was found guilty by reason of insanity and would be committed to a facility for the criminally insane until such time as a cure was found for his RHV. The judge gave up and left the bench as guards, again, descended on the melee.

Harland was rushed out in shackles, not the least bit aware of what was going on around him, or what fate had been decided for him. Agitated, he squawked, but otherwise gave no fight. Sandra looked after him in despair, wishing there was more she could do for him.

"Oh no, Carley, they will put Sterling in an institution, too." Holly jabbered in the back row of the courtroom. "We have to go get him."

"We will. We are; right now, in fact," Carley responded, grimly.

Not waiting for court to be dismissed, Carley grabbed Holly. With Jasmine following closely, they rushed out of the courtroom. Seeing Holly's feathers, which she had tried to unsuccessfully cover, a brutish human who looked apish without enhancements, tried to grab hold of her. Fortunately, they were able to elude him. Now, when everyone was preoccupied with some battle, they would be able to enact their plan for freeing Sterling. Indeed, all the local police were rushing to the courtroom as they rushed out.

Deeply interested in the trial, Robin Birdswell had faithfully attended. She had graciously agreed that Holly's girls could stay and play with Sterling at the estate during the trial. It was routine for Holly, Carley, and Jasmine to stop by each day to pick up the girls, so no one thought anything special about it when they arrived at the estate. In fact, no one paid any attention at all, since they were all focused on the TV, watching the coverage of the bedlam at the courthouse.

In order to ensure that no one would watch what they were doing, Carley left the chattering group of children with Holly and Jasmine, slipping over to a nearby horse barn where all the horses were out in the fields enjoying the sunshine, happily munching on whatever grasses and flowers they could find. Making absolutely sure that no animals were still inside, and feeling a bit guilty and wondering exactly how she had gotten herself into this, she set fire to the barn. All the estate workers converged immediately on the fire, dragging hoses and getting buckets, even though the building's sprinklers had started automatically.

In the confusion from the fire and the bustle of getting the girls into the van, it was easy to slip Sterling in, too. Thinking it was all part of a game, and eager to stay with the girls, he came along readily, though he looked fearfully at the fire. His natural animal instincts alerted him to the danger that Reva and Vera thought was exciting. In fact, it was a bit difficult to drag them away from the spectacle.

Driving sedately, Carley headed for the airport, calling Sandra on her cell at the same time. "I wanted to congratulate you on the verdict. . . . Yes, I know it would've been better if he had been found not guilty on all counts, but under the circumstances, I think you can consider this a win. . . . Listen, I know we all agreed that it was senseless, not to mention dangerous to stay here in the States. The plan was to go back to Argentina today. I wanted to make sure that is still the plan. . . . Okay, I agree. I've got Holly, Jasmine and the kids with me, and we wanted to know what time we are scheduled for take off. . . . Uh, huh. . . . That sounds fine. . . . No, we are all packed and will meet you at the plane. . . . Bye." Turning to talk to the others in case they hadn't heard, she said, "We are right on target. The jet is waiting and we can go right there."

Jasmine nodded nervously, glancing over her shoulder from the front passenger seat to see if anyone was following. Holly barely nodded; she was too intent on calming down the children, and trying to get Sterling into a seat belt to pay attention. It had been a long time since Sterling had been in a car, so he rustled around with excitement, unintentionally making everything harder. Holly could not get her fingers to manage the mechanism, either. Since Sterling couldn't really sit anymore, she gave up trying to strap him in.

"Momma, Sterling is going to go right through the windshield, if we have an accident," Reva announced, authoritatively, Vera nodding in agreement.

"Sterling is okay," Holly screeched at them.

"Aunt Carley is not going to have an accident," Carley said, soothingly. "Look we are almost at the airport."

"Aunt Carley, wasn't that a cool fire?" Vera piped up. "I wanted to watch it." She sulked.

"Fires are exciting to watch, but don't forget they are dangerous, too," Carley said, as she turned into the parking area of the airport. "It was much more important that we get you to safety. And look, you are going to go on a plane ride. Won't that be fun?"

"That's a pretty small plane," Reva scoffed, expertly. She had been to an airport to watch the big planes take off and was not impressed. The twins had never flown, but Reva tried to look superior, not wanting to show how excited she was.

"Well, there are only a few of us going on the plane," Jasmine explained as they all got the children out of the van. "We don't need one of those big planes."

"I can't wait to fly," Vera said, in rapture, grabbing Sterling's hands as she danced him around in glee.

"Stop that", Holly barked. "We don't want to call attention to Sterling."

"You girls have to help us sneak him on the plane," Carley told them, conspiratorially, putting a finger to her lips.

Their eyes wide with questions, the girls kept quiet as they all snuck Sterling onto the plane.

"Sterling, do you understand that you need to be absolutely quiet until the plane is in the air?" Carley asked him, worried that he wouldn't understand and would blow the whole thing by making noise, or worse, coming out of the closet they were hiding him in.

The questions now burst out. "Why are we hiding Sterling?" Reva demanded.

"Is it a game?" Vera wanted to know.

"Some bad people want to take Sterling and lock him up in a mental hospital," Carley explained.

"O-o-o-oh, that's terrible," the twins chimed in, in unison, understanding "bad men" and pretending they knew what a mental hospital was.

Sterling looked scared and Carley hoped that meant he understood what was happening, but would he cooperate? She shut the door gently on him as she heard the other members of their group begin boarding the plane. Turning, she waved her hands to get the kids to move forward, away from the closet.

Nate, Sandra, Rita, and Zack came on board, still gabbing excitedly about the verdict.

"I have to admit that I was skeptical about all this mutation stuff before we got here," Nate said to Sandra. "After what I saw in that courtroom, and on the roads and in the towns, I have to admit you are right. This is much worse than I could ever have imagined."

"We are making the right decision in getting out of the States," Sandra said. "After that verdict, I wouldn't be surprised if the mutants came after me."

Holly gasped.

"Oh, I'm so sorry, Holly. I didn't mean all mutants are that way," Sandra said, giving Holly a hug, and shrugging helplessly to the others.

"What is going to happen to Harland?" Holly stuttered out, her tongue twisting to get out the words. "He will be in a cage the rest of his life." Holly sobbed loudly.

"A bird in a cage," Zack repeated insensitively, earning a dirty look from Rita. "What, what did I say? It's true, isn't it?"

Sadly, Sandra nodded her head. "Yes, I'm afraid it is true, unless a reversal is found." She looked at Rita, meaningfully - hopefully.

Reva and Vera, bored with the adult conversation and feeling self-important with their secret, tiptoed towards the back of the plane, giggling and whispering to each other all the while. Carley shot them a glance to be quiet about Sterling and motioned them into their seats as everyone else settled in, preparing for take-off.

As if in answer to Sandra's look, Rita turned to Zack. "That is one reason I need to work on reversing the devolution. Obviously, Harland will be kept caged until I do. He is our friend and all of us are partly responsible for where he is today. Think of the millions more who are affected, each an innocent person."

"You know I don't make the orders," Zack protested. "However, it is of vital national importance that we uncover RHVs in key positions who can cause irreparable damage to the security of our country."

They continued to bicker as the plane jutted down the runway.

"Look, momma, look everybody," Reva and Vera shouted. They had made sure they had window seats and were busily craning to see everything out them. "There are ape men running towards the plane!"

Jumping out of their seats, everyone rushed to the windows to witness how Sandra's prediction had come true. Converging on the runway were dozens of mutants, most, as the children had noted, devolving along the primate path. Everyone held their collective breaths as they helplessly watched, wondering if the mutants would be able to get to the plane before it took off. The mutants were brandishing guns and sticks. Those who realized they couldn't stop the plane in time even started to throw rocks at it. Pushing the twins down, the adults instinctively ducked as the plane roared into the air, barely clearing the runway. The mutants shook their fists at the quickly disappearing jet. Somberly one by one, they all — even the children — resumed their seats, suddenly realizing they might never again return to the United States.

And then, Sterling popped out of the closet with a squawk.

CHAPTER FIVE

Is Any Place Safe?

"Gabe," Marti hollered, "Honey, it's another abandoned boat." Marti was piloting their boat while Gabe was below resting on his bed. Gabe popped his head out and peered in the direction Marti was pointing. It had become a well-oiled routine with these deserted boats that they chanced upon. As if performing a drill, they set about coming alongside the other vessel, and would prepare to board, only to find no one there. Then they would radio in the boats' whereabouts to the local authorities.

"Ahoy, anybody there?" Gabe shouted out, not even paying attention to the large excursion boat. He was startled when he finally got an answer.

"Si, there are two of us here. Please help us," came a weak shout as a slender young man staggered into view, waving his hands frantically. A young woman appeared next to him. He put his arm protectively around her.

Ratcheting up to high gear, Gabe and Marti pulled up to the other boat and jumped aboard.

"Hi, my name is Gabe Channing," Gabe said in the informal way of Americans, holding out his hand. "This is Marti. What can we do for you folks? Did your boat break down?" He gazed curiously around the open-decked party boat, and then stared at the bedraggled couple in front of him.

139

"What has happened to you?" Marti chimed in at the same time. "You look like you have been through a wringer."

"Please can you help us?" the dark haired young man said again, putting a shaky hand out to grasp Gabe's hand. "Forgive my manners, I am Cori Quilla and this is my wife Chaska. What is a 'wringer?' I am not familiar with that term."

"It's an old-fashioned American term for a clothes washer," Marti said, helpfully. "Never mind that, what has happened to you two? How can we help you?"

With that, Chaska collapsed still clinging to Cori. Cori bent down to her, distractedly, "Chaska, Chaska!" Looking at Gabe and Marti, he said, "It is so long since we have eaten, my wife is weak."

"Let's take care of that right away," Gabe said with concern. "Come on over to our boat and we'll fix that."

Cori scooped up his wife, and with Marti leading the way, Gabe helped him across to their boat. They laid Chaska down as Marti scurried to the galley, returning quickly with two glasses of orange juice. Patting her face lightly, Cori called her name anxiously. Her eyes fluttered open, and she immediately apologized for fainting.

"Don't you think a thing about it, you poor thing," Marti cooed. "You just have a sip of this juice and you'll feel better right away." Marti held the glass gently to her lips, as her husband supported her. With some hesitation, she sipped the juice. Handing the second glass to Cori, Marti said to him, "I'm sure you could use some too from the look of you."

Blushing slightly under his olive skin, Cori gratefully drank it down greedily.

"Thank you so much," Cori began.

"Don't you worry about telling us anything until we can get some food into you," Marti ordered. "Come on, Gabe. I can use some help making up some food for these people." With a salute to her back and a wink at Cori, Gabe followed her into the kitchen as their company sat drinking their orange juice and talking in a foreign language that Gabe and Marti couldn't readily identify.

In short order, Gabe and Marti returned with omelets made with cheese, tomatoes, mushrooms, and onions and a towering stack of whole wheat toast. They had made enough for everybody, not wanting the young couple to feel embarrassed about eating alone in front of them. Besides, Gabe was always ready for some food. They set the meal on the table and encouraged their guests to dig in. For a few minutes, the only sounds aside from the water lapping against the boat and the cry of gulls zeroing in on possible scraps were the scraping of forks on plates as they all busily put away the impromptu brunch in record time.

"That was wonderful," Chaska said, shyly, color beginning to return to her sallow skin. She brushed her long, inky, dark hair off her forehead, her deep brown eyes smiling at them. "We had begun to give up hope of ever being found."

"If you don't mind me asking, what are you doing out here on that big boat all alone? Is that your boat?" Gabe asked, patting his belly, contentedly.

"And how can we help you?" Marti asked, settling herself in for a good story.

"We were on — how do you say — a trip after wedding?" Cori started.

"Aw, you were on a honeymoon!" Marti supplied, giving the two a happy grin.

Chaska blushed, bringing even more color to her cheeks. "We are from Peru. We take our honeymoon on the beaches of Costa Rica," she supplied, carefully saying the word "honeymoon."

Picking up the story, Cori continued. "We saw a weekend cruise advertised to swim with mermaids and mermen. We thought it would be people dressed in costumes. It sounded like fun. When we got on the boat, we saw that all the people really looked like mermaids and mermen, which was quite confusing to us. On the other hand, it made us think the trip would be even more exciting. We were out at sea one day, when all the crew jumped overboard. We hurried into our swimsuits, thinking this was the swim together time advertised, but by the time we got in the water they had all swum away. We went back to the boat to call for help, but all the electronics were smashed. We could not call for help or drive the boat. There was some food in the kitchen area, mainly raw fish, but we have been without food, except what fish we caught, for 3 days now."

"We had begun to give up hope," Chaska said, her eyes brimming, "And then you came. You saved our lives."

"You poor things," Marti exclaimed. "I'm so glad we found you."

"Sounds like you were the unwitting victims of mutants," Gabe said, shaking his head.

"Please, what are mutants?" Cori asked.

"Don't you know about mutants?" Marti and Gabe asked together.

"No, we never saw mutants before. Is that what the mermaids and mermen are?" Cori asked, confused.

Giving Marti a warning look, Gabe took the lead. "Well, there are these pills that are being sold all around the world. They came from a new genetic technology that advertised the supplements would enhance a person's life, like make you smarter or stronger…"

"Or able to swim like a dolphin," Marti added.

"—And medical enhancements, like improve your heart," Gabe continued, wondering if he was going to need to take some for his own heart.

"That all sounds wonderful," Chaska said, brightly.

"Yeah, well, it seemed to be at first, and lots of people started taking them, but you see, the thing is, they weren't tested well enough. Then the pills started causing people to devolve into animals," Gabe explained, uncomfortably, again sending Marti a warning look that meant not to tell their role in bringing the technology to the world.

Marti nodded in understanding. She hadn't been involved directly with exposing the genetic manipulation to public access, but she wanted to protect Gabe's involvement and not embarrass him in front of these nice strangers.

"How is that possible?" asked Cori.

"Well, it is a long story, but basically buried deep within our DNA is our complete evolutionary history. The pills turn on certain dormant sections, causing people to revert into earlier evolutionary states as their cells are replaced through the normal replacement cycle," Gabe elaborated.

"So the people become fish, like the ones on the boat," Cori said, trying to take it all in.

"Yes, fish people, but also other animals, like apes, and birds, and who knows what else. A good friend of ours turned into a bird," Marti said, sadly. "We've been coming upon abandoned boats throughout our travels and we figured the boats had been manned by people who had taken supplements for aquatic characteristics and became fish-like, leaving the boats to live in the water. Since you are the first live people we have found on one of these boats, you confirm what we've been thinking."

"We don't have any of these medicines where we are from," Cori stated, still in wonderment from it all.

"We thought everybody in the world had them by now," Gabe said, puzzled. "I can't believe you don't have them in Peru yet."

"Maybe there are some in Lima," Cori said, shrugging, "but we are Quechua from the Andes. My people are remote from the cities up in the mountains. Most of us don't have much to do with the outside world of cities. We don't take foreign medicine, we trust in the medicine from the earth as our ancestors did."

"If you don't mind me asking, you speak English well. How did that come about with your people being so isolated?" Marti asked, curiously.

"My family has a textile business that exports Quechan crafts around the world. We were educated in a missionary school as children, where we learned English. Then I attended any Ivy League college in the United States — Cornell University," Cori said, proudly. "We do much of our exporting to the United States, so we have to keep our English in good practice."

"I must say, you speak it well," Marti exclaimed.

"I still can't understand how, if you run a big export company out of Lima, how you haven't come across any word of what these mutants are doing in the world," Gabe said, incredulously.

"I travel through the villages doing the buying, and Chaska was working in our collection center in Cuzco when I met her," Cori explained. "Our company is big; and I am not often in Lima. And for the past few months, we have been busy having our wedding and honeymoon." He put his arm around Chaska and shyly ducked his head.

"I hate to clue you folks in," Gabe said somberly, "but from what we've been told, there are millions of people who are affected. And this has caused chaos just about everywhere. Just like those mer-people abandoned the boat and destroyed the electronics on it, the mutants everywhere have been not showing up for work, forgetting how to do their jobs and as a result doing them wrong. In some cases they have gotten violent and purposely sabotaged things around them. I'm surprised you were able to get a plane safely out of Lima, many of them have been grounded."

"There were many cancellations, but we were too preoccupied to care," Chaska said with that ready blush.

"Too busy having a honeymoon," Marti said dryly, arching her eyebrows. She was enjoying have this young couple aboard, even though she felt bad about the horrific event that had brought them there.

"Haven't seen any newspapers either, I take it?" Gabe asked, playfully.

Cori and Chaska shook their heads.

"Well, there are horrendous things happening around the world from the mutants, plus global warming and a bunch of natural disasters, too. I guess, though it is hard to sort out what's causing what. You young people need to get somewhere safe and hole up there. Put in lots of supplies and be prepared to wait out a long period of time until this all settles down," Gabe advised. "That's what we are doing, staying out on the water, away from all the craziness going on in the supposed civilized parts of the world. The United States is one of the hardest places hit."

"Maybe that is why we are having trouble with some of our buyers, now that I think about it," Cori said to Chaska. "After our honeymoon we were going to take a trip to the US to see what the problem is."

"I think you kids need to be getting on home to those isolated villages you were talking about," Gabe warned.

Nodding their heads, Cori said, "Si, I think you are right. If we can just get some of our things off the other boat, we would be happy if we could travel with you until we reach a place we can stop imposing on you and...."

"Cori is worried about his charrango," Chaska teased. "He brought it to sing beautiful music to me."

At Gabe and Marti's looks of incomprehension, Cori said, hurriedly, "It is like what you call a mandolin. It is made from the shell of the armadillo."

"Let's go get your charrango," Gabe said standing and throwing a companionable arm across Cori's shoulders.

"Maybe you can play for us," Marti said spritely, as she began to clear the dishes, Chaska jumping up to help her.

*   *   *

For almost ten seconds, it was as if someone had yelled, "Freeze frame" on the set. No one moved and no one spoke, since most had their mouths hanging open, dumbfounded. Then pandemonium broke loose as everyone started speaking and moving at once. The twins ran to Sterling and clasped his stubby fingers in theirs looking both mischievous and defiant at the same time, as if it had been their plan to spirit Sterling on board. Holly moved to block the view in front of Sterling, as if she could erase what everybody had seen. Sandra, Rita, Nate, Zack and the two flight attendants were questioning and exclaiming loudly, each trying to be heard above the others, as they tried to find out how and why Sterling was on the plane. Carley started aggressively to explain. Sterling, upset by all the commotion, squawked loudly, twitching his arms as if he wanted to beat the air but couldn't because the girls were hanging on. Jasmine sunk deeper into her seat, not wanting to be a part of the racket. The two flight attendants were protesting they knew nothing about it.

Finally, Holly screeched loud enough to shut everybody up. "I did it. I brought Sterling. I don't want him in a cage like Harland. Rita, you must help him."

"How could you get Sterling out by yourself?" Sandra demanded.

Rita kept saying, "Of course, I will try to help Sterling, too."

"I helped her rescue him," Carley said, jutting out her chin defiantly, ready to take on all comers. "We couldn't save Harland, but we could save Sterling."

"Bringing Sterling with us is not an option," Zack snapped. "We need to turn this plane around immediately, and turn him over to the authorities."

"And why?" Sandra demanded, heatedly turning on him. "Let the authorities take all of us into custody? I don't think so!"

"Sandra's right," Nate said, reasonably, trying to dial down the volume and inject some order to the chaos. "Let's all sit down and think this through. Zack, you know we were labeled terrorists by the government just a few months ago. They aren't going to look too kindly on us for making off with one of their prize mutants."

"We had nothing to do with it," Rita objected, then felt ashamed for saying that. "I vote for continuing on to Argentina where we will again be guaranteed asylum if we need it." She thought about having to explain this escapade to her father with a grimace.

Standing up and striding back and forth on the short aisle, Zack was most insistent. "I'm employed by Homeland Security, so I certainly can't be complicit in kidnapping a mutant child that is a ward of the same government that employs me. We have to turn this plane around right now. I will guarantee immunity for all of you who weren't involved in the escape, and I'll do what I can for those of you who kidnapped Sterling." He headed determinedly towards the cockpit.

While everyone else protested loudly, Rita jumped between Zack and the cockpit door.

Zack stopped. Only Rita could've stopped him dead in his tracks without it becoming physical. She put a hand beseechingly on his arm and turned her luminous liquid eyes on him. Zack knew he was lost.

"Please Zack. You don't want to put this orphaned little boy in a cage, do you?"

Rita spoke in her most beguiling voice, stroking Zack's arm. "Just let him come to Argentina with us, where he will be loved and cared for, and maybe I can help him?"

"We can always say he snuck onboard and we didn't know anything about it,"

Nate suggested. "That should cover you with your bosses. Once Sterling is in Argentina, they can scream and holler all they want, but Don Perez is in charge at his estate. He wields great power with the Argentinean government. The U.S. government and you have no jurisdiction then."

"No one saw us take Sterling," Carley put in. "Maybe they will think he just escaped on his own."

"We can claim we know nothing about it," Sandra said regally. "We'll be a continent away. How will they know any different? They won't even know we have him. Besides, we are on an Argentinean plane in international airspace already. You have no authority here."

"I'm sure Homeland Security has more important things to worry about than what happens to one little boy," Rita pleaded, continuing to stroke Zack's arm.

Not wanting to do anything that would stop Rita from caressing him, Zack reluctantly said, "Okay, I won't contact Homeland Security. Maybe everyone will think Sterling escaped on his own. We'll just pretend we don't know anything about it. But, it'll be my head if they ever find out."

"Your head will be just fine in Patagonia," Rita said, giving him a grateful little peck on the cheek. Zack leaned in as if hoping for more. Patting him on the chest, Rita smiled up at him and moved away, turning to the two attendants.

"Marco and Inez, I know you will not tell anyone what you have heard and seen about this boy," Rita said, pointing at Sterling, whom they were both ogling.

"Si, Senorita. You know we have worked for your father for a long time and can be trusted," Marco said, earnestly, a bit miffed that Rita even had to ask.

"Si, me too," Inez asserted, nodding in agreement. "I have one question. What about all the other people on the estate? Of course, they are all loyal to the Senor, but people will talk in the village." She shrugged her shoulders as if to say, we will deal with that when we have to.

"I have a possible solution for that," Nate interjected. "I can keep Sterling up at my ranch, except for the times that Rita needs him. He'll have lots of freedom there."

"I want to have Sterling with us," Reva spoke up. The children had watched the interplay of the adults wide-eyed, but now felt it was time to speak up. Vera nodded, vigorously. Sterling said painfully, "Please." No one was able to decipher what he said, but they got the general idea.

"I think it would be a good idea for Holly and the girls to stay with Nate, too," Sandra decided, as if she was in charge, since it frequently seemed she was. "And Jasmine also," she added, catching a pleading look from Jasmine, who was taking it all in from her spot on the sidelines.

"Sure, why not?" Nate agreed, mentally counting bedrooms and people and wondering how his romance with Sandra was going to proceed with all these houseguests. One look at Sandra assured him he had made the right decision in that regard if he wanted it to proceed.

Just then, the intercom squawked, causing Sterling to startle. Both girls quickly reassured him. Inez went to answer it. "The captain would like to know what the disturbance is all about. What should I tell him?"

"I'll handle it," Rita said as she left for the cockpit. Not knocking, she walked right in. The pilot and co-pilot, long time employees of the Perez family, turned around in surprise. The co-pilot turned away, doing something that Rita could not see. The pilot tried to surreptitiously pull his shirt cuffs down further over his wrists, but not before Rita got a fast peek at feathers.

"Captain Sanchez," Rita said, formally, drawing herself up and speaking with the weight of her father's authority. "You have been taking the supplements, against my father's expressed orders. What of you, Miguel?" Without waiting for permission, she grabbed the co-pilot's arm and pulled his sleeve up, then gasped as she saw tiny, feathery down covering his arm. "I will have to report both of you to my father."

"Oh, please, Senorita, don't make me lose my job. Don't tell the Senor," Captain Sanchez pleaded. "Who will feed the little ones? I only took the pills because I heard they would improve my eyesight, so I could see better when I fly, since my eyesight was starting to go bad. You know I have worked for your father for many years. I just took them so I could do a better job." The older pilot was blubbering, incoherently, trying to get his story out and plead for mercy at the same time.

The co-pilot, an insolent young man of Rita's age, who had grown up with her on the estates and did not have the servile feelings of the older, more loyal workers said cockily, "What I choose to eat or drink is my business. Don Perez has no right to tell me I can't take vitamins that will make me stronger and healthier."

Pushing his wrist up into his face, Rita said, ferociously, "Do you look like you are getting healthier, Miguel? You are turning into an animal, you fool. You defy my Papa, who only has your best interests at heart. He even paid for your training to be a pilot." She threw his hand away from herself, in disgust.

Turning to the Captain she said sadly, putting her hand on his shoulder, "My old friend, I have no choice but to tell my father. Both of you will continue to turn into birds. You will soon not be able to fly the plane whatsoever."

"What will happen to us?" Captain Sanchez asked, mournfully.

"I will help you, just like I am going to help my friends who are aboard the plane. I will speak to my Papa on your behalf and we will take care of your families. If we are able to reverse this process, we will see about you getting your old jobs back, but you must stop taking those pills at once," Rita ordered, looking at them sternly.

The pilot ducked his grey head in compliance, but Miguel, while not challenging her again, looked contemptuous.

"I almost forgot why I came up here," Rita said. "We have guests aboard this plane who are in stages of devolution similar to you. You must not talk to anyone about any of these guests. Do I have your word?"

The pilot nodded a quick agreement. When Rita gave him a strong stare, the co-pilot nodded too, though as Rita turned to leave the forward cabin she was not sure he could be trusted. She then returned to the main cabin with a heavier heart.

Dinner was being served by the flight attendants as Rita came back and gracefully sank into her seat. The wide screen TV was tuned to a satellite station that was broadcasting global news of worsening disasters around the world. The coverage was sporadic, with reports suddenly getting cut off in mid-sentence. Frequently, the screen would go blank for minutes at a time. Nate was having the same kind of reception on his laptop, and clicked it off because it was annoying him.

As usual, the children finished their meals first, making them full of unexpended energy. Roaming around the cabin, they were drawn to the western-facing windows by the sun setting over the Gulf of Mexico.

"Come look at the sunset," Vera called to the adults. They got up good-naturedly to look out the windows with the kids.

"I've never been to the Gulf of Mexico," Carley said, momentarily as excited as the kids were. "Does the water always look that dark and smooth?"

"That's an oil spill!" Sandra exclaimed. She had seen quite a few in her years as an activist and recognized it right away. "Look, you can see it pouring out of a tanker that's on fire way down there in the south." She pointed helpfully, clucking miserably.

Craning his neck, Nate said, "I think I see several tankers leaking oil. From here it looks like it covers the whole Gulf!"

"Momma, why are all those boats just going in circles?" Reva wanted to know.

Holly tried to frame words, but her tongue was starting to fuse to her lower mouth. She was having increasing difficulty talking. Rita, patting Reva on the back, guessed, "I think those are boats that have been deserted, like Gabe and Marti have been telling us about."

"There are animals on that boat," Vera announced, looking through binoculars at a large, overturned vessel.

Taking the binoculars from her to see, Rita said, "Those are aquatic mutants. Some look like mermaids and mermen, but some appear to be seal-like, sunning themselves on top of the boat and sliding off into the water." Fortunately, there were enough sets of binoculars, because everyone wanted a glimpse of the sight.

"Wow, look at them diving," Jasmine said enviously, her devolving body longing to be down there in the water, too.

As they continued south, the oil spill continued and they spotted small islands covered with many mutants, as well as more overturned boats wandering around unpiloted.

"Everything is changing and deteriorating so fast," Sandra said somberly. Everybody else nodded gravely, struck dumb by the evidence in front of their own eyes.

Zack had not joined the others at the window, but had slumped morosely into his seat, ignoring everyone. It was fine and dandy for everyone to say how easy it would to disclaim any knowledge of Sterling's disappearance, but after all, he was the one who was going to have to sit in front of the phone screen and convince Homeland Security. He wasn't sure he was that good of an actor. While he didn't think there was anything wrong with the bird-kid coming with them, since Rita was the person most likely to be able to help him anyway, he still felt a tug of loyalty and responsibility to his job and especially to his country, though he wasn't sure if the two were on parallel paths anymore. Since he was not at the windows, he was the first to notice that the TV screen had gone dead. He jumped up and fiddled with the remote, but there was no response. He tried to power up his laptop, but received a reoccurring empty screen. He tried his phone, too, but with no luck.

"Uh, guys and gals, I think all our communications systems have gone down," Zack called out to the others. "We're cut off from the rest of the world."

No one paid any attention to him, though, because they all zeroed in on a brilliant burst of bright, fiery light in the distance. Sterling got spooked and started flapping around the plane. The girls and Holly chased after him and got him corralled and calmed down.

"What was that?" Nate whistled.

"I think that was two planes colliding," Sandra stammered, shuddering, for once not the self-assured woman they were used to seeing. Nate put his arm around her as they all watched debris fall from the sky. It had been sort of fun watching the sea creatures playing around in the water. This was no longer fun, as they thought of the lives that had been on those planes. Rita wondered if they were safe themselves with mutants flying their plane.

" Uh, guys and gals, I think all our communications systems have gone down," Zack called out to the others. "We're cut off from the rest of the world."

As they turned to look at him, trying to take in what he was saying, even though they were still in a state of shock over what they had just seen, the lights went out in the plane.

As panic began to set in Rita once again took charge and found her way up to the cabin. In the midst of an argument between the pilot and the co-pilot a switch inadvertently was flipped turning out the lights in the passenger section of the plane. With the lights back on calm settled back in and the rest of the trip back to Argentina was without incident. Out the windows they continued to see more of the same but they eventually landed safely.

*   *   *

"How's it going Rita?" Nate asked by way of a greeting as he strode into her lab, looking like a rancher on a mission. "I'm on my way to town to stock up on more supplies and wondered if I could get you anything while I'm there?" Holly, the twins, Sterling, and

Jasmine trailed in after him, calling out their own greetings. Nate had transported them down from his ranch for their daily session with Rita in her lab where they patiently submitted to all her pokes and prods.

"Oh, hi guys," Rita said, looking up from a microscope. She still liked to look in the actual microscope even though the images were displayed on one of the screens in front of her. "No, I can't think of anything I need today. Between you going into town every day, and my father's foreman going in every day, I keep well supplied." She laughed.

By now, they had all settled into a working routine: Rita and the mutants working in the lab, Nate running into town, and Sandra and Carley working the crops in the garden, canning and freezing as much as they could to lay in food stores for the coming winter. Zack maintained contact with HSA and was the one who kept track of what was happening in the world.

After what Nate had seen on their trip to the States and what they were learning on the news, he had become a firm believer in what Sandra had been saying. He realized, to put it baldly, that the world was falling apart. Not only were the stocks dealing with genetics and pharmaceuticals that made supplements in trouble, he could tell that there would be a worldwide crash of the financial markets, so he had decided to sell off all the stocks and paper assets.

"We've got to lay in supplies for a long siege," Nate said. "I'm beginning to find empty shelves and lines at some of the local stores. From the intermittent worldwide reports we get on the news, everybody is stocking goods, and there are long lines and shortages everywhere. Of course, goods are not getting to stores because of mutants walking off jobs, attacking shipments, and rioting in the streets. Just this morning they were showing on the news again the long lines of vehicles trying to exit all the major cities of the world. Of course, the roads are more parking lots these days than they are roadways. People keep abandoning their cars and heading off on foot. I can't imagine where they all think they are going."

"What exactly are you stocking up on besides non-perishable food?" Rita asked.

"I think I've got enough food laid in for a few years," Nate laughed, then looked worried. "Who knows how long this is going to last? I keep thinking I should get just a little more. Then, I am getting storable and renewable energy sources, though both of our ranches are already self-sustaining. What we need now are weapons and ammunition," he finished, trying for nonchalant.

"Weapons!" Rita exclaimed. "I didn't think you knew anything about weapons."

"I'm learning fast," Nate responded defensively.

"What does Sandra think about that? I can't imagine that she would go along with owning guns," Rita said, skillfully steering the twins away from breakable beakers they had decided to play with and setting them in the seats she had them occupy each time they came.

"I haven't gotten a chance to mention this to her yet," Nate said uneasily. "I'm sure that when it comes to self-defense she'll see reason."

"I wouldn't wait too long to have that conversation with her," Rita advised. "I don't think it's going to be as easy as you hope it will be."

"I'd better get going. Maybe I'll beat the crowds," Nate said, ducking the topic of telling Sandra about the firepower he was buying. A man had a right and a duty to defend his home and he intended to be ready if it came to that. He wasn't going to let Sandra stop him with her hippy philosophy of "let's make peace not war." This was a different world now and she would have to understand that.

"Okay, Holly," Rita said, turning back to her test subjects. "Let's test your vitals, and get some blood to see if what we tried yesterday has changed anything."

* * *

Media coverage was sporadic at best, fading in and out, with total blackouts from some areas of the world, spotty coverage from others. Zack fiddled with the channel controls trying to find another station when one went dark.

"Public water and sewer systems are failing. Electrical grids are flickering on and off," reported Rake Yardley on CNN, and then that signal flickered out, so Zack switched channels again. Before he was able to find another one, he got a beep on his phone screen. It was Jamie, checking in for the day.

"How's Dr. Perez doing with her research into a test to isolate mutants?" Jamie began, without any polite preamble. They never knew how long they would be able to talk without being cut off.

"It's not any different then she has been saying for weeks. There is no current technology that will allow for a universal test that detects devolution in humans," Zack repeated for what must have been the millionth time.

"Never mind that," Jamie said, impatient as always. "We want her to keep concentrating on that, but we want her back on looking for a cure. There are only a few remote places left in the world where research can be done. There's a facility in the Antarctic, one on a small island near the Marshall Islands, and one on a mountaintop in Nepal. That is it."

Zack gave a low whistle. This was the worst news he had heard yet. Of course, he didn't mention that Rita was already working on reversing the process with their small group of mutants.

"There is no effective way to maintain physical contact. Communication between these facilities can be maintained, like with you, via satellite links. Finding techniques to maintain the systems is getting tough. I'm afraid they are each going to be on their own. Tell Dr. Perez that the world is depending on her or there will be an end to civilization," Jamie continued in almost a monotone.

Zack had never heard her talk so hopelessly. Jamie Whiteman was always a person with an angle, with a new approach to problems. Her attitude was such that she believed anything could be accomplished. This apathy on her part, more than anything else, convinced Zack that things were out-of-control.

"I thought that people had stopped taking the supplements, after the pharmaceutical companies had stopped making them. Certainly there are enough humans unaffected to round up the ones who are," he almost pleaded.

"The mutants don't just come along willingly," Jamie snapped at him, sounding more like her old self. "The fighting between humans and mutants has escalated. There is violence overrunning all the major cities in the world. The mutants are maniacal and will fearlessly charge right into a storm of bullets. Without being able to tell who is mutant and who isn't, those at the front lines frequently turn on each other. Some human tree-huggers, now mutant-huggers, throw themselves down in front of mutants that are being collected for containment camps."

"Then there are some mutants who banded together with humans against other mutants. We don't know who is enemy and who isn't. Just because a mutant is aquatic doesn't mean a thing. If they go pre-mammalian, they seem to develop the characteristics of sharks, predators, if you will. If they stay mammalian, like dolphins, whales, and seals, they are friendly and usually off cavorting in the water, not bothering anyone. The ape-men are the most vicious."

"There is a new wrinkle that you must convey to Dr. Perez, which might have an impact on her research and testing. The mutants are now breeding with each other." Her voice hushed as she said this. Did Zack hear her right?

"You mean apes and seals are mating?" he said, incredulously, trying to picture the action in his mind but falling short.

"Don't be ridiculous. There is not interspecies breeding — at least not yet," Jamie answered, sounding somewhat uncertain. "They are seeking out the ones in the same devolution path. And the gestation periods are patterned along the lines of the animal they resemble. Avian mutants are having clutches of 4-8 eggs and hatchlings are growing to adult status in months. Aquatic mutants are harder to follow, since many give birth in the water, but the friendly mammalian ones, especially the highly intelligent dolphins, are cooperating with us and letting us monitor their pregnancies. They are following right along the path of normal dolphin pregnancies, including births and growth cycles. Of course, the ape-men are similar to humans, though they reach adulthood quicker than humans do. Do you understand what this means? They can build up armies of mutants from their own children at a rate much faster than we can. In no time they will outnumber us." Zack felt as shaken by the news as Jamie was. Maybe it would have been better if they were totally cut off from the rest of the world, oblivious to the horrors going on out there, and just living their lives in their own isolated, peaceful world. Zack wondered darkly how long it would stay peaceful and isolated.

"Maybe this horrible news will have a silver lining for the scientists studying the RHV process," Zack said. "Maybe it will give them new ideas of courses of study and research."

"We need less study and research and more action," Jamie said, tartly, clicking off abruptly.

Shaking off the desperation he felt at Jamie's dire warnings, Zack stood up to leave his office. The great thing about these updates was that they gave him additional excuses to drop in on Rita, Zack thought optimistically as he headed for her lab to break the news.

* * *

Like a duck out of water, Jasmine thought, unoriginally. That's how she had been feeling for the past few months. Though she had managed to get included when Carley and Holly decided so abruptly to leave the bar in Annapolis, she wasn't part of the inner circle. Carley and Holly were her bosses, and while they had been nice to her, they hadn't been pals. Now she felt as if she wasn't part of any circle. The humans were a tight-knit bunch that she didn't fit in with because she was a mutant. So was Holly, of course, but she had been with them on their initial grand adventure, which made her close to them. She didn't fit in with the other mutants, because so far everyone else was going down the avian path, while she was aquatic. She felt isolated and lonely amidst the crowd. She felt no one was able to understand what was happening to her, the changes and needs that were taking over.

She glanced over at Holly and the girls with Sterling on the edge of the pool beneath the waterfall. While all birds love water, they only stay in the shallows where they can bathe while keeping their head above water, or where they can scoop up fish to eat, which is what Sterling was busy doing. Jasmine could identify with that at least. She felt a desire for raw fish, too.

"Reva, Vera, come out here and swim with me," she called, stroking gracefully towards them. While the girls were pursuing the avian track, too, they weren't as far along as Sterling and their mother, and they still liked to play in the water like normal seven year-olds.

"Look Jasmine, I can swim with my head under water," Reva boasted, suiting her actions to her words.

"What about you, Vera?" Jasmine asked.

"I don't like how the water feels on my eyeballs," Vera answered, shaking her head and backing away as if someone was pushing her head under the water. Jasmine suspected that Reva had done just that.

"Keep your eyes closed," Jasmine suggested, floating on her back near Vera.

"You're a big fraidy cat!" Reva taunted Vera.

"I am not," Vera responded, heatedly. "Momma, tell Reva to stop teasing me."

"Girls," squawked Holly, awkwardly. "Both of you be nice." She splashed some water over her feathers and began preening.

"Sterling, don't you want to come in and play," Reva wheedled. Just then, Sterling speared a fish and swallowed it whole, ignoring Reva. He looked proudly at everybody as if for applause.

"Oh, we forgot about the goggles Aunt Carley gave us," Vera said with relief, picking up a pair and putting them on. She stuck her head in the water to show everybody she wasn't afraid of it.

"Can you swim where the water is over your head?" Jasmine asked Reva and Vera, diving under the water and taking a few strokes towards the middle of the pool.

For a second, instinct pulled on the girls to stay near shore, but they shrugged it off and paddled happily after her. Giggling and dunking each other under the water, taking turns climbing on Jasmine's back as she dove deep, they had a wonderful time. The girls tired before Jasmine did. As they swam lazily back to shore, Jasmine felt the need to dive deeper than she had before. Near the waterfall, the pool was extremely deep, so she hadn't gotten to the bottom yet. She wondered if there would be sand on the bottom that she could rub her belly on. Down she went, glorying in her ability to hold her breath for half an hour at a time if she wished and the freedom of not having to worry about it. This freedom in the water was the benefit she had sought.

She followed the rock wall below the waterfall until she came upon an opening. It looked like a cave, and since she didn't have to worry about breathing for awhile, she wasn't afraid of getting trapped in it. She swam inside and found it turned into a long tunnel. There was a current coming out of the tunnel but it wasn't strong enough to prevent her from exploring up it a little ways. The way back will be coasting, she thought as she headed up the tunnel. The tunnel was wide enough for a number of people to swim through together, and Jasmine bemoaned the fact that there were no other aquatic mutants to enjoy it with. Maybe some of the humans could put on scuba gear, she thought with a superior sneer. When did I start thinking of myself as a mutant and them as humans, she asked herself, troubled that she was internally distancing herself from humanity.

Then she had no further time for introspection as the tunnel opened into a large underground cavern. Jasmine broke through the surface. Her eyes had now adapted to the darkness of deep water so she was able to see everything clearly without a source of light. That was fortunate, since the cavern was in total darkness. In fact, she realized, bright lights had begun to bother her.

The water was warm and pleasant as she free-stroked to the other end of the cavern, which seemed to stretch for miles, but she estimated it was probably the length of a couple football fields and at least fifty feet high. She called out, and her voice echoed all around her. At the far end, Jasmine discovered a hot spring and knew this was the reason the water, even in the pool under the waterfall, was so warm. It was fed, not only by the waterfall, but also by an underground hot spring.

There was a level area of beach near the hot spring. Jasmine climbed out of the water to investigate and to have some rest. Her muscles were tired from fighting the current through the tunnel. She was surprised to find that though there was no sand, the earth felt soft, not rocky. Since she had encountered no other life forms in her exploration of the cavern and beach, she felt as if she was the discoverer of a private new world, a place she could have all to herself. If it wasn't for the fact that she hadn't found any fish in the cavern, she could live here comfortably alone, not having to worry about how she was changing from everyone else, and not being aware of their oh-so-discreet glances at her webbings. She felt that she could not stay here forever. But for now she still felt some responsibility to help solve the problem of mutation with Rita. She was the only aquatic mutant here and that made her unique. Maybe I hold the key, she thought. Reluctantly, with a last longing look around, Jasmine slipped back into the thermal water and headed back to the world of humans and their struggles and conflicts.

* * *

"I promised Rita that I would level with all of you, which is what I am doing," Zack said, telling the group, gathered at Nate's for dinner and an evening of catching up, what he had learned from Jamie. Zack and Rita had driven up from the estate to join those already staying there. While Nate had not formally asked Sandra to live with him, she was at his ranch more often than not.

"The mutants are having babies together?" Nate repeated as if he hadn't quite heard Zack right. He casually put his arm around Sandra in its accustomed position.

They were all gathered at the table for the impromptu buffet Sandra and Carley had pulled together. Since it was fall in Argentina, they had been busy harvesting the gardens and orchards and there were plenty of fresh veggies and fruit for everybody. Raw sushi had been prepared for the members of the group that were now big fish eaters. Sandra could not bring herself to kill and prepare dead animals, even fish, though she recognized the needs of the avian and aquatic members within their group. Carley had thoughtfully handled those details, with Holly hindering, more than helping, after the swim by the pool. Carley also cooked steak for Zack, Rita, and herself on the outdoor grill. Sandra had insisted that she didn't want the smell of meat in the house. Carley was irritated that Sandra was so autocratic when she didn't even own the house. In deference to Sandra's sensibilities, Nate ate vegetarian.

"At the rate of the species they are mutating to," Zack continued, no longer feeling like he needed or wanted to keep any secrets from the group. "You know, there is such total chaos everywhere in the world, we are almost cut off. Essentially, the United States government is fractured and ineffective. I don't even know who or what I have allegiance to anymore. I mean, sure, I am in touch with Jamie, but how can I know what is really happening within Homeland Security. According to her, there are only three groups of scientists, besides Rita, left in the whole world working on reversing the process of RHV. How does she even know that anymore? I hate to say this, but I think we are on our own."

"Welcome to the group," Sandra said, grandly.

"What do you mean?" Zack demanded.

"While you've been briefing Homeland Security and have been receiving briefs, we've all been preparing for a long siege," Nate explained.

"Surely not here," Rita said, anxiously. "I know you and my father have been stocking up with supplies, but I really don't think we will be overrun with mutants in Patagonia." She looked apologetically at Holly and Jasmine. "I mean unfriendly mutants."

"You didn't think any of your father's workers would take supplements either, until you found out the pilot and co-pilot had," Sandra reminded her. "There is no place that is safe. It's not a question of if, but of when."

"I even sold off all my investments," Nate announced, as if that cinched the argument. "Because the market has crashed, there are no safe investments left other than hard goods. In fact, I doubt there will ever be a stock market again." He shook his head as if the idea was beyond comprehension.

"I told you to sell everything off a long time ago when the market was still firm and prices were high. I bet you took a bath," Sandra ribbed him, digging an elbow into his side.

Nate nodded, not wanting to get into a fight with her, all investment professionals have to deal with Monday morning quarterbacks.

"Can we be excused?" Reva and Vera said together. They had been patient with the adult talk while there was food to dig into, but now they were brimming with energy from the sugars and proteins they had consumed, and they wanted to run. Actually, they wanted to fly, but couldn't quite pull that off yet. Holly gave them a nod and pulling Sterling along with them, they ran out on the long sloping lawn to play tag. That acted like a signal for everyone to get up. Then they all pitched in helping to clear the table. After dealing with the dishes and all they settled on the veranda to watch the sunset with a couple bottles of estate wine.

Carley plopped down on the porch swing with Jasmine. Jasmine didn't realize it, but Carley also felt a bit like an outsider. Of course, she was close to Holly and the girls, but they were changing in ways she couldn't understand. She did not feel the tight bond the others had with each other from their shared experiences. Carley was sensitive to the feelings of other people, and she recognized that Jasmine was feeling even more left out than she was.

"You've been quiet during dinner," she said softly. "How was your swim today?"

Jasmine turned to Carley with bright silvery eyes, forgetting the fact that she wanted to keep the cavern a secret for herself. She was so grateful for Carley reaching out to her. "I discovered a large cave behind the waterfall."

"Do you hear that everybody?" Carley said loud enough to make everybody pay attention. "Jasmine has found a cave under the pool."

There were exclamations from everybody at the same time as they all encouraged Jasmine to tell them about it.

Her eyes getting dreamy, Jasmine described her plunge down beneath the waterfall, her discovery of the cave and then the long tunnel leading to the cavern and hot spring. She looked at them all wistfully, now wishing they could all share the experience with her.

"I've got some scuba diving gear," Nate announced. "I for one would love to see this cavern and hot spring. Is anybody else up for it?"

Sandra, Carley, and Zack quickly agreed, though the others had no scuba diving experience. Realizing that diving lessons would be his responsibility in this new world, Nate offered to give lessons to any of the others who were interested. Rita timidly expressed interest, but Holly just shook her head. Her swimming days were over, maybe for good. They chatted about the discovery, Jasmine beaming at being the center of attention and wondering how she had felt excluded with this friendly bunch.

"You know, we haven't heard from Gabe and Marti for awhile," Carley said, thinking nostalgically about her friends and the good times at the bar, that would be no more.

"Let's give them a call in the morning," Nate suggested.

"I'm sure they have all kinds of interesting escapades to tell us about," Sandra laughed.

"They are certainly brave to be travelling with everything in turmoil." Rita said.

"I'm sure they are fine. What could happen out on the water?" Zack said lightly, knowing just like all of them did, that many things could be happening, as they had witnessed crossing the Gulf.

"Look, look Aunt Carley, we found a turtle," the twins yelled running up to show everybody, the turtle equally held by both of them, Sterling flapping and hopping awkwardly behind them.

Everybody dutifully inspected and exclaimed over the turtle as they peacefully relaxed together, enjoying the orange and aqua spears shooting across the sky with the dying sun, the sense of camaraderie of being together and, of course, the wine.

* * *

"Vera and Reva, do you think you could hold onto Sterling's arms while I take this DNA swab? I can't seem to get him to understand that he needs to hold still," Rita asked the girls on their daily visit to her lab, shaking her ponytailed head in frustration.

As the weeks turned into months, it steadily became harder to communicate with Sterling. He had lost his ability to speak quite awhile ago, but until recently he responded appropriately to anything that was said to him. Now, he seemed to be losing the ability to understand English and the gestures humans use to communicate with each other. If it wasn't for the strong bond he appeared to feel for the twins, Rita didn't know how they would manage him. She didn't want to think about what would happen when that bond dissolved. Maybe I need to add another task to my list, she sighed to herself, like how to communicate with mutants. She was already feeling overwhelmed with trying to reverse the DNA switch and find a way to identify mutants with a simple generic test, though that one had pretty much fallen to the wayside for the time being, since she didn't know where to go with it.

Glancing over at Zack, who had dropped in to give his update from Jamie, and Carley, who had driven the mutants down to the lab for their daily tests, Rita scrolled through the group to see if someone else might be able to take this job on. Sighing again, she realized that it would probably fall to her, since she was the only scientist of the pack.

"Sure, we can do that, Aunt Rita," Vera said, moving into position readily, grabbing hold of one of Sterling's arms, though it got increasingly hard to think of them as arms, instead of wings.

"Stay still Sterling and open your mouth," Reva ordered Sterling, instead of complying with Rita's request. She demonstrated standing still and opening her own mouth. Sterling stood still and opened his own mouth, obediently. "See, Aunt Rita, we don't have to hold his arms. He'll open his mouth for me." She fluffed her own feathers, proudly.

"You do have the magic touch," Rita acknowledged admiringly, quickly sticking a Q-tip in Sterling's cheek and taking a swab before he changed his mind and clamped down on her fingers. "I wish he would do that for me. How do you get him to do that?" Maybe the girls can help me figure it out, she thought half-seriously. She turned and wrote some notes about the girls' ability to communicate with Sterling.

Before Reva could answer, Rita's father, Ronaldo, burst through the open doorway, sweat pouring down his face as if he had run a long way, as indeed he had.

Sounding winded, he wheezed out, "Rita, is Zack here? . . . Oh, there you are, Zack."

He stopped to catch his breath, as Rita ran to her father to support him, crying out, "Papa, are you alright?" She looked him up and down to assure herself that he wasn't noticeably injured. "What happened? Is something wrong? Is Mama okay?"

Zack came over right behind Rita, saying, "How can I help?"

Turning to Rita, Rinaldo calmed her down. "I'm fine and your mama is fine." Without skipping a beat, he turned to Zack, still gasping a bit. "It is Jose. He was grabbed and pulled into the sea by a fish-man."

"Papa, have a seat. You need to take a moment to breathe," Rita insisted, more intent on her father's physical distress than on registering the words he said. She forced him into a chair, as everybody gathered around , except for Sterling who stayed right where he had been for the test as if nothing had happened. Rita got her father a glass of water and made him drink before she would let him continue his story. A bit of color returned to his face, and he became more coherent.

"Who is Jose?" Zack asked, wanting to get the story from the beginning.

"Jose is one of my best vineyard workers. He has been with me for 20 years. He is family — loyal. I stood up with his baby when he was born, and now his son is going to work in the vineyard too. His wife, she helps out in the hacienda." He began to sob loudly, while Rita patted him ineffectually. She and Zack exchanged puzzled looks, still having no idea what all this was about.

"You said Jose was grabbed by a fisherman, Sir?" Zack gently prompted.

"No, no, a fish-man! He was taking a nap by the sea during his break from work in the vineyard. Jose, he likes the water. Suddenly a fish-man, one of those mutants, comes out of the sea and just grabs him as he lays there asleep, and pulls him into the water, then down under the water. Other workers were taking their breaks there, too, and they saw it happen, but it was over so fast they had no time to stop it. They jumped in the water, but Jose was gone, all trace of him is gone," and again Rinaldo sobbed loudly.

"Oh, no, Papa, not Jose," Rita cried out, collapsing against her father and hugging him to her, sobbing along with him.

"But, the aquatics have all been friendly, you said so yourself, Zack," Jasmine pleaded, looking around for someone to back her up, but no one was paying attention to her.

The children, caught up in the emotions in the room, while not understanding them, began to shriek and cling to Holly, who tried to enclose all three children with her arms at once.

"I'm going to round up the troops, and head to the beach," Zack said curtly, impatient with all the emotion. He immediately got onto his communicator to the six soldiers he had brought with him to guard Rita's lab. "Sir, did you check the main gate, when you came in?"

"Si, yes, I locked the main gate," Rinaldo answered, gaining control over his emotions by discussing practical matters.

"It's been so peaceful since we got here," Carley exclaimed. "Just when we were all beginning to feel like we were safe."

Concentrating on Rinaldo, Zack began to issue commands. "Senor, I need you to round up all your workers and get them behind the walls of the main compound. Pick your most loyal men, ones you are sure are not mutants. Then send them to patrol the perimeter. Rita, get on the horn and alerted Nate and Sandra about what has happened. Tell them to get into the house up there and lock the doors at the ranch until we give them an all clear. Then, you and Carley get these, these..... people." He gestured towards Holly, Jasmine, and the children, "over to the main house and stay put yourselves until you hear differently from me."

"Zack, do you think we are under attack?" Rita demanded, going eye-to-eye with him.

Grimly, Zack placed a hand on her shoulder. Even in midst of the crisis, he wished he could pull her into his arms, "I don't know what we are up against, Rita. We need to take every precaution as if we are. All I know for sure is that we aren't safe in Patagonia anymore, not even in the isolation of this estate. Now hurry."

With that, Zack strode off to join his men while the others, looking at each other anxiously, set about the tasks they had been assigned to do.

"Does that mean we can't go swimming today?" Reva demanded, tearfully, easing the tension somewhat, as they all had a moment to laugh.

CHAPTER SIX

Mankind Hides

"Scuba gear is all fine and good, at least for humans," Carley declared. "But what about Holly and Sterling, and the twins?" she continued, "I don't think they can use scuba gear to get to the cave."

Things had deteriorated rapidly during the weeks since Jose had been snatched off the beach, with the compound having come under siege from mutants trying to scale the walls and take over the hacienda. With many of the mutants having ape-like skills, making them good at climbing and swinging across the wall, it was found to be impossible to repel them peacefully. It was also discovered that many of Ronaldo's employees had been secretly taking the supplements and were no longer to be trusted. Many of them were in cahoots with the outsiders and were aiding them in gaining entrance to the barricaded property. In full retreat, all the unaffected occupants of the Perez estates had retreated to Nate's ranch as a temporary measure, but mutants had been spotted scouting out the situation from the woods and fields around the ranch. It was no longer deemed secure, and everyone agreed a frontal attack seemed imminent.

A meeting had been called in the Nate's large, roomy living room, which was now very crowded with all the people gathered there, to determine what they should do to protect themselves from being overrun. It was quickly decided that the ranch was indefensible in the long run. The opinion was nearly unanimous that the mutants had no respect for human life, and that they had banded together to eliminate humankind, though no one was sure why. As a scientist, Rita had suggested their motivation was survival of the fittest, and with no one objecting, they went with that. No one really cared why the mutants were in attack mode. Instead the focus was on the fact that they were. Standing around and theorizing about it was the last thing on their minds.

Jasmine had timidly suggested that the cavern she had discovered might be an option as a place to live, that no mutant would ever guess it was there. Several of the group had already visited the cavern individually using the one set of scuba gear that Nate had been able to scrounge out of storage at the ranch. They were amazed at the spaciousness of the cavern. The desperation of the group was such that they immediately latched on to this idea, and had been actively discussing how to make it work, as quickly as possible. Everybody felt they were quickly running out of time. Ever the champion of the disadvantaged, Carley, had spoken out about how to get their little group of avian mutants to the cave. Everybody was silent for a moment, as they pondered this wrinkle. To their credit, it never crossed any of their minds to abandon Holly, Sterling, and the twins to the mutants, hoping they would instead be accepted by all. Most of the group was genuinely committed to Holly and the children. Everyone recognized their importance towards Rita's research, which each recognized as the only hope to save the human race and restore the world to its natural order.

Zack, accustomed to making snap decisions in times of crisis, spoke up first. "We will tunnel down to the cavern from the rear and disguise the opening. We'll put on a heavily fortified door that only we can open. Our mutant friends can get in and out that way. Strategically, we need a back escape route in case the front of the underwater tunnel is discovered by enemy aquatics; and anyway, we need to vent the cavern for good air circulation. I'll get the soldiers right on it. I'm sure we can use some of the excavation equipment you've been using to improve your property, Nate." Nate nodded

169

unnecessarily, because Zack wasn't asking. He was taking charge, naturally slipping into command mode.

Everybody perked up immediately when they heard Zack's plan and saw his leadership. Holly looked gratefully at Carley, tears in her eyes, unable to articulate how she felt. Carley reached over and squeezed her hand.

"We need to form work crews," Zack continued. "We will need more scuba gear to get all the humans to the cavern. Nate and Sandra, you can go into town to get what we need. But be very alert when you go, this is war you realize. Until they get back, Jasmine, you and I, using the one scuba set we have, are going to be the only ones who can get supplies through the underwater tunnel. The rest of you need to start sorting and packing up what we need to take. Rita, it is vital that you be able to continue your research, so make sure you have everything you need."

"We need to be in communication with people in the outside world," Rita added. "I especially need to maintain contact with the three other groups of scientists we know about who are working on reversing or stopping the devolution."

"There may be other groups of humans like us, who are surviving in remote areas, and might be able to communication with us," Nate said, thinking of Gabe and Marti, tooling around the world in their sailboat.

"You and I can take care of that," Zack affirmed. "I would say that communication with the outside world is as important as Rita's research."

"I will take charge of the provisions," Rita's mother, Eva, spoke up. Everybody automatically nodded in appreciation at that. If anyone could make sure they had enough food, and feed them well to boot, it was Eva Perez.

"While we are in town, I think Nate and I need to load up on anything else we might need. I was thinking specifically of medical supplies," Sandra put in.

"I will help you make a list," Eva spoke up again. "Having helped run the estate for all these years, I have treated many injuries. Being a momma, I know about illnesses."

"I've had a bit of first aid training myself," Sandra said. "I'm sure between the two of us we can cover most medical problems." Though Sandra acknowledged quietly to herself that if anything serious happened they wouldn't have the resources to handle it. She didn't mention this to the others, deciding they all had enough worries for the moment. While foresight was wise, there was no sense in adding to the anxiety. She nodded to herself, causing Nate to glance at her, quizzically. She gave him a little grin, but kept her own counsel.

"Of course, I will organize the workers who came with us to construct whatever shelters and amenities we can manage," Rinaldo put in, authoritatively. He wasn't sure he was as comfortable as everyone else seemed to be with Zack assuming control. Because he was accustomed to being the boss, he wasn't ready to relinquish that role easily. "I do have another concern. I'm sure there are other people out there who are also hiding out. I think it is important to see if any of them would like to join us." He looked challengingly at Zack, who just waved for him to continue. "I propose to send some of my men out into the countryside to look for isolated people and extend the offer."

While he didn't want to offend Don Perez as the father of Rita, Zack was mindful of the time and space constraints they were operating under. He carefully voiced his concerns. "I think that is an excellent plan, sir. We need to be aware that we can be attacked at anytime. We need to get into the cavern in the shortest time possible. I respectfully suggest we put a limit on how long your men look for people, and how many we can take. We already have about thirty people here ourselves."

Rinaldo nodded graciously, having won his point.

Rita had a troubled expression on her face, her soft heart working overtime. "How can we refuse anybody who needs us?" Rinaldo turned gently to his daughter, "We must be practical as well as compassionate. We can't risk the survival of our group by filling the cavern beyond what it can hold to sustain life." Rita's brother, Pedro, looking at his wife and children, who were busy playing with

Sterling and the twins, nodded emphatically. Still looking disturbed, Rita nodded, reluctantly.

"Enough talk," Eva said briskly, getting up. "It's time to work."

Agreeing, everybody headed off to get started on their assigned tasks.

* * *

Peering around the corner, Nate pulled back quickly and placed his index finger on his lips, motioning Sandra to be quiet, something she had trouble doing in the best of times, he thought, wryly. "There are mutants down the road this way," he mouthed, soundlessly.

They had left the jeep at the outskirts of town after successfully and uneventfully making it down to town from Nate's ranch. They had agreed to scout out the town on foot before roaring into the village announcing to everybody within hearing distance that they were there. Surprisingly, they had initially found the town to be deserted. The grocery stores had been ransacked and there was nothing left worth taking. Every house had been broken into and likewise emptied of anything of value. Wanton destruction of cars and property littered their path. It looked like the mutants had taken everything they wanted, had their fun, and then moved on to new pastures, one of which was the Perez estate. This was the first sign they encountered life in the town, all of whom were ape-like creatures. They appeared to be having a grunting guttural disagreement about something. They stood directly in the pathway between Nate and Sandra, and the local tourist dive shop.

Turning on tiptoe, Nate and Sandra reversed direction, searching for a way to the back entrance to the store. It was obvious they couldn't drive the jeep into town now, and would have to pack out the gear. Sandra silently groaned to herself.

Finding an alley behind the row of shops, they slipped down it, counting doors until they came to the dive shop. The door gaped open, as had many of the doors along the way. As they cautiously entered, they saw that the place had been ravaged. All manner of diving equipment was thrown senselessly all over the place. Diving knives had been used to slash hoses and suits apparently at random. Nate and Sandra looked at each other with resignation. This was going to take a lot longer than they had originally thought. Resolutely, with one eye on the windows at the front of the shop, they began to sift through the mess, looking for undamaged scuba gear. After a search that lasted beyond their comfort zone, they gathered together enough for half a dozen complete kits, not anywhere near enough to outfit everybody in their group. That would slow down the work considerably, but it was the best they could do. Making like ghosts, they started the task of transporting the gear to the jeep.

After several trips to the hidden jeep, they stopped for a breather.

"I think we should leave now, while the getting's good," Nate said, gulping down water from a canteen. "The sooner we get the scuba gear to the ranch, the faster we can get the supplies to the cavern."

"I disagree," Sandra said, shaking her ponytailed head. "We don't know if we will ever be able to get back here again. We need to do as much as we can while we can."

"If we get attacked and killed by mutants, we won't be doing anybody any good," Nate responded reasonably.

Sandra stubbornly shook her head. "I'm not leaving here without medical supplies. If you don't want to come with me, I'm going back by myself." She started off.

"Okay, okay. You are definitely one hard-headed woman," Nate joked, giving in. He grabbed a crowbar out of the jeep as he hustled to keep up with her. "While we are at it, I have another idea of something we need. I spotted the sporting goods store and that gave me an idea." He eyed Sandra, nervously. She stopped walking and looked at him suspiciously, her highly-active mind working overtime.

"And what would that be?" she asked, with narrowed eyes.

Nate continued to walk. "Come on, I'll show you."

Unlike their first trip into town, they saw no further sign of mutants.

They quickly came to the sporting goods store. Unlike the other stores that had been torn apart, this store had a sturdy lock and iron bars on the windows that had protected it from the attacking mutants. Nate had taken in these details as they had been lugging the scuba gear to the jeep on their many trips and had brought the crowbar along to see if that might help them get in. He tried to pry the lock open while Sandra kept a lookout, but had no success.

"How about the iron bars?" Sandra hissed back to him while continuing to watch for trouble.

After inspecting the bars, Nate found that they were pretty rusty. Some were loose from age, so he was able to force a few of the bars out. When he did it, the bars broke the window. The noise made them flinch and duck for cover. But with no signs of mutants they proceeded to squeeze through the opening. Since he had been there many times before in his runs for supplies, Nate rapidly made his way back to a locked case and used the crowbar to break it open. Sandra, who was bringing up the rear, gave a gasp as he whirled around, holding a gun.

"NO!" she cried out, instinctively, all her pacifist beliefs rushing unconsciously to the forefront.

"Yes!" Nate said, with steely determination. Gone was the Nate who was always trying to play up to her, the man who would twine her hair around his little finger. "This fight is a matter of life or death, our lives or theirs. We have to be able to defend ourselves."

"But, I could never take another life," Sandra pleaded. "I'm even against the death penalty for serial killers."

"What if someone was attacking one of those sweet little twins?" Nate asked, not giving an inch, but still wanting Sandra to understand.

For a moment, Sandra looked like she would go into her standard debate mode, but then she lowered her eyes and gave an almost imperceptible nod. This was not the same as chaining herself to a tree to save it from being cut down. It was truly a fight to the finish. While she still believed she would never be able to shoot someone, at least not to kill, she realized they needed to be able to defend themselves. Wearily, she nodded.

Relieved that he didn't have to fight Sandra about it, Nate began to load them both up with weapons and ammunition. Sandra mutely accepting whatever he gave her.

It required yet another trip into town to get medical supplies. They found the hospital abandoned and the same mindless vandalism there as they had elsewhere in town. Dispiritedly, they loaded up on everything on the list that Sandra and Eva had put together, in addition to other things that caught their eye as possibly useful. Aware that they had pushed their luck with the number of trips they had made already, they headed out of town and back to the ranch.

When they returned, the ranch was a hive of activity, so much so, that they had to unload everything they'd gotten themselves. Though tired from their journey to town, after grabbing a quick bite, they swiftly donned scuba gear to help transport supplies to the cavern, knowing time was of the essence.

* * *

"Hola, Senor," a member of the returning search party called out.

It had been an industrious week. Zack and his soldiers had devised a plan to add secure vents to the cavern, making one a wide path out the rear of the cavern for entry by Holly and the kids, and a speedy exit if it came to that. The work was well under way. Meanwhile, Rinaldo and a few of his men were preparing the hideout. Zack and Nate had set up a communication system in the cavern to link them to Jamie Whitehead and Homeland Security, the other research facilities, and anyone else in the world that had access to technology to contact them. Rita had her lab underground started, and the scuba gear was being used full-time to transport goods.

Taking a short break for lunch, they were gathered picnic-style under the spreading trees, when Rinaldo was hailed by one of his approaching workers who had been sent to look for others who were hiding out from the mutants. Straggling up the path behind him stumbled exhausted people of every age and size. It looked as if the line of newcomers went on forever, but when the count was done, there were fifty people added to their numbers. The two groups eyed each other, warily.

"Welcome, you must all be starved!" Eva said, breaking the stalemate and bustling towards the new members of their little tribe. "Come, sit, and have some wine while we get you some food. You must be famished, you poor dears."

With that, the silence was broken and both groups rushed to introduce themselves to each other.

* * *

Their luck had run out. Sandra and Nate realized it as they screeched to a halt in the jeep. They had been making yet another run into town and were on their way back when, turning a corner, they spotted a road block up ahead. They looked at each other in muted dismay. They had been making these trips into town with impunity. In fact, they had thought the town was essentially deserted. They had become complacent and lax in watching for mutants. Now they had been caught unaware. Not only were the mutants still in the vicinity, but they were organized enough to plan and execute a road block. These thoughts went through their minds at lightning speed as Nate reflexively put the car into reverse.

As if it was a signal, a hoard of ape-like mutants poured out from behind the rocks on the side of the road. They had been ambushed!

"Nate, watch out!" Sandra yelled, needlessly, because Nate had seen them as soon as she did.

"Grab the gun, Sandra!" Nate hollered, trying to be heard above the unintelligible shouts of the wild half-humans surrounding them, as he tried to steer away from them unsuccessfully.

"I can't do it. I can't shoot a living creature," Sandra said wildly, grabbing the gun even as she denied her ability to use it.

"Just shoot in the air to scare them away," Nate screamed impatiently.

There was not enough room to maneuver. There were too many mutants to break through with the jeep. The mutants swarmed their vehicle.

Mutants were throwing punches and swinging aggressively, hopping on top of the vehicle. Nate was trying to fight back, though boxing had never been his sport of choice. Sandra used the gun as a club and whacked at hairy hands reaching for her, but they were greatly outnumbered and it was obvious that the ferocity of the attack would soon overwhelm them. Sandra took a second to glance over at Nate to see how he was doing. She froze. An especially large ape had his huge mitts around Nate's neck and was slowly squeezing the life out of him. Nate was struggling to pull the hands away, but they were as strong as immovable rock, making Nate a virulent shade of eggplant.

Sandra had no time to think or debate with her conscience. She raised the gun and pulled the trigger instinctively. Startled, the mutant released his grip on Nate's neck and all the other half-humans dropped back a few steps. They rallied quickly to commence another attack, but it had been enough time for Nate to slam his foot on the accelerator. The jeep leaped forward towards the road block.

The ape-men cheered, inhumanly, thinking that Nate and Sandra were truly trapped. At the last moment, Nate went off-road and headed across country. The mutants wasted no time and hurried after them, but the jeep easily outstripped them. Before long, Nate and Sandra found themselves deep in a land of fields, rocks, and sudden ravines. When they had gone a safe distance and knew the mutants were lost behind them and could not catch them, they stopped for a moment to get their bearings and take a good breath.

"My kind of hippie-chick," Nate said admiringly, looking at the gun that was still in Sandra's hands.

Sandra looked, too. In reaction, her hands began to tremble. "I can't believe that I shot at another living being."

"You did what you had to do," Nate said with a nonchalant shrug. "I'd be dead if you hadn't."

"I don't know how I'll ever live with myself after this," Sandra wailed in despair. "I've just betrayed everything I believe in." She buried her head in her hands and sobbed.

Like most guys, Nate was exceptionally uneasy with female tears. He leaned over to put his arms around her. "Seriously, Sandra, you saved my life."

"You were beginning to turn a bit purple around the gills," Sandra giggled with a mercurial change of mood.

"Hey, don't kid around about having gills," Nate protested in mock horror, relieved that the waterworks had turned off and Sandra seemed back in balance. "Are you okay now?"

"This is going to require some extensive thinking on my part," Sandra answered, shaking her head solemnly, "but I think I'm going to be okay. Did I hit him?"

"I don't know," Nate responded. "I was a bit preoccupied at that moment. It would be a miracle if you did, if that was your first time firing a gun. My guess is you just scared him and the rest of that gang."

"Well, that makes me feel much better. I don't mind the idea of scaring them out of their skins to save our hides," she joked gamely.

"Now for the important question," Nate said, straightening up after a satisfying kiss. "Where are we?"

"And better yet, how do we get where we want to go?" Sandra chimed in.

They pulled out a map and closely studied it, trying to figure out their location and how to get back to the ranch without encountering any more hostiles. They drove off slowly, mindful of the fact that unknown gullies that could spring into their path.

It seemed that it was no longer safe to go into town since the mutants had been laying in wait for them and would be watching for them again. They marveled at the planning that had gone into the ambush and the intensity of it.

As they discussed this aloud, Sandra continued to review the shooting in her mind. She would never know if she had actually shot a fellow human, no matter how devolved. She realized it didn't matter morally whether she had or not. Her intent had been to shoot him, and that was what mattered. That was what she was going to have to live with and try to resolve within her belief system. Reality had set in, but she kept all this quiet and put on a cheery game face for Nate's benefit as they cautiously made their way cross-country.

*   *   *

"Watch your step right here," Zack instructed the small party of mutants and humans. "We've disguised the opening so that no one chancing upon it would recognize it for what it is." He looked at them, triumphantly.

The group looked around expectantly but could see nothing on the hillside that appeared out of place or unnatural. If anyone had asked, they would have sworn the dirt, rocks, and plants had not been disturbed since the hill first pushed out of the ground, instead of being a beehive of activity for the past few weeks. Even though they all knew the area where all the activity had taken place, they still weren't able to spot an opening.

With the added help of the newcomers, the pace of preparations increased dramatically. In short order, most of the systems for the cavern were in place. The main air vent and entryway was completed and Zack was proudly demonstrating it to the avian members who would have to use it. Holding up a remote control, he dramatically pushed a button. A concealed door opened out of the side of apparently impenetrable rock siding. The group buzzed with excitement.

Continuing his show, Zack said, "See how the door can be opened only enough for one of our avian friends to slip in? In case anyone is able to get through the first one, we added a second door of bars. This will prevent a pack of mutants from being able to come in at the same time. This vent is not only secure, but has the ability to withstand a direct missile strike. Watch what happens when I close it again."

The door closed, seamlessly, leaving no trace of where it had been.

Impatiently Reva spoke up, "Can we go into the cave now, Mr. Zack?" She and the other children had no interest in the finer points of the construction of the entry; they just wanted to finally get a look at the cavern everybody had told them about.

"Holly, you can have the honor of being the first to step across the threshold," Zack said, with a grandiose gesture of his hand towards the opening.

Bobbing her feathered head in acknowledgement, Holly hopped on her spindly legs to the portal, shepherding her twins and Sterling along with her. Carley, Sandra, and Rita followed her eagerly.

After everyone was in Zack closed the door behind them. They wound down the well-lighted path, feeling a strong current of air going with them. There was a steady but gradual decline to the cavern floor. The humans had spent many hours inside the cavern getting their respective areas set up, but it was the first time Holly and the children had seen it. They were awestruck at the immensity and the level of improvements that had been accomplished since the cavern was discovered.

"Oh look, Momma," Reva said, pointing to all the lights and buildings.

"And the water," Vera added.

Sterling squawked uneasily as Holly nodded in understanding. Birds were not comfortable with being so far underground. The twins tugged at Sterling and he followed them off to explore. Meanwhile, Zack led the adults to the command center.

"The topside door can be opened and controlled from here as well. I'm sure none of you noticed the cameras placed up there," he said smugly, pointing to the live-feed of the outside of the opening and the vicinity around it. Nate, who had helped install the electronic equipment, sat at the controls and showed the interested group which buttons to push to control the entryway.

"The vent also improved the air flow into the cave. I'm sure all of you noticed the slight breeze as you walked down," Zack said, resuming his lecture. The group nodded obediently. They all drifted to their areas of responsibility and went back to work.

Sandra had taken over the task of group librarian solely on her own initiative. Now that the trips to town were probably curtailed permanently, she could devote her time to downloading all the knowledge on the remaining internet sites that she could find. Onto flash drives and hard drives, she had downloaded Wikipedia, E books, and Virtual Earth, among many other websites. Who knew how long servers and satellites would continue to function. She was determined that she would save and preserve as much data as she could while there was still access to it and memory left to fill. She recognized what an excellent job Nate had done in setting up their communications console, with proprietary pride, as she settled in for more hours of downloading.

Rita headed to her well-equipped lab, glad now that her test subjects were readily accessible to the cavern lab, since the temporary ranch lab had essentially been dismantled to make this one. She continued to be frustrated in finding any way to stop or reverse the devolution, let alone impede it. As a scientist, she saw every closed door as additional information that narrowed her pursuit of an answer. She wasn't giving up by any means. A number of the newcomers had been drafted as lab techs, and that streamlined and reduced her workload of routine tasks, freeing her up to concentrate on devising new tests.

Carley took the time to show Holly around and get her acclimated. Calling the kids to her, Holly followed Carley into a tent that Sandra and Nate had acquired in their forays to town. It was where she, Sterling, and the twins would be sleeping.

Bouncing on her bed, Reva announced," This is comfortable. I'll take this one."

"Mine's closer to the door," Vera responded, plumping up the pillow on her chosen bed.

Holly gently moved Vera away from her choice and pointed her talons at a bed in the back of the tent. She had almost lost her ability to speak and the twins seemed to respond more to her gestures. She propped herself on the bed near the opening.

"I guess your Mom wants to be near the door to protect you," Carley interpreted.

"More like to keep us from sneaking out at night," Reva said, sourly. Vera nodded in agreement as she reluctantly switched beds.

Holly vigorously dipped her head at that, giving a weird chuckling sound.

Carley introduced them to the cavern kitchen, where Mama Perez was giving orders to many hands. She stopped long enough to offer refreshment to the newest cavern dwellers. "Would anybody like a drink of this delicious spring water?"

"Yes," the youngsters accepted, with alacrity, Holly and Carley taking their drinks too. Carley noted that Holly and Sterling would not be able to hold cups much longer as they struggled to wrap their finger stubs and talons around them. She had taken it on herself to see that the ever-changing needs of her friend and the children were met, while everybody else was busy with the cavern setup. She made a mental note to look into alternative drink containers.

"This is so exciting," Vera exclaimed, grabbing hold of Reva and Sterling and twirling them around, much to the consternation of the other kitchen workers.

Eva Perez, however, shook her head wisely. For now, let the children bask in the novelty of it all. Before long, it would wear off as they settled in for a long siege, not knowing if and when they would ever be able to go out again.

* * *

"Wake up Gabe! I think I hear someone moving on the deck," Marti urgently whispered to Gabe, giving him a hard nudge in the ribs with her elbow. She knew from experience how difficult it was to get Gabe to wake once he was deeply asleep.

"Huh?" Gabe loudly mumbled as he was startled awake.

"Shhh!" Marti hissed. "Listen. Can't you hear someone moving around?"

It's probably just Cori or Chaska going to use the head," Gabe grunted, burying his own head back into his pillows, ready to resume the tantalizing dream he had been so rudely and unnecessarily awakened from.

Marti wasn't having it. "Whoever is out there is being stealthy," she insisted, pulling Gabe's pillows out from under him.

Grumping, Gabe sat up and answered with annoyance. "I'm telling you that it is Cori or Chaska and whichever one is out there is trying to be quiet, not stealthy, so we aren't disturbed from our sleep. It sounds like an excellent idea to me. Give me back my pillows."

Marti and Gabe had sailed the young Peruvians back to their port in Costa Rica with the best of intentions to leave them there. The conditions just in the harbor area had so deteriorated from the mutants ravaging the docks that they all decided the best course would be to keep the newlyweds on board and take them back to Peru. Cori and Chaska had readily accepted this plan, enjoying the cruise and the company. They were eager to avoid the hassle of trying to figure out how to get back to Peru from Costa Rica on their own given the total chaos of the transportation system and infrastructure there.

Since no one was in a hurry they were leisurely heading down the coastline of South America. Having found themselves in the notoriously swift currents near the Galapagos Islands in a dense fog and light drizzle, where navigation was difficult in the best of times, they anchored in a cove of an uncharted uninhabited island for a good night's sleep, hoping the morrow would bring improved weather conditions and better travelling weather.

Gabe and Marti had the large cabin to the fore of the galley. Aft of the midline, there was another cabin below deck that was being used by Cori and Chaska. This arrangement gave both couples privacy, while allowing for social interaction during the day. The only drawback was that the main bathroom was off the galley, not too far from where Gabe and Marti were sleeping. Thus, it was not unreasonable for Gabe to suppose that one of guests was just making use of the facilities.

Marti shook her head, impatiently. After spending days with Cori and Chaska, she knew their habits. This did not sound to her like it could be either of them.

"I'm going to investigate. Someone is being downright sneaky. You stay in bed, old man, and let a real woman handle it." Throwing back the light sheet they had been sleeping under, she was on her feet before she had finished speaking, tying on a silky robe.

"I'm coming," Gabe muttered, finishing under his breath with something that sounded suspiciously like, "you ornery, obstinate woman."

Just at that moment, there was a loud bang, followed by a stifled cry. Abandoning caution, Marti and Gabe hurried out to the deck, brandishing hastily grabbed flashlights. Half expecting that Gabe had been right, and that it was just Cori or Chaska, Marti gasped as they caught a strange man in their beams. She pulled closer to Gabe, reflexively.

"Who are you?" Gabe demanded. "What are you doing boarding our boat in the middle of the night?"

Throwing his arm across his eyes that were being blinded in the glare, the stranger quickly answered in English, not knowing if he had guns trained on him or not. "I didn't know anybody was on this boat. I mean you no harm."

"So you just make it a habit of exploring unknown boats after dark?" Marti said, derisively.

"Please, my family and I have been stranded here for days," the tall, lanky man pleaded, gesturing to another boat that Gabe and Marti could now discern was tied up to theirs. Gabe directed his beam towards the other boat, while Marti kept hers trained on the intruder. Through the murky haze, it was still easy to see the silhouettes of a woman and three young children at the railing of the other boat, gazing fearfully at what was transpiring on the deck.

"Let's get some lights on, and then you can tell us all about it," Gabe suggested. Suiting action to words, he lit up the whole deck area. Hearing the commotion above, Cori and Chaska poked their heads out from below deck. "Come on out, Cori and Chaska, it appears that these folks have a story to tell, one you might be familiar with."

"Tell your family they can come over here," Marti told the man. "We might as well all get comfortable while we sort this all out. Anybody want something to drink?"

Not waiting for an answer, Marti hurried to the galley with Chaska following her. She pulled out a large pitcher of iced tea, gathering enough glasses for everyone. She didn't want to take time with drink orders and wasn't sure at this point that she wanted to share any of their diminishing store of wine with these newcomers, not that the children should be having any anyhow, and they all needed clear heads at the moment. Tea could wake them all just fine. Some bartender I've turned into, she thought wryly, bustling back to the deck.

Everyone had been preoccupied with getting the other family members safely onboard while Marti and Chaska were gone. Now everyone stood taking the others in awkwardly.

The dark wavy-haired man who wore glasses on his narrow, foxy face had his arm protectively around a delicate, pixie-ish woman, her face masked by the long black curtain of hair that hung in front of her face as she looked down at the children. She, in turn, was trying to hold the three children at once, a babe of indeterminate gender in her arms. One was a girl toddler; the other a boy of about five years of age. The children, all with short dark hair and emaciated frames, were clinging to her in a mixture of fear and shyness.

Marti's eyes softened at the sight of the youngsters. She secretly regretted never having children of her own, a thought that almost overwhelmed her. Brusquely, she said, "Here have a seat," motioning the mother to the comfortable deck chairs.

Hesitant to leave her protector, the mother sank into a seat gratefully, pulling her husband along to stand ill-at-ease next to her.

"I guess we'd better explain," the man said, speaking quietly as he patted the baby's head. "First let me ask, do you know about the mutants?"

"Yes, we are well-aware of the devastation that is occurring everywhere in the world," Gabe replied, certain he knew where this story was heading.

"We are from California and things are in complete turmoil there. I thought that I needed to get my family away from there and find a country to hide out in where the mutants had not taken over yet. I thought that South America might still be unaffected and I had some business contacts down here that could help us. I rented a charter boat, telling them we were going on a long cruise, though I intended that we would go ashore and never return. We should have been more cautious about the people who were manning the boat, but the agent who booked it for us seemed unaffected. In fact, the person who showed us to our cabin appeared to be normal. It wasn't until we were at sea that we found out that the other crew members were aquatic mutants."

"They abandoned the boat for the sea, smashing up all the controls before leaving," Cori interjected sympathetically.

"How did you know that?" the stranger asked, in astonishment.

"The same thing happened to us," Chaska responded, quietly, "when we were on our honeymoon." She did the usual blush that Gabe and Marti had become so used to seeing.

"Gabe and Marti rescued us," Cori added.

"We've been travelling round in my ship for a few months," Gabe explained. "It has become a common sight to find abandoned boats. Those aquatic mutants can't resist the instinctual urge to return to the sea. We were surprised to find a boat occupied when we came upon Cori and Chaska. Mind telling us your names?"

"I'm sorry, where are my manners? First I break in on you while you are sleeping, then I don't even introduce myself. I'm Avram Goldstein; this is my wife, Sun, and our three children: Andrew, Rachel, and baby Josef." Avram gestured to each of his family members in turn. Sun raised her head and nodded gravely, giving them all a first look at her exotic features and dark, dancing eyes. The children, getting braver by the minute, stared openly at their new surroundings, each smiling tentatively as their father said their names.

"As Cori said, we are Gabe and Marti," said Marti, continuing the introductions. "This is Cori's wife, Chaska."

Gabe, ignoring the introductions, was now staring fixedly at the newcomers. Something about them was nagging at him, because something did not seem quite right. It was like an itch he couldn't reach. He noticed that each of them, including the children , had fine dark hairs poking out from the necks of their shirts and around the sleeves and pant openings. There was a heaviness to their features that didn't look natural, even to the petite features of Sun. He turned to Avram, sternly. "I think there is something you aren't telling us." He stood up, aggressively. Marti was astounded.

Avram responded, meekly, "I see you have guessed our secret."

"You are mutants," Gabe accused, jabbing his finger at Avram. In disbelief, Marti, Cori and Chaska jumped to their feet and minutely examined the strangers with their eyes. "What is your real purpose in sneaking aboard my boat?" Gabe demanded.

"Everything happened just like we said," Avram said, hanging his head. The rest of the family looked dejectedly at their feet. "After we had been abandoned and were without food, we found a vitamin bottle in one of the cupboards in the galley. We thought that taking vitamins would sustain our strength longer, so we took them, even mashing one up for Joey. It wasn't until we started noticing small changes that we realized the mutants on the boat had hidden their supplements in vitamin bottles. We should have suspected something when we saw the bottle was already open. But, we were hungry. . . . You can't imagine how we felt when we found out that we are becoming the thing we were running from."

"You are going to have to immediately leave this boat," Gabe ordered. "We can't trust you now."

Sun, with the desperation of a mother, threw her head back and cried out. "My husband was just trying to find food for us. Can you at least give us some food for the children? They will die if they don't get some food."

Marti could not bear the thought of hungry children. Truth be told, neither could any of the others. Ignoring her own fears about the strangers, she walked over to Sun and took her hand. "Let's see what we can find in the galley that your children might like. You look like you and Avram could stand a bite as well." She and Chaska shepherded the little group into the kitchen as Gabe and Avram continued to face off.

"Sir, we mean you no harm. We are not violent," Avram said, peaceably, holding out his empty hands in supplication. "Could you at least take us to land where we can find our own way?"

Gabe was torn apart with uncertainty. It was obvious, now that he knew what to look for, that this family was developing ape-like characteristics. Everything he had read and heard led him to believe that ape-like mutants were totally unpredictable and vicious. As an old newspaperman, Gabe knew that the media sensationalized everything and that horrific news made it to the front pages. The good, heart-warming stories were rarely told. Maybe there were ape mutants that were not mindlessly brutal. After all, he knew about Holly and Jasmine, who were still good people. On the other hand, maybe these folks hadn't mutated enough to show their true nature yet. Would they become fierce and aggressive over time? Then again, there were the children, who were still children no matter what they were devolving into. Gabe shook his head in confusion and Cori looked to him for a decision.

"I'll tell you what," Gabe offered. "We have another cabin. I can let you have it for the rest of the night, if you let me lock you in. In the morning, we can see about the possibility of putting you ashore."

"Oh, yes. That is so kind of you," Avram effused. "I promise we will not be a problem. We are gentle, caring people, people of faith. There is not a mean bone in our bodies."

Not unkindly, Gabe said, "At least so far. Even you do not know the outcome of what all the changes will do to your bodies and minds from those pills changing your bodies."

"I know you are right, but I can't help believing that our true natures will dominate even though we are helpless to the devolutionary physical changes," Avram asserted with quiet dignity.

"I hope you are right," Gabe agreed, with Cori and Chaska nodding. "Let's get you some of that grub. You look like you're about ready to fall any minute, man." He led Avram in to join his family at the table. Secretly he still wondered since there was no mention of what became of the Captain.

188

*   *   *

"Where are all the people?" Marti asked rhetorically, since no one on board could know the answer any more than she could.

In the light of day, the uninvited guests looked less threatening and more like a woebegone little family in need of help. After a hearty breakfast, they had taken advantage of the change of weather and headed to one of the inhabited areas of the Galapagos Islands for fresh water, fuel, fruit, and other supplies, and to see about leaving the Goldsteins in a populated area; only to find it eerily deserted. They hunted through the once-thriving town, finding the all too familiar signs that even in this remote place, mutants had ravaged and wreaked havoc.

"Cori and I spotted some shops that have supplies untouched in them," Chaska reported. All had gathered back together after breaking into teams to explore the area.

Reading from a guide book, Marti parroted, "At last count there were 40,000 people living in these islands, and 97% of the land area is preserved as parkland, 95% of the original species found here still that remain as a result of protecting so much area. This was Charles Darwin's playground, where he wrote *Origin of the Species.*"

"Forget about that now. We can't stand on ceremony and hope that the inhabitants come back. We need to stock up," Gabe declared impatiently. "Every man for himself, I mean, every person for... whatever," he corrected quickly after a blazing look from Marti. She tossed her head at his interruption and clumsy attempt at rewording. "Lead us to those shops you found, Cori and Chaska."

They all trooped along, obediently and grabbed as many goods as they were able to carry and take back to the boat. Though no one said anything, on everyone's mind was the problem of what to do now about the family they had acquired the night before. Could they leave them to fend for themselves in this desolate town, all alone with three young children to care for? Or, should they bring them along, not knowing if they would turn on them suddenly as they devolved? (They might even be viewed as potential meals by them. After all, some apes are meat-eaters.)

Once the boat was stocked with everything it could hold, the group gravitated to the beach, putting off any immediate decision on what they should do next. Without discussion, everybody started gathering firewood to make a campfire as the children cavorted in the ankle deep surf. Before long, a cheery fire was going and everyone felt more relaxed lounging around it.

Breaking the long silence, Marti suddenly spoke up. "I vote we hang out here a few days while we try to figure out what to do next. There is plenty of water and food here. We have no place we have to be immediately. There are plenty of interesting animals and plants to look at, too. Let's take a break for a few days."

"We are in no hurry to get to Peru," Cori said. "From what we have seen everywhere we have gone, Lima is probably now a disaster area too. It will be difficult and dangerous for us to make the trip into the mountains. I too vote to stay here for a few days. What do you say, Chaska?"

"This is an interesting place to investigate, and though I am worried about our families, I feel they will be safe here, tucked away from civilization. I also am not eager to run into anymore trouble. Who can be trusted?" Chaska responded, thoughtfully.

Clearing his throat, Avram spoke up, hesitantly. "I know you are all still trying to make up your minds about us, and if you feel you must leave us here, there is plenty of food and water to sustain us for a long time. However, I would greatly like you to stay with us a few days, so that you can see we are just people like yourselves, even though we will be going through horrific changes."

"Speaking selfishly, I feel we need your support to see us through the process we face, especially with the children," Sun put in, looking at Rachel who had curled up in Marti's lap for a nap with the unconscious trust of a child. Marti looked down at the little girl, hugging her gently, a fierce wave of protectiveness sweeping over her.

Everybody looked to Gabe for his two cents and he didn't disappoint. "I don't see any harm in staying on the islands for a few days, but I'm not comfortable with the idea of staying in town. We have no idea if any of the natives will return, and if they do, whether they will be friend or foe. I would suggest we move around the island to a sheltered cove in the parkland. We will be close enough to here if we find we need anything else, but not be sitting ducks, or should I say sleeping ducks, as we were last night." He raised an eyebrow at Avram, but smiled to take the sting out of his words. Nevertheless, the lesson they had learned the night before had hit home. They all readily agreed with Gabe's amendment to the plan. Gathering up weary little ones, they put out the fire and returned to the sailboat.

*　*　*

"Look at the birdie's red shoes, Daddy," Rachel exclaimed, pointing to a large bird reminiscent of a penguin perched on a rock nearby.

"Those aren't shoes; those are its feet," Andy scoffed. Then he looked anxiously at his father for affirmation.

"Birdie," parroted Joey, reaching out with his hands towards the bird, fortunately unable as yet to be a serious threat to it.

"That is called a Red-footed Booby," Marti recited. Acting as tour guide, Marti religiously carried her guide book and read snippets of information to the group about the flora and fauna they came across as they investigated the island. They had been amazed at the abundance of wildlife as they watched fur seals and sea lions along the shore, with whales out in the sea so near they felt they could swim with them. There were sea turtles coming up onto the beach to build nests and lay their eggs. Marti cautioned the young and old alike not to disturb them. Andy was especially fascinated by the iguanas, so much so, that his parents had to keep an eye on him to prevent him from straying away from the group to get up close and personal with one.

"I hear something rooting in those tall grasses," Sun exclaimed, fearfully. She pointed at a section just off the trail they were following. This nature walk was fine and dandy, but she had been a city dweller her whole life and did not feel comfortable with the great outdoors. No sooner were the words out of her mouth, than a large pink pig lumbered across their path. Startled by his mother tensing up, more than from the pig itself, Joey howled.

"Piggie," squealed Rachel, clapping her hands in delight.

"Who cares about an old pig," Andy said, trying for nonchalance and failing miserably. It was easy to see he was just as thrilled by the pig as Rachel was.

"Pigs are not indigenous to the islands," Marti informed them, reading again from her book. "In fact, they are considered to be harmful to the native animals. For one thing, they destroy turtle nests! The islanders were encouraged to shoot them to get rid of them."

"Looks like that old sow was too wily for them," Gabe joked.

"We have many pigs in our homeland," Chaska said, sternly. "We do not consider them a nuisance."

"Kill piggy," Rachel exclaimed, her eyes as big as saucers. Then she inexplicably began to cry. Having just calmed Joey down, Sun turned her attention to Rachel. Marti held her arms out for the baby, unthinkingly.

"We are not going to kill this piggy, Honey," Marti said, soothingly, as Rachel's sobs diminished to sniffs under her mother's ministrations.

Looking for a way to change the conversation and distract the kids, Gabe said, "Hey, look, a lemon tree. We can have fresh lemons." He pulled one off, puckering his lips up comically for the benefit of the youngsters, who laughed.

"They are not indigenous to the islands either," Marti intoned.

"I don't see how they can be doing any harm," Gabe asserted, handing a lemon to each of his admiring young audience. He quickly put his hand over Marti's mouth as she started to explain why the lemon trees should go. She gave him a playful bite, kindly wrapping her arm around his as they continued their hike down the path.

* * *

The time to make a decision had arrived. Their time in the park had been idyllic, but everybody realized it was time to discuss what their options were and make some choices. It had become their custom to cook their evening meal over a campfire on the beach, and by unspoken consensus, they knew this was when they would have their serious talk. The children were played out and lay on blankets on the sand, drifting peacefully into dreamland as the adults settled down to business.

"I think it's time to figure out when we want to leave this island, and where we want to go next," Gabe said, starting things off. "I'm sure everybody has their own ideas on what they would like to do, and it may be that we can each just do our own thing."

"I suppose we have to go home to Peru," Cori said, reluctantly. It had been an adventure to be away from home. Being confined to their small village and afraid of contact with the outside world did not sound attractive to him. He knew he would be subject to the dictates of his elders. It seemed restraining to a young man who had travelled and had begun to feel his oats, and who had started his own family. He gazed fondly at Chaska.

"It is our duty to go home and help keep the families safe," Chaska agreed, without enthusiasm. She had enjoyed having Cori all to herself and knew they would have to fall into traditional patterns if they went home, a role that would be difficult for a woman who had broadened her horizons and been exposed to the equality women like Marti and Sun had.

"I don't know if you have arrived at any decision about us?" Avram ventured. "If we have any say in what happens to us, we would like to stay with the rest of you. We do not want to be isolated by ourselves on a deserted island."

"How would we protect our children from dangerous wild animals or from mutants? What if they get sick?" Sun put in, focusing her plea on the maternal instincts of the other women, both of whom looked downward, not meeting her eyes.

"Maybe you could come to Peru, too," Cori suggested, half-heartedly. "Maybe you could find others like you in Lima."

"You can't lump us together with every ape-like mutant since each of us is an individual. Surely you have seen by now that we have no harmful intent. We are just people trying to puzzle our way through this dangerous world just like you," Avram said, fervently. "What else can we do to prove ourselves to you?"

"I believe you," said Chaska. "You can come to our mountaintop with us. I know my people will accept you."

Cori looked belligerent, but kept his tongue.

"I've got another idea," Marti spoke up. Spreading her arms to encompass everyone, she urged, "Why don't we just stay here together? We have supplies a short sail away. There is plenty of fresh water and fruit. We know and like one another. I think we would be good for each other. What better way is there to ride out the storm that is lashing the world right now?"

The others looked at each other warily. Cori and Chaska communicated silently with each other, both reading each other's distaste for returning to Peru. The Goldsteins felt like Heaven had opened up and granted them their deepest wishes. Gabe, however, was not as easily won over.

"We've managed to find supplies everywhere we've travelled. What's to say that some of the natives here haven't gone mutant and will find us and attack us in our sleep? I'm not saying it is a bad idea," he added hastily, seeing the mutiny building in Marti's eyes. "We need to think about this a bit. I say we sleep on it over night. Meanwhile, we will contact our friends in Argentina and find out what they know about global conditions, particularly the conditions in Peru. With the breakdown in worldwide communication, all of us are batting in the dark."

There was unanimous agreement to table the decision until the morning. They all needed time to mull over Marti's idea, and fact-finding would be useful. Rounding up the drowsy lumps of children, they turned towards their cabins, with Gabe carefully locking in the Goldsteins.

* * *

"We are going to live in the cave," Nate finished after telling the tale of finding the cavern and what had led up to their decision to retreat to it. Marti and Gabe and the others on the boat were grouped around the telephone. After a restless night on the boat, the small group had had difficulty raising their friends in Patagonia.

Sandra added, "Zack has been in intermittent communication with Homeland Security. Rita is in contact with other scientists around the world who are working on the problem of devolution. There does not seem to be a safe place anywhere in the world. I think you are right to hole up for awhile rather than take a chance of finding ports that are secure and harmless."

The group was silent for a moment as they reviewed all the information they had heard. Especially troubling was the tale Rinaldo had told them of his worker being pulled into the sea by aquatic mutants, never to be seen again. The dangers of being at sea took on a whole new aspect. They were always wary of the peccadilloes of Mother Nature, but they had never considered that mutants could rise out of the waters to attack them. Gabe flashed back to the Navel officer returning from the Marshall Islands and the story of Harland's Dad. The issue of mutants attacking brought them squarely back to their quandary of unexpected guests.

Gabe cleared his throat, glancing at the Goldsteins. He continued, determinedly. "We have a family of mutants here who are developing ape-like characteristics. Since they seem friendly enough, do you think we can trust them?"

"Well, you know that we have mutants as friends of ours who haven't developed any violent tendencies. I truly think that individual personalities factor into how people devolve," Rita answered, authoritatively. "However, we have never met these people. Therefore, we can't make that decision for you. You're just going to have to trust your own instincts on that one."

Though he remained quiet, Avram stuck his chin defiantly in the air. It was not easy to be discussed by others as if they were not there, as if they were objects to be shunted around based on others' opinions. Sun put a restraining hand on his arm, shaking her head imperceptibly.

After a few other comments, Gabe signed off. Turning to the group he said, "I think it is time for a vote. I suggest we vote by secret ballot so everyone feels comfortable in voting his or her own mind.

To start with, let's make it simple. The vote is YES we all stay put here on the island, or NO we don't want to stay on the island. If there is a NO vote, we will decide from there what will happen next."

Personally, Marti thought the whole vote idea was silly. Obviously, if she and Gabe wanted to leave, it was their boat to go. Thus, they had the deciding vote, no matter how anyone else voted. However, she kept her own counsel and played along. If they were going to live together on the island, the others needed to feel they had an equal say in being there. She marked her ballot and threw it in the basket, passing the basket on to Chaska. The basket made the rounds, returning to Gabe, who methodically tabulated the votes.

"It appears unanimous; everyone wants to stay on the island," he announced. There was a huge sigh of relief from Avram and Sun, who had tensely been holding their breaths. They felt they had the most at stake in the vote and saw the vote as a tacit acceptance of them by the group. There were tears in Sun's eyes as she turned to embrace Marti. In truth, everybody was in a celebratory mood. Although they all knew the world was in a desperate plight and that their island sojourn was not going to be a visit to paradise, for a moment they allowed themselves to bask in the fellowship of goodwill. The children, sensing the lightened mood, as children always do, ran around laughing and playing up to the adults, who momentarily shed their adulthood and played like children themselves for a while.

Whether from age or because he had been a long-time crusty old bachelor and a hard-headed reporter, Gabe came back to earth first. Reluctantly, he called everyone back to serious discussion. It was decided that he and Marti would take the boat and patrol the coast and look for others on the island in need of the safety of numbers and would thus want to join their band. They would also ferry supplies back and forth from the deserted town. Having located a fresh-water spring during their explorations, it was decided that the rest of the group would begin to build a secure compound near it.

Nobody addressed the continued uncertainty of living with their mutant members. For now, there was an unspoken truce with a wait and see attitude. The Goldsteins were aware that every action of theirs would be scrutinized minutely to determine whether they were going rogue or not. It made for an uncomfortable situation for everyone.

Clearing his throat, Avram said simply, "Thank you. I don't know how else to say it, except to say thank you for giving us a chance. We won't let you down."

That night, Gabe did not lock them in their cabin, though he made sure his gun was close at hand as he went to sleep.

*   *   *

The she-dragon returns, Erin Blaine thought to herself as Jaime Whiteman tromped into the room. I wonder what new orders she has for us this time.

"I have just come from a meeting with Collier and the other top brass," Jaime announced, unnecessarily, as both Erin and Brad knew where she had been. Did she just say "top brass", Erin marveled, sardonically. Her wit was improving the more tired she got. Had she been home at all in the past week, or make that, month?

"We are implementing Phase One of Mission IKE," Jaime continued, eyeing Erin suspiciously. There was an amused glint in Erin's eye that didn't fit with the severity of the situation. Must just be the way the light was hitting her glasses, Jaime surmised, not wanting to put any effort into figuring it out beyond that. "It was decided that we need to secure our top people for their own safety."

What she really means is that it is too late to stop the chaos in this country; Erin interpreted to herself, studiously keeping her face neutral. She caught a suspicious glance Jaime sent her way.

Mission Ike was originally devised during the Eisenhower administration, in the midst of the Cold War. The federal government built large underground facilities designed to protect certain government and private sector personnel in case of a nuclear attack. Throughout the years, the facilities were expanded and further hardened to withstand stronger blasts. Ike had been slowly expanded to include safe places all around the country. The HSA was in charge of maintaining the list of people to be safely whisked away to these facilities.

Brad Cho looked up, expectantly, anticipating what was coming next.

"You two are to spearhead getting the top officials and research scientists transported to the secure facilities around the country," Jaime explained. The minute she had said to implement Phase One of Mission Ike, Brad and Erin already knew what they were to do.

Looking down at the culled list, Erin knew that the task had sadly diminished from what it would have previously entailed. The results of all the testing for mutants had cut the list to only a quarter of its original size. Unlike the friends in Patagonia and the small group with Gabe and Marti in the Galapagos, the government had decided that all mutants were alike. The "top brass" had decided in their all-knowing wisdom that no mutants were to be trusted and would be summarily excluded, no matter how much knowledge and experience would be lost by doing that. Erin shook her head and swiveled towards her com link. Hers was not to reason why, hers was but to do, or die, Erin quietly thought to herself. She pushed the button and got static. Trying again, she got through and began the job of segregation – uh, make that protection.

*   *   *

"The President of the United States is going to be live on TV in ten minutes," Nate broadcast over the PA system that had been set up in the cavern. Everybody, including those who couldn't speak a word of English, dropped what they were doing and hurried over to the communications sector to watch the speech. There was good-natured jostling for the best seat. Nate wondered if he should serve popcorn for the show. When the network anchorman came on the screen, a hush fell over the crowd, as even the children sensed that something important was happening.

"In just a minute, the President of the United States will be talking live to all the people of the world from the Oval Office," the anchorman intoned portentously. "This message will be heard on every channel and station in every nation in a show of unity and solidarity during this time of chaos." He listened solemnly to his earpiece, and then added, "I've just received word that the President is now entering the Oval Office. We go there now, live."

"My fellow Americans and citizens of the world, I come to you this evening during this time of global crisis to let you know that our government has everything under control. We have planned for every contingency, and at this moment, action is underway to restore order to our great nation and to all the nations of the world." Turning away as the President droned on, Zack whispered to his friends who were sitting together. "I got word from Jaime that they have already implemented Phase One of Mission Ike. The President is sitting safely in an underground bunker tricked out to look like the Oval Office."

"I remember everyone thinking that Osama Bin Laden was trapped in some underground cave, unable to show his face for fear he might be killed or captured," Sandra quipped.

The group chuckled quietly. Then everyone went silent, realizing that they, too, were sitting underground, hoping their cave would remain safe.

CHAPTER SEVEN

The War Begins

The honeymoon was over. At first there was harmony and good-will as the rescued groups helped establish the underground cave. All felt their lives were in danger, which gave them a united purpose. The rescued ones felt grateful for the hospitality and those who extended their hospitality felt magnanimous. With a united mindset, supplies were swum in through the underground tunnel, and brought in through the narrow passage built to accommodate the mutant members of the group. Privacy tents were pitched, making the cave reasonably comfortable for all.

On hearing about Project Ike, the group speeded up the process. The wonder of living there lasted for a couple of weeks until the new daily routine kicked in.

The two men hit the ground exchanging punches, neither achieving dominance over the other. A large group of people gathered around, some cheering on one, some cheering on the other. The fighters provided excitement, a real break from the monotony, until one of the contenders started spouting blood. Then Zack and Nate rushed in.

"What's going on here?" Nate asked, doing his best to hold onto one of the fighters who was still struggling to get at the other man while Zack held the other fighter.

Suddenly, Rita entered, out of breath from running. "Javier, what's going on?"

Javier, whom Zack was holding onto, shook Zack off and faced Rita with all the dignity he could muster. Javier dabbed at his bleeding nose then gingerly felt it to see if it was broken. "Senorita, you know I have been your father's overseer for many years. I was telling this worthless hombre that he had to take his turn emptying the self-composting toilet his family uses."

Rinaldo Perez, with his interest in having an environmentally friendly estate, had put self-composting toilets out in the vineyards for the workers. Nate had followed this practice, moving the toilets to the cavern. While the practice did provide rich material for use on the fledgling underground garden, it still had to be emptied. Javier, as long-time vineyard boss was accustomed to assigning this task fairly among his workers.

Paolo, the other fighter, and one who had been rescued by Javier, protested loudly. He had tried to break free from Nate, but Nate's strength kept him secure. "Who gave you the right to tell me what to do?" he said, practically spitting on Javier.

"Senor Rinaldo put me in charge," Javier said, smugly.

"Is it true, Papa that you told Javier he was in charge of all the workers?" Rita asked. She turned to her father, who appeared after hearing the commotion.

Rinaldo stiffened his resolve. "Since he was the boss in the vineyards, he should continue in that role."

"Meaning no disrespect, sir," Zack began, aware that Rita was hanging on his every word, "we are not on your estate. In fact, we are technically on Nate's estate, which would put him in charge until we all agree on some other form of governance."

Nate started at this. In no way did he want to oversee all the workers and others with everyday jobs. Give him his com center and the occasional forays into town with Sandra, and he'd be satisfied.

"Excuse me, but I thought I was in charge of the medical department, including sanitation," Rita replied sweetly.

"Actually, Sandra and Carley are running the garden, so the distribution of composed material probably defaults to them," Nate suggested almost apologetically.

"I think this whole place should fall under the purview of the United States government," Zack said a bit pompously, immediately regretting that comment. Everybody started to protest at once, and no one could be heard over the din.

At that, Paolo shook himself loose from Nate. "No one is telling me and my family what we have to do, especially not that hombre," he said with finality, jabbing a finger at Javier. Before anyone could grab him to prevent another fight, he spit at the ground and walked off to his tent.

"It looks like we have a serious problem here that needs to be decided," said Sandra, calmly. "I suggest we schedule a meeting soon."

* * *

That evening, the central campfire where everyone gathered for convivial get-togethers did not have a cozy feeling, as tensions ran high. Zack began the evening with a little speech about how the United States was sponsoring the crucial research that Rita Perez was doing to try to save the world as she coordinated similar efforts around the globe. Zack reiterated what the President had said about the government was working on dealing with the world's chaos and how their small band should be a part of that effort, though under the auspices of the United States. "This is a time of war," Zack continued. "The United States is under martial law, and we should also be. If we are attacked, we need a clear line of command. As the senior representative of the United States, the burden of leadership falls on me."

Pedro, Rita's brother, was angry. "This is Argentina, not the United States of America. We will not kowtow to the U.S.!" Dozens of people spontaneously sprang to their feet, agreeing with him.

After the ongoing cheers for Pedro quieted down, Sandra spoke. "With respect to the United States government, of whom I am a citizen, I agree with Pedro. We have to make our own way in this place; and as you can see from the reaction to what you said, Zack, most people do not agree with you. This needs to be a group decision, for us to live together peaceably."

Muttering "tree-hugger" under his breath so no one could hear him, Zack nodded curtly, as if he was giving permission to people to speak.

Speaking up, Rita said, "I thought things were working out well with each of us taking an area of responsibility. I obviously am in charge of the research, and have taken on with my mother," she winked at Eva, "responsibility for the medical care and health issues that include sanitation. Sandra has been doing an excellent job of organization, overseeing the setup of the camp and garden, seeing to the storage of the world's knowledge. Nate is handling the communications set-up with the world with Zack's assistance, and you, Zack, are in charge of defense." She trailed off, looking at the eighty people gathered in the cave, suddenly aware that she was assigning all the authority to the group of friends, while leaving out the majority of the people now in the cavern.

"As I said earlier," Javier spoke up, trying hard to look dignified with his bandaged nose, "for centuries we have lived with the Senor, and his family before him, in charge of the estate. We have all known our place and been happy to have the Senor over us. He has treated all with fairness and kindness, allowing us to depend on him. I say, let's honor the old ways!"

Rinaldo bowed his head to his good friend. He was about to speak when Paolo butted in, "Most of us do not come from the Perez Estate. The number from that hacienda is small compared to the number of people living here. Most of us do not want to be under the rule of Senor Perez. I purposely have lived as a free man for my entire life, so I don't intend to start now having someone tell me what to do." Many of the rescued folks started nodding their heads, agreeing with him.

"This is not my estate, old friend," Rinaldo said to Javier. "I was out of place to give orders. As Zack said before, we are actually on Nate's property, and he should have a say in what we do."

Again, Nate looked uncomfortable in being thrust into this position, but clearing his throat he said, "It sounds to me like the bigger issue we are discussing is what form of government we want in this cave." Many nodded their heads at this summation. "Zack is in favor of martial law because of the rapid response that is possible in times of war. Some of you sound like you want a beneficent ruler, while others sound like they don't want anyone to be in charge, but with all having an equal say in decisions. That sounds like a democracy to me, and that is what I am in favor of."

"Are you saying there should be no leadership?" Zack asked incredulously, eyeing the large number of peasants that had been gathered. "That will be sheer chaos. Nothing will get done if no one has responsibility for getting it done. Every team has a leader. There has to be organization."

"I don't think Nate means that no one should have any responsibility," Sandra retorted, shaking her blond locks. "He means more of a one for all and all for one attitude, all working together for the common good."

"Oh, great; now we're going to be communists," Zack sneered.

"I do think that food and medical attention need to be equally available to everyone," said Rita sincerely.

Figuring he had lost Rita's support by this point, Zack continued with his attack, "So you are saying that we should all share equally, even when guys like Paolo don't kick in their fair share of work?"

Indignantly, Paolo jumped to his feet, his wife trying to hold him down. "I never said I wouldn't work," said Paolo. "I've been swimming in supplies almost as much as Jasmine. I just don't want other people ordering me around. I have a right to take care of my family any way I see fit." His macho stance may have even worked if his wife hadn't dragged him down.

Nate gave Paolo the strong stare. "I'm not saying that anyone here doesn't intend to pull their fair weight, but those who don't, shouldn't get the caviar and champagne."

Ultimately, his words were translated to everyone's satisfaction, though some had never previously heard of caviar and champagne. When it was explained to them, some laugh heartedly, easing the tension in the camp. Nate was quite pleased with his wit and the admiring smile he got from Sandra. Of course, there was no caviar and champagne to share at all. But, everyone got the meaning, and by the nods, it seemed that all were in agreement that everyone needed to continue to work for their keep, as they had been doing to this point.

"I think we need to put the matter of a desired form of government to a vote," Sandra said.

And that is what they did. It was voted that they would have an egalitarian society with everyone expected to do their fair share. No one would be denied basic needs, but when the caviar and champagne appeared, the slackers would not be invited for the feast. They all knew that this was the beginning stage of agreeing together on their form of rule and division of labor and goods. It would be discussed and debated many times as they further refined what they meant by equality for all. But, they had made a good start, and most went off to bed content.

Zack, not so easily mollified, gathered his soldiers around him. He knew defense could not and would not wait for votes and debates when the attacks came.

Finally, Javier spoke, announcing his words to an empty campsite, "Someone still has to empty the pot."

* * *

"Nate, I think I hear something," Sandra whispered, pointing Nate and the others to her side near an outbuilding.

"From where?" asked Nate.

"From the woods," Sandra answered.

"Stay here with the others, while I take a look," Nate whispered.

Sandra threw her head wearily, hoping not to have this argument again. Sure, Sandra had been hesitant about using a gun to start with, but she had also proven she would shoot now, and brains still counted for something. Ignoring Nate, she started towards the woods. Nate had no choice but to follow.

While it was deemed too dangerous to make more forays into town, Sandra and Nate still continued to make trips to locate anyone else that might need rescuing. Sandra particularly was haunted by the idea of isolated families fighting off mutants, trying to survive alone. True, their cave was getting full, but they had room for a few more families, and Sandra was determined to find them if they were out there. It wasn't easy to find people, because they were hiding out, no longer living in abandoned houses, they were taking to the woods, and in many cases reduced to living like animals. It was tedious and harrowing work to locate them, and then, even harder to persuade them to come with complete strangers to safety.

Such was the case now. They were standing near a storage shed on what looked to be a previously well-maintained farm. After careful reconnaissance, on the lookout for mutants that might have established residence in the deserted farm, the group had determined that while the place had been ransacked of everything useful, there were no mutants in residence. They were about to call it quits for this trip and take the couple of families, that included children, back to the cave, when they were stopped.

Before Sandra was halfway to the edge of the woods, a large blond-haired man with a ruddy complexion, holding a shotgun, stepped out and pointed the gun at Nate and Sandra. Nate immediately drew his weapon, holding it easily. This was not the first time they had to overcome initial hostility.

"Do you speak English? We come to help," Sandra said quickly, gesturing Javier up to her side. Javier was the natural choice to lead the search and rescue team, since he had headed up the original group of estate workers who had gone out looking for unaffected people. He knew the areas they had covered already, knew the places they hadn't been, and knew the terrain better than Sandra and Nate could ever hope to. It was also thought wise to get him away from Paolo and let that situation have some time to cool down.

Javier repeated what Sandra had said in Spanish. "Who are you?" the burly man asked in English, never lowering his gun. "What are you doing here?"

"We come from the Perez Estate," Sandra said, citing the most well-known place that the man might know. "We have gathered a group of people together in a large cavern for safety from the mutants. Those are the ones who have taken the pills, you know?"

"I don't know anything about pills," said the man, shaking his head as he lowered his gun a fraction. "The creatures that have raided our farm must be what you are calling mutants. They had the form of men, but they also had features of animals. My family and I tried to reach town, but all communications have been cut off, and the creatures were blocking the roads. We fled to the woods and have been living there for weeks. Though we are able to live off the land with hunting and gathering, the winter is coming and I have been despairing of how to take care of my family. We have young children . . ." he trailed off, his exhaustion from the life they had been living, and the worry for his family showing plainly in the lines on his face.

"Let us help you," Sandra said simply, holding out her hand. "My name is Sandra. This is Nate and Javier, the foreman from the Perez Estate."

Raising the shotgun again, the man said suspiciously, "I heard that the Perez Estate was overrun with these half-men."

"That is true," Nate put in, "but I own a ranch up in the mountains, and we discovered a huge cavern that was only accessible underwater. We've been setting it up for months now and have about 80 people safely living there. We have everything your family needs: food, water, medicine, shelter from the elements. And we are able to maintain communication, such as it is, with others like us around the world. You are welcome to join us."

Switching his shotgun to his left hand and setting the stock on the ground, the man held out his hand. He said, "I am Horst Schenck. I have been praying for someone like you to come." After shaking hands with the three from the group, he turned and bellowed, "Liesel, bring the family out!"

In addition to his blond wife, Liesel, four equally blond children popped out from the trees, followed slowly by a woman who was probably the grandmother of the brood, leading an ancient feeble man. Sandra and Nate exchanged glances. They were certainly adding to the number of children that Holly's kids could play with, but they didn't have any others quite as old as this man appeared to be, an octogenarian at least. Medicinal care flitted through their minds, but was immediately suppressed in getting the introductions made as the other families they had found surged out from behind the storage shed to meet the Schencks as well.

Pointing to the elderly gentleman first, Horst began the introductions of his family, "This is my grandfather, Gebhard Schenck. And this is my mother, Sonje, my wife Liesel, and my four children, Christiane, who is twelve, Dieter, who is nine, Anika, who is six, and Amelie, who is two." The adults and children politely shook hands with everybody as Javier started the introductions of the other two families they had found: the Alvarez' with their two children and the Flores' with their six."

Antsy with all the time spent getting everybody acquainted, Nate said, "We've got to get a move on before any of the mutants return."

"They haven't been to the farm in days," said Horst. "After they killed all the animals and raided everything, they all left. I was tempted to take the family back to the house, but who knows when the mutants might return. Those flying men are scary—"

As if saying the words were an omen of bad luck, a squad of avian mutants swooped overhead.

As Nate, Javier and Horst raised their guns to fire, Sandra shepherded the families quickly to cover. Nate and Javier managed to get off a few shots, slightly wounding two of them as they flew off.

"I can't believe they can fly now," Nate said, his eyes widening in disbelief.

"Well, you know that Sterling has been trying to—" Sandra started, then realized what she was saying; and shut up, though the damage was done.

"Do you know these flying men?" Horst asked, sharply, his original suspicions returning as he herded his family into a tight group.

Giving Sandra a look that said "someone has a big mouth," Nate quickly explained. "We have five mutants living with us in the cavern, three of whom are children. They are all friends of ours who took the pills without knowing what would happen to them. They are trying to help our research scientist, Senor Perez's daughter, Rita, to find a cure for the mutations."

"We know nothing of pills. But, we do know that these mutants are dangerous," Horst declared. "I will not subject my family to them."

"These are peaceful people, just as Nate said: two women, and three young children," Sandra said. "We have been studying the effects of this mutation from the beginning. In fact, we know the first person who was affected. Our research tells us that not all mutants become violent. They take on characteristics of the animals they mutate to, but somehow their basic personality comes into play. Some mutants are aggressive while many are passive and loving, like the ones with us in the cave. Why don't you come see for yourself? You can always leave again if you feel the cave is unsafe."

It was a hard decision for the Schenck family since they were surrounded by the remains of their beloved farm. It was so easy to be seduced by the idea that if they stayed close to the farm, then maybe they could find a way to return to it. Yet, thinking of the incident they had just experienced, and the frailty of the grandfather, the decision to try the cave seemed inevitable.

"We will come with you and see this cave you talk about," Horst said reluctantly after getting a nod from his wife, mother and grandfather. The kids jumped around excitedly. "But if we do not like it, we will leave."

"That sounds fair to me," Nate said. "Let's get a move on it."

Sandra was thoughtful as she followed at the rear. Now that there were flying mutants, it was no longer as safe to venture out of the cave. In fact, it could become impossible to safely leave the cave. But something else bothered her. They were leaving the option open to the Schencks to leave the cave. Did that mean that everyone was free to leave? Suppose some did leave? Could they be trusted to keep the location of the cave a secret once they left? Who could tell for sure what any of them would do? Was their bunker as secure as they thought? Should they refuse to let anyone leave? And how, would they even begin to enforce that in the free society they had voted for? Deeply troubled, she knew she would have to discuss these new concerns with the inner circle. She didn't want to borrow trouble in advance, but there was no sense of shutting the barn door once the horse was let out either. Squaring her shoulders, she quickened her pace and resolutely set her feet to the path.

* * *

Marti looked around to see if anyone was on the boat with her. Once it appeared that the coast was clear and the others were off exploring for resources to start building the compound, she relaxed. "Oh, hi Nate, can I speak to Rita?" said Marti, speaking quietly to the view screen. When Rita came into view Marti rushed into her main concern. "Rita, I don't know what to do about medication for Gabe. He has been taking a cholesterol medication, and meds for high blood pressure that were given to him in Barbados. He's about out of them and I don't know what to do. He thinks I don't know about it, but I think he is secretly having chest pains and may have had a minor heart attack if there is such a thing. I'm so worried about him!"

"I don't know what to tell you," said Rita. "We all face the same problems here. We loaded up on all the medications that we could scrounge from the pharmacies that were deserted in town, but they'll eventually run out. We have elderly people here, even an octogenarian that just came into the camp. I'm not a medical doctor, either, though I did study Pre-Med before switching to genetics, and of course, I know a lot about biology, but I shouldn't be prescribing medicine for anyone."

"We raided the pharmacy here, too," Marti admitted, glancing over her shoulder to make sure Gabe wasn't nearby. "Some of the medications say they are for cholesterol and high blood pressure, but they sure are different from the ones Gabe is taking. Is it even okay to use those? I'm just an old bartender. All I know how to do is mix drinks, not medicines." She chuckled at her own little joke.

"Calm down, Marti. We'll just have to do the best we can with what we have," Rita soothed her, though not even convincing herself. "When Gabe's meds run out you will have to put him on other meds. Sandra has downloaded tons of medical data, and we will help you with dosages."

"What happens when all of them run out?" Marti wailed. "I've got two young couples and three children here. One of the families is mutating, too! I feel responsible for all of them; and I haven't a clue how to take care of medical emergencies or anything else that might arise." She brushed at the tears that had dripped down her face. "What if Gabe has a serious heart attack?"

"We're all afraid," Rita answered quietly, her heart wrenching that Marti had such a small crew of people with such limited resources, though her own situation was not much better. While she had more people with more skills, and probably lived in a more secure location, with more people there were also increased medical problems, accidents, and fights, remembering Paolo and Javier's dust up. Obviously, that could have gotten much uglier. "Everybody here is scared, too. Just think of the old clichés, like 'take one day at a time' and 'plan for tomorrow but live for today.' Regardless, that won't change the fact that we are all facing an unknown world and have no idea how long we will have to live this way. I wish you were closer to us."

"Oh, so do I. That's the hardest part, feeling so alone and overwhelmed while dealing with all of this. Are you coming up with any answers to the devolution?" Marti responded longingly.

"I wish I could tell you I have," Rita said. "However, I am in touch with the other facilities that are working on similar problems. All of us are coordinating with what we are working on, so there aren't any research duplications. That way, we can brainstorm in ways that lead to new approaches to research. It gives me hope with so many brilliant minds working together. I can't tell you when, but I can tell you that we will figure this out. Our little group of mutants is so cooperative with everything I want to try on them. I think they are saints!"

"Hey, Marti, are you in here?"

"Please Rita, don't let Gabe know I was talking about him," Marti said hurriedly, then called out, "I'm down here Gabe, talking to Rita! I was just asking how the research and everything else is going." She put her face up for a kiss, then casually turned back to the viewing screen and said, "Could we speak to Holly? I haven't had a chance to chat with her in ages?"

"Yeah, I really miss Holly, Jasmine, and the kids, too," Gabe said, sitting down next to Marti and snuggling close so he could fit into the view screen.

Rita had a trapped look and didn't answer them right away. She looked everywhere but at them in the screen. She sighed, squaring her shoulder and facing them. "I should have talked to you about Holly before now. She can't talk to you guys."

"Is she sick or busy? What's wrong? Why can't she come to the phone?" Marti and Gabe asked together.

"She has mutated so much now that she can't speak anymore," Rita admitted. "Sterling has begun to fly, though there isn't much room in the cavern for that, and Holly is trying to fly. The girls can still talk haltingly, though somehow they all can understand each other. It is really fascinating to see them communicate. If I had time, I'd love to study it." She looked at Marti and Gabe's faces and realized the impact of her words. She continued to speak, hurriedly, "Jasmine spends all her time in the water. She can still speak a little, but doesn't seem to want to, though she has been cooperative in tirelessly swimming supplies into the cave."

Marti's face crumpled and she buried it in Gabe's chest. He patted her back and made "there, there" sounds, though he did not feel much better himself. Wasn't it forty years that he had been going to that bar? He had watched Marti take over ownership, had seen Holly and Jasmine start their jobs, and watched them blossom, becoming great friends with them all in the process. He definitely knew how hard it was for Marti. She was like a grandmother to Holly's kids, having them over her house and taking them out for fun, even when she wasn't babysitting for Holly. To hear that they were not able to communicate like humans anymore was shocking. Gabe realized they were going to witness the same deterioration with the Goldsteins. How would they be able to handle that? Then he remembered that some gorillas were able to learn sign language.

"I want to see her; and I want to see all of them," Marti demanded. "I don't care if they can't talk back to me. I want to tell them I love them and always will, even if they can't understand me."

"Oh, they can still understand us," Rita said, relieved she had something positive to report. "As I said, they cooperate beautifully with me and all the instructions I give them for experiments of different treatments. I hope they never lose their ability to understand human speech. I do wonder sometimes, though, especially with Jasmine, that they seem to be impatient and uninterested in human speech and human concerns. They are more involved in the new interests in their lives, and the interests of the species they have mutated to. . . . I'll get them for you."

Marti and Gabe tried to hide their consternation as they viewed their former close buddies. If they hadn't known before who was coming to the view screen, they would never have recognized the mutants. Of course, they had never had an opportunity to get to know Sterling well, but, from what they could see, he had become an eagle-like bird, just like his father. He was larger than a normal bird, but not by too much. No matter how hard they looked, they could not recognize anything human about him anymore. Holly still had some of her old personality traits that identified her as Holly, an air to her, or maybe it was just wishful thinking by them. It was especially painful to look at her. The twins were still human-like, though it was as if they were birds who had some human characteristics, instead of the other way around. It was hard to realize that they would soon have nothing remaining to mark them as human. Jasmine was still humanoid, though her skin had developed into a rubbery texture. Her arms had shrunk and her legs were fusing together, her mouth and nose pushed out, giving her a perpetual and engaging grin.

"How are you all?" Marti asked.

"Hi, Aunt Marti," the girls squawked in unison, their words barely distinguishable. Holly and Sterling bobbed their heads and squawked.

"Hi, Marti and Gabe," Jasmine said in a high-squeaking chirp. "Holly and Sterling can't talk anymore, but I can, though I'm not interest in talking much anymore." She gazed yearningly to the water. Then, remembering her old self, said, "How are you both doing?"

"We are fine. We just wanted to see all of you, and let you know how much we love you and miss you," Marti said. Gabe was having a hard time saying anything. The words seemed to catch in his throat. "We are glad to hear the research is going well."

Jasmine nodded, uninterestedly. "Rita keeps trying things out on us. I know it is supposed to be important, but I can't really understand why anymore. I'm happy the way things are. I don't know if I would want to change back."

"But, surely, you want to be human again?" Gabe said incredulously, finally finding his voice.

"I don't know. . . I love the feel of the water. . . I can stay down for a long time now . . . I can't imagine not being able to do that again — to glide and leap through the water . . . I just wish I could get to the sea . . . now, um, good talking to you." and with that Jasmine was gone, heading back to the water.

"Girls," Marti began, frantically, "I bet you can't wait to be all human again — to ride bikes and go shopping with me for pretty dresses?"

"I want to fly, Aunt Marti," said Reva, flapping her arms. "Sterling can fly already and it's a real bummer that I can't yet."

"Who wants a bike when we can fly instead?" said Vera, derisively, running around in circles trying to take off.

"Holly, oh Holly, let me know you know who we are," Marti pleaded. Holly continued to nod and squawk. "Oh, Gabe, I don't think she recognizes us."

But then Holly darted forward and pecked the screen. And, to be sure they got it, she pecked it again.

"Oh Sweetheart, you do know us!" said Marti. "You are still Holly under all those lovely feathers!"

"We are always here for you, Holly," Gabe said inadequately, knowing that the miles that stretched between them yawned like an impassable canyon. They couldn't be there for their friends, at all. Instead, they were going to hole up with strangers, including mutants that were ultimately going to be just as inhuman as Holly and Sterling were, only without a bond of friendship.

"We love you Holly — you and the girls," Marti reassured them repeatedly until it seemed like no one knew how to break it off.

Gabe cleared his bothersome throat. "Uh, would you mind if we talk to Zack for a moment? We need to discuss how to build a fort and make it defensible."

Rita, who had been watching the painful exchange, said, "I need to take my favorite test subjects over to the lab now. Bye, you guys. Talk to you soon. . . . Oh, here's Zack now." She hurried the mutants away. Marti had tried to keep them in sight as long as possible. Of course, it was not the last time they could talk to them since they could see them anytime they called. So why was there a feeling of ending, of finality to the conversation? She was being morbid, she thought to herself. Then, she gave herself a shake, though no amount of shaking would remove the images of the non-humans she had just seen, or the struggle to try and reconcile those images to her memories of her friends.

It was hard to switch focus as Zack moved into the view screen, but Gabe swallowed the lump in his throat and got down to business, "Hey Zack, we are looking for some pointers in how to go about setting up a compound to live in. Any ideas of what we can expect if we are attacked? It's not that we've seen any mutants around here yet, any hostile mutants, I mean. What should we do for defense?"

"We have officially closed the gate here," Zack answered. "Nate and Sandra were attacked by avian mutants on their last foray out to find people who needed refuge. The avian mutants can actually fly now. You need to prepare for an aerial attack, as well as a land attack. Do you have any caves there?" And then he remembered about Jose getting grabbing by an aquatic.

215

"No, there are no caves big enough for all of us to fit in. There are just small lava caves close to an inactive volcano on this island, but they are all at sea level and subject to filling at high tide. They're too small to be of any use," Gabe responded anxiously. "How in the world could we ever protect ourselves from attacks out of the sky when we are sitting ducks out in the open?"

"You are going to need a stockade of some sort, preferably with spikes pointing outward, and some kind of a roof," Zack said.

"There isn't much for trees around here to make a stockade or a roof with," Gabe said, scratching his head worriedly. "There are lots of fruit trees, but we need them for food. There is a bit of bamboo and a mangrove swamp along some of the coast, though we haven't been able to explore the whole island yet. Marti and I intend to go out and look for people who need shelter, like you folks have. We have six adults here, two of them mutants. Who knows how long they will be of help, or even if we can trust them in the long run. Honestly, I'm still wrestling with that one."

Irritated, Zack shrugged his shoulders. He was at a loss as to how to advise Gabe and he didn't like feeling helpless. "It sounds like you could use more people to help you build your fort and watch for hostiles. Anyone you find will be of benefit to you as much as you will be to them. I would make that my top priority if I were there. Of course, building a durable shelter is important, but at least you can stay on the boat until you get something built — unless you do get a lot more people. I don't know what to tell you, Gabe. You're the man on the ground. You are going to have to build with whatever materials you can find. Pull up bushes and make dense piles of them if you have to. In fact, that would probably be the fastest way to go to keep wild animals out. Then you can work on a sturdier fence after that's in place. You need to set guards around the clock. Just because you haven't seen any mutants doesn't mean they aren't around. Somebody once lived in that deserted town you mentioned…. and maybe you can take apart some of the structures there." He raised his eyebrows, trying to emphasize his point.

The conversation continued in a similar vein for a few more minutes. As Zack signed off, Gabe and Marti realized that he couldn't be of any practical help anymore since he didn't know their island and its resources. His hands were full managing the defenses of the cavern and the one hundred people there. They looked at each other with brave smiles, each trying to mask the fear for the sake of the other. They were definitely on their own!

*   *   *

"Hey, Andy, did you ever hear of Robinson Crusoe?" Gabe asked the five-year-old boy as they pulled up bushes together. That is, Gabe pulled up the bushes, while Andy "helped" by getting in the way.

"My Dad told me a story about that guy," Andy nodded, not sure he wanted to attempt saying the name. "He lived on an island like us."

"That's right, Andy. Um, do you think you could drag those bushes over to that pile I've been making over there?" Gabe gestured towards where he was building the hedge. "We are going to make a Robinson-Crusoe-type fort. Isn't this fun?"

"Is this where you want them, Captain?" Andy asked, full of himself for being considered old enough to help. His sister, Rachel and Baby Joey were being watched by his Mom. He had taken to calling Gabe "Captain" because Gabe had a boat. His parents had finally given up after repeatedly trying to get him to say "Mr. Gabe." Truthfully, Gabe was kind of tickled at the name, and little Rachel had started calling him that, too.

"Is Andy getting in the way?" Sun asked, arriving with a baby in her arms and Rachel dancing along behind her, popping Andy's bubble of self-importance.

"Mom, I'm helping the Captain," Andy said, trying to regain the feeling of worth he had moments ago, tugging on a bush twice his size.

"I don't know what I would do without him," Gabe said stoutly, stopping what he was doing and giving the boy a pat on the back. "Andy and I are partners."

Andy beamed proudly.

"I feel so useless," Sun said, sitting down on the ground near where they were working, and setting Joey down. . "I can't do anything to help with these children to watch. Joey, stay here. See what I mean?" She ran her hands through her beautiful long hair causing a clump of hair to come out. Both she and Gabe looked at it, knowing its meaning; her mutation was causing her to lose her once luxurious hair, while short, wiry hairs grew into place. Gabe tried to think of something to say to take her mind off what was happening to her.

"Taking care of the little ones is what life is all about," Gabe said, while removing a twig from Joey's hand that was just about to go into his mouth.

"I can help, too," Rachel declared. Standing next to her brother, she pulled ineffectually at the bush.

"Mom, Rachel is getting in the way. Make her stop!" Andy yelled, shoving his sister to the ground.

"Andy, leave your sister alone!" Sun scolded, picking Rachel up and dusting her off as she examined a skinned knee.

"There's a first aid kit on the boat," Gabe said, stopping again to dispense sympathy as Rachel sobbed dramatically. "I'm sure you can find a band-aid to put on that knee. Would you like a band-aid?"

Rachel nodded as Sun scooped her and Joey up into her arms. And feeling very harried she hurried them off to the boat.

"Ready for another one, my man?" Gabe asked Andy, pulling up another bush and pushing it over to where Andy was waiting.

"Aye, Aye, Sir Captain," Andy replied with a salute. He then struggled to pull the bush to the pile.

* * *

"I was wondering if that fog would ever lift," Marti said as she and Gabe put out to sea. "It really hindered us from being able to search for folks."

"At least we were able to get a good start on a brush hedge to surround the compound," Gabe said. "I feel bad that I'm cruising around out on the boat while the others continue to do all the hard work."

"You know what we are doing is just as important," Marti said as she scanned the horizon with the binoculars. "We are getting materials from abandoned towns to build safe houses. And, if we bring back more people, not only will we help them, but we will have more hands to help us get the fort established and better guarded."

Cruising among a number of small islands as they encircled their large island, Marti and Gabe found many abandoned boats. This time, instead of just being content with being sure there were no people that needed assistance, they boarded the boats looking for supplies that could add to their wealth and, if the boat could be lived on, they towed it back. They confiscated flare guns, extra tanks of gasoline, first aid kits, ropes, tools, and anything they could lay their hands that remotely seemed to have a possible future use.

"Look Gabe, on that island over there!" Marti shouted, running back to Gabe, who was at the controls. She handing him the glasses. "Do you see those, I don't know what they are, over on that island?"

Gabe took the binoculars and took a long look, so long, in fact, that Marti grew increasingly more impatient. Finally, she tugged at his sleeve. "Well, what do you see?"

"I'd say those are unfriendly ape-mutants. They're waving sticks at us."

Rummaging around on the shelf below the controls, Marti came up with another pair of binoculars. "Gabe, now they are throwing rocks at us. I think you need to get farther away from that island."

"Already on it," Gabe replied, laconically, not particularly worried about rocks. He remembered something on the Discovery Channel that he learned, that apes can't swim because their muscles are too heavy. Fortunately, they wouldn't be any threat to their island.

"Gabe, one of them has something shiny in its hand he's waving around," Marti said. Trying to see more through the glasses than she could, Marti continued, "I think it might be a gu—"

Simultaneously with hearing the sound of the gun going off, they felt a smack on the side of the boat. Pulling Marti down out of the line of fire, Gabe hollered, "Let's get out of here! They're clearly not friendly!"

Once they were out of the gun's range, they looked back at the ape-men who were jumping up and down in frustration, still shooting ineffectually at the boat. Gabe couldn't put it out of his mind that Avram and Sun, yes, and little Andy, his helper, and Rachel and Joey were becoming like those creatures on that island. He felt helpless at the inevitability of it all, and was sad and worried about what that would mean to all of them.

"Look, Gabe, over there, on that island," Marti said.

This was becoming a déjà vu drag, Gabe thought, obediently sighting in the direction Marti was pointing, expecting to see more hostile ape mutants. Instead, he recognized instantly, after just seeing Holly and Sterling and the twins, that these were avian mutants. The bird creatures seemed to be different species from what Holly and the children had mutated into. In fact, they were all different species! They attempted to fly, and some were getting off the ground and going for a few feet, before crash-landing onto the island or in the water, squawking loudly. Not wanting to risk finding out whether they were hostile or not, Gabe and Marti sailed on, knowing that for now their island was safe from these mutants, but realizing that it might not be like that forever. Would bird-like mutants feel the need to explore away from their own island? Would they attack like the ones who had attacked Sandra and Nate?

* * *

This time it was Gabe that spotted activity on the shore of their island, not far from the deserted village. He had been doing his job of trying to find people on their island instead of sightseeing other islands. "Look Marti," he said, proud of himself. "I think we have found some people." He steered the boat cautiously toward the shore.

Immediately the group of people he had seen blended into the landscape, leaving one brave soul on shore to greet the boat. Making herself visible and non-threatening, Marti called out in her friendliest voice, the one that had stood her in good stead all those years of running the bar. "Hello. We have come to help. Do you speak English?" Then, as aside to Gabe, she said, "Maybe we should have brought either Chaska or Cori with us to speak Spanish."

"Too late now," Gabe said.

They were in luck, as the man on the beach answered readily, "I speak some English." He reached out to catch the line Gabe was throwing him. Being such a tourist area, many locals of the Galapagos were used to American visitors and were bilingual. Gabe and Marti jumped into the water and waded onto the beach. Gabe stuck his hand out to shake in a typical American gesture.

The slim, dark-skinned, bedraggled, fortyish, man with the build of a bullfighter gratefully reached out and shook Gabe's hand, ducking his head in Marti's direction. "Did the government send you to rescue us?" he asked eagerly. Then he shook his head at his own mistake, adding quickly, "No, that can't be, you are Americans, no?"

"Yes, we are Americans, and we are stranded on this island just like you are," Gabe said. "My name is Gabe Channing and this is Marti Svonski."

"You are stranded, too," the man said, sadly. "Then you will be of no help to us after all. How can you be stranded when you have a boat?" he added suspiciously.

"You are obviously right, we do have a boat," Gabe answered, "but we decided that we had to find a place to hole up, that there was nowhere in the world that was safe anymore, and we couldn't just keep going until we ran out of fuel. Besides, we have two other families that we found, well, one of them found us actually, but that doesn't matter. Anyhow, we decided to establish a camp further down the island on the other side of the town, but far enough away from it to be safe. Are you from the town?"

"Si, Senor. I have — had — a small hotel in town for the tourists. The town is very small, and one night we were attacked by these creatures that looked like apes. We fought them, but we are a peaceful people and they were quite strong. I gathered my family together and we ran. Since then, we have been hiding, afraid to go back to town. We live off the land, but it is difficult. We joined with another family from town . . ." he trailed off, as he remembered all the hardships they had been through.

"Well, we've been to town," Marti said. "It's deserted and stripped of almost everything of use. Buildings were wantonly destroyed and ransacked. There is almost nothing usable left and nowhere to stay. We decided it was too unsafe for us, as we would be sitting ducks, if you know what I mean." Then a bit shame-facedly, she admitted, "We helped ourselves to whatever we could find that was left."

"Oh, my beautiful hotel, my family, what will we do now?" the man said, wringing his hands.

"That's why we are here," Gabe said. "We are out looking for people who would like to join us. You can share in everything we have and are planning, and with your help we can have safety in numbers and build our compound faster."

"Oh, excuse me, my name is Emilio Torres. Let me call the others. Everybody, come out, these people are here to help us!" He called out loudly. As if coming from the woodwork a rag-tag group of people suddenly appeared. Putting his arm around a plumpish woman with long dark hair and burning, brown eyes, he said, "This is my wife, Mayra," then pointing to a trio of teenagers he said proudly, "These are our children: Florencia, Natalia, and Rafael." He pulled a shy youngster out from behind the teens, adding, "And this is Anabella, our beautiful little one."

Gesturing to another bunch of people who had huddled together, he continued with his introductions, "These are the Cabreras, Rodrigo and Yanina, Rodrigo had a bait shop in town, and Yanina worked at our hotel in the kitchen, Yanina's madre, Senora Sofia, and their sons — Frederico, Mateo, and Luis."

All the names were a blur to Gabe and Marti, so many teenagers; it would take years to sort them all out. It crossed Gabe's mind that teens would be able to help out much better than if they had found families with a lot of younger kids, not that he didn't adore the Goldstein children already. They held out their hands and all greeted each other.

Marti, on the other hand, looked at the meaningful glances exchanged by Florencia and Frederico, and thought, "teenagers — oh, no!"

"So, would you folks like to come aboard and take a little cruise with us to see where we are setting up?" Gabe asked, worried about being vulnerable the longer they hung out on the beach.

With many "Si's" and nods, the group went and gathered up the meager belongings they had managed to take with them when they escaped from town. Gabe especially eyed a nice axe that Rodrigo was holding possessively. That would certainly come in handy! They hurried everyone onto the boat, and set off for the settlement.

*   *   *

"I can stand guard, too," demanded thirteen-year-old Luis. "I can watch out for mutants just as well as Mateo can.

"Fine with me," Mateo, 16, responded with a sneer. "Who wants to stand around all night with nothing to do? I will gladly let you take my place."

"You've got to be loco to want to stand guard," Natalia said with a sniff. "I, for one, am glad that I'm not old enough. You should be thankful you aren't too."

"Your sixteenth birthday is not too far away," her sixteen-year-old brother, Rafael reminded her. "It won't be too long before you'll be doing it, too."

"Enough, we will have quiet and respect for Senor Gabe when he is speaking," chided Emilio, doing his best to look threatening. "The group has decided that sixteen is the cut-off age. Everybody over sixteen must stand guard. That's it!"

"I want to stand guard, too," announced Andy. "I'm the Captain's partner, and he said he couldn't do without my help." He looked challengingly at everybody.

"And you are a huge help," Gabe said hurriedly, putting his arm around the boy. "There will be important jobs to keep everybody busy, you too Luis."

Luis would not be mollified. He continued to sulk. Not only wasn't he being treated like the teenager he was, but he was being lumped in with a five-year-old mutant.

After the shock of the two groups seeing each other for the first time, and after the newcomers were calmed down when they found out that mutants were in the camp, they all agreed to work together to build the enclosure. There was now not enough room on the boats for everybody. The settlement had to go into immediate use, even though it was far from ready. Overnight, they had more than doubled their numbers and with that came jockeying for power and control. Out went the easy camaraderie the small band had shared up until then. It became increasingly evident that a chain of command was needed, so Gabe called everyone together for a meeting to make some imperative decisions along that line.

Since every adult there had run their own business previously; nobody seemed willing to take orders. It was agreed that there would be a system of shared defense, though in the case of extreme emergencies it was recognized that there needed to be a preapproved command system, and Gabe was appointed commander-in-chief, more by default than for any military reason.

Guarding the fledgling settlement was the first order of business, so it was agreed by all the adults that everyone sixteen years of age and older would be assigned guard duty, which had led to the colorful discussion among the teens. Round-the-clock shifts were assigned with much haggling among the teens about their new partners. Marti shook her head, congratulating herself on knowing that having teenagers around was going to be a problem.

Their parents seemed at a loss to control them, or maybe they gave up long ago. Marti was surprised that the teens were allowed such freedom of speech. Maybe it was because of all the American tourists they had been exposed to for all their lives. Or, maybe it was because of the time they had been in hiding that they acted that way. The teens were being asked to pull the weight of adults in order to survive, which changed the dynamics of who was in charge. Regardless, being forced to grow up fast and face adult responsibilities, they still had teen hormone levels raging through their bodies.

The meeting continued with plans for growing food with everyone not assigned to guard duty, or building the structures, required to help. It was carefully explained that existing food would have to be rationed until they could get a viable garden to grow. The garden inside the fort area would be a community garden and shared alike. Each member could, at his or her own risk, create additional plots for his or her own use, but only after the day's work on the community garden was completed. It was agreed the work for the common good came first and foremost. Only after they were secure and self-sufficient as a group could people branch out into individual endeavors.

Fortunately, there were wild fruit trees to supplement their meager supplies. They also planned to round up the goats that ran wild on the island, which would provide milk. They also discussed ways to trap the wild pigs for meat. When that subject arose, Sun hurriedly took Rachel and the baby away, since Rachel could not bear to think of anything happening to "piggy." Andy sturdily resisted going with his mother, and Avram stepped in to keep him with the group. The five-year-old was going to have to grow up quickly.

They then talked about the medical situation. They were obviously extremely low on medicine, which needed to be used sparingly. Marti secretly vowed to squirrel away all the heart medicine, since Gabe was not going to admit to anyone about his heart condition. He didn't even admit it to himself! Mayra and Yanina, having nursed eight children and two husbands between them, not to mention overseeing the many medical emergencies that happen in a hotel, agreed to be the camp nurses. Everyone realized that as a group they were woefully short on medical knowledge and experience, as well as medical supplies. Even though Rita was just a call away, that didn't give much peace of mind. And, who could be much practical help at such a distance anyhow?

It was agreed that as future issues arose they would vote on how to handle matters. For the moment, work was more important than meetings. The vote issue created another surprisingly heated discussion, with Rafael leading. "If I'm old enough to stand guard, and maybe take a bullet, I'm old enough to vote," he insisted, looking at the other teens for support, which he quickly got.

Natalia, who suddenly did not like being left out at fifteen years old, joined Luis in his protest. If they were going to work like adults, then they should vote, too!

Gabe thought back to the Vietnam era when the eighteen year olds said the same thing, though they wanted to drink alcohol. In fact, before all this horror from the devolution had hit the fan, he had heard college kids campaigning again for the same thing, since the legal age for many things had crept up to twenty-one after the war had ended. With the war in the Middle East, the attitude again in the United States was, "If we can die for our country, we should be treated like adults in every other way too." "If only that was the only problem today's youth had to face," Gabe thought, sadly.

The adults made this decision after some debate and fortunately agreed again that those sixteen and older should have a vote, otherwise they might have had a mini revolt on their hands. Florencia, Mateo, and Rafael looked complacent. Frederico, who was already eighteen, just shrugged He assumed he was an adult anyhow. Now, Natalia couldn't wait until her next birthday. Luis looked like a thundercloud, so Gabe made a mental note that he needed to find something quick to occupy the young man's attention to make him feel more important. Anabella, 6, had fallen asleep long ago in her father's arms, not the least bit interested in the immense decisions and debates going on around her.

Wearily, Gabe announced that enough had been decided for one meeting, so they all trudged off to bed, except for Cori and Chaska, who were standing first watch. Gabe and Marti exchanged glances; the extra hands were a big help in getting their compound established, but they could've done without all the angst and egos. What had they gotten themselves into?

"Is it too late to take off in the sailboat again?" Gabe asked plaintively. Marti gave him an understanding hug, knowing what he meant.

*   *   *

"How are you coming along on getting all the people on your lists?" Erin asked her counterparts while on a secure communications link. She was on the line with five regional offices of the HSA: Colorado Rockies, the Badlands in the Dakotas, Upstate New York in the Adirondack Mountains, the Ozarks in Missouri, and Austin, Texas. The subject of the conference call was about how to transport important people to the bunkers under "Project Ike." Brad and Erin were in charge of the sixth facility at the Biltmore Estate in Asheville, North Carolina, which they were directing from the DC office. Brad, sitting with her, was updating the information on the computer system as fast as she was getting it.

The responses of all were similar. It was difficult to find people because many had gone into hiding. Those with greater resources had escaped out of the country. Massive manhunts were underway, since some people on these lists were important to maintain the government and rebuild the country in every industry: economics, business, science, politics, military, resource management and the arts. Some people had refused to come for various unknown reasons. Because there was no time to try to reason with them, military force was implemented to drag the individuals and their families to secure facilities.

There was also fighting in the streets and countryside, making it almost impossible for military personnel to reach the homes of some individuals on the lists. Soldiers were shooting mutants on the streets in New York, Washington, D.C., Los Angeles, and all other major cities in the United States. Obviously, the mutants were resisting them, with skirmishes occurring everywhere, leading to dwindling ammunition supplies. Mutants had the edge in major cities and areas with heavy tree coverage, which allowed them to hide effectively. In some cases, people were joining with the mutants under confusing loyalties and miscommunication. Major offenses were frequently needed to get to the people they were trying to reach. Erin listened to it all, it was nothing new, as her region was experiencing similar problems.

227

Once the people were found and safely moved to the underground bunkers, a process began of separating normal people from those who had devolved. Thus, only healthy, normal people, who had not taken any supplements, would be housed in the facilities.

"How is the processing going once you get the people rounded up?" Erin asked.

"Believe it or not, we are having a problem with separating out the people who show signs of devolution," said Evans, from the Dakotas. "It's a subjective process to single out people based on looks."

"Can't your screeners recognize feathers or scales when they see them?" Erin said, scoffing.

"Yeah, those that are far enough along the devolutionary process are easy to spot, but even with all the warnings telling people not to take the supplements, there are people who recently took them and are in the early stages of devolving. How stupid can you get? These are the people the government thinks are crucial to the country. Then, there is the opposite problem. Some of the people who have never taken the pills look like they are devolving."

"That's ridiculous," Erin said, "Normal humans don't suddenly start sprouting feathers." She shot Brad raised eyebrows, and he shook his head in response.

"Well, no, but there have been some guys who look decidedly ape-like, especially ones who exercise. Some are knuckle walkers . . . It slows down the whole procedure if we have to screen for the supplement before we can separate out the normal people from the contaminated ones."

"Yes, I know that is a problem. The whole process is too subjective. We need to know definitively whether people have taken the supplements or not. But we can't wait for definitive. I'm instructing you to screen everyone medically, whether they look seriously devolved or not. I will clear this change in policy with Deputy Director Whiteman, but begin implementing it now until you are notified otherwise," Erin directed her opposite numbers in their bunkers. The protests were loud and long.

"That will slow the whole process down even more," complained Twiss from New York, her high pitched voice sounding above the din.

"Sorry about that, but it can't be helped," said Erin briskly. "We can't afford a mistake in either direction. If we let devolved people into the facilities they could wreak havoc. And, we can't afford to lose someone who is vital to the needs of the country by sending that person accidentally to a containment center based on the opinion of a screener just eyeballing that individual. Not to mention, can you imagine the media headache if we sent a child off accidentally?"

"If you ask me, most children look like little animals," Brad joked quietly for just Erin's ears. She gave him a dirty look. It wasn't the least bit funny with the problems they faced right now.

"How is the separation process going?" Erin asked, continuing the conference.

The next step in processing people in the bunkers, after determining who had taken the supplements and who were normal, was to separate out those who were devolving and send them to what were euphemistically called "treatment centers." The hope was that at some future date, there would be a cure, reversing mutation. The term "treatment" was used to assure the rest of an individual's family that the mutant was being taken away to help that person. In truth, the mutants were being warehoused in large dormitory-like containment centers under armed guard, many in former maximum security prisons. Erin thought uneasily of the Jewish camps in Nazi Germany. Squaring her shoulders, she reminded herself that it was all being done for the survival of the country; the continuity of the human race was at stake. It was war, and hard choices had to be made in war. It was like confining the Japanese-Americans in World War II, which was done for national security reasons. At times, Erin didn't like her job, but she had to carry on, as the whole country depended on her.

Brad nudged her. She'd been so caught up in her thoughts that she had been missing what the others were saying.

". . . of course, it is hard to separate the families, especially when a child has devolved. Most of the time it is a teenager who was experimenting, or had something slipped into the candy bowl at a rave. We've had cases of children as young as four years old, even when the parents are fine. It's impossible to figure out how a four-year-old got a hold of a pill, and you certainly can't get a coherent story from them. The parents fight like crazy to keep us from taking the kids. Mothers beg to go with their children. There is a high rate of burn-out of the personnel who are responsible for forcing the separation. It is hard for anyone to watch a four-year-old screaming for her parents," said Hiffert, from the Ozarks.

Erin couldn't help herself, "Four years old?" She caught herself, and went on hurriedly, "Are you encountering any problems at the containment centers?" There was no mincing of words with her counterparts, as they all knew there was no treatment at the centers.

""Aside from the expected problems of mutants trying to escape, fighting with the guards, trying to commit suicide, caring for children without parents, we are having difficulty in culling out the truly aggressive ones," said Chris, from Colorado. "Some people appear violent when they are first taken from their families. Later, ironically, some of them become model detainees. Maybe there should be a second stage to allow for that cooling-off period before deciding who has truly anti-American tendencies? Or maybe there should be a waiting period before rushing to the decision that a mutant is intrinsically dangerous to society?"

Looking at the middle-age Chris, Erin thought to herself, "She must have been part of the Kum Bi Ya movement." Erin said, "Those are valid arguments, which I will mention to Deputy Director Whiteman. Regardless, unless we have new orders, you are to continue identifying violent mutants and sending them to the high-security facilities."

"Even if the mutant is a screaming four-year-old who is battering the day care worker because she misses her parents?" asked Hiffert.

Gulping, Erin said, "It is not for us to make judgment calls. Our jobs are to follow the directives we have been given. I assure you that there will be further screening done at the high-security system." Erin crossed her fingers, hoping what she said was actually true, since she had no clue what went on when the mutants reached the last stage in the separation process. Surely this once great government espousing strong family values had a comprehensive screening process in place at the highest level that would catch a four-year-old and recognize that a young child was probably not a danger to society?

After a few more items of business, Erin scheduled the next conference call and signed off.

"Uh, Erin, I couldn't decide whether to show you this or not," Brad began, uncharacteristically diffident. He was holding a copy of a Presidential order.

"How did you get this?" Erin asked as she grabbed it out of his hands.

"It was in this folder of the updated lists that Jamie gave me," he answered. "It must have been filed wrong."

"How does a top-secret document get filed wrong?" Erin asked rhetorically noticing first the brightly stamped words stating that it was "Top Secret." She knew she shouldn't read it, but in these times of mayhem with everybody's life at stake, including her own, it was too dangerous for her to even go home anymore, she felt justified in reading it. The paper fluttered to the ground dropped by her nervous fingers. She stared at Brad wordlessly, and he stared back. Neither of them could give the horrible orders life by putting them into words.

The President of the United States had signed an order authorizing the extermination of all mutants showing aggressive behavior in a containment facility. Violent mutants were being put to death. That was what Erin had just condemned the four year old to. She dropped to the ground moaning out loud. Later, she wiped her tears and sprang up, reached for a button to reactivate the conference call. However, Brad's hand enclosed her wrist, stopping her before she blabbered about the inevitable truth that would happen.

"What are doing?" he hissed.

"The four-year-old — I have to stop it," Erin babbled, struggling to break away.

"Are you crazy? Think of your job. Think of yourself," Brad urged, holding on tight.

"But, that little girl is going to be exterminated at my order," Erin wailed, her eyes pleading with Brad to understand, flailing ineffectually with her other arm.

Gently, Brad said, "It is already too late for that little girl. From the way Hiffert spoke, the separation procedure had already occurred. And besides, is the sixteen-year-old teenager any different, or the entire family that gave the pills to their children as vitamins? This is war, Erin. There are civilian casualties in every war. You can't override the President's order. At the minimum, you will get yourself fired, and someone else will oversee carrying out the command. At worst, you might be thrown in with them."

Erin slumped, hearing the truth of his words, but not wanting to accept them.

"Think of all the people you are saving from harm from the brutal actions of the really dangerous mutants," Brad urged, letting go of her wrist, but still watching her closely.

"I've got to think about this," Erin mumbled, not looking at him.

"There's something else," Brad said.

"How could there possibly be any more?" Erin asked lethargically, still processing what she had already heard.

"I was looking over the latest list of people to be housed at the Biltmore. It says it is the final draft, and you and I aren't on it," Brad said, holding out another sheet of paper to her.

"What? That's impossible!" Erin ran to the computer and began checking the final list against the one Brad had just given her. "They just left us off because we are already part of the personnel running the project. They couldn't do without us. We are too important to the mission. Why, we are in charge of Project Ike. Who would run it if we weren't included?"

"Plausible deniability," Brad said succinctly. "Face it. We are peons. We don't have any fantastic skills or knowledge. In fact, we know too much. Once the program is completed, they no longer need us, and would be better off without us and what we know."

"This has to be an oversight," Erin blustered. "I'm going to call Jamie and get this straightened out." She reached again for the call button. Again, Brad stopped her.

"Let me. You know she has a thing for me," he said blushing, not meeting Erin's eyes.

"You know about that?" Erin asked, momentarily diverted. She gave a half-heartedly chuckle. "I didn't think you had a clue that the Deputy Director had the hots for you."

"It was obvious enough for even someone as dense and socially inept as me to see," Brad said, ducking his head and turning back to his computer. He pushed the call button and Jamie Whitehead appeared on the screen.

"Oh, Brad, I'm kind of busy right now. What is it?" Jamie tried to preen, while looking officious to someone who was obviously in the room with her. She didn't succeed at either.

"I just need a moment," Brad said, giving her a flirty look, or what he supposed was a flirty look. He didn't have much practice with flirting at all, let alone with a woman who could be his mother. The thought made him gag and he covered it up quickly. "I was just looking over the final draft of the list of people to be housed in the North Carolina facility, and noticed that Erin and I were not on it."

Jamie blinked, and her eyes darted to someone else in the room with her. Brad wished he had a way to see who it was. Then, blandly, she said, "I'm sure it is just an oversight — a typo. Don't worry about a thing. I'll take care of it as soon as I can. Of course, you are too important to the project to be excluded." Unspoken was the obvious message, "and to me too."

"And Erin," Brad pursued.

"Oh, of course, Ms. Blaine is vital to the mission, too," Jamie droned robotically. "I've got to go, Brad. Uh, stay right there." Her eyes darted to that unseen person again, and she gave a barely perceptible nod. "I'll be down to see you shortly." Unstated, but obvious to both Brad and Erin as she signed off was that Deputy Director Whitehead had not given a second's thought to Erin and was just trying to pacify Brad. It was also apparent that she wanted them to remain in the office for some reason other than a visit.

"Well, at least you are safe," Erin said, sardonically. "Deputy Director's little sugar baby."

Ignoring her last remark, Brad answered, "I don't think I'm going to make the cut either. You saw the way her eyes flickered to whoever was in the room. I think she's getting orders not to include us. The question is what are we going to do about it?"

Erin, emotionally overwhelmed with the two discoveries they had just made, could not muster an answer. She was having a hard time getting her mind around the fact that after years of faithful service, she was going to be denied the safety provided for the chosen few, and was being thrown on the mercies of the chaos of the country, forced to fend for herself.

"We have to get out of here," Brad continued when she didn't answer. "There are millions of people who are not going into the bunkers. I'm sure some of them have banded together for safety from the mutants for their survival. We need to find one of those groups and join with them."

"How would we even start to find people like that?" Erin asked, her mind frantically searching for other solutions. "We've been so tied down here, concentrating on Project Ike, that we have no intel on the resistance groups around the country."

"I think we need to get out of here now, as in right now. Jamie Whitehead was way too casual in the way she answered me. And there was the insistence on her part that we stay here so she could visit us. Suppose they are coming to get us because we now know too much," he jumped up, grabbing Erin's wrist again, trying to pull her towards the door.

"Wait a moment!" Erin said, getting away from him. She ran back to the console and scooped up all the papers, including the President's extermination order. "Someday, when and if the world gets back to normal, people need to know about Project Ike and the President's order to eliminate the threatening mutants. If for no other reason, we need to get these papers out of here. Okay, let's go."

They hurried out of the building, unaware that minutes later armed guards had come to their offices, looking for them, under orders of Deputy Director Whitehead. Without trying to return to their homes, instinctively sensing the urgency to flee, they headed west on foot, since no road was safe, all the while unknowingly following the path Harland had taken just months earlier.

CHAPTER SEVEN

We Lose

"The patient in 143 did not eat his food again," Ski announced to the guards as he brought a full tray of raw bloody meat back from Harland's cell in the wing of the prison that had hastily been converted to hold the mutants judged criminally insane. "Do I look like an orderly?" Murphy, a retired MP, now a guard at the facility, growled. "Do I look like I care whether the inmates eat or not? I'm here to make sure they don't escape, or kill each other. Though, in my opinion it would be better if they did kill each other, it would save the taxpayers a lot of money." He rubbed the belly that had inched its way further and further over his belt as the years went by.

"Easy for you to say," Twinkle groused, her full-bodied, prematurely gray hair, and sour demeanor, contradicting the name, which actually was a derivative of her last name Twinkler. Nobody was very original when it came to what they called each other. "You have your military pension to fall back on. I need this crummy job to feed my three kids."

"Maybe if you stayed married to one of the many husbands you've had you wouldn't have to worry about that," Murphy sneered. "Besides, don't you have truckloads of child support rolling in?" He got up and peered at the tray that the orderly was still holding in front of him. "Yuck, what are you feeding that bird-man now?"

"It's just raw chopped meat, but he doesn't seem to like anything that comes from a cow. It is so hard to come up with a diet for all these different mutants. Each one needs something different," the orderly complained. "It seems all the bird-man wants are rodents and fish." He shuffled off to return the tray to the kitchen.

"You try to live on what I get in child support. Besides, I can't even get that money most of the time now, since my exes were having their wages garnished by the State, and now that system is completely down," Twinkle retorted, continuing the conversation as if there hadn't been a break. "Maybe if I marry Rodney, I won't have to work in this place. I think I'm going insane from having to work here."

"Try living on a military pension," Murphy answered her back. "I thought I'd go directly into being a cop after being a military police. Affirmative action ruined that. Then I thought I'd at least get in a regular prison – you know, with humans. I never expected to get stuck in this hellhole with a bunch of violent mutants. And, I'm having trouble getting my checks too. Seems the mutants have destroyed all the computer systems. We are lucky to be in a small town out in the boonies where we haven't been bothered that much. We were all too smart around here to take any of those supplements. Hey, would the Rod-Man be your fourth victim? When are you going to learn that none of these losers are going to be a ticket out of here for you?"

"I've only been married two times before, two of the guys I never married, and Rodney is different. I'm thinking this one might work out," Twinkle sniffed. She hoisted her short body out of the chair. "You know what I hate, is having to take these cretins out for exercise. Good thing we carry tazers, but I think a cattle prod would work better."

"You mark my words, Rodney will be just like the others, get you pregnant then take off," Murphy advised. "That cage they threw together to exercise these bozos in is a joke. It's so rickety that I'm afraid it will fall down when the ape-men climb all over it."

Twinkle swatted him angrily, "They don't leave me, I leave them. And, I took care of things so there won't be any more babies – no more surprises. Guess we'd better start getting the prisoners, I mean patients, to the exercise cage. It is such a pain that they can't all go at once, that we have to separate them according to supposed species. Like how can we even tell what some of them are?"

"At least we don't have any aquatic ones here. They can't stand to be out of water. I heard their bodies collapse on themselves from the weight if they are out of water too long. Good thing they put them in a closed down aquarium. At least the guards there don't have to take them out for exercise," Murphy said, sharing his little bit of knowledge.

"But, I heard they have to hire divers to clean the algae off the insides of the tanks," Twinkle said, as they headed down the wing that housed the criminal mutants. "How much fun would that job be? Especially with shark-like mutants attacking you the whole time? What are we going to do? Take the ape-men first?"

"Didn't you get the memo? They've divided themselves into two separate gangs, and they fight if they are taken out all together. We have to take them out in two different groups now," Murphy grumbled, acting as if the new directive was too much to bear.

They walked through a barred gate and slammed it locked behind them.

"Good thing they are segregated into individual cells that are numbered. I can't tell those apes apart from each other," Twinkle joked, as they reached the first cell. "What was that?"

There was a loud hissing noise and suddenly the lights went out.

"Don't worry kid, the back-up generator will kick in," Murphy reassured her, trying not to panic himself.

But, the back-up generator did not come on. Twinkle and Murphy lit up their flashlights that they used for bed checks. There was a clanging noise and they turned to shine their lights on the gate they had just passed through. The lock had disengaged when the power went off.

"Are you thinking what I'm thinking?" Murphy asked, shining his light in Twinkle's face.

"Get that out of my face, you moron," Twinkle said, whacking the flashlight out of his hand. She turned her own light on the cell door they were standing in front of. In the glare they could see clearly that it was unlocked. She swept her beam towards the other cells, and they were all unlocked. "Oh, no, Murphy, the cells are unlocked. What are we going to do? Call for back-up?"

"Not me, Sister," Murphy whispered. "Shhh, don't let the inmates know the doors are open. They don't pay me enough to deal with rioting crazies in the dark. And, you know there is no back-up. We are chronically short-handed since people have stopped showing up for work. I'm out of here. Suddenly that pension looks adequate." Not waiting for her reply, he hustled away as fast as an out-of-shape sixty year old with extra tonnage could.

Twinkle stood there indecisively a moment, until she heard the cell door rattling from the other side. Those ape-men were pretty smart despite their mutation. Abruptly she realized that her life would not be worth anything if they got loose, and she turned and high-tailed it back down the hall, running into Ski walking purposefully into the wing with another food tray. "Run, you idiot," she hollered at him, "the doors are all open and the mutants will be on you in a second. Run." Suddenly life with Rodney and the kids looked pretty appetizing.

Following her lead, Ski dropped the tray and ran as mutants burst out of their cells and gave chase. But, he was too slow to react. The ape-men quickly caught up with and overpowered Ski, and as they set to attacking him with a will, Twinkle made good her escape.

Harland had been sitting alone in his padded cell, staring fixedly at the door, when the lights went out. By now Harland was fully an eagle, though much larger because of his original human size. No former friend of his would be able to find anything recognizable about his features, nothing that told them he was still Harland, in either his physical presence or his behavior. During the time of his crime, while he was devolving, Harland's emotions, thoughts, reactions, and behaviors were in a jumble, complete chaos, so he didn't know up from down or what he wanted or what he was; now everything had settled into all the attributes of the species into which he had devolved. He did still have moods. No bird could be locked up and not be morose and despondent, if human emotions can be assigned. And, while his thoughts were distinctly those of a bird, he still had razor sharp intelligence that was directed towards the mysterious concerns of birds.

He knew his offspring, Sterling, needed him, and it deepened his depression that he didn't have Sterling with him, nor did he know what had happened to Sterling. No one thought it important to tell him about Sterling, assuming that as a bird he couldn't understand. That was one of the strange things about this mutation; he could still understand human-speak, he just could not communicate back to them, and even if he could, he no longer had any desire to, except to find out where Sterling was.

Harland was quite able to fly now, but had limited opportunity to build up his flying muscles. The rinky-dink cage they brought him to for exercise barely allowed him a few strokes before he was at the other end of the enclosure. He tried flying the perimeter, but that wasn't much help either. Back in his cage he flapped his wings repeatedly to try to keep up his strength, but he had quickly learned that the humans became afraid of him when he did that. At the beginning, he had thrown himself at the walls, and they had tried all kinds of restraints on him. He had gotten cagey, and modified his behavior when the humans could see him. He no longer screeched at all hours.

He tried to be a model prisoner, except when it came to food. Initially they had tried to feed him human food, but he could not stomach it. He refused to eat and got weaker and weaker. The ACLU got involved, and insisted that each mutant had to be fed a diet that fit the dietary need of that specie. Since Harland was the very first mutant, and the very first mutant prisoner, or patient, as they euphemistically called them in the asylum, he was the first guinea pig. They were still trying to get his diet right, which was pretty silly, since any imbecile could look in a bird book and see what eagles prefer to eat.

Harland cocked his head. The lights were not coming back on. That didn't bother him. He could see quite well in the dark. In fact, his eyesight was superb. Then he heard a click on the cell door. For a moment, he stood silently, trying to puzzle-out what it meant. Suddenly his door was thrown open by an ape-man.

The ape-men had run amok all over the prison, throwing open any door they saw, indiscriminately freeing all the other prisoners, even the ones in the human areas of the building. The ape-man chattered to Harland, and then advanced on him. Not caring whether the action was meant to be aggressive or not, Harland instinctively lashed out with his beak, barely missing the ape-man's eye. The ape-man about-faced and rushed off to join his fellow escapees, knowing there was safety in numbers.

Harland hopped over to the door and peered out at the mayhem in the hallway. He tried to stretch out his wings, but the hallway was too close and congested for him to be able to fly over the heads of all the mutants scurrying around. Instead, he sidled along a wall towards freedom.

In short order, he came upon the escapees who were beating on Ski. Though Harland had no particular feelings for him, seeing him as just a source of daily food, he thought Ski might have some value. But, what really concerned Harland was that the ape mob was blocking his way towards a complete escape. Harland began pecking and clawing indiscriminately at the ape-men, trying to force them out of his way, his wickedly sharp beak and talons doing great damage in the process. The ape-men howled, retreating from his deadly beak weapon. Greatly bruised and injured, Ski jumped up.

"Thanks Man," Ski shouted over his shoulder. "I'll never forget this." Harland didn't even blink. He had no interest in what any human had to say. His intention was to clear his own path. He hurried after Ski, dimly aware that the human must know the way out.

By now, some of the braver, or more foolhardy, guards had arrived on the scene, busily trying to quell the riot. They waded into the brawls, not paying much attention to the eagle quietly making his way towards the front door. The lights remained out, so their flashlights were focused on the melee of ape-men.

Harland reached the front door of the facility only to find another skirmish happening between a few guards outnumbered by the many prisoners trying to escape. Again, Harland used his beak and talons to his advantage, not caring who he ripped at. At that moment, all the prisoners made a concerted effort to rush at the remaining guards, causing all of the guards to fall down. All were looking at the long fence surrounding the complex, as mutants and humans rushed to the front gate. Some tried to climb the fence which was no longer electrified, while others batted at the manual lock, which was still in place. Shots rang out from the perimeter guards who had real guns, but they were shooting in the dark and seldom hit a prisoner.

Harland stood by the building, carefully surveying the scene. Did he have enough take off room? Were his wing muscles strong enough to get him over the fence? He knew he had to chance it, even if he had to laboriously climb to the top of the fence by using his beak. He also knew he would be an easy target in the dark, a silhouette under the half-moon! Regardless, Harland spread his wings and flapped furiously. Slowly, he gained altitude, and with sheer determination, he was soon ascending into the air his powerful wings lifting him over the man-made fence. The guards vaguely saw a shadow crossing the moon, causing them to impulsively raise their guns and shoot at the figure, knowing it wasn't human.

Harland escaped unharmed. A half hour later, he landed in a field far away from the asylum. He had rapidly hopped and flapped away from danger! Although it would take much practice to strengthen his muscles to fly long distances, this was quite an accomplishment! Soon he would take off again, to fly to wherever Sterling was, hopefully back at the family cabin where they had last seen each other. Harland hopped and flapped and flew, steadily making his way towards the mountains.

* * *

A rabbit froze, raising its nose into the air as it sensed danger. But from where was the danger coming? Without waiting for more information, he frantically hopped toward his safe hole, but to no avail. Harland swooped from the sky and stretching out his talons grabbed the defenseless creature. It squealed briefly, but Harland had already snuffed out its life. Not even stopping to fly to a safe height, Harland ripped apart the rabbit while in mid-air. Harland's hunger was enormous, needing the food to help him grow in strength, to ultimately become a full-fledged eagle. Belatedly, he scanned the area for danger, knowing instinctively that anywhere on the ground made him vulnerable to predators. Harland flew, ascending to a high ridge to survey the great vista of countryside.

Because it was summer in the Northern hemisphere, Harland would have no problem finding sufficient food to feed his intense appetite. The hunting skills Harland had developed during his winter stay at the cabin were now very useful. From high in the sky, he could easily spot streams for drinking and small animals to eat. He lazily drifted with the wind currents, finding his way as he felt his muscles developing.

Obviously, his initial trips to the cabin had been in the comfort of a car. He now had an avian brain, with an avian sense of time and place. He could see for many miles and easily fly in a straight line towards a destination that he sensed in his mind but could not explain with any words. While he had never flown that route before, his power of instinct was also developing. Was it the magnetic field of the Earth that he was feeling? Ever fearful of predators (humans, and now, mutants), he avoided human population centers, flying steadily towards the wildest countryside he could find.

Descending to a ridge near a stream, Harland vaguely recognized a cabin. He was aware of two humans hiking along a path, no longer viewing them as members of the same species. He noticed that he now viewed them as a threat to his life, even though he had no intention of living in that cabin and confronting them. He was disturbed that they were so close to him. They might scare Sterling off, or have even scared him off already. He flew up to a high ridge where his eagle eyes enabled him to watch their every movement.

*   *   *

A few days earlier, Brad and Erin had found the cabin in terrible shambles. Erin thought it looked like wild animals had been living in it, unaware of how accurate she actually was. Because it was in close proximity to a stream, they decided it was a good place to stop and catch their breaths. Unfortunately, they were out of options. Their original plan, to connect with a band of humans survivalists, seemed to be a pipedream. How would they find such a group without access to Homeland Security information? Their hope was to stumble across others who were hiding, ultimately joining with them. But, so far, they had had no success, and were worn out from their struggles to make it in the wilderness on their own.

Neither of them was a hunter. In fact, neither of them was ever a weekend camper. They had no idea which berries were safe to eat and which were poisonous. Brad remembered something about red berries, but he couldn't remember if those were the good ones or the bad ones. He had reasoned that strawberries and raspberries were red, so they must be good. Erin had disagreed, pointing out that she was pretty sure holly berries were poisonous. Thus, they tried to only eat wild plants they thought they recognized.

Knowing HSA was on the lookout for them, they had immediately headed across the country with the limited resources of their clothes, Brad's pocketknife, and Erin's bottomless pocketbook, making it a testament to their perseverance that they had made it as far as they had. Fortunately, streams were plentiful in the Virginia countryside, so drinking water was not problematic. So far, they had slept in abandoned barns and had, desperately, broken into a few deserted farmhouses. Along the way, they had acquired a gun, fish fillet knife, string and fish hooks, a couple sleeping bags, and various additional objects they could carry that they thought would become useful. Items taken from a deserted frozen food store had stood them in good stead for a few days, though eventually they somewhat learned how to fish and hunt. However, they had reached the end of their ropes, weary to the bone, when they chanced upon the cabin.

For the first few days in the cabin, they cleaned out the skeletons of dead rodents and fish, in addition to debris that had blown in through an open, hanging door. Aside from that, the cabin was in good shape, and a welcome summer retreat in the Virginia Blue Ridge mountain range, with beautiful views all around. Maybe this could become their base camp, offering a relatively safe haven from the long reach of Homeland Security and wild animals. The portions of each day not spent gathering and storing food supplies for the winter were spent on long day hikes in various directions. Aside from establishing in them a joy of nature, the hiking trips also offered them hope that ultimately they would find another band of people in similar circumstances. "Safety in numbers," Brad would repeat, and repeat. They were on one of those hikes, following a well-trodden path, when they spotted an eagle high on a ridge looking down at them.

Stopping to admire the eagle, Erin said, "Doesn't that bird look too large to be an eagle?"

"You can never be sure of the actual size at this distance," Brad answered, judiciously.

"A long time ago, before all the animals got loose from the mutant sabotage, I saw an eagle at the National Zoo," she said mournfully, thinking about the fate of all the animals accustomed to being fed their two squares a day. Now those animals were left to fend for themselves, quickly forced to relearn long-dormant survival skills. "I still think it looks kind of large," she insisted, referring back to Harland, who was now gazing at an area behind them. "Do you think it could be a bird mutant?"

From their safe (but not cushy) jobs at Homeland Security, Brad and Erin had heard much about mutants, even seeing pictures of them televised from secure satellite feeds. By now, most network and cable stations were decimated, giving greater purpose to the secure Homeland Security feed. In the beginning, when they were travelling back and forth to work from their individual apartments, Brad and Erin had seen devolving gangs of half-humans trolling the streets. At that time, no person had fully devolved, which meant that many of their former human characteristics were still intact. In time, they had to sleep on cots provided by Homeland Security because it was no longer safe to travel back-and-forth from home to work. Consequently, they had never seen a completely devolved bird-man mutant in the flesh making recognition of one difficult.

"You know, I think you might be right!" Brad queried. "I wonder what he is thinking about. Can he still think like a human?" No one had wasted much time in speculating on the thought processes, or the remaining humanity of the mutants. The whole thrust of the offensive had been to neutralize them at whatever cost to their natural lives. "Do you think he might be dangerous to us?"

Brad grabbed Erin and pulled her behind a bush before she could respond.

"I'm sure he is too concerned with eagle matters to care about us. Eagles don't naturally attack humans," Erin responded tartly, brushing herself off from the leaves and twigs that had fallen on her following Brad's rash action. "He sure is magnificent. What would it be like to be able to see for miles, and soar over all these obstacles we have to climb over?" She stood and cautiously returned to the path, lightly kicking a boulder alongside their pathway.

"I wonder what he's planning?" Brad mused. He shamefacedly came out from behind the bush. He then half-turned around to see if anything was behind them that might attract an eagle's attention. Just then swooped down, lunging at them.

And that was when the mountain lion sprang! Apparently, the mountain lion had picked up their scent and began to stealthily stalk them, soundlessly creeping up on them. Before Brad and Erin could react let alone gasp Harland had swooped down from his perch, his eagle eyes seeing the mountain lion from a great distance, and connecting the threat to the humans.

Brad drew the gun that he had fetched at one of their past breaking-and-entering stops and pointed it clumsily at Harland, thinking the eagle was attacking them. He then shot and missed it, causing Erin to grab a branch for self-defense.

Ignoring the humans as if they were irritating gnats, Harland landed on the big cat and sunk his sharp talons into its throat, pecking at it with his rapier sharp beak, and beating it with his wings. With a ferocious roar, the mountain lion whipped around and bit Harland in the leg. Harland hung on, loudly squawking and shrieking in the process. After what seemed like hours of furious fighting (though actually only seconds), the cat lost enough blood and could no longer fight. Harland gave a horrendous wrench to its neck and the lion was dead! Bleeding from his leg, and now too exhausted to fly, quickly Harland turned to face the humans, wondering if he had enough left in him to fight them off too.

Brad and Erin were mesmerized by the brutal battle, staying rooted to their spots on the path. Looking at the hurt eagle, it was now evident that he was a mutant, a fully devolved bird-man, revealed only by the fact that his size was greater than that of a normal eagle.

Brad raised the gun again. They had been programmed to view all mutants as bad, dangerous, even in need of extermination in the worst of cases. To confirm that thinking, this particular eagle had attacked something only a few feet away from them. Sure, it had attacked a mountain lion, but wouldn't it ultimately attack them?

Then Erin batted Brad's gun downward. "Don't you realize he saved our lives?" she said. "He's wounded. We need to help him." She edged carefully towards Harland, the mutant bird.

"Are you crazy?" Brad shouted, trying to grab Erin to keep her from going to Harland. "He's going to come after us next."

"He risked his own life to save ours," said Erin, staying out of pecking range of his wicked beak. "We have got to help him, Brad. You know that we were appalled, anyways, that HSA was arbitrarily putting mutants to death, even young ones. Suppose some of them are good, or at least not harmful to us. As far as I'm concerned, this eagle mutant was helpful to us, even saving our lives. Let's fix his leg and get him to safety." Turning to Harland she spoke to him directly, speaking slowly as she reached out a friendly hand to the mutant.

Harland looked at her and then swiveled his head, looking fixedly at the gun in Brad's hand. Following his gaze, Erin looked pointedly at the gun. "Oh, put that away Brad! You've already proven you couldn't hit the broad side of a barn with that thing. Give me a hand with our new eagle friend."

Still not sure they were doing the right thing, Brad put the gun away. He gradually rationalized that if the bird-man was ever going to attack them, he would have done it already. Then, further observing the eagle's injuries, he worried that though the mutant did not have the strength to attack them now, what was to say he wouldn't hurt them when his strength returned?

"Okay, we'll try it your way — for the time being."

Erin continued to talk to Harland, crooning as if she was talking to a baby. Harland cocked his head and listened closely, almost remembering human speech from a different life. Erin's desire to help him affected him. She started talking, and mentioned the "cabin," a word Harland recognized. Since he was heading that way, he hobbled after them as best he could, even allowing Erin at one point to put out a hand to steady him when he could've fallen.

Naively, they brought Harland to the cabin. His first reaction was to balk, refusing to go inside. In the meanwhile, Erin went inside and got bandages and warily patched Harland's wound as best as she could. She tried everything she could think of to coax him inside where he would be safer, but Harland would not budge.

"As a bird, he is probably afraid of closed-in places where he can't spread his wings and fly away easily at the first sign of danger," Erin said, bravely stroking Harland's feathers.

"As a man, he should be used to it," Brad said, a bit nastily. Brad was still uncomfortable within the proximity of the bird, thus he carefully watched its every movement. He kept his gun in his pocket, sometimes stroking it to reassure himself that it would protect him against the mutant.

Brad and Erin had no idea of how many months Harland had been confined in a smaller space within the asylum. He still had a combination of fear from being a prisoner coupled with his natural fear about being within an enclosed space, unable to fly. At the same time, Harland knew he needed to stay close to these humans inhabiting the cabin he had inherited, because Sterling might come at any time. Harland also realized he was too weak and hurt to fly and hunt for himself. Reluctantly, he admitted to himself that he was probably dependent on these humans to help heal him. Vaguely, he was aware that the female human had nurturing intentions toward him, especially since she had already patted him, and bandaged his wounds. The male human he was unsure of, thinking that all males wanted to stake out their territory, something Harland understood. He would stand and watch them both. For now, they would be friends at least until Sterling arrived.

"I think in the long run we can all help each other," Erin declared. "Once he's better, he can spot game and danger from on high. And we can watch his back, too."

"We'll see," said Brad, not at all convinced with her logic, but too tired from the events of the day to argue with her. "Right now, all I want is some grub and a bed. Let's leave bird-man out here, since he won't come inside anyhow. I'll go rustle something together." Brad got up and headed into the cabin.

"Did you actually say 'rustle'?" Erin asked, giving Harland one last pat on the head, that he stoically tolerated. Then she followed Brad inside. The three of them, two humans on the run and an eagle mutant on the run, had formed an alliance.

*   *   *

"Excuse me, Zack; can I get in here to contact the other research facilities?" Rita politely asked, as she moved into the Com Center.

"Oh, sure, Rita, I'm done for now anyhow. It is frustrating trying to get through to anyone. Lucky there are still a few communication satellites working. I just finished talking with Jamie Whitehead and things are looking pretty grim up there," said Zack, vacating his seat for Rita. Lately they had been formal with each other, leaving Zack at a loss at how to break through that barrier.

"How are Brad and Erin doing?" Rita asked. She had gotten accustomed to chatting online with them as Zack talked to them.

"That's a funny thing there," Zack said, puzzled. "Normally they are the ones I talk to, but this time they weren't there at all. I asked Jamie about them and all she would say was there had been personnel changes, and that they were working on another project and would no longer be my contacts. I asked if I could have their new e-lines and she said that they were currently unreachable. She mumbled stuff about 'high security' and 'top clearance', but it didn't sound too convincing. I can't believe she was giving me the shuffle. I thought I was in the inner circle."

"That sounds so strange. Could they be out on assignment somewhere?" Rita tried to sound interested as she took Zack's seat, though her mind was on the conference call she was about to make.

"I seriously doubt that. Everything is in chaos on the outside. That's why no civilians even venture outside anymore. Everyone has been living in their offices, and all key people are now being pulled into hidden bunkers since most of the infrastructure has fallen apart. Even the electrical grids have failed, causing a cascading effect on the rural communities. The metropolitan areas are ghost towns, and even in the small towns people are fleeing the mutants, abandoning their jobs and their homes as the power has failed and no one from the government has come in to help. The military and police are so occupied with fighting mutants, that there is no one available to help defenseless people. The weak are nearly completely on their own," Zack shook his head, ready to head out to check on their own defenses.

"I thought that is what Erin and Brad were working on — getting people into the secure areas."

"I thought so, too, that's why it's so strange that they are not available," Zack said, concerned more about the cave population than what was happening in the states.

"See you later." And with a wave, he was off.

As he exited, Rita wondered when she and Zack became so formal. Making herself comfortable in her chair, Rita began the process of calling the secluded far-flung research facilities. This was their weekly conference call, and they usually spent the first few minutes reviewing the status of their current living arrangements, including security concerns before tackling research specifics.

"How are things on your mountain top aerie, Dr. Hausman?" Rita asked. Dr. Klaus Hausman, the German bio-ethicist had ended up in Nepal. It was astounding that these key scientists were now living continents away from their homes, similar to her. Rita was lucky, though, because at least she was with her family.

"Believe it or not, we are still finding displaced people from the isolated villages here. We are still able to send out a search team to look for people in need of a secure facility, but we are almost at capacity. Before long, we won't be able to help any more people," Dr. Hausman said. "How are you doing?"

"We find ourselves in the same predicament," Rita said, ruefully, as the others chimed in, agreeing with her. "Since we are almost full, it's becoming too dangerous for us to send out any more search and rescue teams. Why risk an air attack from a hostile bird mutant?"

"Survivors have told us stories like that, too. In one case, children were carried off," Dr. Hausman shuddered. Everyone paused for a moment at the horrible picture it created in their minds.

From an island near the Marshall Islands, Dr. Nguyen spoke. "We are stocking supplies we find on forays on previously occupied islands. On these trips, we still find people hiding from the mutants, though that is rare. After we find them and they calm down, they tell us news about aerial and land-based attacks. Some of them are fighting back, using whatever weapons they can find: handguns, sticks, rocks. They talk about the people who have been killed in the battles, and finding human remains. . . . Suddenly we find ourselves having to be medical doctors and grief counselors. We aren't prepared to handle all the needs these people bring with them."

"I know what you mean," Rita empathized. "I'm the closest we have to a medical doctor here. I feel like I'm in way over my head."

"I think we are in the most isolated area," piped up Dr. Breedlove, in Antarctica, "Even though we haven't had any sightings of mutants, we are building our defenses. We have quite a few military personnel who were abandoned here. Their commands stopped communicating with them. There are a couple of tourist groups here, though we have the same thing happening, with their rides home never showing up. What we are really lacking are live and cooperative mutants that we can use for experimentation and . . ."

"Yes?" asked Rita.

"We are starting to worry about our food supply."

"You are helping out tremendously on the theoretical hypotheses," Rita assured her. "You have pointed me in directions I never thought of taking."

Then the discussion turned technical. They hunkered down to the terrifying task of trying to save the world by reversing devolution. The enormity of the task pressed down on them, but like scientists everywhere, they tried to put the big issues aside and concentrate on the daily tasks, taking things step by step, methodically.

* * *

"Lowell Brant Kempfield III, you can do this. Please, a little farther, Baby. We have to find help," Hiawatha pleaded, supporting as best she could her companion who had broken his leg after falling into a shallow ravine off of a mountain path. They had gotten into a tickle fest, which was totally inappropriate while hiking in the wilds, leading to the injury.

Brushing at an insect flying determinedly in his face, Lowell gasped in pain, "I can't go any farther, Doll." He collapsed onto the ground. "You are going to have to leave me here and go for help. It can't be too far until we get to those shots we heard awhile ago. Where there is a gun, there is a person," he added, unnecessarily, for the tenth time now, more to reassure himself than to inform her.

"I can't leave you here," fifteen-year-old Hiawatha wailed. "A bear or a lion could eat you while I'm gone." She looked around them as if expecting one to emerge from the forest at any time. Groaning, she stretched her back. Truthfully, she knew she could not half-carry Lowell another step and that she could make faster time without him.

Lowell's eyes rolled back in his head as perspiration covered his face. With each passing second, he looked like he was fading more and more. They had done their best to splint his leg with tree limbs, but they were woefully ignorant about proper first aid techniques. She rooted around in the underbrush for a long, sturdy branch.

"Lowell, can you hear me? Lowell, answer me!" she screeched, pulling on him, patting his face and covering it with kisses. Soon his lips responded and he regained focus. "Baby, here is a big stick. If anything comes near you, try to keep it away with this."

"Help me move my back to a tree trunk," Lowell directed. "At least I have my knife, too. I'll be all right. Just be quick." He helped her adjust him against a tree, grimacing with pain all the while.

"Okay, I'm going," Hiawatha said, trying to muster the courage to push off into the woods on her own, as she left her love. "I will be back as soon as I can. If I can't find anyone in a few minutes, I'll be back anyhow."

"You've got to find someone. We won't make it otherwise," he muttered, resolutely pushing her on her way.

With many anguished looks back, Hiawatha reluctantly headed along the path, gaining speed as she got out of sight of the most important person in the world to her.

* * *

Brad and Erin were enjoying target practice near the cabin. Based on their encounter with Harland and the lion, they both realized Brad was definitely not a marksman with a gun. Erin had volunteered for gun training with Homeland Security, but Brad, being a computer nerd, had managed to duck that particular course. Now that their survival depended on their shooting ability, they realized that some gun practice would be useful. Fortunately, they took as many boxes of bullets they could from the farmhouse where they had found the gun. Weighing the option of depleting their supply versus improving their shooting had been a tough call, but they decided practicing would improve their aim, ultimately leading to wasting fewer bullets and possibly saving their lives in the process.

Harland fled after the first shots were fired, though it was nothing new to have him fly away for a long stretch of time. Whether it was the noise of the shooting, a need to hunt for food, or just a desire to be alone, Harland would leave for many unknown reasons. For the time it took for his leg to heal, Harland had grown to trust them and even depended on them for his food and water. Now that he was mostly healed, Harland would return the favor, bringing them fresh meat to eat. It took some time for Brad to get over his qualms of skinning and cooking animals that had been alive only minutes earlier, with meat still warm from recently flowing blood, but Erin, endowed with the hard practicality women have for taking care of family above all else, was the first to brave the cooking chores, with Brad slowly catching up.

"That was a pretty good shot for a geek," Erin was saying in response to Brad actually hitting the tree he was aiming at, when a young girl stepped cautiously into the clearing. She had looked like a young deer ready to take flight at any sudden motion. Fortunately, Erin waved Brad to stop shooting.

"Hello there. Can we help you?" Erin said, as soothingly as she could manage.

Hiawatha overcame her initial hesitation at approaching people who were shooting guns when she heard Erin's soft tones. Hiawatha rushed into speech, "Lowell broke his leg and can't go any farther. I tried my best to carry him, but I am small compared to him. I feel terrible that I had to leave him back on the main trail. Please come help him before a wild animal or a mutant eats him." She dissolved into tears, shaking as if she would fall apart. Her long, chestnut hair hid her face as she doubled over.

"Of course, we will help," Erin asserted, going over and putting her arm around the frightened teen. "Do you want to lead the way?"

As if a rod was suddenly rammed down her spine, the young girl straightened herself, revealing her rounded belly. Erin gasped, blurting out, "You are pregnant!"

"So what if I am?" Hiawatha said, defensively. "Come on, you've got to help my Lowell." Then she turned to lead them along the trail back to Lowell.

After travelling silently and rapidly along the path, they came around a bend and spotted a figure backed up to a tree. As they approached Brad suddenly jumped in front of the women, crying out, "It's a mutant." He pulled out his gun and pointed it at the muscular ape-like man.

"That's Lowell," Hiawatha said. Brushing past Brad with annoyance, she ran to Lowell and knelt down beside him. "Baby, are you all right? You've got to help him. He's passed out again. Maybe he hit his head when he fell."

Grabbing at her arm, Brad pulled Hiawatha away from Lowell, "Are you crazy, going that close to a mutant? Don't you know how dangerous they are? Don't you know what he's capable of? He could kill you!" Brad shouted.

"Let go of me," Hiawatha screamed, struggling to get away from Brad. "Lowell wouldn't hurt a fly. In fact, he's my husband."

"Brad, let her go," Erin said, putting in her two cents. "She obviously knows him."

Brad released Hiawatha, who hurriedly returned to Lowell, trying to get him to drink from her water bottle, while Brad continued to protest to Erin. "But Erin, look at him, he's an ape-man. You know all the reports we got in on how irrationally violent they are."

"He doesn't look dangerous right now," Erin replied.

"That's just because he's injured," Brad retorted.

"Come on Brad, let's think this over. We've built a relationship of sorts with a bird-man. How is this any different? Maybe all mutants are not alike, and can't be lumped into one category. Maybe some of them are non-violent, and we've been mislead. Think about it. All our current information comes from the Agency, not from first-hand knowledge," Erin urged, watching the tender ministrations of Hiawatha towards Lowell.

"Doll, what's happening?" Lowell said, trying to pull himself into a sitting position. "I guess I nodded off a bit. Whoa, it looks like you found some people. Are they friends or foes?"

"I don't know, Baby, but they are worried because you're devolving," Hiawatha answered, stroking his coarse, black hair. "I'm not sure whether they are going to help us or not."

"Hey look, folks," Lowell said to Erin and Brad, trying to stay focused. "Looks can be deceiving, man. I'm just an ordinary guy like you." He pointed at Brad.

"You're nothing like me, Buddy," Brad protested.

Erin said, "Of course we will help you. You aren't the first mutant we've helped. In fact, we have a bird-man who has just joined with us. Though calling him a "man" is a probably not correct, since he's pretty much all bird by now." She shut up suddenly, realizing she was babbling.

Holding out his hand, Lowell said, "I am Lowell Brant Kempfield III, but my friends call me Low."

Stepping forward, Erin clasped his hand and introduced herself, "I am Erin Blaine, and this cautious guy with me is Brad Cho. We are holing up in a cabin not far from here."

"And, I am Low's wife, Hiawatha Kempfield, but everyone calls me Hi," Hiawatha said, shooting an unreadable look at Lowell.

,"You are kidding me right?" Brad said, still alert to any danger. "Hi and Low? That is way too cute to be real! And Hiawatha come on, who would stick their kid with that handle?"

"What can I say, my mother loved Longfellow," Hiawatha answered. "Now, are you going to help us or not?"

Erin was saying, "Of course we are," and Brad was reaching out a hand to help, when Harland swooped onto the trail, squawking wildly. He hopped in front of Erin and Brad, protecting them, snapping his beak threateningly at the teens.

"It's okay, Baldie," Erin said, using the nickname she had come up with for Harland. Brad thought it was lame, and that an eagle should be called something more regal, but since he didn't come up with anything better, he also used "Baldie." "They are not going to hurt us. They need our help, just like you once did." She attempted to look deep into Harland's eyes, but with the dead stare of an eagle, it was hard to read whether he understood. Harland, however, backed off, and seemed content to observe everything closely, as Brad got his shoulder under Low's arm. Hiawatha tried to support his other side, but it was obvious to everyone that she had reached her limit and was running on empty. She gave a token protest as Erin gently pushed her aside and helped support Lowell.

Slowly, they dragged Lowell down the trail, though in their minds they were trying to make him walk. By the time they got to the clearing around the cabin, Lowell was delirious. Both Erin and

Brad were beat as they stopped to catch their breaths before stepping into the cabin.

* * *

"So, Hi, do you want to tell us what you are doing out here in the wilds?" Erin softly asked Hiawatha, since Lowell had fallen into a deep sleep after their meager first aid ministrations. Brad plopped down next to them and tried his best to look supportive. "What's to tell?" Hiawatha answered, half-heartedly. "We are escaping from all the fighting like everyone else."

"Come on, Hi, we weren't born yesterday. It is obvious you are both teenagers. Where are your families? How can you be married at your age?" Erin persisted.

"You sure are nosy to people you've just met," Hiawatha said, jumping up and walking away from them. "I guess Lo and I will be on our way once he has finished his nap." With that, she burst into tears.

Erin popped up and went over and put her arm around Hiawatha. "Lowell will not be going anywhere soon. You can both stay here as long as you like. In fact, Brad and I were just saying to each other that we needed to find other people to join with for safety in numbers. But, if we are all going to live together, we have to be able to rely on each other and trust each other. Here, I'll go first. Brad and I are on the run from the government."

"Erin!" Brad exploded. But, of course, it was already too late to take back what Erin had said.

"It's a two-way street, Brad," Erin said, seriously. "People might be hunting us down. We can't put these kids at risk without them knowing the score."

"Really, you're running away from the government? Cool!" Hiawatha said.

Brad gave Erin a look that said plainly — see what you've accomplished. "We all are running away from something," Erin continued unperturbed, taking her glasses off and polishing them nonchalantly. "What are you running from?"

"It's complicated," Hiawatha said, having trouble getting started and afraid to open up to strangers who were also grown-ups, not to mention their initial negative reaction to Low. "When we found out we were pregnant, Low and I wanted to get married. Both of our parents were against it, and because we are underage they wouldn't let us. Like pioneer women were married at thirteen, you know?"

Then Hiawatha stopped to see how Erin was taking it so far. Erin nodded in agreement, keeping her face neutral.

"Low's parents are rich snobs, and they think my family is trailer trash. Since Low was a body-builder, he was into taking all kinds of supplements to improve his health. Then he started taking these new pills and started changing. Well, then my parents were even more against us marrying, not wanting me to marry an ape. I love Low, regardless of what he is! After Low's parents wanted to send him to an institution to get help, we ran away and got married in South Carolina, and decided to come back here and make it on our own." She looked challengingly at Erin and then at Brad.

Erin was pretty sure that South Carolina would not allow kids as young as Hi and Low to get married, and suspected there might be other parts of the story that might not be exactly the way Hiawatha was telling it but she kept these thoughts to herself.

"Sounds like you have had a hard time of it," Erin said, sympathetically.

"Won't your parents get worried about you?" Brad said, not quite as sensitive as Erin was to the nuances.

"My Dad started fighting the mutants and then he disappeared. My Mom took my younger sisters to live with my aunt, but I didn't want to go with them. Low and I are married now, and we will make a life for ourselves," Hiawatha declared with the bravado of youth.

"We are happy to have you stay here with us," Erin quickly said, wondering how she and Brad would deal with a pregnant teenager. Suppose there were complications with the birth? And, aside from the issue of dealing with the broken leg, what would Lowell be like when he further mutated? And what about the child, would it be a mutant or a human? Or, would the child be something in between? It was hard to shake the prejudices that had been ingrained into them at HSA and through the media. It was hard to accept that Lowell wouldn't turn violent as he mutated further. Only their experience with Harland gave them hope that mutants might not all be the same, that some might not become uncontrollably vicious. And then there was the issue of them being teens, with all the raging hormones and angst associated with that stage of life. And, were these kids "wanted?" Were the authorities out looking for them? Erin gave herself a shake. Surely they were too busy to be looking for a pair of runaways. At least Hiawatha and Lowell —Hi and Low — would be safer with them than stumbling around on their own.

Brad, with thought processes similar to Erin's, added his piece, "As I've been saying, there's more safety in numbers. But, if you are going to stay with us, you will have to bear your part of the load. This isn't a free ride for anyone. We all work together. And we have to be able to trust and count on each other." His eyes questioned Hiawatha.

Suddenly eager to please, with the mercurial changes youth are capable of, Hiawatha nodded enthusiastically. "You can count on us. We are hard workers. After Low gets better you'll see he is very strong."

And mutating to an ape will make him even stronger, Brad thought sourly, though he didn't voice this thought.

Just as they were all starting to feel more comfortable with each other, there was a loud knock at the door. Brad grabbed the gun out of his pocket which he kept with him all the time, and looked questioning at Erin. Had the authorities found them, or had someone followed the young people? There was no other exit from the cabin. If someone was here to take them into custody they would have to either surrender or fight for their lives. He looked over at Lowell, who was still sleeping peacefully. Even if they could fight their way free with Harland's help, they couldn't make a run for it with an injured boy and a pregnant girl.

Resignedly, Brad said, "We're just going to have to see who it is, and take it from there."

"Hide," Erin said to Hiawatha. "Then at least if someone is looking for you and Low they won't see you, and maybe we can send them on their way." She also realized that if it was Homeland Security out there, nothing they did would be of any use.

Putting the gun away again, Brad and Erin bravely walked to the door, as Hiawatha hid out of sight.

*   *   *

"What in the world do you folks think you are doing? You are making enough racket to attract aliens from across the galaxy," a bearded, weathered mountain man demanded before they could get the door open a foot. "Do you think you are the only people in these woods?"

With their mouths hanging open, Brad and Erin looked at the man who now pushed his way into the cabin. He was the last thing they expected when they opened that door. Hiawatha popped back into sight, full of curiosity now that she knew it wasn't her parents (or Low's) and that it also wasn't the authorities.

"Excuse me," Brad said. "Who are you? And who do you think you are shoving your way into our cabin?"

"Your cabin you say. Got a deed to back that up? I thought not," the stranger said as he saw Erin and Brad exchange quick, guilty looks. "What I came here for was to save your fool hides!"

"We don't know what you are talking about," Erin began, pulling her dignity about her like a cloak. "We have been taking care of ourselves just fine up until now."

"By shooting up the forest and staying in a cabin near the main trail? You aren't the only ones trying to hide out in these woods. With all the noise you are making someone or something will be breathing down our necks in no time, not that we care if they find you, but they might find us too," he ranted, poking his finger into Erin's face.

"I'll ask you again to tell me who you are," Brad repeated, fingering the gun in his pocket. Then he eyed the shotgun the mountain man casually held. He had no idea how a handgun versus a shotgun would end.

At that, Harland charged from behind the man. Diverted from thoughts of the gun, Brad tried to block Harland, while Erin tried to soothe him down.

"I see you've got mutants living with you," the stranger nodded, looking at Harland fearlessly and casting a glance at Lowell. "Hard to believe you city folks are smart enough to make friends with mutants."

"How do you know we are city folk?" Erin began. Vainly, she had thought they had been doing a good job at blending into their environment, and this guy was blasting all her preconceived notions.

At the same time, Brad repeated his original question, "Who are you?" And then added, "Who are the other people you are talking about?"

"Believe me, you folks are leaving large footprint on the earth, and I'm not just talking about a carbon footprint." The man set his shotgun down against his leg, and looked around. "Mind if I sit a spell? We've got some talking to do."

Feeling that some of the tension had left the room, Harland relaxed, though he was still on alert. At a loss for what else to do, Erin motioned the stranger to a seat, and dropped into one herself with Hiawatha and Brad soon following. This had been one heck of a day, and it still didn't look like it was over by any means. She didn't know if her system could take any more surprises. Then looking at the pregnant teen, she wondered how Hiawatha was standing up to all she had been through.

"Here's a bulletin. You are not the first ones to take to the mountains to get away from the pandemonium sweeping through our country. There are many of us who left at the first signs of trouble. Some of us could immediately read the writing on the wall and see where everything was heading, and we got out," the man began, sitting and now relaxing. "Some might call us survivalists. Be that as it may, some of us have been stockpiling supplies ever since those enhancements hit the market, seeing the way the wind was blowing. We have quite a large encampment up here, and we can't let some fool dandified city folks threaten our safety." He stopped and looked at them as if he had finished saying his piece.

Almost whining, Brad asked for the fourth time, "Who are you?"

"Didn't I just explain all that?" the man said, annoyed as he stared at Brad like he was an idiot. "No, I mean, what's your name? I'm Br…"

"Shhh. No one is dumb enough to use their real names here. While we all think we can trust each other, you just never can really tell about folks, can you? You can call me 'Tracker' if you must. That's as good a handle as any."

Suddenly, Hiawatha looked smug. Erin immediately thought again of the convenient names, Hi and Low.

"So are you ready to go?" Tracker said, standing up and grabbing his shotgun.

"What do you mean go?" Brad asked, confused. Had he missed something? He was still shocked over the day's drastic turn of events.

"Why, with me to the compound, you don't think you can live this close to the main trail and escape detection do you? You have a lot to learn about living in the woods without attracting attention, which is what we can teach you. We welcome anyone on the run," he said, simply.

"Why do you think we are on the run?" Brad said, forgetting they had said almost the same thing to Hiawatha, seemingly hours ago.

"In these difficult times, anyone with half a brain is on the run from someone or something," Tracker said.

"But, we can't just up and head out with you to who knows where," said Erin.

"And what about Low, he can't live out in the open," Hiawatha protested, saying nothing about her coming child, though she patted her pregnant belly.

"Who said anything about being out in the open?" Tracker demanded, now irritated and thinking that someone with more patience should have been sent to deal with these folks. "Didn't you hear me say we've been at this a long while now? Do you think we live in the trees? We've now got a nice compound all established. There are plenty of people there to help you all. In fact, we even have a doctor, well, a guy who at least says he was a doctor in China, and a former Army medic, too. Look, why don't you come see for yourself? If you like it, you can stay." He avoided the issue of how his group would deal with the noisy city folk if they stayed in the cabin.

"That sounds like a good idea," Erin said. "I'll go with you."

"Erin, I don't like the idea of you going off with this stranger alone without me. Pardon me, but you, sir, are a stranger to us," Brad objected.

"Don't be silly," Erin said airily. "We can't all go traipsing off on a trip with Lowell's condition. Hiawatha needs to stay with him. And you need to stay to protect them."

"We don't need protection," Hiawatha asserted, trying to look brave and utterly failing.

Tracker sneered to himself at the idea of Brad being able to protect anyone, but he kept a straight face anyway. Reluctantly, Brad agreed to Erin's inescapable logic since she had an annoying way of frequently being correct in her assumptions. "Can she trust you?" he asked Tracker, knowing it was a silly question when he asked it.

"I'll have her back before sundown, Dad," Tracker joked, lightening the moment, which suddenly made them all feel more relaxed.

"Okay, let's get on with this," Erin said briskly. Before Brad or Hiawatha could comment, Erin was out the door with Tracker, going off into the unknown. Brad and Hiawatha looked at each other, exchanging glances. Would they ever see her again? Harland squawked bobbed his head and then took to the air.

*   *   *

"Are we there yet?" Erin complained. The walk from D.C. to the mountains, plus the weeks at the cabin, reminded Erin of how out of shape she was. Even now with weeks of exercise her muscles still weren't accustomed to climbing over rough terrain. Now she was questioning her decision to follow the mountain man.

With no more than a stern glance at her meant to tell her to be quiet, Tracker gave a bird whistle. Soon the undergrowth near the overgrown path rustled, revealing a huge black monster that leapt out at her. Erin gasped, trying to shrink inside herself, while simultaneously wondering which way to run.

"Here, Lope, leave the lady alone," Tracker said softly, bending down to ruffle the dog's ears. By contrast, Erin saw it as the biggest dog she had ever seen. She grew up with pugs in her house and didn't know any large dogs. And she couldn't have identified a breed even if she tried. She guessed that the grinning, large-headed beast was a mutt, maybe part bloodhound and part Newfoundland. But right now it was wagging its whole body as if seeing Tracker was the happiest moment in its entire life.

"You have a dog?" Erin asked, inanely, all the while wishing she could take back a rather obvious question.

"Yep, I couldn't exactly leave her to fend for herself when I took off, now could I? Don't worry you don't need to be afraid of her. She wouldn't hurt a flea, though she is a good hunting dog. You more than earn your keep, don't you girl?" Tracker said, playing with the dog as if they had all the time in the world. "Fact is we have quite a few dogs here. A number of other folks brought theirs, and we found some strays that were probably abandoned by their owners." He looked exceptionally fierce at that thought, shaking his head as if he couldn't imagine a greater crime.

"Can I pet her?" Erin asked quickly, trying to get him back in a good mood.

"Sure, and she's sweet to all the kids in the compound, too," Tracker responded, proudly.

"Kids?" Erin asked, putting her hand out for Lope to sniff. Lope took a good sniff then rubbed her big head against Erin, begging for a head rub. Erin obliged, running her hands through her long silky fur.

"Sure, we've got a few families with children living with us. That there pregnant gal of yours will fit right in when she has her baby," Tracker said, clucking to Lope he started walking again.

"Excuse me, but how much further do we have to travel?" Erin asked, without moving.

"Why, can't you tell we are here?!" Tracker chuckled. Confidently, he moved towards some dense brush and moved a swath of it aside to reveal a narrow cave opening. "I'd say 'ladies first' to be gentlemanly, but you had best follow me this first time," Tracker warned, walking into the cave, with Lope prancing behind him. Erin had little choice but to follow, though trying to stay as close as she could.

After going down a narrow, claustrophobic tunnel leading into the ground, the cave opened into a warren of larger rooms arranged along an underground riverbed. The rock formations, stalactites and stalagmites, had Erin gasping as she managed quick glances, though always careful to keep a close eye on her feet. The pathway was smoothed flat, and spotlights were strategically placed to light the way. After a number of turns, Erin lost her bearings and gave up trying to keep track of them. She'd just have to trust Tracker to get her back out.

A large cavern opened before them, giving Erin her first sign of life within the cave. People came and went through well-placed passageways, making it difficult to properly count the number of people within the complex. Erin guessed that there were at least twenty to thirty people living there. When she was within sight of the others they all stopped what they were doing and silently crowded around her.

"I see you managed to snag one of those noisy city folks," one of the men called out to Tracker.

A woman, who looked like a picture-perfect Native American, reached out her hand to Erin, warmly saying, "Welcome to our home. You may call me Kaya, which means Elder Sister in Hopi. I don't know if Tracker warned you or not, but we have all shed our past names, and in this new world we have accepted new names. Living along the heavily populated Eastern Seaboard it is not out of the realm of possibility that one of us could be captured and forced to betray the others. Using aliases is one of the ways we guard against this. So, having said that, what would you like us to call you?"

Erin took hold of Kaya's outreached hand, feeling a bit overwhelmed with her long explanation and with the looks of the commanding woman. "I'm glad to meet you. I'll need some time to think of a suitable name, since it sounds like an important decision."

Everyone around her nodded gravely and approvingly, since they had all once faced the same difficult task.

"This is my daughter, Namid, which means Star Dancer in Cheyenne," Kaya continued, pulling forward a willowy girl, 18, with short black hair. Erin stifled a gasp as she realized the girl was devolving along the ape route, obviously farther along than Lowell. She looked back at Kaya to see if there was any sign of devolution in her, but was not able to discern any. All she saw on the lean, medium size woman was intact, long black hair, bright dark eyes, high cheekbones, and a welcoming smile.

"It's nice to meet you, Namid. That is a beautiful name you have chosen," Erin said, offering her hand to the teen.

There was a collective sigh, as if Erin had passed a test from the gathering, as the girl shook her hand, looking her straight in the eye, "My mother helped me pick out a Native American name. Since we have both Hopi and Cheyenne in our ancestry, we wanted to honor both of those cultures in our new lives."

Kaya nodded in agreement. "I'm not going to take the time to introduce you to all these people now. That will only confuse you. You can get to know them at your leisure once you are all safely here. Let me show you around briefly, so we can get your fellow travelers here as soon as possible. I understand you have a young man with you who is grievously hurt? This is Dr. Longwei," she gestured to an elderly man to her right, and then to a woman in her twenties next to him. "This is Medic. They will be able to minister ancient Chinese medicine and acupuncture to him, along with modern military medical practices. I am also dabbling with Native American healing arts, so we have many avenues covered to help with anyone's well-being. For now, though, let me show you around."

Glancing at the rest of the group, Erin gathered impressions of a number of weather hardened, woods-savvy men like Tracker, and many families with a bewildering assortment of children. As Erin followed Kaya on a tour, she recalculated that the cave contained 40 – 50 people instead of her earlier estimation of 20 – 30. Kaya revealed a state-of-the-art computer console, which Erin was relieved to find. The tour continued through a food storage unit complete with shelves of canned goods, a cold cellar, a kitchen and dining area, a clinic, a common room, and a munitions room, along with many private dwelling rooms. There were so many rooms that they all blurred in Erin's mind. She was convinced the cave had even more important areas, though they probably would be revealed on a second tour.

"And this is our Listening Room," Kaya said, finishing and expectantly looking at Erin. It was essentially an empty room with some low seating haphazardly spread around, not at all arranged for a formal meeting.

Erin asked, "I'm afraid I don't know what a listening room is?"

"This is our spiritual center," Kaya said, reverently. "Because we all come from different walks of life with different religious beliefs (or even a lack of beliefs), some of us use this room as a chapel, for some it serves as a temple, for others it fills the need for a place to come and focus on whatever issue is of pressing need. The point of this place is to listen to the spiritual counsel we get from outside ourselves, or inside ourselves. Sometimes we seek counsel from each other here about personal matters, though it is mainly a place to commune quietly within ourselves in whatever way brings us to harmony and peace. We have found that in this time of world crisis, we need a haven like this more than ever." She gave Erin a quizzical gaze.

Since religion had never been a major part of her life, Erin responded lamely. "Uh, that sounds nice. I mean, it must be a comfort to people who need that in their lives."

"I hope you will feel you can take advantage of it when you need it," Kaya said, simply, leading Erin back to the main room of the complex, without further ado.

"Do you have any questions before we bring your friends here?" Kaya asked.

"Who is in charge here?" Erin asked.

"I suppose you could say I am in charge," Kaya answered, with a twinkle in her eyes. "After all, I am the Elder Sister. But, in truth, most decisions are made by consensus, with the advice of the ones with knowledge in key areas relied on the most. But, everybody is expected to carry their own weight since we all are fighting for our survival."

"Would Br—, uh, my friend and I be able to work in the computer area?"

"That would be acceptable, once you get trained," Kaya nodded.

"What kind of training are you talking about?" Erin asked suspiciously.

"Everybody here has to be a jack of many trades. First and most importantly, you will be trained in woods craft by Tracker and a few of the other experts we have in that area. It is most important that when we travel through the forest we do so silently and as one with nature. You also need to be taught how to not leave any tracks. Then, you must learn the skills in all the areas of the compound. For instance, everyone must learn how to hunt and trap, how to cook, and how to administer first aide."

"Why?" asked Erin.

"If a person had a specialty in just one field and something were to happen to that person, who would jump in to take his or her place? Therefore, we all need to be able to work within each skill set in case tragedy was to happen. And, let's face it, the longer we are here, the more we will face unexpected dangers, events and illnesses — be it giving birth, setting broken bones, or handling wounds from a mountain lion. Also, we may face various factions of warring people and mutants. Besides, we are not the only people in these mountains." Kaya paused to see if Erin was following along with her, but of course, Erin did not need any warnings about the chaos the world was in. "Once you have acquired all the skills everybody has to offer, then you can work in the area most suited for you. Regardless, we still take turns at the undesirable jobs — like KP and latrine duty." She gave a soft laugh, and Erin joined in.

Erin was now reassured that she and Brad had found the kind of group they had hoped to find. Of course, they hadn't found the group through their own initiative, but rather through blundering through the forest and carelessly raising a ruckus. Fortunately, a peaceful group had found them and welcomed them with open arms. Erin was now eager to get back to Brad and the young couple they had just found to bring them to this place. The worry of a pregnant girl and an injured mutant was not theirs alone to bear.

Judging from Kaya's daughter, Namid, the group had already accepted peaceful, ape-like mutants. She hoped that they would be equally accepting of Baldie, their eagle ally. She spared a concern for how he would do in the caves, since he would rarely enter the cabin. These last few days had really opened her eyes to the personality differences in mutants. She couldn't bear to think that she had been part of a government system of segregating, imprisoning, and purging the country of mutants. Now she was filled with shame, though with a new determination to avoid prejudice based on appearances; a noble goal, which was harder to practice than it was to preach.

"Are you ready to go get your pals?" Tracker asked. He had been silently waiting as Erin stood, lost in her own thoughts.

Giving herself a shake, she answered, "Let's do it!"

CHAPTER NINE

My God, What Have We Done?

Nate and Sandra wound their way slowly through the encampment, holding hands and talking quietly while most of the others rested after a long day of toil. A few people sat around the central campfire, enjoying some camaraderie. They remarked on all the changes that had occurred during the time they had been in the cavern. In addition to tents, several permanent cabins had been built with more underway. In the tradition of the Amish, everyone helped one another with house-raising, all the while making a party atmosphere of it. They needed non-routine activities that lifted spirits and helped to keep everybody busy. Excessive free time led to depression and mischief, with the mischief not being the sole province of the young.

Hating to break the current romantic mood that was building between them, Nate realized that what he had to say to Sandra would be very important to her, and would have a huge impact on their relationship, hopefully taking it to a whole new level. So, in the long run, he thought it would increase her feelings for him, which was all to the good.

"Sandra, I have something to tell you that I have been thinking about for a long time now," he started.

Not understanding that Nate was about to say something he believed was important, Sandra asked idly, "What's that, Nate?" Her mind was busy figuring out how long it would before she and

Nate had a cabin of their own. The idea sounded so luxurious. Selflessly, she and Nate had decided that the family units should have the housing first and they would wait until that was accomplished before starting one of their own. Sandra had already picked out the perfect spot for it, as far away from the center of camp and the smell of cooking meat as they could get. The distance would also give at least an illusion of privacy, something that was at a high premium in the cavern.

Nate stopped walking and grabbing Sandra's arms he gently turned her towards him. "I've decided to become a vegetarian," he said simply.

"Oh, Nate, that is wonderful," Sandra cried out, and launched into a big hug. The next few minutes were satisfyingly busy with heartfelt kisses. Instead of breaking the mood, this had actually advanced it, Nate thought congratulatory.

Sandra pulled back, her eyes suddenly filled with questions, "Nate, you aren't doing this just for me, are you? I mean, that would be sweet of you to do it for me, but…."

"Sandra, you know I would do anything for you," Nate said, his heart full to bursting. "But, I know that becoming a vegetarian to please you would be insulting to you, almost like I was trying to buy our relationship."

Sandra looked at him with something approaching awe. She hadn't realized that Nate had thought so deeply about this, and was touched that he understood that he couldn't buy into the relationship by catering to her beliefs. He understood how much having a real belief of his own was too vital to his own being to adopt it casually for the convenience of their relationship.

"Wow", she said simply, giving him another deep kiss that took some time.

"Hey, when it comes to buying and selling, I'm the best," Nate joked.

"So what led you to this change in your thinking?" Sandra asked.

"Well, partly it came from listening to you and beginning to understand the horrors of the meat industry and the torture they put

271

animals through. That is unconscionable. I realized I had to accept responsibility for the torturing, the same as most Americans, when I was buying a nice sanitized package of meat. At first, I thought, if animals were cared for properly and killed humanely then it might be okay to eat them. I think the final nail in the coffin was seeing the mutation of our friends. I realized how little we know about what goes on in the minds of other species, and how disrespectful we are of all of nature by putting our own selfish wants, not needs, ahead of all else. I realized that we were devaluing the very meaning of life itself by killing so wantonly. And, I know, like you always say, that I could never kill another creature while looking it in the eyes."

"Now I know how you were able to sell to your investors," Sandra said, applauding him with her eyes. "You don't know how happy you have just made me!"

"Senor Nate and Senorita Sandra may I have a moment of your time?"

Nate and Sandra turned still holding hands tightly, to see Javier striding towards them determinedly.

"Of course, Javier, what can we do for you?" Sandra asked, a little sad that her joyous time alone with Nate had been shattered. She was still overwhelmed with her feelings of love for Nate, and wanted nothing to come between them at this moment.

"I've been turning something over and over in my mind, not sure of what to do. I could be mistaken, and I don't want to accuse anyone unjustly," Javier said a bit breathlessly, his usual authoritative manner a bit in disarray.

"Duly noted," Nate said encouragingly, wanting to get whatever it was out of the way quickly. He gave Sandra's hand a squeeze, and got an answering squeeze back. Resolutely, he forced his mind back on Javier's concern. Even with the decision to have a democratic government most of the people still tended to turn to the initial group for direction.

"Do you recall the last time we were on a mission to find people to rescue," Javier began, "we were attacked; and after thinking a lot about it, I think I know one of the attackers."

"You do?" Sandra exclaimed, appreciating his news, all the while making Javier feel important though that he already had plenty of self-confidence.

"Well, come on, man, spit it out," Nate said, impatiently. "The suspense is killing me."

"It was Miguel," Javier said, triumphantly. He then spoiled the effect, saying, "At least I think so."

Sandra and Nate looked blankly at each other and at Javier.

"Who is Miguel?" they asked in unison.

"He was Senor Perez's co-pilot," Javier said.

"Oh, yeah, now I remember," said Nate. "He was the co-pilot who took us to the States, and brought us back here. Wasn't there some kind of problem with him?"

"If I remember correctly," Sandra began, wrinkling her brow upwards adorably, "Rita said that he had taken the supplements, in fact, both he and the captain took the supplements and were devolving down the avian path. Is that actually correct?"

"Yes, Senorita, what you remember is correct. Captain Sanchez was also devolving, along with Miguel. Senor Perez offered to help both men, though he was angry that they had ignored his directive to not take the pills. He told them he would take care of them and their families, and that they could be included in the trials conducted by Senorita Rita to find a solution to the problem. Captain Sanchez was appropriately remorseful for what he had done, so he threw himself on the mercy of the Senor. He and his family are here in the cavern with us. Miguel, however, was a different story. He became increasingly belligerent and took off never to be seen again."

"And you think you saw him with the avian mutants who attacked us?" Nate finished for him.

"Yes, I'm pretty sure it was him. However, how can I be sure? The creature we saw had mutated so far that he had advanced to the point where it could fly. There was almost nothing left to distinguish him. I would not like to falsely accuse anyone by jumping to a hasty conclusion, especially since the rest of his family is with us. It was just a brief glimpse as we ducked for cover. I've been mulling this over and over in my mind and I thought I should bring it to someone's attention, and then I noticed you two, uh, walking by. Maybe, I should have spoken to the Senor first, though he was not with us that day, and you were."

"I never got a close enough to look at him, and certainly didn't know him well enough to verify what you have said," Sandra admitted.

"It's probably a waste of time to even mention it, but I'm sorry to disturb your evening," Javier said. He bowed slightly then started to turn away.

"Wait a minute. I think this is important," Nate said, a troubled expression on his face. "This Miguel guy knows the estate pretty well, doesn't he? It is probable that he knows something about my ranch from things he overheard before he left. Do you think he knows anything about the cavern? Did he leave before it was discovered or after?"

Sandra looked startled then worried her lightening quick mind immediately tracking what Nate was thinking. Was their secret hideout known? Had all the work to cover their tracks been for naught? Was the location of the cavern already known?

"I think he left before the cave was discovered," Javier answered, judiciously, trying hard to work out the timeline of when Miguel had left in relationship to the discovery of the cave under the waterfall.

"Then we are probably safe," Sandra said, relieved.

"Nevertheless, I think we need to talk this over with Zack so that he can alert his security personnel. We may need to tell everybody at the next community gathering," said Nate, remorsefully.

"Ah, sir, but Miguel's family is here. What a shame and an embarrassment that would bring to them, to have their family name dishonored in front of everyone!" Javier said, pleading. "Please do not subject them to that."

"Javier is right, and so are you, Nate," Sandra said, thrusting her index finger into the air. "We need to put Zack in the know, but there is no reason to humiliate Miguel's family."

Javier nodded, energetically, cleverly looking at Nate for confirmation.

"Okay, I agree," Nate said, not wanting to ruin the evening with Sandra by getting into a disagreement with her. "We'll tell Zack about it, but otherwise keep it to ourselves."

"Thank you. I'm sorry to have disturbed your evening, but I hope the rest of it will be enjoyable for you," Javier said, formally, this time turning away and purposely walking towards his family tent.

Nate looked at Sandra hopefully, though he could see she was wired by what they had heard. He realized there was little likelihood of immediately resuming the romantic mood that they started before Javier's untimely interruption. He sighed, his mind darting in many directions as it tried to come up with a way to return Sandra to thoughts of romance.

"Do you think we need to go to Zack immediately?" Sandra asked, primed for action that had nothing to do with romance.

Somewhat desperately, Nate said, "No, I don't think there is any rush. Why disturb his sleep at this point? Tomorrow will be soon enough. Right now, we are near the Com Center, and I have a nice bottle of wine in there for us." Maybe a couple glasses of wine would return Sandra into a proper frame of mind. They were trying to be frugal with the supply knowing it would not last forever, a fact that Rita's father had bemoaned loudly about every day.

"Since we are here, there is something I would like to look at," said Sandra, leading the way to the computer console.

It was not what Nate had in mind. "Haven't we already spent enough hours on the computer?" he asked, plaintively. He uncovered the fine bottle of wine and following her, he sank into the seat next to her. He poured each of them a glass – still hopeful.

"For some reason I was having trouble accessing some sites yesterday," she said as she typed, frantically, her mind already on what she was typing as she accepted a glass of wine, absently from Nate. "Look, I can't get onto Google anymore."

"That can't be true," said Nate, the computer geek momentarily taking over from Mister Romeo. "Here, let me try this time." He turned to the screen in front of him and tried to launch Google.

"What do you mean — let you try? What do you think I've been doing every day, copying information off Google as fast as I can?

Do you think I don't know what I'm doing?" Sandra demanded, her feathers ruffled, looking quite avian herself at the moment.

"No, I didn't mean that!" Nate stopped, not wanting to dig a deeper hole. Trying to distract Sandra, he hurriedly said, "What about Yahoo?" he said, his fingers stroking away.

"Nope, I can't get on Yahoo either. It keeps saying 'Page Not Found.' Let me try Wikipedia," Sandra answered her mind back on the problem.

"I just tried *The Washington Post*, and the *New York Times . . .* nothing," Nate reported.

"Nothing at Wikipedia either?"

They both tried dozens of search engines and news sites. Now, every site was down and couldn't be reached. They continued to get the "Page Not Found" screen. The earlier mood of the evening was now destroyed as they looked at each other in dismay, about to give up.

"Wait a minute; I've got an idea," Nate said, swiveling towards the keyboard. With a bit of clever computer contortions he was able to find a way into the U.S. Satellite system downloads. They immediately found a view of Earth from space.

"Can you zoom in on that? Something about it doesn't seem right," Sandra said, leaning over Nate's arm for a closer look at his screen. "Can you pull that up on this computer, too?"

Even though he enjoyed Sandra leaning on his arm, Nate pulled up the Satellite system for her also.

"Isn't this Greenland?" Sandra asked, pointing to the first image she noticed on her screen. "All the ice is gone."

"I guess it now finally lives up to its name of *Green*-land," Nate joked.

Sandra whacked him. "It's not funny Nate. This is terrible."

"Look at these massive brownout areas," Nate said, pointing to key locations on his screen. "If I'm not mistaken, these are where nuclear plants used to be. Even roads, houses, and bridges appear to have been vaporized — as if nothing had ever been there."

They looked at each other in horror as the reality of nuclear explosions suddenly swept into their minds, with its ramification of fallout and radiation sickness, including nuclear winters. How far beyond the obvious visual destruction did the effects go?

"The Himalayas are snow-free, too," Sandra noted, still web-surfing over Europe and Asia.

"Does that make it easier to climb Mt. Everest?" Nate joked. Sandra sent him a withering look. What they were seeing was too catastrophic to be joked about.

Nate zoomed into South America and exclaimed, "The Amazon rain forest is burning! And the whole Gulf of Mexico is on fire! So is the entire Pacific Northwest in both the United States and Canada." His mind staggered at the enormity of what he was seeing, unable to fully take it in.

"So are the African jungles!" Sandra reported almost robotically.

Almost in unison, they both panned to and zoomed into the East Coast of the United States, a place home to them only recently. Everything seemed distorted. The atmosphere was thick and hard to see through due to massive fires burning everywhere. With their continuing persistence, they found a closer look, realizing the coast of the United States had permanently changed. They gasped when they realized that the whole Delmarva Peninsula was gone, including Washington, D.C.

"We have no home to go to," Sandra said, inanely, though it was the least of the tragedy.

"Florida is gone, so is most of Louisiana, and a huge chunk of the Texas coast, though that is hard to see because of the fire in the Gulf."

Panning slowly further north, they gasped in horror when they saw that Manhattan, with all its surrounding islands, including Long Island, was gone. Not being able to stand it anymore, Sandra turned away from the screen and buried her head in Nate's shoulder.

"Oh, Nate, this is beyond believable. The cataclysm of nature's fury brought on by global warning, and the destruction caused by mutants occurring at the same time is beyond comprehension. I can't get past the horror of it."

Holding out the bottle of wine, Nate poured them both another glass, not with any hopes of reviving the passion, but more to take the edge off the dreadfulness and awfulness of what they were seeing.

"I think we need to have Rita and Zack see this," Sandra suggested in a shaky voice.

"Good idea," Nate said, jumping up and holding his hand out to Sandra. Any action was preferable to looking longer at those computer screens and trying to imagine the loss of life that went with the physical devastation they were seeing.

* * *

"Wait a sec, just a moment." It was Zack's voice coming from Rita's cabin.

After asking around to see if anyone had seen Zack and Rita, Nate and Sandra were pointed towards Rita's cabin. Filled with the horror of what they had just seen, Nate and Sandra hadn't noticed the smirk that came with the directions. There was nothing unusual for Zack to be in Rita's newly-built cabin, since it also housed the new research lab. He often consulted with her there, even though the hour was admittedly a little late for that. Everyone knew that Rita often worked well into the night. They had knocked without a second thought about it. But, at the muffled sounds of Zack's voice and the noise of hurried scuffling, Nate and Sandra came back to the present, and looked at each other with raised eyebrows. Their suspicions deepened when Zack opened the door appearing disheveled and breathless.

"Is Rita here?" Sandra asked, innocently trying to crane her neck to see around Zack.

"She's in the bathroom right now" Zack answered, trying to act casually but failing miserably unable to look either of them in the eyes.

Nate and Sandra exchanged knowing glances, though they were only momentarily diverted. What they had seen was too horrendous to keep out of their minds for long. They blurted out to Zack about the satellite feed that Nate had managed to tap into and what they had actually witnessed.

"Can you and Rita come over to the Com Center to see what we've found?" Nate asked.

"If you're not too busy, that is?" Sandra said, batting her eyelashes.

"No problem. We'll be right over," Zack hurriedly answered, almost shutting the door in their faces.

Turning away from the closed door, Sandra wryly said, "Looks like Rita and Zack have made it past the awkward stage."

"Do you really think so?" Nate asked, more to keep his mind off what the computers had shown, than with any sincere interest in an answer to his question.

"Surely, you noticed Zack's state of almost undress?" Sandra prodded.

"Rita always acts as if she isn't even aware of Zack," Nate protested.

"'Act' being the operative word," Sandra said as she led the way towards the Com Center.

"What is that supposed to mean?" Nate said, figuratively scratching his head. Sometimes women were hard to figure out.

"Have you ever heard of running just fast enough to get caught?" Sandra soothed, patting Nate's arm as he looked at her quizzically. "It isn't important. And speaking of running, here comes our athletes," she finished as Rita and Zack raced into the Com Center, acting as if nothing unusual was afoot. "Everything okay Rita?" Sandra asked, tongue in cheek.

"Of course, why wouldn't it be?" Rita answered, distractedly. "Zack and I were just going over some of my latest findings," she explained, defensively.

"It would be interesting to know what you discovered," Sandra said, still sticking it to Rita.

Rita shot a look to Zack that begged for help. Clearing his throat and improvising quickly, Zack said, "So show us what you have found that couldn't have waited until morning?" He plopped down in a seat next to Nate.

Relieved to be on solid ground after all the confusing strong emotions that had been swirling in the room, Nate plunged into telling Zack and Rita what he had discovered, showing them everything on the computer screen.

"Oh, you guys just noticed all of that?" Zack said, dismissively. "I've been monitoring the destruction around the globe every day. In fact, I can get us in to see closer with this HSA program." He suited his actions to his words. Soon they were zooming in closer to the East Coast than they had been able to do with the satellite feed they had been using, focusing first on the former D.C. area that was now under water. He panned west until the screen showed empty land.

"Do you see what I see?" Sandra asked, finally diverted from teasing Rita. It was easy to tease Rita. "It seems like a still picture instead of a live video feed. No cars or trains are moving and no people in sight."

It was true. The picture was tight enough that a car's model name could be read. Oddly, there weren't any people in the pictures. Even the bustling suburban areas of Virginia and Maryland, the bedroom communities of Washington, D.C., were abandoned.

"It's nighttime there, like it is here," Rita said, practically, the blush beginning to fade from her face. "Everything is just buttoned up for the night."

"I don't think so, Rita," Zack said, zooming up to house doors that were left hanging open. Graffiti and unspeakable filth covered the walls of houses, with gaping holes where windows once were. In addition, cars were mindlessly overturned and stripped of their parts. There were no house lights or street lights anywhere, just fires burning brightly. There were no boats moving in the waters.

"Seeing these deserted boats reminds me of Gabe and Marti. I can't believe it's been at least a week since we talked to them last. Can you pan to the Galapagos Islands and let's see what is happening there?" Sandra asked.

Zack obliged, allowing them to quickly see that many of the Galapagos Islands had been drowned, leaving only those with tall volcanoes poking above sea level. Zack zoomed close into an island they knew Gabe and Marti had taken refuge on. They could see

Gabe's boat and the fact that thankfully most of the island was still above water. Sadly, they weren't able to see their friends.

Sandra and Rita gasped in dismay.

"I'm sure this means they did such a good job of camouflaging their campsite that we can't see it," Nate said reassuringly to the gals, as he took Sandra's hand and squeezed it tightly.

"We've got to give them a call," Sandra said tremulously, hanging on to Nate's hand. Somehow the fate of Gabe and Marti seemed of supreme importance to her, as if they represented the fate of all mankind.

Zack, meanwhile, had panned back to the northeast coast of the United States. He interrupted the worried conversation about Gabe and Marti, saying, "Look at this. You can see some of the skyscrapers of New York City poking above the water that has flooded it."

Diverted, Sandra, Nate, and Rita peered closely over Zack's shoulder as he moved them slowly over the Jersey coast. Unlike Washington, D.C., this area was not deserted. Horribly, they saw people, like ants, streaming westward, followed closely by an army of attacking mutants. The mutants were overtaking the slower ones, and the view was now so close that they could see people being beaten and trampled to death, the mutants dancing gleefully as they killed children, discarding their bodies like toys. The hardest part was that it continued forever, with bodies continuing to pile up, as people had their limbs torn off, and their faces chewed up. Avian mutants were picking up the bodies and dropping them off from great heights with no discernable reason. The slaughter was beyond comprehension, beyond the ability of the mind to assimilate. They could see people screaming, though they could not hear them. It was like the worst Hollywood horror movie, made more macabre by its lack of sound and mood music. Unlike a movie, there was no end in sight with no hero to ride in and save the day, and no way to reassure oneself that all the participants were actors with fake blood spewing temporarily on a screen. The group seemed frozen in place, unable to turn it off.

Finally, taking the initiative, Zack clicked the screen off. Moaning loudly, Rita sank into her seat. Tears fell down her cheeks and her sobs became increasingly hysterical as Sandra comforted her. Tears were also falling down Sandra's face. The men were having difficulty too. Rita was gulping air and shaking as her sobs turned into a frantic wail. She was headed for a serious panic attack when Zack shouldered Sandra out of the way and gathered Rita up in his arms, saying, "Come on Rita everything will be alright." Although he knew it wouldn't be. Sandra collapsed against Nate, her tears slowing as her concern for Rita grew.

Pushing Zack away, Rita jumped up and yelled. "No, it's not going to be okay. How can you say that, Zack? It is *never* going to be all right ever again. The world is in mass destructing, and it is my fault!"

Thunderstruck, Zack stuttered, "What do you mean — *your fault?*"

"Rita, surely you don't think you personally are responsible for global warming," Nate said calmly, trying to be a voice of reason in the emotional swirl.

Rita looked at him contemptuously. "No, I'm not stupid enough to say I can control climate change. No, I'm just laying claim to how fast it has happened. All the brilliant minds that had been studying climate change argued that we had centuries to deal with the issue. But the chaos caused by the mutants, caused by the pills, based on my research, has resulted in nuclear meltdowns, massive oil spills, raging fires, and all kinds of events adding to the warming trend. There wouldn't be any mutants if I hadn't played around with the program that Pedro wrote, adapting it and fiddling with the genetic code, as if I was God."

"Rita, you were only trying to enhance people's lives with that program, improving things for the betterment of humankind. You hoped to genetically get rid of diseases and to help women who were unable to conceive. I could go on and on listing all the good you intended to accomplish," Sandra protested, trying to reach out to Rita to keep her from tearing around within the Com Center like a tornado run amuck.

But Rita was not having any of it. "Oh yeah, by working on that top secret government project, trying to turn non-human

DNA into human DNA, I learned enough to be lethal. My mother was right when she accused me of messing where angels feared to tread. I thought I was smart enough to do what no one else had accomplished. Who did I think I was? Now the whole world is paying for my conceit. Instead of enhancing people's lives, I have destroyed them. I caused people to devolve into violent animals. I can claim credit for the flooding from global warming and the mutants causing the deaths of millions of people. Innocent babies are dying!" She couldn't go on, falling into tears as she spoke.

Zack corralled her into a corner of the room. She fought him briefly, lashing out with fists and feet, but finally, exhaustion set in, slumping against him as he held her tightly in his arms. "You were just trying to help people," Zack said. "All your motives were noble. You couldn't have foreseen what would happen."

"I should have," Rita mumbled, stubbornly, her face muffled from being pressed into Zack's shirt. "I'm a scientist. I should have tested for any possible side effects before releasing my invention onto the world."

"If anybody was at fault, it was me," Sandra asserted, her eyes becoming steely marbles of anger as her thoughts turned inwardly. "I'm the one who thought the government was using your work to develop super soldiers to secretly modify people with the goal of world domination. I saw the good in your work and wanted to equally share it with the whole world. I wanted it to be that humankind everywhere would have the same access to developing a brilliant new technology that would enhance everyone's lives. I also wished that the United States would not be able to dominate the world with what they learned from their hidden experiments. I'm the one who suggested that we take your program to the United Nations."

"Oh, come on, Sandra. You didn't know anymore than Rita that there were flaws in the program that would lead to devolution. You were just thinking of what was best for everybody," Nate said, giving her a squeeze.

"If anybody is to blame, it's the government," Zack said, firmly, stroking Rita's hair over and over. "The genetic changes from the nuclear testing are what started the whole sequence of events. If the government had been honest and open about what had happened and how they were attempting to correct the genetic monstrosities that had occurred, then you, Sandra, would not have thought we were busy designing super armies, and you, Rita would have known what you were working on."

"Oh, I would've blamed the government for hiding something anyhow," Sandra said, darkly. "Don't forget that I was an activist. I devoted my whole life to exposing the government, positive that they were holding back information we had a right to know and plotting things that would advance their own nefarious agendas that would not be for the good of all people, or for the planet."

"And you were right," Nate said, persuasively. "The government was hiding what they were doing. How can anybody ever trust a government that perpetually lies to its citizens under the guise of protecting them for national security? You had a perfect right to doubt what the government was doing."

"If they had come clean with the problem of devolution, Rita would've known there was a danger in manipulating the genetic code and none of this would have happened," Zack said sourly. "I can't believe I have spent my entire life being complicit in hiding important findings from the American people. I just became so acclimated to that mind frame that it became second nature, or rather, first nature. We all felt we had the right to secrecy to protect the public for its own good. That became an internalized mantra. And of course, the government did not take the proper safety measures they should have with their experiments. Instead, they were always cutting costs and going with the lowest bidder (who normally cheats, anyhow)."

Now it was Rita's turn to calm him down. That discourse effectively stopped her tears, as she cuddled in close, murmuring words the others could not hear.

"Actually, if Wall Street, the Biotech industry, and people like me hadn't been so greedy, the proper testing would've been done in the labs once the formula was released," Nate admitted, shouldering his share of the blame. "Along with every other investor I couldn't wait for those enhancements to hit the market, and put pressure on the companies to hurry products to market. I was thrilled when they avoided the procedures of the FDA by sliding through as supplements and not medications. I got high off buying and trading the stocks, watching our money double, and later triple. I had no qualms about handing that formula off to the UN. All I could see were dollar signs, one million of them to start with. Even when Sandra was warning me to sell all the biotechnology stocks off because of the mutations, I still continued to play the market to make the most out of it. I was consumed by greed." He looked into Sandra's eyes with remorse and apology.

"Hush. Just like you said to Rita and me, you didn't know what was going to happen either. None of us had crystal balls," Sandra soothed him.

Once Nate decided to take on blame, he stubbornly insisted on keeping it, "No, that doesn't work, because as I said, I continued to make money off the technology even after I knew it was fatally flawed, while all of you were already committed to trying to solve the problem." He plopped down into a chair and stared at the floor.

"It looks to me as if there is enough blame to go around for all of us," Sandra said morosely, flopping into a seat next to him. All of them had played a major role in the destruction taking place around the world.

Sitting there shell-shocked and drained from the high emotions of the past hour, no one noticed when the computer uploaded archived footage from the BBC. As they gradually became aware of it, they saw time-sequenced footage of when New Orleans was covered by the rising sea and Paris literally burning. The screen kept looping the same footage over and over again, with terror and chaos visible everywhere. Shuddering, this was the last thing they needed to be watching in their current condition of self-loathing and blame. Nate reached out to turn the computer off when all the sound and video finally went dead.

* * *

Making chimp sounds, Andy swung down from the tree unexpectedly where Mateo was standing guard. Mateo was sitting disconsolately at the entrance to the compound stripping twigs to stave off his boredom.

"Hey Andy, You aren't supposed to be near the entrance to the compound," Mateo chided him, though secretly glad for the diversion. Pulling guard duty during the day seemed like an exercise in futility to Mateo. Who would be dumb enough to attack in broad daylight? And though the younger teens were required to stand guard, they were given the least likely times of the day for an attack. The night hours were given to the adults. It has been proven that teens have much quicker reflexes than adults, Mateo told himself, thinking of how quickly his hand-eye coordination was with video games, totally discounting how experience played into reactions in real-life situations. He hadn't wanted to do guard duty, anyhow.

A big, simian grin split Andy's face as he dropped down next to Mateo. He hopped around, his elongated arms brushing the ground. "The Captain, said I would make a good guard," he insisted, his mouth having difficulty forming the words.

"Captain Gabe means when you are sixteen, like me," Mateo said kindly, used to a younger brother's antics. "Now, go away like a good boy."

Andy did not go away. He continued to caper in circles around Mateo, and then, with a quick dart, he grabbed the shotgun Mateo had carelessly left sitting on the ground.

"No, Andy. Give me that," Mateo pleaded, trying to keep it quiet, not wanting anyone to know that he had lost control of the shotgun. "Be a good boy, Andy. Please, give the gun to me."

He lunged at Andy, causing Andy to scamper away, and climb up into the tree he had come down out of. Mateo reached up to grab him, but Andy just climbed higher out of reach. Mateo tried to jump into the tree, too, but was unable to do so because his arms were too short.

"Great! Now what am I going to do? Andy, you get down here, right now!" Mateo hissed, trying not to make a commotion that would draw attention to them.

Andy chattered away, grinning down at Mateo, finding the game to be great fun. He looked in the end of the shotgun curiously then pointed it at Mateo.

"Andy, no," Mateo screamed, abandoning all thoughts of secrecy. He dove behind the bush barrier surrounding the compound.

Then, Andy pulled the trigger, luckily missing Mateo, who was now hidden. He dropped the shotgun at the explosion of sound that resulted, covered his ears and began to yell. People came running from every direction to investigate the commotion. Mateo came out of hiding and sheepishly picked up the shotgun.

"How did that boy get that shotgun?" his father, Rodrigo, asked sternly. He grabbed the shotgun away from Mateo.

"Andy, come down here, son," Avram said as calmly as he could do. Sun and Marti, holding the two younger children, added their entreaties to his.

Andy wasn't having any of it. He just climbed higher and sat in the tree, rocking back and forth as if in pain. Stretching his long apelike arms, Avram tried to climb to reach Andy, but Andy was high among the slender branches that could hold the weight of a five year old, but not that of an adult.

"How are we going to get him down?" Sun moaned, switching Josef from one hip to another. Her obvious distress communicated to Josef, he started wailing. "It's okay Josef. Andy will be all right."

"Here, Avram, you watch Rachel," Marti said, handing three-year-old Rachel to her father, who was busy hollering orders to Andy. "Let me go get Gabe. He seems to have a rapport with Andy. Maybe he can get him to come down."

Marti hurried off to the boat where Gabe was working on the computer, oblivious to the sounds from the compound. Truth be told, Gabe had developed a bit of a hearing problem in recent years that he still wouldn't admit to. He considered a loss of hearing as a sign of getting old. It was bad enough that he had problems with his heart he didn't want to acknowledge any other signs of aging when so many people were relying on him during such dangerous times.

"Gabe!" Marti yelled, swinging herself onto the boat. She had noticed Gabe's hearing loss, but had never mentioned it. Instead, she just made sure she spoke louder to him. "We have somewhat of a situation with your little pal, Andy."

"What's that rascal up to now?" Gabe asked, indulgently as he chuckled. Five-year-old boys would be five-year-old boys.

"It's not so funny this time. He took the shotgun from Mateo, who was on guard duty at the front gate and shot it. Now he's up in a tree and won't come down," Marti explained.

"Does he still have the shotgun?" Gabe asked in alarm, getting up hurriedly from his seat.

"No, he dropped the gun when it went off. The sound must have frightened him, but now he won't come down out of the tree. No one can climb up and get him. Everybody is too heavy to get as high as he is. The whole group is gathered around the tree, trying to persuade him to come down, and nothing is working."

"Poor little guy," Gabe said, leading the way off the boat, running, and heading towards the compound. "I'm sure he must be scared to death."

"Well, he could have caused someone else's death," Marti responded, tartly, huffing to stay up with Gabe. Gabe could sure run when he was motivated! All those years of jogging kept him in pretty good shape!

Arriving at the tree, Gabe was surrounded by all the other members of their little band, all talking at once, some making suggestions of what Gabe should do, others reviewing what had already happened.

"Okay, everyone, do you think you could all clear out and give Andy and me a little space to resolve this? I'm sure everybody has something they should be doing. If Andy and I have a little quiet time together we should be able to work this out," Gabe said, his look calming everyone. Slowly, and reluctantly, most of the group left to return to their jobs.

Grabbing hold of Mateo's arm, Rodrigo steered his son towards their tent, "You come with me, young man. We have some business to discuss."

"Shouldn't we stay and help you?" Sun asked, including Avram in her glance. "We are his parents."

"I'll come get you as soon as he and I have had a little chat," Gabe said. "But, if you don't mind, I'd like to have a little visit with my partner alone." He raised his voice at the end of his sentence to make sure Andy heard him above his sniffles.

Looking like he wanted to debate, Avram stood his ground. Sun, gave him a beseeching look and a nudge. He capitulated and followed her grumpily away.

"You too, Marti," Gabe said, seeing she was the only one still there.

Giving him an unreadable look, Marti silently marched off.

"Andy, buddy, we are here all alone now. You can come down and join me," Gabe called up into the tree.

"I'm never coming down," Andy sobbed, clinging fiercely to the tree trunk, his widened nostrils flaring.

"Then I guess we will be here a long time, since I'm not going anywhere without you," Gabe replied, sitting down with his back to the tree. "I'd sure like to hear what happened from you, personally."

"I didn't mean to," Andy said in a muffled voice, his head bowed into his arm.

"Can't hear you pal! You are too far up in that tree. The wind is taking your words away," said Gabe, calling up to him. "You are going to have to come down for me to hear you."

He picked up a stick and started doodling in the dirt as if he had all the time in the world.

Andy tried, yelling down to him a couple times. Gabe acted like he couldn't hear a thing. Finally, Andy scooted down a few branches and tried again.

"Captain, I didn't mean to shoot that gun," he said.

"I think I hear something, but you are still too far up for me to figure out the words. Sorry, son, you'll just have to come down a little bit more. I know you didn't mean to shoot anybody," Gabe said, encouragingly, being careful not to look up at Andy.

A few moments passed, and then Andy climbed down another few feet placing him now directly over Gabe's head. Out of his peripheral vision, Gabe saw a hairy leg dangling, knowing he could make a grab for the boy and probably succeed though that would destroy the fragile connection they had at the moment. Gabe wanted Andy to come down on his own.

"I said, I didn't mean to shoot the gun," Andy hollered, almost into Gabe's ear.

"No one thinks you did, Andy. It was just an accident. No one is mad at you, including myself. Why don't you sit here with me, Partner, and we'll talk this out?" Gabe answered softly, causing Andy to strain to hear him. He kept doodling in the dirt as if he would wait forever.

There was a dull plop, with Andy now next to him. Slowly, so as not to scare the child, Gabe put his arm around him. Andy buried his head in Gabe's chest, crying his little heart out.

"It's okay, buddy. Everything is okay now," Gabe soothed.

"I just wanted to stand guard," Andy said.

"I know, son. I'm proud of you for wanting to help. You will make a great guard when you are a little older," said Gabe, agreeing.

"I can do it better than Mateo," Andy asserted. "I wouldn't have left the gun on the ground for the bad guys to grab. I can climb trees higher than anyone, and spot the bad guys first," Andy declared, proudly puffing out his hairy chest.

"I know you can!" Gabe said, ruffling the short hairs on Andy's head. "But, the group made the rules to say you have to be sixteen to stand guard, and we all have to obey the rules. Isn't that right Soldier?"

"I guess so," Andy answered reluctantly, knowing a good soldier always obeyed his Captain.

"I'll let you in on a little secret," Gabe said, his eyes darting around as he pretended to make sure no one could overhear. "Did you know that your job working in the garden is the most important job in the compound?"

"Pulling weeds?" Andy scoffed.

"Think about it. If we don't have food to eat, we won't be able to fight off the bad guys if they ever come. Taking care of our food source is the most essential work you can do around here.

I'm counting on you to keep the troops fed. Can I count on you, Soldier?"

"Aye, aye, Captain," Andy said, saluting him, and jumping to stand at attention.

"And you know what? I think you are ready to go into training for guard duty," Gabe announced, knowing he was going to get in trouble for this bright idea. "I think you can stand guard duty with me once in awhile. What do you say about that?"

Andy whooped like a normal boy, giving Gabe a big hug. "I'm going to tell my Mom and Dad about this."

"Uh, Andy, I suggest you ask them, not tell them," Gabe called after him, as Andy ran off, his normal exuberant spirits restored.

As Gabe got up, congratulating himself on his handling of that, he saw Emilio Torres approaching, "What can I do for you, Emilio?"

"Senor Gabe, I am concerned with what happened today. Mateo could have been killed. It could have been my Florencia or Rafael," Emilio began.

"Fortunately, no one got hurt," Gabe said, diplomatically.

"That little ape-boy is becoming more and more of a problem as that family devolves," Emilio said aggressively.

"Hey, what happened had nothing to do with his devolution," Gabe retorted, hoping he was right. "He was just acting like any other boy would."

"That is what you say," Emilio said, mulishly. "Some of us are not so sure."

Remembering his distrust of the devolving Goldstein family, Gabe understood Emilio's position. "I disagree, as I said. Marti and I know other people who have devolved who did not become violent. We've seen the Goldstein family long enough to know that they are peaceful, intelligent people who are as committed to the survival of the group as any of us. This was just a normal prank that can be expected of a little boy."

"We can't risk this occurring again," Emilio insisted.

"You are right about that, my friend," Gabe said, throwing his arm about Emilio, trying to defuse the high emotions. "We need to take actions to ensure that something like this doesn't happen again. We have learned that we need better training for our young guards. Leaving a weapon on the ground is not acceptable. Better we learn that now, from the antics of a child, then during an attack. We also need to make sure that even the youngest members of our tribe, including your Anabella and Natalia, are kept busy and are made to feel that their contributions are vital to sustaining our community."

Emilio gravely nodded his head, the moment of anger past as he thought of his two youngest daughters and some of the problems he had been experiencing with them.

Giving him a comradely pat on the back, Gabe set off to find Marti, wanting to make sure he was square with her, unsure what that last look she had given him meant. This being a leader was certainly hard work. Who would've thought a year ago, that he would find himself the head of a band of people relying on his leadership abilities? He had always been a loner, and now, not only was he required to be a team player, but the one everyone looked to for answers. Good thing he had Marti to bounce his worries and concerns off of, otherwise he'd go bonkers from the pressure.

Marti was on the boat gabbing with Sandra. Sandra had insisted on calling Marti after their mea culpa session to ensure that the small band in the Galapagos was still okay. She had recounted to Marti all the anguish they were experiencing as they had been reviewing their roles and decisions that had precipitated the worldwide crisis. Marti had filled the Patagonia contingent in on the current episode with Andy, and was in the process of reassuring Sandra that their little group was still doing as well as could be expected given the uncertainty around them.

"We did have to move to higher ground as the waters crept up," Marti admitted. "Since they are still rising, we may have to move again. That is our major concern at the moment. If we run out of room there are too many of us to put on the boats and sail off. I don't know what we will do. Gabe and I have been discussing this and are struggling with it. Should some of us leave now by boat to try and get to the coast, then come back for the others once we find a secure location? Who knows if we would even be able to find somewhere else along the coast that is safe? We have no idea what changes have occurred to the contour of the land. How far away is the coast now? Are areas on the coast rampant with raging mutants? Should we just wait and see? How long should we delay the decision? And who should go? Who do we leave here as vulnerable and without reinforcements? What small group of people would we leave exposed on an unknown coast while we sail back for the rest of our group? Gabe and I would feel very guilty, setting off on our own, and depriving these families with children a means of escape. Then again, it might be the right choice in the long run for everyone involved." She stopped dispiritedly then looked up as Gabe came over and put his hand on her shoulder. "Speaking of Gabe, here he is now."

Gabe sat down and briefed Marti and Sandra on the conclusion of the Andy incident. They all chuckled, bringing some relief to the heavy mood. Then Gabe continued to cite the problem with the growing prejudice and distrust of the young mutant family. That sobered everybody up again and brought to mind all the burdens pressing down on them. They signed off with heavy hearts.

"You know, Marti, this is as much my fault as it is those kids," Gabe said, dejectedly, adding self-blame onto his worries about being an effective leader and his concerns about his supposedly secret medical problems. "I should have been the mature, wiser head of the group when they were all hyped up about selling the formula to the United Nations. In fact, if I hadn't filched their names from that bowl on the bar, and gotten them all together to start with, none of this would have happened. The whole world would not be falling apart."

"Gabe, that is not helping anything, talking like that," Marti remonstrated. "You had no way of foreseeing what would happen when those kids got together. Obviously, you didn't know the first thing about them."

"That may be true, but if I had been trying to put a real story together with hard work and research instead of trying to cut corners, things would be different today. Besides, I had dollar signs in front of my eyes, just like those young people did later. I didn't make a single objection to collecting a cool million dollars, or spending it on outfitting the boat so we could sail forever, wherever we wanted to go. And when you come right down to it, it was my article in *Playboy* that told the whole world about the enhancements. That's what lit the fire worldwide and put the pressure on the biotech firms to mass produce the so-called supplements to meet demand without fully vetting them." Gabe was sunk so deeply into a morass that Marti was surprised he wasn't physically beating on his chest.

"Well, if you want to get right down to it, I'm just as much at fault as everyone else is," Marti said, smartly.

"Oh, give me a break," Gabe protested. "You weren't in on the decision to sell the technology."

"You are forgetting that I am the one who masterminded your group escaping from the Feds at the restaurant," Marti challenged. "If you had all been caught at that stage, it would have been all sorted out and none of this would have happened. Plus, I was quick to sell the restaurant and hop on the ship with you guys. I knew what had gone down and I did nothing to stop it. If I had resisted, I might have prevented your article in *Playboy*, I might have alerted the authorities and they might have been able to get the formula back from the United Nations before it got distributed worldwide. Then, Harland, Holly, and Carley, plus their dear children would not have devolved into animals. Precious little Andy and his baby brother and sister would not be battling prejudice along with the strange changes to their bodies and minds." She trailed off in misery, no longer intent on bucking up Gabe as her own self-recriminations sank into her.

Unable to comfort Marti, Gabe continued with his self-criticism. "Now the big joke is that these defenseless, innocent people are turning to the perpetrators who betrayed them in the first place for direction and leadership. How ironic is that?"

Feebly, Marti shook herself, her instincts to support Gabe causing her to try and mitigate his pain. "In spite of what you think, you are being a good leader to them, Gabe. Look at how you resolved the situation with Andy, and how you defused the bigotry of Rodrigo."

"If I was such a great leader none of this would have happened in the first place. I should have made sure that our guards were better trained and that Andy was kept busy and out of trouble."

"Oh, come on Gabe. As you said yourself, 'boys will be boys.' Besides, you can't be everywhere at the same time and know everything that is going to happen in advance. You are not God, you know," Marti objected, trying to get him to at least look at her.

But, Gabe was not having any of it. He wasn't going to be talked out of his bad mood, instead deciding to dig himself into a deeper hole. "These children would not have to be on alert for attacks from violent mutants if we didn't do what we did. They should be busy playing soldier, not having to be real soldiers. How will I ever live with myself if one of them ever has to take a bullet?"

"I pray that never happens," Marti said, fervently.

"Speaking of God, where is He or She, or It, in all of this? Don't tell me you actually believe that God's hand is in the death of the world," Gabe said, derisively, finally diverting the focus from self pity. "You know from listening to me over the past twenty years, that I don't put much stock in the theory of God anyhow. As far as I'm concerned, it's all one big cosmic joke!"

"Yes, I have heard you sounding off for twenty years, Gabe. I'm not sure what I believe about God right now. I've had some serious questions for a long time now, and what's happening in the world weakens my faith more every day. If there is a Heaven, I'm going to be first in line with my questions. But, one thing I'm sure of is that you are a good man, Gabe Channing, and together we are going to do our best for this small group of people who have fallen into our care. We don't have to be perfect," she warned, stroking Gabe's arm. "But we are going to give it our darnedest; aren't we, Babe?" Softly and simultaneously, she voiced challenge and affirmation. Gabe could not resist Marti's looks, and for her sake, even if he wasn't totally convinced of matters himself, he straightened his shoulders and put his best game face on. Then Gabe gave Marti a resounding kiss.

* * *

"Rita, I've been looking all over for you," said Eva Perez as she bustled into the Com Center. "It's so late in the evening I thought for sure you would be in your cabin."

Rita and Zack quickly exchanged guilty looks. Suppose her mother had bumbled into them the way Sandra and Nate had? There was no place for privacy in this cavern.

"What are you doing up so late, Mama?" Rita inquired back; still listless after the emotional torrent she had been through.

"I suppose this could have waited until tomorrow," Eva began, unapologetically and obviously intent on dealing with what was on her mind without considering whether it was convenient for others at that moment. "Many of the people here are bemoaning the fact that we do not have a church. We would like to start holding church services."

"That's sounds like a good idea, Mama," Rita answered, dutifully, with no real interest in her voice.

"Yes, well, we have a couple problems we thought you could help with," Eva continued, belatedly glancing around at the others in the Com Center as she nodded a greeting to them. "We would like a place to worship, with our own priest, too."

Sandra, who had just signed off from talking with Marti and Gabe, was quick to notice Rita's lack of interest and jumped in. "I'm sure you are welcome to use the community gathering place for your services, Senora Perez."

"Oh, that won't do at all. We need privacy for confession and a place to pray. We can't have children running around as we seek to worship God."

"I think we have an extra tent you can use," Zack offered, trying to ingratiate himself with Rita's mother. "The Schenck family just moved into their newly built cabin, and their old tent is available. Of course, some other people have requested it so that they could divide their large families up into two tents instead of just one." Receiving the gimlet eye from Eva, Zack hastily continued. "I believe establishing a church will take precedent in everyone's mind."

Eva graciously nodded to him, a queen bestowing favors.

"That still leaves us with the major problem of not having a priest. Couldn't you have managed to rescue a priest when you were out on your forays?" she joked.

"One priest, coming right up," Nate quipped back.

"Can't you appoint or commission, or whatever you call it, a priest from among yourselves?" Sandra asked, helpfully.

Eva was horrified. "A priest is appointed by a Bishop, who is appointed by the Pope from the Voice of God."

"We don't even know if a Pope still exists in our world," Sandra said, brutally.

Eva was confident. "Oh certainly there is! God always provides for the safety of the Pope. I'm sure he is safely hidden somewhere out there, just like we are. Otherwise, whatever cardinals are still living would have convened, hearing from God whom the next Pope would be."

Sandra exchanged looks with the others. Obviously Rita's mother did not fully grasp the true condition of the current world. From their satellite globe-trotting, it didn't look like the Vatican was still standing.

"Certainly there must be contingency plans for ordaining priests during times when communication is impossible," Nate suggested, trying to be reasonable.

Biting her lip, and giving her daughter a look that asked why she wasn't more involved in the dilemma, Eva firmly addressed Nate. "Well, if there really is such a plan, then no one here knows how to go about it. In the old days, priests had to travel from village to village possibly only visiting a village once a year. Everybody had to wait for the priest in order to celebrate the sacraments of marriage, confession, and communion. How are we going to do all these holy things without a priest?"

"Well, I can look on the data bases I have downloaded, and see if I can find out anything," Sandra offered, though she doubted she could easily find something of such an archaic nature.

"Oh, would you?" Eva asked wistfully, her gratitude evident.

Rita finally spoke. "You can appoint a lay leader in the meantime, Mama. Whoever it is cannot perform the sacraments, but at least he can lead the congregation in Mass."

"And who knows, maybe God will miraculously bring a priest to our door, or this crisis in the world will somehow end peacefully," said Nate.

Eva was not having any of that; she was no fool. She might not realize the extent of the devastation and pandemonium in the world, but she knew that they were entombed for the long-run and no easy answers were going to suddenly present themselves.

"I guess we can appoint a lay leader, but it could prove to be difficult. After all, we are a humble group here," she reluctantly admitted. "I imagine Rinaldo could lead us."

"If you would like it, I will move that tent to wherever you like first thing in the morning," Zack offered.

"We want it away from all the commotion," Eva advised. "We need as much privacy for our services as possible."

"Your wish is my command," Zack said grandly, thinking to himself that everyone wanted more privacy. The close proximity of everyone was beginning to fray everybody's nerves.

Eva suddenly realized she might have interrupted a meeting. "I'm sorry if I disrupted something you young people were doing, but I hope you understand how critical this is to most of us in the cave. In this time of hardship, our faith in God gives us comfort and solace." She gave Rita a worried look. Then, she bid farewell to the others as she exited, again reminding Zack that she would meet him in the morning.

"That was kind of you, Zack," Rita said after her mother was beyond earshot. "I know you don't believe in God."

"Frankly, I've always ascribed to the belief of survival of the fittest," Zack said, almost apologetically, not wanting to alienate Rita. At the same time, he refused to pretend to have beliefs that were not genuine. "I think evolution has been pretty well proven. All we have to count on is each other."

"I don't believe in God either," Sandra asserted. "I believe we are all equal parts of the universe — you know, very Zen. The key is to be in harmony with all of nature and yourself as part of that nature."

"I beg your pardon, Sandra, but how exactly does the destruction of the world and the devolution of people into animals fit into being one with the universe? That's a bit too pie in the sky for me," Zack said, shaking his head. "Where are you in all of this, Nate?"

Sandra cut off Nate before he could answer. "Did you ever see the movie *The Matrix*?"

"Yeah, so what?" Zack answered.

"Well, if you remember, people are viewed as the ones destroying the greater community of life."

"So," Zack cut in. "The devolution is resetting the world to a less toxic state?"

"Exactly."

That evening, things were not going as well Nate had planned. This religious discussion wasn't helping anything either. "Well, I was raised in a family where as a child I attended church regularly. Because of that, I can recite for you large parts of the Bible and fundamental principles of an evangelical Christian doctrine. Once I got into college I got away from all of that, and haven't given it much thought since then. I guess, if I had to define my current philosophy, I declare myself as agnostic. I believe there might be a God, but not one that is in any way similar to what standard religions of the world suggest. Does God have any involvement in what happens on Earth or on any planet for that matter? How could you explain how a loving God could allow what is happening in the world? Surely a caring God would intervene. I think my concept of God is an impersonal universal life energy force, at best. That is, if I really believe in God at all. Truthfully, I've been too busy playing the market to give much thought to it. None of it seems relevant in my life anyhow." He shrugged, looking at Sandra, hoping to see a reaction.

"You've been quiet, Rita," Sandra said, turning towards her after giving Nate the kind of reassuring smile one would give a small child struggling with a new math problem. "I know you were raised in a strict Catholic home, but I've always been curious about how you fit that in with your work as a geneticist? Aren't the two polar opposites?"

"And doesn't the devolution we are seeing in the mutants from the manipulation of genes support the premise that we all evolved from lower life forms?" Zack asked, half regretting his words as they came out. It was obvious that the last thing Rita needed right now was intense pressure from a friend.

"I don't know," Rita answered, reluctantly, shaking her head as if to clear her mind from the same agonizing ethical question she constantly asked herself. Was everyone now ganging up on her? "Once I became a geneticist, it became evident that evolution had validity; however, a religious person can believe in God and still believe in evolution. Haven't you ever heard of the concept of intelligent design? The belief that God created the initial spark of life that got the whole evolutionary process going? No one has yet been able to create life out of nothing. There is the theory that the supposed seven days of creation were actually complete eras of time, during which evolution occurred. I was comfortable believing in a personal God who cares about all his or her creatures, while still giving a bow to evolutionary beliefs. But, like Nate, I am having a hard time accepting that a God who is intimately involved in our lives would allow what has happened in the world."

She paused, with the rest uncharacteristically respecting her silence. "According to my faith, I would say that Satan is behind what is happening in the world today. We are witnessing a spiritual battle of cosmic proportions occurring in the universe right now. Maybe this is the last battle before Christ returns to Earth and establishes His royal throne on Earth. If that is true, then all of us were the true instruments of evil."

They were all speechless, the earlier guilt compounding with every second.

Rita continued. "The child in me who grew up with trusting God wants to believe that God is going to overcome all things and set everything right. By contrast, the scientist in me is at odds with that approach, forced to calmly at reality with cool logic and calculation. The bitter truth is that I am lost within my own confused beliefs.

Now I may have permanently lost my faith in God because of what I have done. That cold-hearted fact leaves me destitute and ethically confused, without an anchor in this tempestuous sea." She laughed a sad laugh, a somber sound coming from a person who in truth could be a mad scientist. "How melodramatic that is of me."

Not really knowing what to say, all her friends remained silent. Then, predictably, they all started talking over one another, though their words were just platitudes. Unfortunately, none of them had enough wisdom to buoy Rita back to the surface of her sanity. Instead, they were also living within a whirlwind of confusion.

CHAPTER TEN

Brains versus Brawn

"Mr. President, based on all the satellite data and reports we've received from the other bunkers, plus our own intelligence, there have been no sightings of mutants for weeks now," General Tommy Jennings began his briefing. All the President's advisors surrounded him as they met for their daily update in the situation room.

The President was confident, despite the current state of the world. He slowly scanned the faces of those in the situation room. "Are there any recommendations about how we should proceed?" he asked, looking pointedly at his top generals. Facing a dire situation, no one wanted to be the first to make a suggestion and put his or her head on the block.

Eric Collier, Chairman of Homeland Security, glanced quickly at his Deputy Director, Jamie Whiteman. Collier nodded and cleared his throat as he stared at the President. "Mr. President, it is our recommendation that all the bunkers send out reconnaissance parties to assess the immediate surroundings, with the aim being to regain control of some of the surface as soon as possible and finally exit these bunkers."

"Does everybody concur with this recommendation?" the President asked, looking sternly at each person seated at the table. He then waited until each person nodded before he proceeded. In truth, they were all heartily sick of being cooped up in the confined space of the bunker. The bunker was definitely crowded, even though it only contained the top personnel in the administration, key military staff, and distinguished leaders in the business and science communities. Without being able to bring all the staffers who did all the routine work into the bunker because of space limitations, the VIPs were reduced to handling many of the menial tasks that kept offices afloat. Consequently, they had become pretty disgruntled after months of working in that environment.

Jamie Whitehead, for the thousandth or so time, gave a thought to what had happened to Brad and Erin, especially Brad. She hoped they were hunkered down somewhere safe. Moreover, she also realized what an enormous amount of work they had shouldered, as she got up to get Eric Collier a refill on his cup of coffee. She was now reduced to lowly tasks that even administrative assistants used to stick their noses up at doing. Wouldn't it be wonderful to get to the surface again and get everything back to normal? Unfortunately, that was just wishful thinking. She plunked the coffee down unnecessarily hard, causing a few drops to jump out on the papers in front of Collier.

"Sorry," she said, gruffly, as Collier jumped back, narrowly avoiding getting any spots on his wrinkled, tired, and smelly suit. There were showers and laundering facilities in the bunker, though everyone's wardrobe was limited. He stifled a verbal response, not wanting to call the President's attention to the incident since there were more important things occupying everyone's minds. This time he sent Jamie a dirty look because he was tired of having her at his elbow every minute of every day. The bunker was a boring place, with no allowed vacation days or weekends. Obviously, there were no peaceful rounds of golf under glorious sunshine, either. (He never realized he'd miss the smell of newly mowed grass so much.)

"General Jennings, I authorize you to begin implementation of Phase One of Outward Migration," the President ordered, getting up and then heading away to his luxurious suite. Having given the order, his main work was now done. The mission had been meticulous planned out and rehashed interminably over the months they had been imprisoned in the bunker. Everyone knew what their assigned role was and would carry it out without anymore micromanaging.

Standing belatedly, since the President was gone before they could get to their feet, everyone hustled out to initiate Phase One — sending out scouting parties of Special Forces to evaluate the surrounding area and report back on recent mutant activity. There was a buzz of excitement and hope in the air, even among these hardened, experienced leaders of the free world.

* * *

Sgt. Bryce Chicory cautiously stretched his right leg. For close to an hour, he had been laying still in this shallow gulley, watching and waiting for signs of mutant activity. His squad was spread out in similar positions around the perimeter of the hidden entrance to the bunker. While trained to maintain positions like this for hours on end without moving, there was an eagerness in the group to continue the mission. They were the elite, highly trained forces of the military. And, they had been pressed into jobs of running errands and guarding the secret exits to the bunker for months on end. It had been close to impossible to continue training exercises in order to maintain their edge. Therefore, they had been subjected to tedious hours of mind-numbing boredom. Take for example the executive meeting he had to guard this morning. Wasn't it enough that there were secret service guys present to protect the President? In addition, every entrance and exit of the bunker had dozens of troops monitoring electronically sealed doorways impenetrable by even a nuclear bomb. Who was he guarding against? The people who had been brought into the bunker because they were so vital to the survival of the country?

His earphone brought him back to alert. "Chicory, do you have anything to report?" It was the lieutenant, safely to the rear of the forward positions and checking in with each member of the team.

"That's a negative," Chicory responded laconically into the built-in microphone in his helmet. After all, since he was a Texan, he had to maintain a certain image. Once engaged with the enemy, he lost his laid-back veneer and sprang into controlled, calculated action.

Wait a minute! Was that movement he saw to the left periphery? Was it a squirrel? Being summertime now, there was a surprising amount of animal activity, in spite of the given state of the world. No, that was no squirrel! Whatever was rustling that bush was much too large. Could it be a deer? He flexed his nostrils, trying to smell the air, every sense heightened.

Whispering into his mike, he said, "L-T. I'm getting some movement on the left of my position."

"Proceed cautiously to check it out, Chic," he said. Soon he began walking his elbows in the direction of the spotted movement. Suddenly, breaking from the surrounding brush, an ape-like mutant ran off. The orders were to shoot any mutants in sight. Bryce sighted down his rifle and got off a shot, but the mutant kept going. It was now out of range and hidden in a dense thicket. Maybe he had winged it, Bryce thought, hopefully, as he reported in. Moving to the location where the mutant had been spotted, he noticed crushed twigs and broken branches. Was the mutant a lookout? Why hadn't it attacked? Maybe it was just a lone wolf and not part of any organized pack, eating hand to mouth and surviving on its own. If that's all that was left of the mutants, there would be no problem in establishing a base camp outside the bunker. But, hey, that wasn't his decision to make!

After another hour with no further sightings, the squad got slowly to its feet and began canvassing the surrounding forest and hills, scouting for signs of other mutant activity. They came across some evidence that there had been encampments in the vicinity, but these all appeared to be deserted.

Though going carefully, with all his senses engaged, Bryce was enjoying being out in the field again. The woods were alive with twittering birds and hopping rabbits. Scanning the skies, he started searching for avian mutants, but all he saw were normal birds. Climbing up a steep rocky crag, he came upon an eagle's nest, though it was normal size — way too small to belong to a flying mutant. He wondered idly if mutants made nests or had mutant babies. Did mutants lay eggs? He hadn't kept up on all the intricacies of mutant biology, and now wished he had.

Again, he spotted unexpected motion, this time heading towards it without reporting in first. He didn't want to spook whatever it was with the sound of his voice. Moving with all the stealth that had been drilled into him, he worked his way towards the spot. When he got there, all was calm. Shaking his head, he wondered if he had imagined what he thought he had seen. After all, there hadn't been any pause in the forest sounds. Surely a mutant who had been living off the land would know how to blend into the natural order without disturbing it? The mutant seen before sure didn't know how to do that. He shook his head, unable to shake the feeling that he was being watched and tracked, no matter how fast he turned or how slyly he disguised his intentions.

Meanwhile, all the squads reported back to headquarters with some reporting lone sightings of ape-like mutants hurrying into the distance. Shots had been fired, but no one got a clear shot. Most of the troops were ecstatic that there had been no organized resistance or signs of massive numbers of mutants operating in packs. The idea of a random mutants living alone or in small packs was certainly not a threat to the power of the United States military. Obviously, they felt confident that they would be able to secure encampments on the surface as the next phase of the mission anticipated. Bryce stood, slowly shaking his head as the others reported their findings.

"What is it Chic?" the lieutenant asked him in exasperation. "Is there something else you have on your mind that you haven't told us already?"

"L-T, I just got this feeling," Bryce drawled. Special Forces were known for their casual approach to the chain-of-command outside combat situations.

Rolling his eyes, the lieutenant asked, "And what would that be, Sarge?"

Suddenly serious, Bryce answered, "Don't you think it is just too quiet? I mean, where did they all go? They couldn't have just died off suddenly."

"Maybe the radiation killed off large numbers of the mutants," the lieutenant surmised then he said hurriedly, "that isn't our problem to figure out what happened to them. Leave that to the brass. They've got nothing better to do anyway."

Everybody guffawed obligingly.

"I just feel like something has been watching me the whole time I've been out here. There's nothing I can put my finger on, but my gut is still telling me we aren't alone," Bryce persisted.

"It's probably just a cute doe stalking you," the lieutenant kidded. "Come on, let's get you and your 'gut feeling' back to the bunker."

Glancing unconvinced over his shoulder one last time, Sgt. Bryce Chicory followed his team back into the bunker.

*   *   *

"Mr. President, I think it is advisable to give more time to the Special Forces to check out an extended area around the bunker entrance," said Eric Collier. Jamie bobbed her head in agreement, but all the members of the armed forces were actively shaking their heads in the negative.

"We respectfully disagree, Mr. President," said the chairman of the Joint Chiefs. "The Special Forces have thoroughly evaluated the surrounding areas and have issued a report that there is minimal isolated mutant activity that would be easily quelled by our forces. In fact, the mutants encountered our squads and ran into hiding. There appears to be no organization or sophistication among the sparsely populated mutants in these areas. It is viable to move immediately to the surface, and commence recovering control of the country. We have the same reports from all the other bunkers across the country, as well as satellite data to support our findings." He looked challengingly at the others gathered at the table. None of the military heads dared oppose him, regardless of their private reservations.

"It seems that our military is in agreement that we can move out of this bunker with no threat of an attack," the President restated what he had just been told.

Sergeant Chicory, standing guard duty inside the meeting room, had a hard time controlling his reactions to what he was hearing. The lieutenant had called him paranoid since he was the lone voice urging more scouting time. It was definitely not his place to say anything in the presence of the President. He wasn't even allowed to react to what he was hearing. How did the Secret Service guys do this day after day?

Before the President could continue, almost at the risk of interrupting the President, Eric Collier, head of Homeland Security, spoke up again. "I would beg to put in a word of caution. I suggest we proceed with our plan to migrate to the surface, but do it in smaller stages, starting with only a military presence and gradually moving the other people out as the safety of such a move is proven to be sustainable."

Watching the President as Collier spoke, Jamie had the sinking feeling that he wasn't going to pay any heed to what Eric was saying. The President was as heartily sick of the bunker as everyone else was. He had always been given to grandiosity and believed his army was infallible. It had been almost impossible to get him to agree to go into the bunker until repeated threats to his personal safety had convinced him. He had a strong streak of self-preservation, a quality in high demand in politics. She sighed. Maybe everything would be all right. After all, the satellite data supported what the recon forces had already reported.

Perturbed to be stopped mid-pronouncement, the President said, a bit more forcefully than he normally would have, "We will commence Phase Two of Outward Migration immediately, without any modification. Notify all the other bases across the country to coordinate their movements with ours." Maybe he could do something about Collier once they were reestablished in a new Capitol. He was getting a bit uppity. Maybe it was that Deputy of his, Jamie Whitehead, who was the real problem, the President mused.

"Yes, Mr. President," resounded from everyone around the room as the President brought his thoughts back into focus. Then he stood, signaling the end of the meeting. Leaving the room, the President briefly noticed the soldier guarding the room. Had there been a fleeting expression of disagreement on his face? Soldiers who were trained to guard the President were carefully schooled in refraining from facial expression. Then again, these weren't just Secret Service guys guarding him anymore. Some of the guards were Special Forces guys doing double duty. He'd have to speak to the head of the detail to chastise that soldier. Or was the President only imagining the weird looks he was receiving? If that was the case, then he should cut the young guy some slack. After all, they were all under immense strain while in the bunker. No young whippersnapper would dare think he knew better than the President of the United States.

*   *   *

Jamie Whitehead looked around and blinked. It was a cloudy gray day, but after being in the bunker for so long it seemed bright, and the air smelled so clean, the wind moving in irregular bursts instead of the monotonous, steady rate of the air circulating in the bunker. She could not believe that she was now outside. She had survived the crushing atmosphere of stale sour bodies for as long as she had to. Nothing could force her back into that bunker! She was suddenly a believer that all was right with Outward Migration.

People were finally streaming out the bunker doors in all directions. What had started as an orderly migration had degenerated into a shoving match as people, eager to get to the outside pushed their way ahead of others. A mob mentality had definitely been created among the elite of the country. Jamie sneered as she hurried to the hut that had been established as a temporary command post.

Most of the soldiers were busy setting up tents. The plan was to spend the first night within close proximity of the bunker. A perimeter of military presence would be set up and then gradually expanded into the countryside as they ascertained there was no resistance. Bryce Chicory snapped a tent into shape, glad that the old days of pounding in stakes was a thing of the past. Maybe he had been too pessimistic and this was going to work out okay.

Fortunately, there had been no signs of mutant activity since the first scouting mission.

Forgetting their perceived importance, leaders and support staff alike frolicked in the gathering dusk, loath to retire into confinement after briefly tasting freedom. But at last the final diehard headed for sleep and sweet dreams of a new life outside the bunker. The camp was quiet, except for the occasional signals of guards surrounding the encampment.

Chicory, after laboring hard all day was supposed to be sleeping since he had second shift night guard duty. Unfortunately he was filled with unease. He finally sat up, giving up on sleep. Maybe he just needed a nature call to settle back down. It certainly couldn't hurt. He eased out of the tent and silently made his way to the latrines, noticing that many shapes were headed in the same direction. It was hard to believe that there were so many folks still awake this late and on the same mission he was on. The forms melted into the woods and did not continue toward the latrines at all. Something was definitely wrong. All his instincts told him that. It became apparent to him in a rush of insight that the mutants were about to attack. He needed to sound the alarm and report to the lieutenant at once. It was his last thought as something hit him on the head and he went down.

The highly organized mutants snuck a team past the soldiers guarding the perimeter, their familiarity with the woods masking any signs of their passage. The mutants also organized themselves between the humans and the bunker door cutting off any retreat. The size of the mutant army was massive. They had also developed underground tunnels and quarters that were not picked up by satellites or the forward scouts during their brief foray to the front. The alarms sounded, but the military strength of the United States at this particular location was inadequate.

Startled, Jamie awoke out of a dream. She had been dreaming about herself as a slimmer and younger person, reunited with Brad, who was plainly infatuated with her. The noise of shouting and shooting around her was deafening. The smoke blocked her vision. She stumbled into a scene that could only be described as a precursor of hell. Attacks by mutants were occurring in every direction with military might strongly answering them. Strangely disconnected from the fighting, Jamie was at a loss of what she should do. She didn't have any weapons, and had no real role in defense of the encampment. Maybe she should find Eric Collier. Then it hit her —someone had to return the President to the bunker. Unfortunately, she wasn't thinking very straight because, of course, the Secret Service was assigned to that task. She ran, twisting through tents and trees, intent on reaching the command hut where the President was bunking.

She stumbled again, almost falling over a body on the ground. How did she get all turned around? As she groped the body, she realized this wasn't the direction to the command post. To her amazement, the body groaned, it hard for Jamie to discern if it was a friend or foe amidst the lightning streaks of gunfire. The body groaned again allowing her to see that it was an American soldier, one of their own forces. How dare he lay there when he was needed in the fighting!

"Get up," she commanded, nudging him.

Chicory sat up, woozily, trying to focus on the two images of an irate woman in front of him. They condensed into one, allowing him to recognize her as one the higher ups he had seen in the top strategy meetings that he had guarded. "Come with me, Ma'am," he said urgently, grabbing her arm, as he tried to get to his feet.

"No, you come with me," Jamie ordered, tugging in a different direction. "We have to get to the President and save him!"

"The President's men will see to him as I get you to safety," Bryce said, firmly, using such a strong grip on Jamie that she couldn't break free.

Jamie continued to struggle, getting irrational with her insistence of getting to the President. A group of mutants materialized out of the darkness and Bryce had no choice. He clipped Jamie on the jaw and then slung her over his shoulder, groaning at her weight. Even though he had been through grueling training with heavily weighted packs, none had compared to this lady. It was a good thing he exercised regularly! He trotted off unerringly towards the bunker doors, slipping wraithlike between trees, all the while burdened with carrying the woman.

The fighting at the doors was fierce, but the superior weaponry of the military had forced a temporary standoff with the mutant forces allowing the civilians to make a mad dash into the bunker. Unceremoniously plopping Jamie into the bunker, Chicory hurried back out to join the battle.

Fighting continued into the morning with the advanced armament of the humans killing off most of the mutants, with those unharmed wisely making for the hills, vengeful scouts followed. But, the toll was tremendous. Not only had most of the ammunition been used up, but many of the soldiers were dead, injured, or missing.

The President survived, thanks to his trusty Secret Service agents. As Jamie gathered in the meeting room with the decimated group, she saw that Eric Collier was not with them. With a gulp, she remembered getting him coffee only the day before, almost spilling some on him. Could he really be dead? Surely he was not! Slowly processing it all, she realized she was now the acting head of Homeland Security. Instead of the flush of pride she had always dreamed of feeling if this fantasy ever came true, she felt small and insecure, wanting to do nothing else than hide. She furtively glanced around and her eyes lit on the guard standing at the door, instantly recognizing him as the soldier who had saved her life. She could have sworn he gave her a wink, though it was so fast she couldn't be sure if it was true. She squared her shoulders and took her seat to fulfill her responsibilities.

"Reports are pouring in from all the other bunkers across the country that they all suffered the same surprise attack that we did," announced General Jennings, somberly. "It is evident that the mutants are much more organized than we believed and their numbers are much higher than originally estimated." He looked shamefaced as he waited for the ax to fall. It was apparent though there would be no ax, for the forces were too small and too necessary to be chopping heads anymore. Every last soldier would be needed to fight the mutants.

"Must we continue to stay in this bunker forever?" whined the President, giving up all pretext of sounding like the leader of the Free World. Free?

Speaking more assuredly than she thought she would, Jamie was the first to respond. "Mr. President, we have taken enormous losses and are running out of ammunition. The only good news is that we finally have the mutants on the run. I believe we can establish a small military presence outside the doors of the bunker and send out scouting troops to deal with the remaining mutants. Phase Two should continue, but at a slower pace." She unconsciously echoed her predecessor's cautions.

"Is this still viable?" the President asked, turning to the Chiefs of the Armed Forces as he regained some of his posture.

"Yes, Mr. President," they all answered in subdued voices, trying not to look at the empty seats around the table.

"So be it," the President ordered. "And may God help us all."

*   *   *

"It looks like there is a sudden flurry of communications going on between the President's secure location and the other bunkers across the States," said Nate. He and Zack were taking the night shift at the computer console, both feeling disgruntled that this was cutting into their love lives, but not at ease enough with each other to talk about what they were really feeling.

"Let me see if I can break into the stream of chatter," Zack said, turning to his own monitor. "Since they changed the codes without telling me I have been left out of the loop. Their whole focus is on what is happening in the country. They seem to have forgotten the outposts spread around the globe. You'd think they'd have more interest in what scientists like Rita are trying to accomplish." He was miffed for Rita's sake, but equally mad at the fact that his prior high standing was being discounted.

"Nope, I can't get into the communication loop," he said in disgust. Idly, he panned the satellite feed over the terrain surrounding the President's secret facility. His voice took on a sharp, excited edge, he called over to Nate. "Are you seeing what I am seeing?"

Nate came over and peered over his shoulder. "It looks like a huge armed force gathered outside the bunker. Can you zoom in closer?"

Zack zoomed. It was immediately evident to both of them that the forces were not human, but mutant. They could see the mutant army spreading out and around, encircling the sleeping camp. Zack tried to raise Jamie (or anyone else) on his sat phone, but again, the lack of appropriate codes kept him from getting through in time.

They sat in horror, watching the carnage as the mutants attacked. The humans rallied quickly and the fighting was fierce. Zack and Nate felt helpless, able to see everything that was happening while not being able to do anything to help. It was almost unbearable. Nate groaned, putting his head in his hands and then unable to resist watching the destruction once again turning his eyes to the monitor.

"There must be something we can do to help," he said in anguish.

"I'm trying, man. But all communications have been cut off. I can't get through to anyone," Zack said in frustration and rage.

"There's nothing that we can do at this point anyhow," Nate said. "They know what is going on and are fighting back now. Watch out, behind you," he yelled ineffectively at the soldiers on the screen, turning away in horror as the mutants attacked.

They continued to watch until the last civilian had retreated to the bunker.

"The mutants were highly organized," Zack noted, clinically.

"They are a lot smarter than everyone has been assuming," Nate agreed. "Even with having Holly, Jasmine and the children here, I don't think we have given enough credit to their continuing intelligence, just because they can't communicate with us effectively."

"I need to instruct Rita to concentrate some of her energies on the communication issue and not just on trying to reverse the devolution," Zack mused, as if he could easily order Rita around.

"Pull up the island where Gabe and Marti are," Nate requested, suddenly uneasy with the thought that the mutants might have the capability to coordinate worldwide attacks with other mutant groups. A silly thought — impossible even — but it couldn't hurt to check it out.

Without responding, Zack switched to a view of the Galapagos Islands, zeroing in on the shrunken island where Gabe and Marti holed up with their small band. The inadequate barrier around their campground was well-defined. Unfortunately, there was a group of mutants massing outside it.

"Oh, no, this is too coincidental. I've got to warn them," Nate said, grabbing for his sat phone.

Continuing as if he hadn't heard Nate, Zack switched to a close view of their secret door to the surface. With a complete lack of surprise, he said matter-of-factly, "We have a problem of our own to deal with, Nate." Reaching over, he sounded the alarm that screamed throughout the cavern.

"Gabe, there is a force of mutants gathered outside your compound ready to pounce," Nate shouted through the phone. "I can't talk. We are about to be attacked, too."

*   *   *

Namid giggled and whispered something into Lowell's ear in the half-human guttural simian code they had developed between them. Lowell gave a nod and chuckled back at her, a big toothy look splitting his ape-like face. Casually he reached over to groom her hairy shoulder. Sensing a presence next to him on his other side, he ducked just in time to avoid a hard slap across the face.

"Hi — what are doing? Geez, all I'm doing is sitting here talking to Namid," Lowell protested, trying for indignant but not pulling it off. In fact, he looked sheepish more than anything else.

"Don't try to pull that with me, Mister Kempfield the Third. All you do lately is cuddle up with that ape girl and talk gibberish. It's me that's carrying your baby! Or, have you forgotten that?" Hiawatha ranted, thrusting her swollen belly in his face.

Lowell started his defense. "I'm not doing anything wrong. Namid and I have a lot in common. We are going through the changes together at the same time. Nobody else understands what it is like. Even though I love you, you do know I love you, right? You can't begin to understand what it is like for me. Namid does." He trailed off, realizing that Hiawatha was not buying it at all, but was busy preparing her retort. Obviously, it might involve another slap, one that wouldn't miss this time!

"I don't understand you?" Hiawatha began, shrilly. "Who understands me? I'm the only one pregnant around here . . . Yeoowww!" She bent over in sudden pain, huffing as if she couldn't get her breath.

"What's the matter?" Lowell said in alarm, jumping up and putting his arm around her. "Is it the baby?"

Hiawatha disdainfully shrugged off his arm. "It is too soon for the baby to come. Don't try to change the subject . . . Yeoowww!" This time she stayed doubled over. "Lowell — help! I think the baby is coming!"

Lowell stood there looking wildly around, but Namid, who had enjoyed the side play, jumped up and headed off for assistance, going first for her mother, Kaya, who had all the healing knowledge of the ancestors and modern medicine, and then to Erin, who had become a big sister to Hiawatha.

Regaining some of his senses, Lowell had managed to guide Hi to a medical clinic bed by the time help arrived, and was busy patting her hand and stroking her forehead.

"Did the pains just start?" Kaya asked, all business-like. "Do you know how far apart they are?"

"No, I have had some pains all through the day," Hiawatha gasped, lying spent as the most recent pain diminished giving her a breather. "I thought they were just false labor, since this is way too early for the baby. It is too early, isn't it? That's what you told me." She looked accusingly at Kaya.

"What I told you was an estimate based on what you told me," Kaya said calmly, not stopping in her examination of her patient. "Babies mysteriously pick their own times to be born."

"What can I do to help?" Erin asked, feeling useless, but wanting to do something to make things easier for Hiawatha.

At that moment, the alarm system within the whole cave complex blared a warning. Kaya and Erin exchanged glances. Kaya, as the leader, was immediately needed to handle the emergency. The alarm meant that the mutants were approaching their hidden compound and that they were in imminent danger of attack. Kaya was the one with the most medical knowledge, though fortunately not the only one with that type of knowledge within the cave.

"Namid, go get Longwei to care for Hiawatha," Kaya ordered. "Erin, you stay here and assist. Lowell come with me. We may need your strength. Let's go."

"What about Medic?" Erin answered, not sure she was willing to entrust Hiawatha's care into the hands of an ancient Chinese doctor. She moved to the head of the bed, grabbing Hi's hand.

"She'll be needed for casualties," Kaya threw over her shoulder as she ran to her gathering forces and sending a chill down Erin's spine. Casualties? How could they handle a battle which would surely involve injuries and deliver a baby at the same time? It was too impossible for words. Hiawatha let out another cry.

"How far apart are those contractions?" Erin asked, gulping as Longwei and Namid joined them.

*　*　*

"The mutants are getting close to our hidden entrance," Tracker reported to Kaya and the gathered force of fighters from the mountain enclave.

"That is exactly what we don't want them to do — find the entrance," Kaya responded, shaking her head. "Our strength is in fighting them out in the forest and mountains away from our complex. Tracker, you and the rest of our mountain men and women, who know the woods like the back of your hands, need to melt into the terrain and attack in guerilla warfare-style, coming at the mutants from all directions, confusing them and leading them away. You all know your jobs; let's get to it!"

"What about me?" Brad said a bit plaintively. "What am I supposed to do?"

"You can work with the other computer jocks to see where the attacks are coming from and alert our troops," Kaya answered decisively. She paused, thinking. "Do you think you can communicate with the eagle mutant you befriended?"

"I can try," responded Brad, slowly. "Erin and I believe that Baldie's intelligence level has stayed on par with his human level. It seems that he understands everything we say, yet we can't understand what he is trying to say to us."

Harland had avoided human contact for most of the time they had been in the cave system. With an eagle's natural aversion to closed places, he had refused to go into the cave. He was sporadically seen flying high up with other bird mutants, but he never brought any of them around. This led to sharp disagreement in the population of the cave. Some were suspicious that he would reveal, either knowingly or unknowingly, their location to the dangerous bands of rogue mutants wandering the mountains. However, Erin and Brad staunchly defended him, even though they secretly wondered why they trusted their avian friend even though he had saved their lives.

Once a day, Harland would appear at the entrance to the compound and wait patiently, ignoring anyone who approached him. That all changed when Erin and Brad appeared. It was as if he felt responsible for them and was checking up on them to be sure they were all right, even though he couldn't put that into words. Erin and Brad oddly felt comforted by this consistent attention of their eagle friend. Sometimes they would sit for long periods of time, not saying anything, just being together. Other times, Brad and Erin would try to tell Harland about the happenings in the caves, not knowing how much he understood about human concerns, or even if he cared, beyond his obvious devotion to the two of them. He always brought an offering of a recent kill, which they accepted solemnly with gratitude.

"I would like you to attempt to explain our current situation to him and see if he can help with an air attack," Kaya instructed.

"I'll be glad to try," Brad said, relieved to have something meaningful to do. Sure, he could help in the computer center, but that area had been well in hand before he came on the scene. Nerd and Geek were already in control there. He thought highly of his own computer skills until he met those two. Boy, was he quickly humbled by serious wizards. Then, he turned and trotted off to the mouth of the caves.

True to his pattern, Harland was there, patiently waiting for his pals, a dead rabbit at his feet. Brad ducked out the entrance, alert to sounds of gunshots in the distance. Tracker had lost no time in getting his scouts into the field to hustle the mutants, running and hiding and sniping at them, all the while leading them astray.

"Baldie, how are you?" Brad began with his normal greeting. Harland dipped his head in acknowledgment. "We are under attack from savage mutants, as I'm sure you know," Brad continued, pointing to the loud reports not too far away. "Can you help us by attacking from the sky?"

Harland stared at him, unblinkingly. Belatedly, Brad realized he might be asking Harland to attack creatures that he considered to be from his own kind now. Just because he was attached to Erin and Brad did not mean that Baldie supported the human cause, or even cared about their continued existence as a species. Who could know his true loyalties now?

Giving emphasis to Brad thoughts, Harland gave a raucous squawk and launched himself into the air, quickly flying out of sight.

That tears it, Brad thought angrily, not believing he had actually asked a mutant to turn against other mutants. Obviously, Harland has not taken their side because he could have led them there at any time. But, to ask him to turn against them . . . that was another story.

As if to underline his thoughts, a loud crashing sound came from the battle. Rocks rained from the skies. Shielding his eyes, he saw avian mutants in the distance attacking humans from the air. While treetops provided some cover for his eyes, the fight was stacking against them all. Discouraged, he returned to the entry, guessing that his only use was as a backup to the computer geniuses inside after all.

*   *   *

Injured warriors filled the sick bay. Soon, Longwei abandoned working with Erin on helping to deliver Hiawatha's baby and joined with Medic to work on the wounded. They were overwhelmed by the numbers.

"Erin, what is happening?" Hiawatha frantically asked between breaths.

"Keep breathing," Namid instructed calmly. Hiawatha gave her a blistering look, which she ignored.

"The mutants are attacking, but don't worry because we are safe here," Erin said, distractedly. She had never delivered a baby. Heck, she had never even been near a newborn, let alone in a hospital room with a mother giving birth. How was she supposed to deliver this baby all by herself? At least Namid's soothing presence would somewhat help. Erin had never seen someone so in control of herself as she saw in her brief glimpses of Kaya. Kaya even spared a quick moment or two to check Hiawatha's progress, or rather, lack of progress. Did all babies take this long to be born? Who would ever willingly subject themselves to such a torturous birthing process? She was sure she would never put herself through this.

"Get her away from me," panted Hi.

"I'm just here to help," Namid said, unfazed by her demand.

"You're trying to steal Lo," Hi accused, half out of her head with delirium. "Where is Lo? Why isn't the baby coming? Is something wrong?"

"I don't want your boyfriend," Namid said, disdainfully. "We are both going through the same changes now and it helps to have someone to share that with. That's all it is."

"I don't believe you for a moment, you witch," Hiawatha cried out, her chest heaving as another contraction grabbed her.

"Hiawatha, you have to concentrate on having this baby," Erin urged, almost wailing. "Don't think about anything else right now. You know Lowell loves you."

"Then where is he? This is an important moment."

Erin and Namid exchanged looks. Did they dare tell Hiawatha that Lowell had joined in the fighting? They shook their heads in unison.

"He'll be right back here," Erin said, firmly. Then, to distract Hiawatha and possibly because it might be true, she said, "I think I see the head."

* * *

Harland was not avoiding the conflict, or going to aid the mutants attacking the humans. His thoughts and emotions were chaotic during the time of his transformation, but they had stabilized once he had completed his devolution. While a near-bird in thought and actions, he still retained core values he had developed since birth. His military loyalties were deeply ingrained, so he dimly recognized the humans as the remains of the United States of America he had sworn as a human to defend. This had nebulous meaning to him, but it was all in the subconscious, in addition to his devotion to Brad and Erin and his life-bond to his son, whom he fiercely missed. Soon he would be strong enough to hunt for Sterling. He had been slowly building his endurance since his recovery from his injury. For now, his duty lay with the humans that had nursed him to health.

Harland screeched again and again, calling to the other avian of a kindred spirit that he had befriended over the past weeks. Rallying to his call were eagles, hawks, owls, and all manner of bird mutants who were still grounded to their human roots and were ready to help protect their birth species — the humans. They had been secretly practicing maneuvers in the high mountain reaches where few land based creatures would travel. As one unified group, they formed a line and streaked through the sky, ending in formation over the flying enemy. They attacked without hesitation, surprising the enemy who thought they were the masters of the skies. The battle was brutal and there was no help from the ground, because once the fight was joined there was no way for humans or land based mutants to tell which birds were friends or foes. They tore into each other with beak and claws, falling from the sky still entwined.

Brad, who had heard the screeching, had turned back in time to witness the new disturbance. Though he couldn't pick out Baldie in the ensuing melee, he had no doubt that his friend had come through for them. He cheered silently, frozen in place as all thoughts of retreating to the computer center were forgotten.

The enemy was outnumbered. Soon those that were not killed or wounded flew off in retreat. Harland and his combat forces began using the same tactic started by the enemy, dropping rocks on the enemy. They patrolled back and forth along the ridge that protected the hidden entrance to the compound so that no mutant could cross that line.

"This is a land where the sky rains death," Brad thought to himself, giddily. Then, the shooting faded and it appeared that the mutants had retreated. Tracker and his scouts slipped back into the caves, carrying their wounded brethren. Because the death toll was high and there was no clear victory they would never truly be safe while marauding bands could find their base and launch a new attack. But at least for the moment, they were safe.

* * *

Lowell hobbled into the sick bay, aching from a badly twisted ankle. He had been of minimal help because he wasn't a skilled woodsman. His appearance caused some humans to mistake him for the enemy until he called out to them, revealing who he was. At least it had worked to their advantage that one time, when a mutant had thought he was an ally. He had turned his back on Lowell and got brained in the head for his trust. Lowell felt a little bad about that, but he remembered that all was fair in love and war. Speaking of love, he needed to find out right away what was going on with Hiawatha. He felt torn. He knew he should have been by her side, but he was of no real use there. In fact, he felt superfluous. At least out in the battle field he felt like he was doing something.

A strangled scream pierced the air, as Lowell pushed through the crowd that had mysteriously appeared around Hiawatha's bed. Was she dying? Oh, no. Was he too late?

"Let me through. I've got to see Hiawatha. Hi . . . Hi, are you okay?" he hollered as the people parted miraculously in front of him. He took one look at Hiawatha's beet-red face, and saw she was still breathing.

"Here you go, Lowell." He heard Erin's voice from behind him. He didn't pay attention at first. All he could see was his Hiawatha gasping with deep breaths, with sweaty beads pouring down her face. He grabbed her hand, given up by Namid who had moved quietly out of the way.

"Did you see him?" Hiawatha whispered, an unearthly glow coming over her face.

"Who," Lo garbled.

"Your son," Hiawatha said in a stronger voice, triumphantly pointing towards Erin.

"Here he is," Erin said again, handing a squirming bundle to Lowell, who almost dropped him in the process, overwhelmed by the moment.

"A son?" he marveled in wonder as he peeled back the blankets for a closer look. A half-human, half-simian face inspected him back. It was impossible to define the baby as either human or ape. He had characteristics of both, yet when someone tried to specify the answer slid elusively away. He was a combination of the best of both species, a new species all his own.

"Lowell Brant Kempfield, The Fourth," said Hiawatha smugly with self-satisfaction as if she had accomplished the greatest thing in the world. From the hushed awe around her, it seemed all in the group agreed. Amidst all the horror and pain of the injured, the first baby had been born in the compound, signaling to all that life would go on, a new life that they all swore to protect with their own.

"My son!" Lowell said, grinning proudly.

* * *

High over head, Harland watched the orderly retreat of the humans into the caves. His band of avian chased the surviving mutants off in all directions. It was as complete a rout as could be hoped for. His instincts overpowered him and he felt pulled in opposite directions. Surely the humans would need him again. He was sure of that. And, he felt pulled to go in search of Sterling. Surely the friendly avian would continue in their defense of the humans without his continued leadership. It was as if a magnetic force was pulling him. There was no way of knowing where Sterling was, but he had to start looking somewhere. Maybe the irresistible pull was somehow from his son, though he couldn't tell for sure. Giving a squawk at his second-in-command and turning the leadership officially over to her, he lifted his wings and headed south to Sterling . . . to Argentina.

* * *

After having a pack placed onto her back, since she no longer had hands to do it for herself, Jasmine whistled to her band of humans who had trained in the water with her. They had increased their ability to hold their breath for long periods of time, developing superb swimmer muscles. Carley, who had stayed close to her devolved co-workers and who had an uncanny way of understanding their non-human communications, had trained along with Jasmine and the other humans in this squad. Her job was to serve as an interface, an interpreter between Jasmine and the humans. Their job as a team in the pending attack was twofold. In addition to guarding the water tunnel from attack, they were also charged with ferrying out supplies to the fighters whose job it was to attack the mutant army from behind. The radar and infra-red from the satellites had shown that so far there were no aquatic mutants among the mutant forces. It made sense in a lop-sided sort of way. What would a water-based creature want with a cave, when their desires were abundantly satisfied by the richness and extent of the never-ending oceans of the world? Jasmine, thankful for small blessings, took a graceful dive to lead her team through the tunnel opening. Sometimes she too longed for the open seas, but her loyalties to her human friends were strong and they needed her now.

Pausing a moment to watch the impressive departure of the swimmers, Nate hurried back to the com center. His job was to monitor the screens to identify where and how the mutants would attack, what size their forces were, and to guide their small company to strike the enemy. This was made doubly hard now because their friends in the Galapagos Islands were simultaneously being attacked. A coincidence he wondered? He didn't have time to dwell on that now. What he did know was that he couldn't handle two battles at the same time. He hoped that Zack had connected as planned with Sandra to send her to help. Originally Sandra had intended to be part of the force gathering at the entrance to the land tunnel with Zack in charge. Now he needed her more. Ah, there she was, scurrying to the computer complex. He took a moment to admire the rearview before calling out to her.

"Sandra," he called out.

She paused and turned. "I can't believe that Gabe and Marti are being attacked the same time we are," she hollered over the blaring sirens that still sounded throughout the cavern. If anybody hadn't heard the news of the attack he was seriously deaf. Though if they didn't get those sirens turned off soon, they would all be deaf anyhow, she thought, wincing. That would be her first priority when she settled at the console. Hearing each other was as vital as their other tasks. It was amazing that the mutant army above could not locate them from the sound, she thought, as she hustled inside.

"You take charge of helping Gabe and Marti," Nate ordered as she fell into the seat next to Nate. "I'll oversee what is happening here." Normally, Sandra would have taken exception to his assumption of command, but now was not the time for petty bickering, and she knew it was more a sign of stress on Nate's part than his need for control. She nodded briefly and got on the horn with Marti. Gabe had already gone to assemble and organize his small group of humans, a pitiful number of adults with children, and teenagers who thought they were adults.

"Marti, this is Sandra. I will stay with you to keep you informed of what the mutants are doing outside your compound."

"Sandra, thank God. I was feeling so alone here on the boat. Gabe made me promise to take her out to sea after he jumped off. I have never handled this boat by myself before," Marti said, distractedly.

"Marti, do you have reliable communications established with Gabe?" Sandra asked, trying to get Marti focused on what was important.

Taking a breath, Marti steadily answered. "Yes, I do. Gabe, can you read me?"

"Loud and clear," Gabe responded. Sandra could hear Gabe's answer too, since Marti had put the communications on speaker.

"The mutants appear to be staging from three sides with a force of about twenty at each location," Sandra informed them, her heart sinking along with theirs. They were easily heavily outnumbered. Most likely all the mutants were adults with animal strength. "I think they are using a three-pronged strategy of tunneling under your barricade, while trying to go over it and cut through it. Oh, no! The group on your left flank has just set the wooden barrier on fire!"

* * *

"Mama, where are you going?" Rita asked, grabbing hold of her mother's arm as she was scurrying by, thankful that the sirens had finally been shut off. Her mother was weeping copiously. Rita gathered her in her arms.

"I am going to the church to pray," Eva mumbled. "Everyone has a job to do except me. Although everyone must think I am too old to be of any use, at least I can pray and God will hear me, and He will be on our side."

"Mama, you are not useless. Running the kitchen is important to all of us. We have to maintain our energy to be of any use during a fight," Rita exclaimed. She wanted to get on with her own mission of finding Zack, but she did not want to leave her mother like this. She spared a thought to whether God took sides.

"There are many people already working hard in the kitchens, so they are getting along fine without me. In fact, there are so many people there, including children that we all are getting in each other's way. No one will even notice I am gone. And besides, prayer is not useless," Eva said, pulling herself up with great dignity.

"No, Mama, of course, you are right. However, you do not have to be in church to pray. I have something important that you can do that will help me out immensely; and you can still pray while you do it. In fact, it will give you abundant material for your prayers." Looking furtively around, Rita whispered to her mother what she should do.

*   *   *

Zack listened closely as Nate relayed to him that the mutants were massing one ridge over from where the main tunnel opened out. They did not seem to know exactly where the opening was, but the humans did not intend to wait to let them find it. Zack thought darkly about Miguel, the former co-pilot who had devolved into an avian mutant. He obviously had led the other mutants to them. There was no way the mutants could have found them without an inside source.

Since they had not found the land-based entrance and fortunately had no inkling of the waterway tunnel under the waterfall, the mutants were still encamped a short distance away, allowing Zack to send some forces out under cover of dark. As had been previously planned and practiced, Holly would slip out with Sterling and the twins to mount an aerial offensive. If Miguel was involved, there would be enemy avian also present, probably in greater numbers than their little band of four and most likely older and stronger. But Sterling and the others were more devolved and confident in their new-found skills. Plus, their small number made them highly maneuverable, as a group. Zack tried hard not to think about the fact that three of them were children because hard choices were necessary in a time of war. Holly, Sterling and the twins were ready.

Zack cautiously opened the land door, and they hopped out into the countryside, immediately taking wing and soaring off to a predetermined spot on the hillside. If seen by the mutant army, they hoped they would be mistaken as part of the mutant forces. From what they had seen, there did not appear to be many avian joining the land-based mutants. Most large birds were solitary creatures and had little in common land based creatures. Flying free and catching prey, as needed, was all the life they desired. The exception was Miguel, who seemed to have a personal grudge, so he had gathered a small band of his own. Holly and the kids would have their work cut out for them.

The plan had always been that the humans would strike first if they were threatened by mutants. They knew they were safe from harm inside their cavern system, but they also could not afford to be surrounded and possibly starved out. Their supplies and interior gardening site were extensive, but not tested as their sole source of food. They needed to deal decisively with this comparatively smaller force. They did not want news spreading among the mutants that a group of humans were living nearby.

Zack turned from closing the door after the avian left and headed back to the force of humans he would lead outside. Rita remained determined and resolute in her purpose, a confident look on her face.

"What are you doing here?" Zack demanded, harshly.

"I'm going to fight, too," she challenged.

"But, Rita, you know we've been through all of this before. You are needed as a doctor to handle the injuries of the wounded," Zack said, dismissing her position, though her eyes pleaded with him.

"I have turned that over to my mother," Rita announced triumphantly. "You know I am not a medical doctor. For all these months that I have been serving in that capacity, it has now become evident to me that my mother has more medical knowhow in her little finger than I have with all my degrees. She will do fine without me. I am needed here. What's more, this is where I want to be — by your side." She finished defiantly.

Looking at her standing brave as she held a weapon, next to her father and brother and all the people from her family compound and from her country, he was undone and knew there was nothing he could say to stop her. This was no time for an argument in front of his troops. No one else would dare broach his authority at a time like this, but before Rita he melted. Nodding in defeat and turning his back on his grimly resolute company, he led them out.

* * *

Miguel was expertly cruising through the dark skies. Unlike most of the avian mutants who had followed the path of devolution to hawks, owls and predator birds, Miguel had devolved along a different path. He had acquired some enhancement pills that were selling at a bargain price on the black market, after Don Perez had forbidden their use among his employees, which promised to increase his night vision exceptionally. It sounded extremely attractive for a pilot, and Miguel was resentful that he was being denied the right to decide for himself what was good for him. He wasn't a serf within an old-time feudal system.

When he first developed wings, he blamed Senor Perez in a convoluted rationalization. If Senor Perez had not forbidden the enhancement supplements, he wouldn't have tried them. It was all Senor Perez's fault that he was devolving to a bird. Later he noticed differences in the way his wings were forming than those of Captain Sanchez, who had also taken supplements. The more mainstream pills were marketed for pilots, pills that Miguel had sneered at because of their exorbitant price. He was secretly proud of cleverly hunting out a cheaper enhancement. He was not developing feathers on his wings. Instead, his skin was becoming leathery, especially on his wings, a kind of webbing between hard veins of cartilage. He craved blood, but not meat. Dimly, while he was still able to think about or care about such things, he recognized that he was devolving into a vampire bat — a mammal. He was able to see well in the dark using his built in sonar. While he considered the fact that he was still a mammal, he was livid at the idea that he was devolving at all, though it was uplifting to be able to fly wherever he wanted without the confines of a plane. Soon his thirst for blood turned his mind to visions of revenge on Senor Perez. He would not rest until he could drink the blood of the Senor and all his family.

It had not been easy to form an avian squad, especially since the bird brains looked askance at his differences. To make matters worse, he only flew at night, while they preferred the daylight except the owls. He tried to work with the owls, but they wouldn't have anything to do with him. As for his avian squad, there were only a couple hawks and one owl that showed any interest in being involved with the mutant army. He eventually gave up working with most of them, and let them work out their own daytime plans for attack. A loner by nature, he would secretly patrol the skies alone at night. He was the perfect nighttime scout for the mutant army, since no one else could see as well as he could in the dark.

He was also their inside informer. Too bad he hadn't stayed in the Perez compound longer so he could have gotten the specific location of their hidden entrance. It didn't matter though because they would have to come out sometime. As he patrolled the skies, he felt confident they would try to slip people out under cover of dark, revealing the entrance. Then the mutants would be able to attack the proper location, proving his value in their hierarchy and getting him closer to his ultimate goal — the Perez family.

What was that over there in the sky, birds taking wing, and at night? This went against everything he knew about the avian mutants. He remembered rumors that the humans were experimenting with pet mutants. Could this be them? He pirouetted in midair, wheeling over to investigate.

* * *

"Form a bucket brigade," Gabe yelled to Avram.

Their worst fears were being realized — fire! They had hoped that a primitive instinctual fear of fire would prevent the mutants from using fire as a weapon. They had tried to guard against it by daily wetting the brush barrier around their small enclave. With the sea at their backs, they had abundant water to use, though it was a losing battle. The dead bushes got drier and more brittle as each day went by.

A greatly stretched line was formed, of mainly younger children, from the sea to the fire, but it was too small an effort for the conflagration that consumed their flimsy barrier. The smoke and burning stench was overpowering and soon they could not even see one another.

Throwing one last bucket onto the flames, Gabe yelled, "Fall back to the second barricade." He waited until everyone else had made it up the ladder in the trench around the earthen mound that served as their second line of defense. Following them, he pulled up the ladder just as the first mutant stomped through the still-flaring embers of the ruined brush wall. Gabe thought grimly of the complaints among the teenagers when they had to dig that trench and build that wall, especially the younger kids who thought they were only being given busy work. He thought darkly that they were finally realizing how important their work was.

The earthen barrier they had built went right up to high cliffs on both sides of the encampment, one of the reasons they had chosen this location to fall back to when the waters rose and forced them higher. The other reason was the natural harbor between the cliffs on the far side. It would be impossible for the mutants to climb the wall with their stunted bowlegs. They would not be able to manage the cliffs, and swimming was not an option for the top-heavy muscular apes. Gabe realized the weakest points were where the wall met the cliffs. It was only a matter of time before the mutants were able to dig through it.

Gabe braced one of the ladders they had made against their side of the mound and climbed it, shooting down at the mutants who were throwing themselves in a rage against the wall. He hoped the mutants would not have any weapons other than rocks or sticks. Again, it was wishful thinking. Some of them already had owned guns and remembered how to use them, or they had acquired them in the towns they had overrun. Among the people in the enclave, they only had three handguns and a shotgun. It was apparent to Gabe that they were going to be outgunned by the mutants.

Shots were exchanged, but the mutants were openly exposed to being picked off. Though they had superior fire power, they recklessly shot at the mound without any visible targets. Gabe was hopeful that they'd run out of all their ammunition in no time. Animal cunning took over and the mutants retreated temporarily, leaving their dead where they had fallen.

"They're retreating," Gabe announced, descending the ladder, as Avram did the same. He wiped the sweat from his brow.

"We won!" Andy shouted, pumping his hand in the air.

Gabe smiled wearily at the boy. He knew it was only a matter of time before the attack was resumed, and he knew it would be fiercer than before. He didn't want to dampen the boy's celebration. For the moment, let the children revel in triumphant feelings, as reality would soon press on all of them.

As the fire quickly consumed the whole bush barrier all the camp gathered around Gabe waiting for new instructions. Their battle plans had been rehearsed many times, with everyone knowing what their individual tasks would be, yet they still looked to Gabe for orders and, more importantly, for reassurance.

"Marti, the mutants have fallen back temporarily. Can Sandra see where they are now?" Gabe asked, eyeing the solemn group gathered around him. How did he, almost an alcoholic, who had nothing better to do than sit on a bar stool each evening, get into this position of commanding a small ragtag group of humans and mutants in the Galapagos Islands? He shook his head in borderline despair, afraid that he was not up to the job; the weight of their trust pulling him down.

"Gabe, Sandra says that the mutant army, still about fifty strong, is assembling at the east end of the wall, against the cliff. They appear to be building some things, but she can't get a good enough look to tell what they are doing. Is everyone all right?" Marti came through clearly.

"So far, no one has been hurt," Gabe reported, ruffling Andy's short, wiry hair. As usual, Andy was sticking close to his Captain. He had escaped from his mother's care and found his way to Gabe's side. Gabe knew that he was going to have to send him back to the comparative safety where Sun was guarding the smaller children near the water's edge. For the moment, he let the boy stay.

"Okay, we've got a small breather," Gabe said, sounding winded, but not daring to think about his heart. "Any idea about what they might be up to?" he asked as most of the group headed toward the east end of their earthen barrier.

This too had been discussed endlessly, with excellent input from Avram and Sun. It boiled down to digging through or under, or trying to climb over. What they had learned already, if they had not known it previously from interacting with the Goldsteins, was that the intelligence and ingenuity of the ape people was not to be discounted.

"Gabe, they are attacking!" Marti screamed into the phone. "It looks like they have made ladders and shields of some kind."

"Run, everybody! Run to your posts. Andy, go back to your mother," Gabe said gruffly.

"But, Captain," Andy protested.

Giving his son a push, Avram thrust him in the direction of Sun and the other children. "There is no time for argument," he grunted.

With a bit more tact, Gabe hollered over his shoulder as he ran, lugging a ladder. "Take care of the little ones for us, Andy. You are their protector. I'm counting on you." Unable to see if the youngster obeyed, Gabe ran to his assigned post.

Andy defiantly stuck out his lip, mad at being treated like a kid but also trying hard not to cry. Then he thought harder about the Captain's words. Suppose those sneaky mutants got around the camp people and had attacked his mother and baby brother and sister. He would be the only one left to defend them. He squared his shoulders and marched his ungainly little legs over to his mother. Sun distractedly grabbed him, scolded him and held him close at the same time. Meanwhile, Andy just squirmed. This was not how a soldier was supposed to be treated!

*   *   *

Zack led his troops out as stealthily as they could manage, trying for a surprise attack on the mutant forces in the dark. The group that Jasmine and Carley, with their squad of human swimmers had ferried out through the water tunnel, amassed behind the sleeping enemies, and began to creep up on them from the rear. It seemed like a perfect pincer play in progress for the humans and Zack allowed himself a moment of hope.

"The mutants are stirring," Nate's voice came over the sat phone. "Something, probably an avian mutant, flew into the camp and alerted them that you were coming."

The element of surprise was gone.

"Attack!" Zack shouted as the order was quickly passed on.

Nate relayed the orders to the rear team of humans led by Javier and Paolo. And the human force quickly engaged in heated battle from both sides with the enraged mutants.

As if on cue, Holly and the kids swarmed out of the dark, raining rocks on the mutants as they bumbled around, searching for their weapons and struggled to organize. Many of the mutants went down from the barrage, but they could not have it all their way. The enemy avian, who had been sleeping on roosts, sprang into the air. From the left, Miguel swooped in to attack Sterling, engaging in mid-air. Miguel's bat's mouth was no match for Sterling's wickedly sharp eagle beak. In addition, Sterling's deadly claws were sharper than Miguel's tiny claws. Aside from the fact that a bat could never contest an eagle and expect to win, Miguel had not devolved as much as Sterling and was not as adept in his bat-like form yet. Sterling, who was completely devolved, attacked Miguel with rapier speed. He tore into the leathery wings with his claws, and slashed his beak into Miguel's weak face. Miguel squealed and gave up the fight, trying to get away, but Sterling was filled with the blood-lust of battle, and could out fly a bat, even a human, adult-sized one. The battle was hardly started before it was over, Miguel's lifeless body falling to the ground.

Sterling turned to see Holly fighting with two hawks, while the twins were harrying an owl. As he looked, the owl took flight and headed away, no longer interested in the fight. It did not like the sharp beaks, and suddenly forgot why it had wanted to fight with the mutants anyway. Sterling and the twins flew over to help Holly, who was bleeding profusely from numerous wounds inflicted by the hawks. Being an eagle, and more fully devolved than the hawks, she was larger and stronger than they were, but she was also outnumbered. The tide changed when Sterling and the twins joined in on the uneven contest. And the hawks, similarly to the owl, suddenly lost interest in the fight and weakly flew away, barely able to stay aloft from their wounds. They would hunt easier prey that couldn't fight back after they had recovered. What did they care about the concerns of land-based mutants or humans anyway?

Supporting Holly, who was hurting badly, Reva and Vera helped her make it safely to the ground. Then they guarded her until she limped into the entrance, where Eva met her.

"You'll be okay, Holly," Eva clucked, maternally, overseeing her transport to the sick bay. Eva had her first casualty to deal with, and human medical knowledge was going to be sorely tested in helping a mutant bird.

"Squawk, squawk," the twins cried worriedly after Holly. Then reluctantly turning their backs on their mother, they gathered more rocks with Sterling and again took to the air, back to the battle.

* * *

Mateo went down in a ball of fire, rolling on the ground, shrieking. His father, Rodrigo grabbed a blanket and started whacking at the flames. Gabe threw a bucket of water on Mateo yelling, "Chaska, go get Yanina and Sofia." Chaska took off running to get the women, who were standing ready to minister to anyone who was injured. Bringing up more buckets of water, Frederico threw them at his brother, not caring that tears were streaming down his face. The fire was out, but all of Mateo's clothes had been burned off of him and he was barely conscious. Yanina and Sofia came hurrying up with Chaska, Yanina wailing as she saw her son's charred flesh. Sofia had seen great hardship over the years; she courageously pushed past her daughter and began to check out Mateo's injuries. "Get ahold of yourself, Yanina," her mother chided. "Your tears will not help the boy."

Coming to her senses, Yanina fell to the ground next to Mateo, and called out to him softly. "Mateo, can you hear me, bambino?" Then, switching to drill sergeant mode, she barked out orders to her husband and oldest son, "Pick Mateo up and carry him to the sick bay." Gingerly they complied, afraid to touch the injured boy for fear they would hurt him more.

"Everyone else, back to the wall," Gabe hollered, setting the example by climbing the ladder he had been fighting from.

The battle had been fierce. Somehow the mutants had pieced together metal shields, probably taken from parts of buildings in towns they had raided. These shields had deflected bullets, and firebombs that Gabe and his small group threw at them. As Sandra had reported, they had been building ladders. For a while, the defenders were able to push the first ladders over, but the sheer numbers of the mutant force were overwhelming the small group of friends.

"Fall back to the sea," Gabe yelled through the smoke and sounds of heavy shooting. He and the other men continued the fighting as the women and teens ran for the water. Marti had brought the boat back to shore, and those who were assigned to the boat piled on. The boat's life raft and a couple of wooden rafts constructed specifically for this purpose were shoved out to sea. Mateo was carefully lifted onto the sailboat, unaware of what was going on around him.

The mutants swarmed over the mound, with nothing stopping them. They threw firebombs at the structures in the compound and soon everything was on fire, burning wildly out-of-control. Now, visibility for defenders and aggressors was equally difficult.

"That's it, men, to the life boats," Gabe called out and turned to provide covering fire for his fellow warriors. Suddenly, he was hit with a bullet in the right shoulder, his shooting arm going limp as white hot fire shot down his arm and through his chest. Grabbing his useless arm with his other hand, by sheer force of will he kept to his feet and lunged after the retreating men, followed closely by howling ape-men. The only advantage they had was their superior knowledge of the camp.

The boats had already pulled away from shore, so the last defenders had to swim out to the nearest rafts. Fleeing the flames themselves, the screeching mutants followed uncomfortably close behind. Gabe fell into the water, then again struggled to his feet as mutants closed in on him. As he tried to swim one-handed to a raft, an especially large ape grabbed hold of his left leg. Gabe kicked at him with the other leg, as Emilio and Cori tried to pull him onto the raft, but the mutant had a strong hold, and others were coming on fast. From the boat, Marti screamed in anguish, only the strong arms of the other women keeping her from throwing herself into the ocean and rushing to Gabe's aid.

Suddenly there was a hard solid whack into the mutant's side causing him to reflexively release his hold on Gabe. As the mutant disappeared under the water, Gabe scrambled with a renewed adrenalin rush onto the raft, looking behind him to see what had caused the mutant to let go.

It was a dolphin, or more accurately, a pod of aquatic mutants who had long ago devolved into dolphins, accompanied by sea lions and other sea mammals. Unknown to the humans, and only dimly recounted in oral history among the sea creatures themselves, these animals were direct descendants of Shaka and Devi, the humans who were originally trapped on the Marshall Islands and exposed to the nuclear fallout that resulted in the first devolution. Some of the DNA from these first victims had started Rita on her first experiments.

The sea mammals attacked the mutants with a vengeance, butting them in the sides and legs and darting away. The enraged mutants switched their target to the sea mammals, giving the humans a chance to get on the rafts and head out to sea. Firebombs were useless weapons in the water, and the mutants could not effectively get good shots off at the fast dolphins, which were able to quickly dive deep and twist away to escape injury. Following the boat and life rafts, the dolphins created a barrier between them and the attackers. Finally, the mutants were trapped. They could not continue any deeper into the water, since they were unable to swim with their heavy muscle and bone structure, and the sea mammals were guarding in that direction anyhow. Nor could they return to the land, either, because of the fires.

Bringing the life rafts alongside the sailboat, Gabe was helped into the boat where Marti grabbed him as if she would never let go.

"Gabe, are you all right?" Marti wailed, taking in the blood pouring out of his wound.

"I'll be just fine . . ." Gabe began then he collapsed onto the deck next to Mateo.

*   *   *

Rita sighted down the gun the way she had practiced regularly with her father and brother as a teen. She got off a shot that felled another mutant then she quickly ducked behind a tree. She looked for Zack and spotted him a few feet away, engaged in hand-to-hand combat with two mutants. He appeared to have lost his gun and was getting a beating from the powerful arms of the apes. She raised her gun again, trying to get a clear shot, but Zack was in the middle of the melee, and she couldn't be sure she wouldn't hit him. Looking around herself desperately, she spotted a large rock. Grabbing it, she rushed out from behind her tree, and waiting until a mutant head was right in front of her, she brought the rock down with all the force she could manage, giving the mutant a hard kick at the same time for good measure. The mutant went limp. With only one mutant to fight, Zack was able to use his training in martial arts to effortlessly throw the ape-man, recover his gun, and put a bullet in his head.

With a grim grin of acknowledgment, Zack looked at Rita.

"You're welcome," she said.

Surveying the battlefield, it was apparent that their three-pronged attack had the mutants on the run. It was important to let none escape to tell where they were located. Zack's forces were overpowering the few remaining hard-headed mutants who were doggedly fighting to the finish. Holley and kids were zooming down on a few who were about to escape and raking them with their claws. The battle appeared to be just about over.

"How does it look from above, Nate?" Zack asked.

"I don't see any more forces near you they definitely are on the run," Nate came through clearly, though he sounded a bit weary. It had been a long and hard fight, and Nate had been on top of the action directing the fighters the whole time.

"Are we done yet?" Rita said, jokingly trying to sound like a little kid fed up with doing chores. She didn't quite carry it off, though her smudged, tired face fit the image.

Pedro trotted along with Javier. "Zack, a few managed to get away, but we've taken care of the rest," they reported. Rita didn't want to think about what "taking care of" meant. "We've sent the marines after those who escaped."

"Casualties?" Zack asked in as professional a manner as he could manage.

"We are still counting, but there are surprisingly few," Pedro responded. "The advantage of surprise certainly helped us. There are wounded, and my mother has her hands full, but we have had no reported deaths."

"I'd better go help her," Rita said. Suiting actions to words, she was off before Zack or her brother could say anything else.

"You've got your hands full there," Pedro said to Zack with a smile, tipping his head at Rita's departing back. "Believe me, I know my sister."

Ignoring Pedro, Zack turned to the others, reporting in and giving orders for mop up operations.

* * *

"Whew, it's over," Sandra said limply, slumping back into her chair. "It didn't go too well for our friends in the Galapagos. They were outmanned and outgunned. Gabe has been shot, and one of the teenagers, Mateo, is badly burned. I don't know what they are going to do now. They are stranded out-at-sea, some of them only on hand-made wooden rafts." She looked at Nate despondently. "I did everything I could to help."

Nate, who was jubilant at their local victory, suppressed his celebration and immediately turned to hug Sandra. "I know you did all you could. There would have been many more injured without your help. I find it amazing that you were able to direct a battle a continent away through just satellite data. I still can't believe we were both coordinating two battles simultaneously." He couldn't quite keep down the self-congratulatory tones.

"We did help, didn't we?" Sandra marveled, returning his hug. "And everything will be okay for Gabe and Marti; I know it will."

* * *

A huge avian plunged from the sky, coming to a landing in front of Zack and the other leaders. Zack immediately raised his gun, assuming it was another enemy that had avoided detection, but something about the eagle's non-aggressive manner kept him from pulling the trigger. If he didn't know better, he would have thought this strange avian mutant was trying to communicate with him the way Holly and the kids did. It was bobbing its head and flapping its wings, craning its neck to look into the sky. It spied Holly and the kids and let out a loud, scary squawk.

Before Zack could get any further in his thoughts, their own bird mutant friends dropped from the sky and began leaping excitedly around the newcomer. Sterling rubbed himself against the big eagle, and Holly butted heads gently with him.

"Get Rita back here," Zack called into his sat phone. "We've got a visitor she needs to see right away."

They all watched in guarded amusement at the antics of the avian mutants, who obviously delighted with the visitor. Having just come from a serious battle, they were not ready to accept the stranger so easily, but waited patiently for Rita to arrive.

It wasn't long before Rita arrived followed closely by a curious Sandra and Nate. At one glance at the large eagle man, Rita stopped, thunderstruck.

"It's Harland," she shouted, throwing herself at him and hugging him. Sandra and Nate joined the group hug, all maniacally dancing together. Sterling, Holly and the twins raucously squawked with glee.

"Harland?" Zack asked stupidly. In his mind, he quickly reviewed all he had heard about Harland. "Was this the criminal who had killed a Navy nurse?" He brought his gun back up, wishing Rita would get out of the way.

"He was temporarily insane," Sandra said, putting her hands on her hips and thrusting herself in front of Zack, spoiling his aim.

Harland, whose homing instincts from the imprinting of the Earth's magnetic waves into his newly morphed dominant DNA components had guided him to the place of his avian birth; Patagonia. It may have been a coincidence that Sterling was here, or maybe there was some telepathic communication over distances that birds had that humans did not understand. Who had ever been able to figure out the way birds, whales, and even dogs could travel thousands of miles to places they had not seen in years? Harland was exhausted, having flown straight without stopping except for food or sleep. He rubbed his head against Sterling, content at last to finally be home with his son.

"Put that gun down, Zack," Rita commanded her arms as far around Harland as they could reach. Feeling somewhat foolish, Zack complied.

CHAPTER ELEVEN

The New Order

Sweat poured down Gabe's face, blocking his vision. He was dizzy and unfocused as he placed his fist on his chest to soothe the pain, instinctually feeling that if he pressed on the pain it would lessen. He felt like he was in a tunnel looking out a long distance. His stomach heaved, though nothing came up, aside from his intolerance of the terrible, gnawing nausea he felt. The pain was worse than any Gabe had ever had, shooting up his left arm and nearly crushing his chest. As he lay in his berth on the boat recovering from the wounds he had taken in the battle, Gabe immediately recognized it as a classic heart attack.

Gabe had lost a lot of blood from the gunshot, so his recovery was progressing slowly. This pain was nothing like those angina pains he'd been getting off and on, all unbeknownst to Marti. He knew he should take his nitro pills, but more importantly, he dimly remembered he was supposed to take an aspirin. As he lurched to the galley, the hand not holding his chest, batted around in the overhead cupboards in the galley of the boat, alternately searching for the medicine bag that held the aspirin bottle and struggling to keep himself erect. Bracing himself against the sink, he finally found a medicine bottle. He squinted at it, hoping it to be aspirin, though he was not certain.

He remembered to only take a single pill, without dividing it. Finally, he dared to take his hand off of his chest so he could shake a pill from the bottle into it. He dry swallowed the pill, grasped his chest again as pain continued to pound at his chest. No longer in control, he blindly reached for the radio to contact Marti, now on land, where she was organizing the new village they were establishing on a deserted island they had found after fleeing their burning compound. The batteries were too weak, though, and there was no time or way to reach her. There wasn't time for anything. Gabe thought about how much he loved her as he fell to the floor, now unconscious. Solidly, he hit the deck, the pill bottle falling next to him, spilling out its remaining pills.

* * *

"I can't raise Gabe or Marti on the sat phone," Sandra announced, swinging around and facing Nate.

"They must just be on the island getting things established," Nate said, reasonably. "Give them a try later."

"Duh, you think?" Sandra replied with a toss of her hair.

Nate leaned over from his seat and gave Sandra a long, satisfying kiss.

Of course Zack and Rita chose just that moment to pop into the com center. Zack smirked, so Rita playfully punched him for it. Pointedly ignoring them, Nate and Sandra took their time finishing their kiss. Zack gave an exaggerated yawn.

"Did you come for anything other than to interrupt us?" Nate asked, finally sitting up, though leaving an arm around Sandra.

"It has been weeks since we have had any activity from the mutants. I have a feeling that any organization they once had has since broken down," said Zack.

Puffing, Carley entered. "I'm afraid I have some bad news. The gardens seem to have gotten some kind of sickness. Everything is beginning to wilt and turn brown. What are we going to do? Without the garden we won't have enough food."

"Maybe I can find something on the computer that will tell us how to treat that," Sandra suggested helpfully. She was always the one with an idea for a solution.

"We are almost out of medical supplies," Rita added.

"All of this fits right in to what I was going to suggest," Zack continued. "I think we need an expedition to the surface to get a lay of the land and to see if it would be feasible to start moving out of the cave. Sitting here, we aren't going to know what is happening on the surface."

"We always have the trusty computer to show us," Sandra protested, giving the monitor a pat like it was a loyal pet.

"Nothing like firsthand intel," Zack said briskly. Truthfully, he was getting antsy after all the weeks with no activity, as were most of the people in the cave. Supplies were getting low and everyone needed a new purpose, a mission in their lives.

"I've been thinking I wanted to go check out the ranch, see if there are any crops left, or if they were all destroyed, or eaten," Nate said as he made a face at the thought of his ravaged ranch. "I especially want to find out what happened to my horses."

"Nate!" Sandra said with reproof in her tone at the same time Rita was saying, "Zack!"

"You have no idea how dangerous it is out there," Rita said, worriedly.

Carley didn't have the same strong emotional attachment to the guys that the other gals had. "Something has to be done; otherwise we will all starve. We can't just hope for a miracle cure from your little computer," she said, rudely directing her comments towards Sandra. "Even if it does diagnose the problem and tells us a cure for the plants, who says we will have the ingredients for a proper treatment. No, I am with the guys. We need an exploratory trip to the real world. I, for one, have no intention of living underground forever." She put her hands on her hips and thrust her jaw out for emphasis.

"Sandra, we promise to be careful," Nate wheedled. "We'll have our avian friends keep a lookout from above. They'll be able to spot danger a mile away . . . as will you on the computer," he added hastily.

"We won't be gone long this first time," Zack said. "Just Nate and I will go with only a couple of others. That means we won't have a large contingent to make much noise and to spark attention . . . not that we expect any attention at all," he finished quickly as he saw Rita about to object.

Sandra and Rita looked at each other, helplessly. They both knew that the "boys" would do what they wanted to do, no matter how much they protested. There was no sense in wasting their breath arguing. It wouldn't do any good. Reluctantly, they nodded their heads while holding the fear tightly controlled in their hearts.

Carley clapped her hands. "Yes! I will pack up some supplies for you both. You'll see, this will be the beginning of life returning to normal." She bustled out, single-mindedly intent on her task. The guys, not wanting any last minute changes in the minds of their ladies, hurried after her.

Sandra and Rita exchanged long looks both thinking of the things they had witnessed, heard, and seen through the satellite communication they were still somehow lucky enough to have. The remains of past human civilization had been virtually wiped out. The fires, the rising sea levels, the nuclear explosions, not to mention the mutant desire to destroy the "unnatural," had rendered all transportation systems unusable. All the major coastal cities were also gone, where ninety percent of humanity once lived. Plus, all vehicles were corroded and burned beyond use. Most of the computers in the world were destroyed. There were no remaining power grids or power either, with all modern conveniences now gone. Virtually no medicines remained and the small amounts still available were rapidly dwindling. Books in libraries had been burned long ago, used as fuel. No, life would not be returning to "normal" anytime soon, despite Carley's cheery optimism. Wordlessly, the women followed the men out to help with the preparations, as each kissed her guy good-bye.

*   *   *

Nervously, Erin looked over the gathering of people spread out in a large circle before her. There was no reason to be nervous, she scolded herself. She had been with these people for months now, fighting alongside them against the enemy mutants. She helped with the daily chores of survival, working side-by-side with them, even delivering a baby. She grinned at the thought and glanced fondly at Hiawatha, holding her infant son with Lowell standing protectively and proudly by her side. No, she had nothing to fear from any of these people. They were her friends. In fact, they were now even "family." Regardless, she was still nervous.

She reached out to Brad and gave his hand a squeeze, which he squeezed back. Of course, Brad had already been through this with his Naming Ceremony. When he discovered that "Nerd" and "Geek" were already taken, he quickly settled on "Chip" without a second thought. While "Chip" suited him, and Erin called him that in public, in private she still called him Brad, and would always think of him that way.

Erin had taken longer to come up with a new name. She had struggled long and hard over her choice, answering to "Hey you," or "Hey good-looking," whenever Tracker spoke to her. Everybody patiently waited for her to come up with a name and never asked her real one.

"Are you ready, Little Sister?" Kaya asked.

With a gulp, Erin nodded, solemnly, though she kind of liked being called "Little Sister" and wasn't sure she wanted to give that up.

Taking Erin's hand, Kaya turned to the assembled group of mountain men, women, survivalists, young families, Native Americans, and half-mutants. In all, they were a highly diverse group.

"Our sister has a chosen a name, and would like to share it with us," Kaya announced, stepping back to give Erin the stage. They were gathered in a meadow out in the forest. Little by little, they had come out of the mountain cavern system, establishing a base camp near the river. In time they would fight small skirmishes with isolated bands of mutants, but for now they were finding little resistance as they slowly expanded outwards.

Letting her eyes slowly roam over the people who watched her in anticipation, Erin finally found the calm she had sought. "I thought hard about a new name," Erin began softly. "I wanted something that was meaningful to where I am in my own life, and where the world is now. Yet I wanted a name that would stand the test of time. It may sound egotistical to some of you that I would put such stock in a name. It seems to me that finding a new name came easily to all of you, especially since they all fit you so well. I couldn't think of one that fit me. Although I have never been a person of faith, after spending time in the Listening Room I am aware that I want more out of life. I want renewal for myself, not only for myself, but for each of you and for the world as a whole. Since there is no guarantee that any of this will happen, the best we can do is to believe that it will happen. I want to believe the earth will heal. I want to believe that all the species on earth can learn to live together in peace. I want to believe that I can grow spiritually as a person inside myself and also as a member of this community. For all those reasons, I have chosen to name myself 'Hope.' I love that name because I want to be filled with 'hope' and now I can have that feeling define me." Suddenly shy, she mumbled, "Thank you." Her last words were drowned out in a rousing round of clapping and raucous cheers from those gathered, as they all began to chant "Hope! Hope! Hope!" Everybody rushed forward to either embrace her or give her a hearty slap on the back.

A lavish spread of food had been set out for the celebration. After congratulating "Hope," everybody started eating. The children frolicked and Tracker started to play a tune on his guitar that people started dancing to.

Standing back uncomfortably, Hiawatha and Lowell had not come over to congratulate Erin. She purposefully went over to them. "Is anything the matter, Hi?"

"No, everything is just fine," Hiawatha said, quickly. "Congratulations on your new name."

Erin, who, had degrees in psychology and human behavior and the intuition to back them up, looked at her shrewdly and said, "You know, I have always wondered why the two of you did not want to change your names and have your own naming ceremonies. In fact, you haven't even named the baby yet." She paused, leadingly.

Hiawatha gave Lowell a quick look. He gave her a slow nod.

"That's because these aren't our real names," Hiawatha announced, miserably, while trying to hold her head high. "We changed them when we ran away from our families. Because of that, we don't know how to name the baby. I'm sorry we didn't trust you, Erin, I mean, Hope. Our real names are—"

"No, don't tell me. That's the whole point of new names. We have all been given a chance to remake ourselves with a fresh start. You just did it first," Hope interrupted, giving Hiawatha a careful hug because of the baby in her arms. "I always suspected that 'Hi' and 'Low' weren't your real names." She smiled at them, affectionately.

"You caught that, huh?" Low said, ruefully, his ape grin returning to his face.

"Kaya, Kaya, come over here for a minute," Hope called out, waving her one arm to catch Kaya's attention, her other arm firmly around Hiawatha's shoulder. Curious, Kaya hurried over. "Kaya, we have another naming ceremony you need to perform. In fact, we have three names to share with the community."

Turning to Low, Hiawatha said excitedly, "We can keep our new names forever, Lowell. And we can name the baby."

"Can I ask you what you are going to call him?" Hope whispered in her ear, while playing with the baby's fingers, as Kaya called the community back together.

"Why, this is Lo the Second!"

* * *

Bryce Chicory was glad to be out in the field again, watching for hostiles. He hated standing watch at all those dull meetings. Not that they had encountered many hostile mutants as they had spread cautiously and slowly this time out into the countryside. The ones they did chance upon were solitary and quickly disappeared into the forests, showing no desire for confrontation.

There was no doubt that there were plenty of mutants alive and well in the world. But for now it seemed they had given up on attacking humans. There was wild speculation on what the mutants were planning. The right-wing hawks that were left of the decimated human population insisted that the mutants were busy plotting future attacks. The remaining handful of soldiers needed to go on the offensive and vigorously hunt them out. The more moderate leaders postulated that the mutants had decided to establish communities of their own, with no further interest in being bothered with humans. Many scoffed at the idea that the mutants had the self-discipline and intelligence needed to establish a cohesive society on their own. They were quietly reminded of the cunning displayed by the mutants in surrounding and attacking their own camp. Wiser, calmer heads had prevailed. In the end, everybody agreed that they no longer had the force necessary to pursue the mutants as long as they kept to themselves. The mission was to verify the safety of the land they were reclaiming as they pushed their way outward.

During the past weeks, the Special Forces had continued scouting further out, heading towards where the capitol had once been. No one quite knew the rational for this, since Washington D.C. was long ago under water. But the President had ordered the scouting missions to proceed in this direction and Bryce was happy to oblige.

Going it alone, Chicory sniffed the air, enjoying the scent of pine trees and the wonderful springy feeling of pine needles under his feet. All his senses seemed to be drinking in the wildness and beauty of the forest around him. That meadow to his left looked promising for a settlement, he thought as he headed that way. There was even a sweet stream running through it for fresh water. Chic was keeping his eye out for a place away from the herd where he might put down roots for himself one day. Who could ever fathom that a boy from Texas could find his heart in the mountains of Virginia? In the meantime, this meadow would do for a temporary campsite. Or maybe he should keep this one quiet so it didn't get mucked up and trampled to pieces. He could just see the President claiming sites for his new government. They might commandeer it for a hidden location of their ongoing experiments on the handful of captive mutants they had brought to the bunkers. Chicory had chanced past the top secret area where the scientists were conducting their secret testing. That's where he had heard the screams and seen the dungeons before the guards had warned him off. He shuddered making him more than a little surprised that anything would negatively affect him after all he had been through. His reaction was difficult to explain maybe it was because these mutants were, technically, still his fellow Americans.

He fell to the ground, hidden by the tall grasses. What was that sound he had just heard? What direction had it come from? For a moment, all he heard was the normal sounds of the forest, but then he heard it again. It sounded like sniffing. It was probably just an animal, though a really noisy animal.

At that, Lope walked into the clearing, heading unerringly for Chicory. Warily, Chicory sat up, automatically stroking the dog with his left hand while his right reached for his weapon. Suddenly he was staring up into the muzzle of a rifle. Withdrawing his hand slowly from his gun, Chic put it up in the air, his mind absorbing the situation. Within a microsecond, he realized that it was not a mutant, but another human. Then, calculating at the same time the moves he would make to reverse the situation, he never doubted what he could do. Some instinct of his prevented him from putting that immediately into play. Maybe it was the dog that did it, who was still slobbering all over him, industriously licking his face.

"Give it a rest, Lope," said the tall, lean, bearded mountain man. The dog instantly, albeit reluctantly, stopped, looking inquiringly at his handler.

"Mind if I get to my feet?" Chic asked, casually suiting his words to action without waiting for a reply. He didn't know why, but his keenly honed senses did not detect danger from this man.

"Are you alone, son?" asked Tracker, eyeing the advanced weaponry that Chic had on his body. As the community from the mountain caves gradually branched out over the past weeks, they had run into isolated humans who had gladly joined up with them.

This young man did not give off the vibes of someone who had been living alone by his wits for months. He looked a little too well cared for, Tracker thought, sincerely doubting that any isolated individual would have that type of high technology.

"I'm a forward scout for the government," replied Chic, tentatively holding out his hand.

After a moment, Tracker gave it a shake and dropped his rifle down to his side. "What government would that be exactly?"

"The United States government . . . of course," Chicory said with great surprise. "May I ask who you are, sir, so I can introduce you when I take you to our leaders?"

"Now hold on there, son. You aren't taking me to any new place. I have my own leaders, well — that is — we have our own community. I'll have to consult with the others before we decide whether or not to meet with your group," Tracker said, laconically.

Sensing this was going nowhere fast, Chic became more forceful. "I am here at the behest . . ." (did I just say "behest," he asked himself) ". . . of the President of the United States. He would greatly like to meet with your leaders at their earliest convenience." Geez, he was admitting to himself that he was beginning to sound like a politician. It must have come from spending too much time uselessly guarding those endless meetings, he guessed.

"And where was that President of the United States when we were all under attack?" Tracker challenged the young upstart. "Was he hiding away somewhere while the rest of us were left to fend for ourselves?"

"We've done plenty of fighting with the mutants," Chic answered, wearily. "We've lost seventy-five percent of the people we started with. You don't hold an exclusive on mutant battles."

There was an uncomfortable silence for a moment that neither stubborn man knew how to break. Kaya chose that instant to come out into the opening to join in the conversation that she had been listening to. "Hello Soldier. My name is Kaya, and I am the token leader of this group of people. Tracker, here, is protective and suspicious, as he should be, after what we all have been through.

However, we are interested in a time of peace, and would gladly meet with the President with that goal in mind."

Relieved to be talking with someone in charge who seemed inclined to cooperate, Chic held out his hand to her. "Sergeant Bryce Chicory, ma'am. If you'll come with me, I'll take you to our current camp and get with the President's advisors to establish a meeting for you with the President."

"Why don't we say tomorrow morning?" Kaya said, regally. "I need time to discuss this with my advisors first. While they call me the leader, we are really a democracy with everybody getting an equal say. I can't make this momentous decision all on my own. And, I need to get together some of the others from our community to come with me."

"Sure, I understand. Of course, the United States has always been a democracy. We can set this up for tomorrow," Chic agreed, uncomfortably, not sure that this woman should be dictating a meeting time to the President of the United States.

"Sadly, Sergeant, the United States has not been anything close to a democracy for a long time," Kaya answered, quietly. "We'll meet you here again tomorrow."

Without further words, she and Tracker melted into the trees as if they had never been there. Lope spoiled the effect by giving Chic another hand-lick before he leaped after them.

* * *

The sobbing, weeping and wailing was heart breaking. Marti didn't know which was worse, watching Yanina (Mateo's mother) screaming her anguish as she beat on her husband, Rodrigo, while he stoically stood there holding her as if he were a marble statue that would never move again, or seeing little Andy yowling in his mother's arms. No matter where she looked, there were signs of the grief they all felt at Mateo's death. Anyway, looking at these people was better than watching Emilio and Frederico carefully lower the shrouded body into the freshly dug grave. Marti had been doing a good job of holding back her own tears and ministering to the grief of the others. She knew she would lose it completely if she watched.

They had tried everything they could for Mateo, but his burns were too extensive. Marti tried to tell herself that he wouldn't have lived even if he had been in one of the premier burn centers that used to exist in the world. At least they had enough morphine left to lessen his pain. Each day that passed gave his family false hope that he would live. But Marti, with the awful knowledge she had gleaned from the computer, knew better.

How could God let this happen to a sweet, beautiful sixteen-year-old boy — a boy who never wanted to be a soldier? At his age, he should have been busy going to school and chasing girls. Then again, who wanted to be involved in a war? None of them wanted the children to be exposed to this horror. Sobbing, Marti caught her breath before it could escalate and control her.

At least she had spared Gabe from having to hear the stumbling words that Emilio had tried to say over the grave, and to watch the slender form being taken away from his family forever. Gabe was still too weak from his wounds to have made the trip from the boat. It was such an easy lie to tell him that she was helping to establish the new compound today. It wouldn't be so easy to answer questions about Mateo when he started to quiz her about how the boy was doing.

Beginning a new compound was one thing. Supplying it was a whole different issue. They were low on critical supplies, like medicine and food. Even their ammunition was now virtually all gone. Except for the boats, there was no real shelter for them. How was this little community going to survive at all? Knowing that dwelling on those thoughts could lead to madness, Marti resolutely pushed away her worries about her own survival.

She would not, however, push aside her concerns for Gabe. Constantly thinking of him, Marti continually felt uneasy. It was almost as if she was having a premonition of impending doom, though she tried to shake it off. If any person was the practical, non-mystical type, it was Marti. She didn't believe in a sixth sense or any other New Age mumbo jumbo; however, the crushingly brutal atmosphere was getting to her. The more she tried to dismiss it, the stronger the feeling became that something was wrong with Gabe. Now it was overwhelming her to the point where she could no longer stand still for another minute without determining that Gabe was okay. Mumbling an incoherent excuse, she turned from the mourning group, and half-ran to the boat.

"Gabe honey, are you all right?" she hollered as she climbed onto the ladder, unable to wait until she was onboard for reassurance. Only silence met her call. Going first to their bedroom, she immediately saw that Gabe was not there. A quick glance at the bathroom, showed the door open and the room unoccupied. Her calls became more frantic as she hurried towards the galley, trying to tell herself that Gabe was just hungry and probably went to make himself a sandwich, ignoring her strict orders not to move until she was back.

And there he was — on the floor of the galley. Screaming, Marti dropped to her knees and frantically tried to see if he was breathing. Was there a pulse? Yes, he did still have a pulse, though a weak one. He was still breathing, too, though he wasn't responding to her. She sat down and pulled his head onto her lap, rocking him, begging him to wake up.

Marti had questions swirling in her head. Did he pass out from walking too soon? Did he have a heart attack? Doing a more in-depth survey of Gabe's condition, she noticed his hand was clenching his chest. Sweat was all over his forehead and his face was flushed. Without a doubt, she was certain that Gabe was the victim of a heart attack.

"Gabe, wake up! Speak to me, Honey!" she urged, terrified at the idea of losing him. It rushed through her mind again that they had no medications left in the community. Gabe still had his nitro on hand, in addition to aspirin. He was supposed to take an aspirin if he felt a heart attack coming.

She noticed his other hand was open at his side, with a medicine bottle on the ground only inches from his clenched fist. Her first feeling was a small measure of relief that Gabe had been able to ingest the aspirin in time, increasing his chances of reducing the effects of the heart attack. Surely, he would recover with an aspirin in his system, she thought. She reached for the bottle, but knew, before she got it up to her face to read, that it was not actually the aspirin bottle. She read the label, knowing already what it would say.

"Supplements, not approved by the FDA for medicinal purposes," she read aloud. The label promised strength and virility, plus the ability to stay underwater for long periods of time. Marti groaned loudly, as it was she who had originally flirted with the idea of taking the supplements. By contrast, it was Gabe who had been staunchly opposed. Why didn't she fling them out a long time ago? Oh why, oh why had she kept them? Marti berated herself.

With that, Gabe stirred and mumbled something she couldn't hear.

"Gabe, what did you say?" Marti urged, hugging him closely and pleading with him to wake up and return to a conscious state.

"Did you take one of these pills, Gabe?" Marti asked, gently.

"Yes. I just took one aspirin," Gabe muttered, trying to open his eyes, but not quite succeeding.

"I love you, Marti," Gabe murmured.

"Oh, Gabe, everything is going to be okay," Marti said through tears that were now blinding her. "I love you too, Gabe."

Resolutely, she opened the bottle and slowly brought one of the pills to her mouth, swallowing the supplement. "Wherever you go, I will be with you, forever."

*   *   *

Nate and Zack on a low rise, grimly looking at the ruins of the ranch, though Nate thought he was prepared for this moment- he wasn't. Jasmine, while she still had the ability to speak, had told him that the ranch was no longer standing. This had been substantiated by the fighters who had been spirited through the tunnel to the surface of the pool during the battle. He had believed there would be at least something left. If not for the charred embers, he wouldn't have been able to tell where the house had once stood. It had been gutted and then burned to the ground. Since the house was no longer blocking the view, it was also evident that the outer buildings had suffered the same fate. Skeletons of animals, picked clean of their edible meat by the mutants and then the vultures, lay scattered everywhere. The others avoided looking at him, giving him a moment to collect himself.

"Now I can rebuild it exactly the way I want it," Nate managed, trying to sound optimistic. He tried not to think of how hard it would be to construct a house from scratch without much in the way of tools or supplies. Nate was a stock market analyst, with little experience in building a house aside from refurbishing his ranch after he bought it. With all that had happened, it seemed like eons ago.

"As you said, Nate, now you can design the house any way you want it. Or, should I say, the way Sandra wants it?" Zack said with a bit of a snicker. His intent to lighten the mood served its purpose and Nate gave a grin as his mind pictured Sandra directing the construction. Now that he thought about it, this could actually be fun to do this together.

"Let's go look for the horses, since that was one of the reasons we came here in the first place. We already expected to find the ranch like this," Nate responded.

Without waiting for an invitation, Pedro and Javier started trudging through the remnants of what had once been a thriving estate to the woods and pastures. They all knew it was unlikely that any of the horses survived, but Nate was determined. And, as if providence had smiled on them amid unending chaos, they came upon half a dozen of Nate's horses that had returned to a fairly small pasture of grass between a heap of rocks and the stream.

After months on their own, the horses were skittish. Following the devastation, they had returned to their natural wild state, but their memories of working in concert with humans came back as Nate and the others gentled them into it. Since there were no saddles, the men had to ride bareback, something Nate and Zack had never done before. As a result, their ride was definitely a slow one.

"I'd like to see what is left of our home," Pedro said with a grimace. Of course, they all knew it had been burned down and demolished long ago by the mutants, but there was a necessity to grieving that required them to revisit their homes. It was also important to assess whether rebuilding was feasible in the old location or whether new homes should be placed elsewhere.

Travel on horseback was certainly faster than walking, even at the pace of amateur riders. Soon they secured leads for the two additional horses so they wouldn't wander away. Building a shelter and corral for the horses that also was secure against a mutant attack moved up on the priority list in Nate's mind.

It didn't matter which way they went, since their mission to scout out mutant activity could be served by striking out in any direction. They all readily agreed to the plan to head to the coast. After a couple of hours of leisurely, uneventful riding they got to the coast, with its altered coastline. Because of the drastic climate change, the risen sea level drastically changed the coastline. Much of what had been the Perez estate was now under water, hidden in the sea.

"My family home is gone," Pedro shouted, frantically looking around him in every direction, as if the casa would suddenly reappear in its former glory.

"Maybe we came the wrong way," suggested Zack, again trying to ease the situation, totally unlike the gruff Zack of old. Living in tight quarters with strangers for a long period of time had improved his diplomacy skills.

Giving him a disgusted look, that had to do with more than just Zack's idiotic suggestion Pedro got off his horse and fell to the ground weeping. "I know this land as if it were my bones. It is in my blood since the first day I was born, in the blood of my family for generations." He swept his hands wide in a grandiose gesture that encompassed everything in his sight.

"We can rebuild, Pedro. It will never be the same, but your family has survived through many hardships in the past and they will do so again," Javier said, formally. In a more personal tone, he said, "You have to be the strong one for your Papa and Mama, and the rest of the family."

Accepting from Javier, the long-time companion of the Perez family, what he would not accept from Zack, Pedro got to his feet and went to grasp Javier's hands, making a silent pact that they would see this through together.

"If the sea level is still rising, you might want to rebuild further inland," Nate observed. "In fact, to start with at least, we all need to live close together. It is going to be hard enough to survive a winter and possible mutant attacks as a group."

"You are right, my friend," Pedro responded, turning to him. "Because all of us suffered losses, we cannot dwell on what is past when we have a pressing need to take care of the people who have been entrusted to us. It is going to be hard to tell my Mama and Papa about this." He remounted his horse, somberly.

At that moment a large shadow flitted across the ground and they all looked up to see Harland flying overhead. They had not been the first to brave the hard, new world, Harland and the other mutant avian friends never returned to the caves after the battle. They had formed an aerie near the top of a close mountain. They did maintained friendly relationships with the humans, coming by occasionally to allow Rita to continue her research.

It seemed that Harland had followed them on their trek, keeping a lookout from on high. Nate felt cheered by this, and looking at his companions it appeared they were happy, too. He acknowledged Harland by waving to him, knowing that his eagle eyes would easily see that.

"We've probably gone as far as we should for this first trip out," Zack said. "I think that we need to take another way back so we can check out more terrain and scout for more mutants. It has been much quieter than I expected."

"Maybe the mutants are forming their own communities," Nate said, hopefully. "There is obviously nothing left for them to take, so why would they bother coming back to our old homesteads?"

"Do you think you can understand an animal's mind?" Zack asked. "Why attack us at all, for that matter? None of their actions seemed to make much sense. Their thought processes, if they have any, are alien to us. It's time that we finally face the fact that they are our enemies. We can no longer let down our guard."

Agreeing with him, Pedro and Javier nodded. However, Nate was not so easily convinced. "What about all the peaceful, friendly mutants? Maybe a day will come when we can all live side-by-side together in this world."

Nate's visionary dream was burst by Zack returning to his old character, sneering, "In your dreams! My advice is that you keep a loaded gun under your pillow.

Ignoring Zack, Nate said, "We need to check in with the home base before we start off again, though they are probably watching us via satellite." He waved at the sky, which made the other men grimace. Pulling out the sat phone, Nate punched up the signal to speak to those in the cave. They had done this periodically on their trip and had no difficulty talking to the others waiting behind. But, this time nothing happened. "We aren't getting a signal."

"Here, give me that," Zack said impatiently, tired of Nate's foolishness. He grabbed the sat phone and pressed the button, as if only he knew how to do it. The result was the same.

"Maybe there is some electrical interference," suggested Javier.

"That's not possible," asserted Pedro, adjusting his engineer hat.

"Do you think there could be a problem at the cavern? Maybe no one is in the com center," Nate offered.

"The mutants cannot get into the caverns," Zack answered. "You know as well as I that Sandra and Rita are glued to their seats, awaiting our every call."

"It's the same with the whole community," Javier affirmed. Indeed, all the people in the cavern were eagerly waiting for word on how this first venture back into the countryside had gone. By now, they were all sick of being cooped up and would gladly rush out on their own if encouraged to do so.

"We'd better get back there right away," said Nate, trying not to look worried. He didn't really think anything could happen to the people in the cavern, but he wanted to see for himself that Sandra, and of course, everyone else, was okay.

They all turned their horses around and forced them into a fast trot. Javier led the way, showing them a path through the woods that he said was a shortcut. He informed them that it would bring them around to the door that led in to the cavern from above. Not thinking of their own isolation, or of how Harland would not be able to see them under the trees, they followed Javier's lead, thinking only of their loved ones.

Suddenly, a group of mutants dropped from the trees and knocked them off of their horses. It was immediately apparent that they were outnumbered. With the surprise attack they were unable to reach for their guns. The mutants swarmed around them, badly injuring all of them, hitting their heads with rocks and sticks and kicking and biting them from all sides. Powerless, the humans fell to the ground.

*   *   *

The meeting had begun pleasantly, with Kaya arriving with a large contingent of her community. The President with all his advisors had been completely gracious, welcoming back citizens of the United States into the fold. Then things deteriorated rapidly as members of Kaya's group were identified.

"Brad, and Erin," Jamie blurted out, spying them among the mountain people. "Can that possibly be you? You survived? I mean, of course you survived. Yeah, why wouldn't you have? I am so glad to see that you are well." She trailed off as she saw the unfriendly stares of Erin and Brad.

"Aren't they the staff personnel who accessed top secret material without authorization?" said the head of the military police. Without awaiting confirmation, he bellowed an order. "Arrest them."

The Secret Service personnel guarding the meeting, along with Sgt. Chicory and a few other Special Forces soldiers who had been detailed to this meeting, looked questioningly at the President. None of them reported to the head of the military police and they weren't sure if he had any authority here or if they should obey him.

"You must be mistaken," said Kaya, smoothly understanding immediately that there was a problem in including Erin and Bran in

360

the proceedings. "This is Hope and Chip. Each of them is a member of our community, and each is protected as such."

"You heard the man," bellowed General Jennings. "Arrest them."

Both sides reached for their weapons. Fortunately, it was Jamie's quick thinking that averted a possible exchange of fire.

Jamie, who wanted no harm to come to Brad, quickly said, "I'm sorry I just mistook you for someone else." Her look at Erin and Brad said in no uncertain terms that they owed her big time and she would be sure to collect.

"Surely this is meant to be a peaceful meeting between two groups who have survived the ravages of war and come together to see if we can work together and present a unified, stronger front to those who mean us harm," Kaya said, looking directly at the President.

"Leave them be," the President ordered. "Immunity is granted to every person in this group who came to this meeting, at least for now. However, once you have been assimilated back into the protection of this great nation, you will have to adhere to the laws that govern it." Kaya's spine stiffened at these words, as did the spines of everyone with her. Before she could begin to protest, the General picked that moment to speak again.

"It appears that they have mutants with them," he pointed out, unnecessarily. It was obvious to everyone that Namid and Lowell were mutants. In fact, they had been included in the group going to see the President for that specific reason. "They will have to be placed with the mutants that we are doing research on."

"That's definitely not going to happen," said Kaya, firmly. "As far as we're concerned, these mutants are equal members of our community. In fact, this one is my daughter. Lo here is the father of the first child born to our community. I don't think anyone would or could subject them to any research without their permission."

"It is vital that we learn how to reverse the condition of devolution," the General pontificated. "And we have to study the mutants to know what they are capable of. It is a matter of supreme national security."

"As I've already stated, the mutants in our company will not be subjected to any experimentation without their approval."

"Why?" he asked.

Kaya was unrepentant. "They have the same rights and privileges as any other member of our group," Kaya repeated, ignoring the General and talking directly to the President.

The President silenced the General with a glance. "Ma'am we will do our best to accommodate all the members of your group into our nation. Surely, General, we have enough mutants to run tests on that we can leave these alone?"

Erin, who had been standing there, seething, could no longer hold in her contempt. "You mean torture, don't you?" She squared her shoulders as every head swiveled in her direction. Brad reached out a remonstrating hand, which she promptly shook off. After all, they had just ducked an almost certain arrest. Now, Erin was calling attention to them again, risking everything as she gave Brad an apologetic glance. "Yes, I am Erin Blaine. I am the one who read the documents about you torturing and killing completely innocent mutants. I also read about how people who were suspected of having mutant blood were actually separated from their families and put into concentration camps. That's where you killed those innocent babies." Her voice broke into a sob. "I can only imagine what kind of experiments you are doing right now on citizens of this country."

"Arrest her!" thundered the General and the head of the military police, simultaneously.

Tracker and the rest of the mountain folk surrounded Erin, making it clear that those trying to arrest Erin would have to go through them to fulfill the order. For a moment, everybody stood frozen in place, hesitant to take the first step that would send them down a path impossible to turn back from.

The President cleared his throat. "Tommy, I have granted immunity, temporarily, to everyone at this meeting, stand down soldiers. I'm afraid the exigencies of war have forced us to use measures that some might consider to be inhumane. Let me assure you that all that we do is necessary for the survival of this great country."

Bryce Chicory, who had been watching this particular meeting with great interest, was especially attracted to the fiery "Hope." He remembered his own venture into the halls where the research was being done on captured mutants. He winced at the memory of their squalid living conditions, living within earshot of surreal tortuous screams. He had a hard time keeping his tongue still. Fortunately, his many years of military training kept him in line.

"Mr. President, I fear this meeting has been for naught," said Kaya. "It is apparent that we have many areas of disagreement on how to live. Since I do not see any possibility of us joining our forces together, we will be on our way." She turned, signally for the others in the group to follow her.

Jumping to his feet, exhibiting his famous temper, the President bellowed an order. "Block them from leaving!" This time the soldiers jumped to obey him brandishing their weapons.

"All of us are citizens of this country," he thundered, "and now some of you will witness our judicial system. Each of you will swear allegiance to the United States, immediately stopping this stupid nonsense. I think we've all now tolerated as much of this stupidity as we can."

"Wait," Jamie cried. "As the acting head of Homeland Security, I can confidently say that I do not see how any of these people can pose a threat to our government."

Erin looked at her curiously, amazed that Jamie would risk her own hide to go against the flow.

Jamie continued, doggedly, ignoring what might be facing her. "I don't see any reason we can't live side-by-side peacefully. By the way, Kaya is a Native American name, isn't it?"

"Yes, you are correct; I am a Native American," Kaya acquiesced, puzzled at where Jamie was going with this.

"Then Mr. President, her rights to this country supersede those of our government," Jamie continued, grasping at straws, wondering to herself what she was doing. She knew that she was tired of fighting and that they needed new allies because the world was now full of enemies. "After all this fighting, sir, we need allies right now, not enemies. There are barely enough of us left to even form a viable community of our own. With this group added to ours, we have much better of a chance of survival. We need to rebuild not only the infrastructure of our country, but successfully defend ourselves against hostile mutant action that we might encounter in the future. Speaking for myself, I see no threat from these people. Instead, I see allies that we can work with and live in peace with. Personally, I am ready for a little peace."

With admiration, Chic looked at Jamie. Now he knew exactly why he had saved this ornery woman

The President, too, was thoughtfully looking at Jamie. He also didn't want another fight. He knew that if these people were successfully arrested that they wouldn't have enough guards secure them. Thus, it was better to pretend to appease their terms, for now. As the country strengthened and the number of loyal Americans increased, there would be plenty of time to deal with renegades. He nodded, sagely, as if he, himself, had thought up Jamie's words.

"We are dedicated to setting up a peaceful nation, and though we would gladly accept you as part of our community; it would be to all of our benefits to live in harmony with each other," he said ponderously, attempting to retain his presidential appearance.

"We agree, completely, Mr. President," Kaya said, diplomatically, knowing full well that her people would not peacefully coexist with a government where torturous atrocities were being committed. "If you will excuse us, we will take our leave now." Inclining her head, she led her people out.

As Brad followed her out, passing the armed soldiers, he gave Jamie a little wink.

* * *

The death was sudden and dramatic, though not noisy or unexpected. By this point, they knew their generators were running out of fuel, so they needed to conserve energy in every way imaginable to keep the computers running and the sat phones charged. By this point, people were using candles for light and fires for warmth and cooking. At least they had been able to keep the computers and sat phone operational, until now.

"The computer is dead," Sandra announced quietly, surprising everyone.

"So is the sat phone," Rita added.

A soft groan permeated the room, since the bad news had happened at the worst possible time. With their first expedition above ground, they had no way to find out what was happening. It had been hours since the men had checked in, and now they would not be able to check in at all.

Sandra had a vision of Nate casually picking up his phone and to call her and suddenly finding out that he couldn't. Knowing Nate, he would be worried about the people in the cavern.

All that Sandra could envision was that their scouting team was suddenly cut off from any help that they could need. It was now painfully clear that they were all on their own. She should have gone with them. In the past, she always traveled with Nate, taking trips together on the surface to scout out more supplies before they had shut themselves beneath the ground. If it wasn't for the flu she caught, she would've been with him this time, too.

"The men will be okay," said Rinaldo. "Since they were only going to stay out for the day, they should be back before nightfall. Besides, the last time they checked in they said that there had been no signs of mutant activity."

"It's starting to get dark above ground," said Sandra. "They should be coming in at any minute now." Her words sounded reasonable, in spite of a sinking feeling in her stomach. Oh no, that was a queasy feeling. She lurched to her feet and headed to the nearest latrine.

Rita, who was also feeling the same early affects of the flu, was trying to convince herself that she was just tired. She tried not to think of Sandra vomiting, in order to keep her stomach under control.

They all worried as they waited for hours, with no sign of the men returning. Eva Perez was the most outspoken, even as Rinaldo and Rita were busy trying to reassure her.

Horst Schenk, who was stationed at the entryway, ran into the com center. Hearing him, they all ran towards him, relieved and initially confident that he would bring them word that the men had been spotted, ending their fears. Unfortunately, his face did not show any form of good news.

"That mutant, Harland, kept rapping at the door, but I couldn't figure out what he actually wanted. All I know is that it definitely isn't the right time for you to do your research with them, at least not this late at night, right Rita?" he asked, almost apologetic to interrupt them with such a small matter.

"Maybe Harland has spotted our travelers and is trying to bring us word about them," Rita exclaimed, jumping to her feet. She raced to the tunnel, finishing first, with Sandra a close second, and the whole community running behind them. Most of the people had to be content with waiting at the beginning of the passage, since the tunnel could not hold all of them.Harland stood perched outside the doorway. When he saw Rita and Sandra he got excited, instinctively ruffling his feathers. Then he hopped around, squawking and throwing his wings into the air as he mindlessly bobbed his head up and down. Within his bird brain, he imagined himself imitating the men passing under the trees and the mutants dropping down on them. Nevertheless, to the humans who watched, he just seemed to be acting like a bird.

"Harland, we can't understand you," said Rita. "Are you trying to tell us something about Zack, and Pedro, and Nate, and Javier?" Rita was as patient as she could be. After all, she had the most experience dealing with mutants and, therefore, the best chance of deciphering what Harland was trying to communicate.

Harland dramatically kept bobbing his head up and down, now cocking his head quizzically, with the 'yes' and 'no' nods that had become the staple of avian-human communication.

"He's saying yes," said Sandra, excitedly.

"Are they almost here?" Rita continued. Again, Harland tried to pantomime what had happened to the quartet.

"Just give me a yes or no, Harland," Rita urged. She could sense the frustration he was restraining. Meanwhile, Harland just kept shaking his head back and forth, vaguely signally 'no.'

"Has something delayed them?" Sandra interrupted, impatiently.

Harland vigorously nodded his head.

"They are all okay, aren't they? Please tell me they are all okay," Eva begged, holding her hands high, prayerfully in the air.

Slowly, Harland shook his head 'no.' Waves of sympathy were pouring off of him.

"Oh, Dios, my little bambino," Eva cried out, falling to the ground as she sobbed her words. Rinaldo gathered her in his arms, himself full of dread for the welfare of his son and lifelong friend and the other two young men he loved as if they were his own blood.

"Can you take us to them?" Sandra asked, completely forgetting her upset stomach. If she could only go to him, she was sure he would be okay. In her mind, he had to be!

Harland restarted his complicated dance, this time alternately signaling 'yes' and 'no.' No one could decipher his rhythms.

Rita tried rephrasing the question a different way. "Do you know where they are?" Somewhat responding, Harland repeated his undecipherable actions.

Frustrated, Sandra gritted her teeth. Time was slipping away fast, and they were getting nowhere. They needed to get to the men to help them. Who knew how precious each moment was if they were injured? Was this actually a matter of life or death? Doing her best her mind quickly veered away from that thought, which wasn't as difficult as it could have been since she didn't want to go there in the first place. In fact, she refused to go there.

"We can't waste time with this," she said, forcefully. "We need to get together a posse, as quickly as possible to go out and search for them."

Rita was not willing to give up on Harland so easily since she was sure vital information was locked in his brain that he was trying to communicate. "Sandra, we don't know where the men are unless Harland helps us."

"All we know for sure is that with their last communication they were heading for your family estate," Sandra snapped. "How hard can it be to follow the road there? I'm sure we will find them if we try, right?"

"Well, there is more than one way to get there," Rita responded, calmly, refusing to get angry at her friend's flippant statement. After all, they were all under stress. Meanwhile, she tried not to think of Zack and her brother. "Besides the road, there are different paths through the woods."

At the mention of the woods, Harland started hopping up and down, nodding his head, excitedly.

"I think he may be trying to tell us they were on one of the paths through the woods," Rita said, triumphantly. "Can you take us to that path?"

Again, Harland nodded, emphatically. He hopped a few steps to the left as he and launched himself into the air.

Just give us a minute to get some gear together, and we'll go with you," Sandra said. With that, she vomited in front of everybody. Seeing her do that, Rita was no longer able to control her own stomach, causing her to vomit along with her.

"You girls are not going anywhere," Eva asserted. "No, no, no, don't even think of protesting," she added as Rita and Sandra weakly tried to do just that. "You would be more hindrance than help at this point. Come with me. Liesel, give me a hand getting these girls back to the camp." Still trying to protest, Sandra and Rita were led back down the passage.

Rinaldo and Horst hurriedly formed a search-and-rescue party and followed after Harland.

"I feel fine now," Sandra asserted, trying her best to get up from the cot she was laying on."Me too," Rita said, determinedly, though she didn't put actions to words.

"You girls have got to take care of yourselves," Eva assured them. "That is the most important thing you can do right now since it is too late for you to catch up with the men."

"I can't just lie here doing nothing," Sandra railed, protesting.

"Waiting is always the hardest," Eva said, nodding her head. "I, too, want to run off and find my son."

Ashamed, Sandra hung her head. In her own fear for Nate, she had forgotten that Eva's son was out there, too. All she could think of was Nate. This waiting was terrible for everyone involved.

"How long has it been, Mama?" Rita asked.

"A few hours, it's now daylight outside."

"Only a few hours," Sandra raged, thinking of how much could happen in a few minutes, let alone a few hours. "If only we hadn't come down with this beastly virus."

"I can't believe we both got sick at the same time," Rita added.

"You girls are kidding me, right?" Eva asked, suspiciously eyeing them.

"What do mean, Mama? How could any of us joke at a time like this?" Rita said, affronted.

"Isn't it obvious that two intelligent, worldly girls like yourselves would know what is making you sick," Eva said, incredulously.

"Isn't it a virus?" Sandra asked thoughtfully. "I suppose it could be food poisoning since the food we are growing doesn't have natural light."

"You really don't know, do you?" Eva said, shaking her head, wonderingly. "I guess I'll have to tell you then. Both of you are pregnant."

A bomb going off next to them would have hit the women with less force than that quiet announcement. Sandra and Rita looked at each other, questioningly, both fearful and excited.

"So you and Zack," Sandra asked Rita?

"Well, it's not going to be a virgin birth," said Eva, contemptuously.

"How can that be? We've been practicing the rhythm method, religiously," Rita protested.

"That's how I had your brother," Eva informed her.

"Weren't you on birth control pills?" Sandra asked.

"No, I never expected to . . . I've never felt the need . . . I didn't know we were going to —" Rita blushed, embarrassed and unable to complete her sentences in front of her mother.

Roger Marshall with Cathy Newman

"Lot of good it did for me. I just ran out, myself. I thought it took about a year for the body to recover," Sandra mused, aloud.

"Girls your age think they know everything," Eva informed them. "All babies come from the good Lord. Maybe you don't realize that, but both of you are about to become mothers. It's about time, too, Rita. I want a grandchild."

Overcome with the wonder and joy of the situation, the women marveled silently for a moment. They were actually carrying new lives inside of their bodies! It seemed evident now that they had been told. The reality of the situation now crashed down on them. Was it actually true that their men were missing and no one knew what had even happened to them? If everything turned out for the best — as they fervently prayed and hoped that it would for— who wanted to bring babies into a devastated world like this?

They heard a commotion outside the building they were resting in. Forgetting everything in their eagerness to see Nate and Zack, Sandra and Rita rushed outside. Thankfully, the search party had returned and were milling around a couple of men on the ground. Shoving their way through the spectators, Sandra and Rita finally got to the center of the circle. To their dismay, on stretchers were the severely injured bodies of Javier and Pedro. Falling to her knees next to her brother, Rita took Pedro's hand.

"Pedro, are you alright?" Rita needlessly asked. Her gaze swept over the bandaged head, the swollen shut eyes, the bleeding lips, and the arms and legs in hastily-constructed splits.

Trying to answer, Pedro groaned and groaned and groaned. How else could he communicate with her? Looking over at Javier, it was apparent that he was in no better shape, either. Silently, tears rolled down Rita's cheeks as she cradled her brother, until she was rudely pushed aside by Eva, who gathered her son to her bosom.

Rinaldo gently pulled her away. "Careful, Mama, you don't want to disturb his injuries, or you will worsen them. At least we don't think that there are any internal injuries. We definitely need to get them to the clinic, as soon as possible." Now, Eva and Rita fell into each other's arms, sobbing until their tears would run out. The two people with the most medical knowledge were completely undone, paralyzed with pain.

Sandra, though deeply concerned with the condition of the two men, kept looking through the throng. She was certainly puzzled and expectant, unsure of what to do next. If Nate and Zack were not among the injured, then surely they were there among the search party, right?

"Nate?" she called out. "Nate?" A terrible foreboding feeling hit her. It couldn't be! She couldn't put into words what was in her mind at that moment. Grabbing onto Rinaldo's arm she entreated, "Where are Nate and Zack?"

Rinaldo bowed his head, not immediately answering, alerting Rita and the rest of the community to become quiet so they all could hear. But what would they hear?

"Oh no, Papa," Rita screamed, clinging to him. "Tell me Zack is not dead."

"No they are not dead, at least we pray that is so, as far as we know right now," Rinaldo said, looking at his daughter and Sandra with sorrow in his eyes.

Just then Zack and Nate came stumbling out of the trees. Rita and Sandra rushed to them as they collapsed into the arms of the women they loved.

The world had just entered a new phase. Mankind was back and yet the mutants were still very present. A tenuous balance existed. Would it continue?

The End